MONTROSE PARANORMAL ACADEMY

Book 2

Crossing Nexis

Barbara Hartzler

ISBN: 9798583234677
Imprint: Independently published

Printed in the United States of America

First Printing, 2020

Editor: Rachelle Rae Cobb (2019), Rachel Garber

Cover Design by Barbara Hartzler

For Sam, my husband, my partner, my best friend.
I will always love you.

You left this world singing with the angels.
I can't wait to see you again.
Until then, I know you've always got my back.

CHAPTER 1

Snowflakes splatted on the windshield as my new boyfriend's car charged uphill through the slush. A shiver slithered down my spine as I grinned at Bryan's profile. Fits of sleet and snow assaulted us on the three-hour drive from New York to Pennsylvania, but my heart felt lighter with every mile between me and Montrose Paranormal Academy. My junior year had started with the hope of a new beginning, only to end with my crazy ex stalking me a thousand miles to try to kidnap me. Not your average semester.

But then again, I found out I wasn't your average girl. In just a few short months, I'd discovered I had the power to see the unseen world of angels and demons. And become an angel conduit. Yeah, still trying to figure that part out. Not exactly a gift I'd asked for, by the way. Nope. Apparently, the McAllen family came from a centuries-old firstborn bloodline dating all the way back to Noah the Bible guy. I just lucked out it was my turn to carry the mantel of the Seer. At least now I had a new boyfriend to help train me.

"Lucy, here we are. Good old Harrisburg PA. At last." Bryan squeezed my hand with his rough fingers, bringing me back to reality. We coasted into his hometown—more like a snow-encrusted Thomas Kinkade village.

The car shuddered to a stop at the red light.

"It's beautiful, all wrapped up in snow." I couldn't help but smile at the welcome distraction.

Quaint little shops lined the streets, their roofs capped in snow. White Christmas lights twinkled in the eaves. Street lamps with red bows flickered on as dusk gathered around Main Street.

"It's the envy of all other towns." Bryan's blue eyes sparkled as the light turned green.

"It's okay, you can admit it. You live in one of those towns. The kind with festivals to commemorate the first snow." I blinked at him, just staring at his profile. I still couldn't believe this guy was my boyfriend. Earlier today he'd told me he loved me and somehow convinced my dad to let me go to Pennsylvania to meet his family. What a guy, right?

His brow bunched up as he stared at the road. "Uh oh. I forgot about this crazy festival. Looks like we'll have to go around."

"What festival?" I turned to look out the windshield. A barricade I hadn't noticed blocked the street in front of us, frosted enough to blend into the snowy backdrop. Bundled-up people lined the sidewalks, waiting around for something.

Those blue eyes snapped toward me, suddenly haunted. "Lucy, I'm sorry. I'm such an idiot." His jaw twitched as he flicked on his blinker and turned left past a stone chapel, blanketed by ice.

Glancing at his stone profile, I spotted two rows of elementary schoolers lined up on the sidewalk. "What are those little girls doing? It's too cold for them to be out." I sunk my teeth into my bottom lip. Yep, I just sounded like my mom. Too scary.

He ignored me and slammed his foot on the accelerator, eyes as wide as marbles.

"Bryan, slow down." My heart thumped away as we skidded past the church. "What's going on?"

I squinted at the strange scene in front of me, my heart beating just a little bit faster.

Little girls in flowing white robes with red sashes swarmed from the church doors. Two nuns glided among the white-on-red huddle. One placed electric candles in the girls' red-mittened hands, while the other plunked holly wreaths on their heads. The candles flickered like real firelight.

Then I saw it—a giant banner next to the chapel. *St. Lucy's Day Parade Entrance.*

Dread slammed me right in the pit of my stomach.

I gasped, a choking breath that stilled my lungs. Automatically, I flipped my left wrist over. The tiniest scar still singed my skin. Remnants from the last time I stepped into a St. Lucy's church in Harlem, where a lunatic member of the Watcher Corps tried to brand me with a hot iron to mark me as the Seer. *Breathe, it's over now,* I told myself. But the memory flashed back, clear as day.

Bryan snatched my hand like a lifeline desperately yanking me back to reality. "Sweetie, I'm sorry. They do this stupid parade every year. I totally forgot it was today." He sucked in a breath. "We're not Catholic, so we don't celebrate it. But any event that goes on in this town is a big deal. They make a production out of everything."

My hands trembled as his words crackled in my ears like radio static. White-gowned girls floated toward me in two perfect lines. Almost as if they had one mind synced together by the cold. A little blonde girl locked her eyes on me.

My heart pounded with new speed, and suddenly I could see. All the visions of St. Lucia I'd ever envisioned lined up one after another—like a playlist of terror.

St. Lucia appeared before me with creepy jeweled eyes of diamond and topaz, her long hair blowing behind her as she stretched a pale hand toward me. My pulse kicked into high gear as I tried to blink the image away.

But the image didn't go away. St. Lucia morphed into the version of her I'd seen in the Nexis book, with hollowed eyes. Her face contorted as if to warn me. All my breath seized in my lungs.

Would I share the same fate, and have my eyes gouged out by the Watchers?

I shut my eyes against the horror as my stomach curdled. The darkness faded into light as a new vision of St. Lucia emerged from the shadows. This time she had eyes of light surrounded by the rays of heaven. A warm, peaceful feeling enveloped me, washing away all remnants of terror. St. Lucia stretched out her arm again, this time to beckon me closer. I shook my head. I didn't want to hear her warning, whatever it was. With my refusal, she faded into nothingness.

My vision cleared, and the world righted itself. I was back in Bryan's sedan, stopped in a line of parade traffic.

I turned to him. "Can we get out of here already? Doesn't this hunk of junk have four-wheel drive or something?"

"Don't worry, I'll get us out of here. Right now." Bryan's jaw hardened into a stony line as he spun the wheel hard to the right to escape the traffic jam.

The tires slipped in the slush and the car fishtailed as he peeled out. I wrapped my fingers around the seat and held on tight, my stomach twisting even as I silently urged him to go faster. With a few deft maneuvers, he righted the car and slid onto a desolate two-lane highway. Soon we were headed in the right direction. Away from this sick celebration.

I didn't care where this country road took us. At least I could breathe again.

Bryan's palm encircled my scarred wrist. "I'll never let something like that happen to you again."

"I know." The trembling stilled, my heartbeats slowed.

"I'm not just a Guardian," his fingers laced through mine, "I'm *your* Guardian now. I'll do anything to protect you."

"Thank you," I whispered. Leaning over, I planted a kiss on his cheek.

His body went rigid, except for a lone muscle twitching in his cheek. And that's when it hit me. He was just as scared as I was. Only he was afraid *for* me.

My heart curled in on itself. Angling my face to the window, I watched as pines blanketed in white buzzed past the window. I never wanted this. Never asked to be the Seer. The gift could've been given to many more worthy people—like my brother James. This so-called power was taking over my life and hurting the people I loved. Being the Seer felt more like a prison than a privilege. Even so, I would never trap anyone else in this prison.

So, I pasted a smile on my face and let three empty words tumble from my mouth. "I'll be fine."

"Are you sure?" He didn't look at me, just flicked on his blinker and turned his car onto a snow-packed road that coiled like a slinky through the forest, winding and curving for miles.

"I'm hardly ever sure of anything." Except one thing. I couldn't put this burden on anyone else's shoulders. It was my cross to bear. I needed to learn to be the Seer and figure out how to use that gift. Bryan said his family would train me. Now more than ever, I hoped he was right.

"I'm not naive." Gulping in a major breath, I clenched my fists. "I know you can't protect me from everything. That's why I'm here. To learn how to fight. To stand up for myself. So bring on the Seer training. I'm ready for it."

"That's my girl." He squeezed my hand. "You'll be awesome at this."

I closed my eyes against the whiteness, but the truth still smacked me in the face. It iced the breath in my lungs. I wasn't even close to ready for this.

><

Who-knows-how-many miles outside of Harrisburg, Bryan turned onto a deserted road that wound through luscious fir trees. His shiny sedan plowed her way through inches-deep snow, then angled down a winding driveway that dead-ended in front of a house large enough to be a lodge.

"This is where you live? It's breathtaking." If I snapped a photo right now, of this lodge nestled among the evergreens, it'd make the perfect Christmas card.

"It better be." He shut off the car as two bundled-up figures trudged through the snow toward us. A golden retriever lolloped along behind. "The Guardians lorded over every detail of this place, from design to construction."

"The Guardians?" I cocked my head at him, unsure if I'd heard him right.

"Incoming," he pointed at the passenger side window. Subtle.

As soon as I opened my car door, Bryan's mom wrapped me in a giant hug. "I'm Cindy. It's so good to finally meet you."

"Nice to meet you, Mrs. Coo—, uh, Cindy." I hugged her back.

"Brooke has been talking about you non-stop. Ever since she got home with Abby." She put her arm around me. "You've been so good for her, helping her come out of her shell. We're so grateful."

The golden retriever jumped up, its paws landing near my shoulders. Foul breath assaulted my frozen nose as I dodged its lolling tongue.

"Down, Ginger." Cindy patted the dog's golden fur. Ginger landed on all fours and followed Cindy to the front door. At the porch, she called back. "Mark, don't forget the bags."

Mark towered over me, offering a lanky arm. "Hi, Lucy, nice to meet you. That's my cue." Hard to guess where Bryan got his broad shoulders.

I plowed through the snow after Cindy, leaving the guys to their luggage duty. She ushered me into the foyer where I shook off snowflakes under a vaulted ceiling.

As I hung my parka on the coat rack, Brooke rushed up to me. "Lucy, I'm so glad you're here." She squeezed me tight around the waist.

A lanky girl hovered behind Brooke, unable to hide because she stood a good six inches taller. She fidgeted with her long blonde hair, twirling it around her index finger.

"Don't be shy." Brooke motioned the girl over. "This is my older sister, Abby."

"Nice to meet you." Abby's face broke into a smile as warm as her mom's. "You look so much like your brother."

"Hello, she's a girl. That's not very nice," Brooke scrunched her forehead at her sister.

"Oh, that's not what I meant. I'm sorry. It's just with the dark hair and those big brown eyes. Just like James . . ." Abby's blue eyes darted from Brooke back to me as she resumed her hair twirling.

"Don't worry about it. I actually think that's a compliment, especially now." I shrugged it off as my brother's goofy grin flashed in my mind. I wish James was in Europe somewhere, having the time of his life no doubt. *Yeah, right. I wish.* More like running from Nexis, no doubt. Pressure built behind my eyes at all the what-ifs whirring in my brain. But I couldn't go there. Not right now.

"I'm sure you miss him a lot." Abby grabbed my hand, just like Bryan would if he was here. "I know just the thing to cheer you up. You wanna see your room?"

Without waiting for an answer, she gripped my hand and tugged me across the fluffy entry rug, then down a hardwood-lined hallway.

"Here we are." She gestured to the perfect little white and oak room. "Maybe later we can talk about your brother, if you're up for it."

"I'd like that." I couldn't help but smile at that. "I love talking with people who knew James."

"Great. Maybe tonight after dinner." She offered me a James-like grin. Then she slipped out of the room, her long blond hair swishing in waves behind her.

The guest room was small but comfortable, complete with soft white carpet, a white quilted bedspread, and matching oak furniture. I padded over to the window, taking in the snowy scene outside. Tall pines fringed the backyard, almost like the landscape hanging over the bed. The cavernous ceiling was pristine with beautiful rustic beams, but it wasn't *my* room. Back home, I'd filled my room with color and random doodles—my own organized mess.

Out of nowhere, an overwhelming wave of homesickness washed over me, gnawing my bones with its icy loneliness. This would be the first Christmas I'd ever spent away from home. Even if things weren't right with my family, they were still my family. And I missed them.

I reached for the phone to dial my dad's number, but my finger froze mid-air. What would I say to him if he answered? *Hey, Dad. Sorry I don't wanna come home and face all the drama of my stalker ex-boyfriend and keep secrets from my sister about our brother who is really our half-brother.* Yeah, I'm sure that'd go over real well.

Instead, I set the phone on the nightstand in easy reach in case they decided to call and check in on me.

Tucking my suitcase under the bed, I curled up in a ball on the giant four-poster bed. In a house full of familiar strangers, I felt so alone. All the emotions I'd held in since the attack swirled in my gut, threatening to bubble over.

Sheer anger rose to the surface. My blood boiled as I tried to shove the memories of Jake back into the dark pit from which they'd come from.

I couldn't understand it, couldn't wrap my brain around it. Flashes of that night played in my head. Jake shaking me, yanking my arm out of its socket. Trying to take me God knows where so Nexis could do who knew what with me. If it wasn't for Angel, my angel, who knew what would've happened? To think, I used to date that guy. And the whole time he'd been some Nexis lackey, spying on me. I shuddered at the thought.

One question lingered like a neon sign. What happened to Will? I wondered if he was okay, or if he was secretly in cahoots with Jake and somehow got beat up in the process. I'd find out in a few weeks when winter break was over.

Even though Will had called two dozen times since that awful night, I ignored every call. Erased every voicemail. Pressure built behind my eyes. I was too afraid Will was in on the plot. Call it magnetic charm or a latent self-destructive streak, but for some reason I felt drawn to him. No more. I couldn't let him get any closer. Couldn't let that night repeat itself.

If I let my mind wander down the what-if road, I'd be consumed by the shadows of what could've happened.

Before I left Montrose, my trauma counselor told me, "Don't let the darkness consume you." And that stayed with me.

I couldn't dwell on that horrible night forever. I had to find a way to shove it aside and move on. Or it'd eat me alive.

Instead, I vowed to focus on the good things in my life—to feed my spirit with much-needed light. Angel, as I had taken to calling him lately, *did* come to save me when I need him. He helped me find and unlock my gift, and help me choose the right path. Which brought me to the next step in my journey. Staying with a warm and welcoming family who could protect me and train me to fight my own battles. Probably the safest place I could be right now.

I unfurled my limbs from my self-made cocoon. The shadows dissipated, and a sense of calm enveloped me like a warm blanket. I was safe. And I was stronger than I ever thought I could be. Soon, after Seer training, I'd be even stronger. I smiled at that thought, even as my fingers curled into fists. Seer training was just the next step in my journey.

Chapter 2

The mouth-watering scent of garlic tinged with onions wafted into the room. "Mmmm, heavenly," I murmured.

Slipping into my favorite canvas shoes, I followed my nose down the hall to the kitchen. Immaculate granite countertops lined a peninsular island that led to the chef's corner, complete with a giant gas stove. Cindy hovered over a stainless pot and wiped her hands on her apron.

"Hi, Lucy. Would you like to help?" She handed me a ladle and motioned toward the heaping plate of pasta on the counter.

"Sure." I rolled up my sleeves and dunked the ladle in the sweet-smelling spaghetti sauce, pouring it all over the noodles.

"Perfect." She gave me a warm smile as she sprinkled parsley on top and set the family-style dish on the rough-hewn kitchen table. "Come and get it."

If she'd rang a dinner bell, it couldn't have been more perfect. Footsteps pounded toward the kitchen as Mark, Abby, Brooke, and Bryan all rushed in and sat down at the table.

Bryan pulled out a chair. "For our guest."

I didn't even try to hide my smile as he tucked himself in next to me.

"Shall we say grace?" Mark extended his hand to Abby and me, and everyone followed suit. "Lord, please bless this food, the hands that prepared it, and our guest of honor. May your guidance be ever-present as we seek you for our next steps. Amen."

When I glanced at my plate, someone had piled it high with Parmesan-crusted spaghetti. "Thanks, Bryan."

"You got it." He mumbled through a mouthful of pasta.

My tummy grumbled as I spun the pasta around, shoving it in my mouth. The tomatoey-goodness hit my tongue as I reached for a flaky piece of French bread. I let my gaze wander across the table to Abby and Brooke, who looked so much like Cindy with their blonde hair and round cheeks. Abby must've gotten her blue eyes from Mark, just like Bryan. On my left, Mark's tall, broad-shouldered build mirrored Bryan's stature.

My fork plopped on my plate. The whole picture made me choke up a little. The Coopers' camaraderie reminded me of my family. Except Mom's betrayal had shattered our once happy family. Truth be told, James didn't really look like my dad. He never had. But still, it had taken a trip to Montrose Paranormal Academy and a conversation with the reigning Nexis president himself for me to see the truth. Of course, the truth didn't change the way I felt about James. I'm sure Dad would agree. But the perfect family portrait was tainted. I hated it.

Abby downed a gulp of water. "It's so good to have you here, Lucy. Brooke's told me so much about you. Bryan, too, of course."

I shoveled more noodles in my mouth and could only manage a nod.

Abby leaned in, her tone quieting. "So, are you guys like boyfriend/girlfriend now? You make such a cute couple."

"Excuse me." I coughed as a huge lump of spaghetti lodged in my throat. "I'm not sure." I glanced at Bryan in time to see his jaw fall open.

"What?" Abby's face turned red. At least she had the decency to look outraged for me. She turned to her brother.

"You've been going on and on about this girl for months. Why haven't you asked her to be your girlfriend yet?"

Cluunck. My fork plunked onto my plate about the same time my jaw fell open. I turned to Bryan. "Yes. I'd like to know, too."

"It's complicated." Bryan stopped eating, averting his gaze to Abby. "I haven't got the Guardians' approval yet," he mumbled more to Abby than to me.

She jutted her chin out. "Have you even asked them?"

He shook his head. "Not yet."

Now he wouldn't even look at me. He just stared at his plate and jammed food down his throat.

"Abby, you of all people should know there's a protocol to these things." Cindy shot her sideways glance from the other end of the table.

"Mom," Abby practically growled through clenched teeth, eyes darting toward me for a split second.

Bryan heaved out a sigh, shaking his head. "Thanks, Abby." Reaching under the table, he took my hand and finally turned those blue eyes my way. "I'm sorry, Lucy, but my mom is right. There's a lot of red tape that comes with dating someone outside the Guardians, let alone the Seer."

"Oh." I slumped down in my chair, the spaghetti fermenting in my stomach.

Brooke gnawed on her lip, looking more unsure than ever. All of the Coopers were staring at me now, pity plastered all over their faces.

I couldn't look at them anymore. I stared down at my lap, wrapping my fingers around the sides of my chair till my knuckles went white. The knots in my gut twisted up as a freight train of fury chugged through my head.

"Excuse me." I scraped back my chair. "I need to get some air."

><

Standing all alone in the middle of nowhere, I stared up at the sky and inhaled the frigid air. It soothed my flaming cheeks. Stars twinkled down at me, icy dots of hope waiting to reveal their secrets. Yet they didn't say a word—just like Bryan.

"I'll never understand that boy. Why does he keep secrets from me?" Of course, the stars didn't answer. They just blinked their benign little twinkles as if it wasn't news to them.

Whoosh. The sliding door opened behind me on the snowy deck. A familiar bomber jacket slid around my shoulders.

"Peace offering." Bryan held out a steaming mug of hot cocoa as if it could make up for his omission. "Lucy, I'm sorry about the Guardians. I really am. If I could change things, you know I would."

I took the mug without looking at him, giving him a dose of his own medicine. Then I blurted out the question I couldn't hold in any longer. "Are you going to let them have the final say in our relationship?"

"No, I'm not planning to." He puffed out a warm breath near me. Too near. "Even if we have to keep it a secret."

My face caught fire again, molten lava sizzling through my veins. I did *not* want to be anyone's secret girlfriend. Period.

Snow crunched as he turned to face me, his paws landing on my shoulders. "Tell me what you're thinking."

"Sometimes I just don't want to do this. I never asked for this gift. And I certainly didn't ask for the Guardians to have a say in who I date." Sipping at my hot chocolate, I raised my eyes to meet his.

His hands slid down my arms, then dropped to his sides. "I forget that you haven't grown up with all of this. In my world, it's normal for the Guardians to get involved in something this big. After all, you are the Seer."

His words shivered down my spine, making me feel cold for the first time since I'd stepped onto the deck.

"You're right. I am the Seer," I whispered the last word into my cocoa, disturbing the floating marshmallows. "I have this crazy power. Shouldn't I have a say in what my life looks like?"

"Like I said, it's complicated . . ." he trailed off, his eyes turning from me up to the stars. "If you could just join the Guardians without a war being declared, everything would be fine."

"Right. War." All the fight in me died at that word. Like my allegiance could start a war. It was crazy. Darkness curled around my vision. "I understand," I mumbled.

"I feel like I'm not doing this right." Bryan dragged one hand through his dark hair. "I don't know how to juggle you and the Guardians. My feelings complicate things. They cloud my judgment."

"I see." My insides melted a little as the darkness dissipated. "I'd argue that your feelings make you a better protector."

"Hey, I like that. Maybe we can use that and make our case together." Moonlight illuminated the curve of his lips. "So you're not mad?"

I gulped down the chocolate dregs as the last remnants of anger melted away. "I didn't say that. I just understand this is complicated. Our relationship is complicated. Whatever that means."

"That's fair." He moved in front of me again, studying my face. "You know, I'm crazy about you. Have been since I bumped into you at orientation."

"Is that so?" My heart shuddered as my mouth curved to match his.

"I know I just told you this morning," he inched close enough to smell his aftershave and took the mug from my hands, "but I've loved you for a long time." His nose brushed mine, warming my face.

Icy tendrils burst into a shower of sparks in every nerve ending. Did I dare tell him the truth? With all the resolve I had left, I rose on my tiptoes to take in that frozen sea of blue.

"It's been about a month for me," I whispered.

"Really?" His eyes lit up with stars of their own as he cupped my face with his hands. "I love you, Lucy."

"I love you, too," I murmured against his lips as they brushed mine. Warmth curled down my neck as his mouth drank me in and his arms wrapped around me, drawing me close.

When he pulled back, his cheeks were red. "If only all our fights could end like this."

"Don't even go there." I punched his shoulder. "I hate drama."

"Even if it leads to this?" His lips mingled with mine again, and I huddled into his arms.

"That's so not the point." I couldn't help but smile up at him, even as I pushed the Guardian drama out of my mind. For now. I guess love really could make a fool out of you.

><

Shadows unfurled in the night sky, blotting out the moon. Charcoal curls, midnight tendrils of mist. Their fingers crawling toward me, ready to engulf me. Forever.

Jake's face emerged from the black mist. Tendrils of darkness unfurled from his back like strings, attached to every limb. He stared at me, the look in his eyes pure torture. He shook his head vehemently like he was just as scared of the shadows as I was.

Snap. A fireball crackled through the air, glowing orange above his head, red-hot in the center. Jake froze in an instant. Shadow-strings lowered from the red orb in the center of the fireball, attaching to Jake's limbs like tentacles.

Tick, tick, tick. With clock-like rhythm, he walked toward me. His motions were stilted and robotic as the fiery shadows moved in tandem with him. It was Jake, but it wasn't Jake. As if the shadows made a puppet out of him.

Yeoow. With an ear-piercing shriek, Jake's right hand landed on my neck. Then the left. Squeezing. Choking.

I clawed at his iron grip. And screamed into the blackness.

"Lucy, wake up." Strong hands gripped my shoulders. Shaking me. "It's okay, angel. You're safe."

Panic hissed in my ears as my heart banged around in my chest. Remnants of the puppet-like shadows lingered in my hazy mind. Wait. It was just a dream.

"What's going on?" I asked Bryan, taking a deep breath and rubbing the shadows out of my sight. "What time is it?"

"I don't know, two a.m. I think?" His voice was groggy. "I woke up. Heard you screaming. You must've had a nightmare or something."

I scanned every nook and cranny of the dark room. The shadows were gone. Bits of silvery moonlight streamed through the blinds, outlining the contours of Bryan's face as he yawned.

He perched on the edge of my bed in striped pajama pants and a faded Yale shirt. Ready to fight off all my bad dreams. I wanted to reach for him. But I couldn't. Something held me back.

"Was it about him?" he asked.

I nodded, the pressure building behind my eyes. I couldn't get it out of my mind. Jake's tortured face. Surrounded by shadows.

This time I couldn't help it. I reached for Bryan, my hands landing on his chest. In a nanosecond, he curled his arms around me. Nuzzled his scratchy chin into my forehead.

"I'm here, sweetie. It's going to be okay now."

I shut my eyes tight, but hot tears slipped out anyway. Dying a damp death on his warm t-shirt.

"Do you want to tell me about it?"

I arched back to look at him and my insides went pitter-patter. The wings of a hummingbird sprang to life. Quivering a tumult of hormones.

No boy had ever been in my room in the middle of the night. Especially not a guy I was dating.

Suddenly I was all-too-aware of his proximity. The warmth seeping from every pore of his body begged me to come closer.

"You don't have to tell me." His gaze traveled down past my chin.

"I want to, but I don't know where to start." Just like that, all the hummingbird hormones screeched to a halt. I couldn't do this. Not now. I wasn't ready for this kind of intimacy. It was too much. Too soon after Jake.

Bryan's breath hitched in his throat. One. Two. Three seconds and he stood to his feet, leaving a cold space beside me.

"What's wrong?" My heart thumped like crazy.

"It's just. You're so ..." His eyes flicked to a spot lower than my eyes.

Fire sizzled up my neck, gathering in my cheeks. I yanked the covers up to my neck. "Sorry."

"Don't apologize for being gorgeous." He raked one hand through his dark hair, mussing it as his gaze darted between me and the ceiling.

My heart skipped a beat. A smile toyed with my mouth. "I guess I won't ask you to stay then."

"I shouldn't." His lips twitched. "But I'll go ask Brooke or Abby if you'd like."

"That's sweet." I yawned, slumping back under the covers. "I don't want to wake them."

"If you're sure. I just want you to be okay." Moonlight cast slatted shadows on his face as he stared at me. "Do you think you can sleep?"

I shrugged. I couldn't answer that. Not with the shadows threatening every time I closed my eyes. "Couldn't you just stay until I went to sleep?"

"I would if I thought I could." His eyes made their way back to me, but he didn't move to come any closer. "You know, I'll have to tell the Guardians about your nightmare."

"What?" I sat up straighter, covers slipping. "Why do they need to know?"

"So we can protect you." His face hardened to marble, his gaze fixed. "It's my job. You know that."

"I know," I mumbled to the blankets. "I guess I just thought that since you're *my* Guardian now, you might be able to keep some things between us."

"Some things, yes. But not everything. Not this." All of a sudden his voice turned gravelly. "I'm sorry."

"I understand." My heart sank a little. "I'm glad you came and woke me up, at least."

"Me too. Get some sleep. You need to get some rest. Your first training session is tomorrow." With that, he vanished. His footsteps thudded down the hall.

Why did I think he'd suddenly change? He'd always put the Guardians before me. The struggle, the emotions at war in him were obvious. I just wanted to win a battle, for once. Why couldn't I ever find a guy who would put me first? He couldn't even sit across the room until I fell asleep.

The hope he'd stirred up in me dissipated into the night. At least I could punch my frustrations out in training tomorrow. It'd better be worth it.

CHAPTER 3

A whiff of bacon wafted to my nose, rousing me from my fitful slumber. Rubbing my eyes, I sat up in bed. I hadn't slept much last night after the shadow puppet nightmares.

Bzzzt. My phone buzzed on the nightstand. Five missed calls and a bazillion unread texts greeted me when I picked up the phone. All from Will. My heartbeat ticked upward as if he might show up and I'd have to run away from him. Again. Couldn't this guy take a hint? Still, a part of me was curious about what had happened to him that night. But I couldn't deal with that now.

Yawning, I twisted my hair into a messy bun and wriggled into my slippers. I slowly shuffled down the hall until I reached the foyer.

Suddenly, a blast of cold air whipped me in the face.

"You look cute in fuzzy slippers." Bryan burst through his own front door and raced down the hallway, leaving slush footprints on the carpet.

"Where's he going in such a hurry?" My cheeks caught fire as I padded to the kitchen to help Cindy with brunch. At least his mom had enough sense to start breakfast at ten a.m. instead of eight. This place already felt like home.

"It snowed a little last night." Cindy's smile warmed the kitchen as she handed me a steaming mug of coffee. "He's just rushing to get his chores done and get things ready for after brunch."

"Why, what's happening after brunch?" I poured creamer in my mug and cocked my head at her.

Her eyes lit up, then the rest of her face. "It's time to start your training."

"I can't wait to—" I bit my lip before the truth oozed out.

Cindy gave me the faintest nod like she knew exactly what I was thinking.

After last night, and everything that happened in the past month, I relished the chance to punch something. An overwhelming urge to fight back beat against my ribcage. I was more than ready to release some aggression.

The rest of the family trickled in, and we ate our brunch in relative silence, with Brooke and Abby making small talk amongst themselves. I munched my bacon and eggs, letting the sweet coffee warm my insides.

When I finished the last bite, I rose to help Cindy clear the dishes, but she just patted my hand. "Don't worry about it, hon. You need to go get ready for training."

"Get ready?" I gulped, glancing at her then toward Brooke. "I didn't bring any workout clothes. Someone surprised me with this Seer Training invite."

"We got you covered." Brooke tugged me out of the kitchen, past the living room, then down the hall. "Anything can happen in Seer Training."

"Really?" I followed her down the basement stairs, blinking at the vast basement that spanned the entire length of the house. More like an underground bunker, really.

Personal gym didn't quite describe it. The entire room was laid out with black rubber tiles and sectioned off into four quadrants complete with blue mats, punching bags, and weights and machines on the left. One quadrant housed an odd assortment of weapons on the right. In the back, sat a collection of objects that could only be described as an obstacle course. Indoors.

"What *is* this place?" I whispered, my jaw dangling on a string

"Oh, you know, just your average secret society training facility. No big deal." Brooke scowled as she stared me down.

"I'll say." I couldn't stop gaping at the facility made just to train me. "I can't believe underneath this peaceful lodge is a secret boot camp."

"The Guardians don't call us the official Seer Trainers for nothing." Brooke's motioned for me to follow her to the nearest door.

"No wonder Bryan had no problem standing up to Jake. He was probably playing nice." I followed Brooke around the corner to a bathroom big enough to be a locker room. With actual lockers. "Wow, you guys really have everything."

"You bet we do. The Guardians make sure of it." She opened the nearest locker and pulled out a set of pink-and-black workout clothes, with matching shoes. All in my size. "We'll call this an early Christmas present, compliments of the Guardians."

"I'll take it." Shooting her a grin, I slipped into the nearest stall to change into my new clothes.

"And whatever Bryan did," Brooke's voice filtered through the door, "I'm sure he wasn't playing nice. He's never been a fan of guys mistreating girls."

"Can't say I disagree with him there." I mumbled, forcing back images of my nightmare as I knotted my sneakers.

When I opened the stall, Brooke was fishing through a plastic tub.

She handed me some black leather pieces. "Strap these on. You'll be glad you did. You've got your shin guards and your arm guards."

I gawked at her as she velcroed the padded gear into place on my extremities and around my torso. Then she bent over the tub again.

"Here's what I like to call the pièce de résistance. Your helmet, my lady." Hoisting it high like a crown, she proceeded to shove it down over my head. Hard. After she velcroed it in place, she boxed my ears on both sides. "Yep, she's on there pretty good."

"Ya think?" I cupped my hands around the helmet. "My ears are ringing."

"That'll wear off in a minute." She barely glanced back at me as she strapped on her own gear. "We'll probably start as sparring partners today. But you'll have to fight the boys eventually."

"Seriously?" The pads weighed down on my limbs like anchors. I felt like a sumo wrestler in a rubber diaper. "Is all of this really necessary?"

"You bet it is." She nodded vehemently. "You think because it's your first day that I'm going to go easy on you? Fat chance."

I tried to shrug, but it came out more like an arm flap. "Maybe just a little easy, okay?"

"We'll see about that." She gritted her teeth and pranced out of the locker room.

I waddled behind her to the sparring quadrant, planting my feet on the blue mats. "What now?"

Bryan marched over, clad in full boxing gear, too. "Don't you look cute?" His gaze flickered up and down my outfit. "Too bad cute won't cut it today."

"Trash talk? Seriously?" I cocked my padded head at him. "You must think you know what you're doing."

He inched closer. "Good thing for you, I do." Suddenly his lips hovered near mine. Butterflies flitted through my stomach. I leaned in closer. Then he pulled out a mouthguard and shoved it between my teeth.

"Smooth." I tongued the plastic into place.

Mark lumbered in behind his son, clapping his hands. "Ready, kids? We'll take it easy on Lucy today. Just show her the basics." Then he turned to me. "Lucy, welcome to your first Seer Training session. For a gift as unique as yours, the Guardians have designed a very special training regimen tailored to your needs. It's a three-phase system handed down through generations of Guardian trainers. The first phase is physical warfare, learning how to fight to protect yourself from Nexis."

"And now the Watchers, apparently," I mumbled through my mouthguard.

"How true." Mark's brow quirked, but he kept going. "The second phase is spiritual warfare. It's all about learning to use your angel conduit abilities to summon the powers of heaven to fight with you, especially your designated guardian angel."

I blinked at him. "Huh, I never thought about him like that." But it was true. Angel was always there when I needed him most.

"And the third phase combines the physical and the spiritual. You'll learn how to call upon your angel conduit powers and pair them with your fight moves to enhance your physical power against humans and demons alike."

"You mean I get to learn how to use superpowers? Heck, yeah! Sign me up for that." I pumped my fist in the air as excitement bubbled in my chest.

Mark leaned in and grabbed my hand. "I'll warn you, phases two and three take more energy and skill to learn than the physical training. Our brain and our senses aren't made to access the spiritual realm. Even though you've been given that gift, it can be quite taxing if you don't harness it right."

"Oh." My eyes widened as I studied his face. That familiar Cooper jawline was rigid. He meant every word he said.

"Don't worry. We'll help you learn the proper techniques. You aren't the first Seer the Guardians have trained. We have certain methods we can show you to amplify your power." He turned to Bryan, Brooke, and Abby, who must've come in mid-speech. "Kids, it'll be your job to assess what level she's at today. Sound good, Lucy?"

"I guess so." I forced a smile around the mouthguard.

"Great. We'll start with square one. Fight stance. Show her." He snapped his fingers in Abby's direction, and just like that Seer Training was on.

Abby nodded and her blonde ponytail swished as she moved to my side. "We've updated parts of the traditional Seer Training. For you, we've chosen the Krav Maga fight stance because you're small and will need to maneuver easily."

She demonstrated moving her legs and rocked back and forth on her feet. "Put the right leg back, and the left leg forward."

"Like that?" I tried to match her stance.

"Almost." She shook her head at me. "Point your feet forward and don't plant them. You want to be able to rock back and forth on the balls of your feet in case you need to kick someone."

A grin spread across my cheeks. "I like the sound of that."

"Good, Lucy." Mark positioned Brooke and Bryan on the mats in front of me. "Okay kids, show her how it's done. Lucy, try to follow along. Mimic what they do."

As if on cue, Bryan and Brooke circled each other in a dance they seemed to have down pat. First, they threw straight punches at each other, then jabs, followed by uppercuts.

I moved my oafish legs along beside Brooke, trying to learn the footwork timing as best as I could. At this point, I didn't have time to worry about the actual punches. Instead, I just let my body remember the techniques I learned from my Dad in our family training sessions. Back then he'd called it firstborn powers training. How ironic.

"Great, Lucy. It looks like you've done this before. You've got good form." Mark's booming voice echoed off the walls. "Let's try kicks now."

The dance drifted to their legs as they moved into a series of straight kicks, side kicks, and roundhouse kicks. Struggling for breath, my lungs screamed for oxygen.

"Not like that, Lucy." Mark's voice filtered in snatches through my wheezing. "Tighten your core."

After a few rounds of trying to keep up, I doubled over, hands on my knees. "Can we take a break? That's definitely more exertion than I'm used to."

"Fine, take five." Concern washed over Mark's face and he barked out orders. "Brooke, get the girl some water. And a towel. Bryan help her to the flat bench. Now."

"Yikes, do I really look that bad?" I sucked down as much cool air as I could inhale. Black dots swam in my vision, and my cheeks were probably Christmas red. "Man, you guys are really in shape."

"Kinda have to be. You'll get used to it." Brooke handed me a towel and plopped down on the bench next to me.

"Not bad for a pip-squeak." Bryan's mouth twisted as he handed me a water bottle.

"Thanks. I'm stronger than I look." I wiped my forehead without looking up at him. Who wants to see their girlfriend all sweaty and gross?

"I don't doubt that." Mark's shadow towered over me. "Now that we've got you warmed up, you want to try phase two training?"

"Really?" I peeked up through my lashes. "You think I'm ready?"

"After what Bryan told me about what happened at Montrose, I think you have a natural ability. I want to see how we can help enhance it." Mark glanced and Bryan with a quick nod. "Would you like to give Lucy her first summoning lesson?"

Bryan's blue eyes lit up like fireworks. "Absolutely."

"Here you go, son" His dad pulled a small velvet bag out of his pocket. "You do the honors."

Bryan took the black pouch from his father, grinning ear-to-ear. Then he turned to me. "Do you remember what we told you about the sacred stones in that secret tunnel we found last month?"

I scrunched my forehead at him. "Sacred stones? Yes. Brooke mentioned that each of the Three Societies have their own sacred stone. The Guardian Amethyst, the Nexis Ruby, and the Watcher's Sapphire. Why?"

His baby-blues darted toward me, then back to the bag. With a flourish, he pulled on the gold cord and slid a sparkling silver and amethyst necklace into the palm of his hand. Gingerly, he turned it over.

"Oh, my," I gasped, stepping back. "It's breathtaking."

And it really was. A large oval amethyst took center stage as three silver rings looped around the centerpiece dotted with rows of tiny amethysts. Even Abby and Brooke stood with their jaws hanging open, appropriately silent.

"This is a piece of the Guardian Amethyst." His face went slack as he slipped the necklace over my head. "It protects the Seer and helps them to harness their power. Since we're in the training bunker, we have permission to show you how to use its powers."

"That's a hot commodity, Lucy." Abby's gaze landed on the new piece of jewelry around my neck. "If it ever fell into Nexis hands, who knows how they would bend its power to their own will?"

A rush of electricity jolted through my body as the amethyst landed on my collar bone. My hands couldn't help but play with the shimmering stone around my neck. Glints of lavender and flecks of violet danced in the light.

"You know, the Guardian Amethyst has special powers, right?" Brooke's voice filtered in from somewhere beside me.

I tore my gaze away from the purple stone. "Yes, I think Bryan and I talked about them once. But he was too distracted to finish the conversation." With a grin, I elbowed him in the ribs.

"Each of the sacred stones has its own special powers. It's what each respective society is built around." Brooke's eyes were wide as she stared at me.

Abby elbowed her sister in the ribs. "Way to go, Brooke. Now she's probably more confused than ever."

Brooke shrugged. "I just thought she should know."

"What do you mean by special powers? Can each of the Three Societies harness power from the stones?" I could feel my face doing the bulldog scrunch, but I didn't even care at this point. Why couldn't I remember this? It seems like a never-ending carnival funhouse of secrets being revealed at every turn. Except it wasn't fun anymore.

"No, silly," Brooke shook her head, causing her blond bangs to swish in front of her glasses. "Only the Chosen Ones can wield the power of the sacred stones."

"Oh, right." Her words rolled around in my brain like a loose marble. "So there's a Chosen One like me for Nexis, and the Watchers, too?"

Brooke nodded and Abby shook her head. Why did I get the feeling I didn't want to know the answer to my own question?

"The only thing you need to worry about right now is the Guardian amethyst. It helps the Seer harness their powers." Bryan's fingers wrapped around my hand and I stilled, glancing up at him.

"Excuse me?" Taking two steps back, I dropped his hand. "If the amethyst does that, what do the other sacred stones do?"

"My son is right." From the back of the circle, Mark cleared his throat and stepped forward. "Don't worry about the other sacred stones yet. We'll teach you about them later. Let's focus on the amethyst, and how you can use it to help you."

"Okay," I mumbled, frustration mounting behind my eyes. Clenching my teeth, I gulped down all my clever comebacks. I guess my sacred stone questions would have to wait.

Mark crossed his arms over his chest and stared at me. "Tell me how you've summoned your guardian angel's power in the past."

The necklace warmed against my skin. "I never thought of him that way before, like a sweet little cherub or something."

Beside me, Brooke barely stifled a giggle.

"Is that what you think we are too, sweet little cherubs?" A laugh rumbled from Mark's chest. "Guardian just means protector, and this angel is your protector, right?"

I bit my bottom lip, debating how much to divulge. At this point, they were probably way past thinking I was crazy. "That's definitely how I would describe him. He's strong, much more powerful than the idea of angels I always had in my head."

"Good." He scratched his chin. "But you still haven't answered my question. How did you summon his angel powers to protect you?"

"Oh, that." I studied my sneakers as the truth spilled out. "I don't know. I sort of talk to him in my head and my arms tingle with angel fire. Except that awful night . . ."

"Lucy, I don't want to make you relive something painful." Mark placed a hand on my shoulder until I met his eyes. Kindness loomed large enough there to keep the memories at bay. "But this is part of your Seer training, learning how to summon your angel fire, among other powers. The Guardian Amethyst only works with your natural process. So whenever you're ready, I'd like to hear about that night and how you talked to your angel." He dropped his hand and stood there, waiting.

I couldn't look at Bryan's dad and picture my angel. So I shut my eyes, focusing on the truly awe-inspiring moments of that night—how my golden-eyed angel came when I called, how he split that tree in two, freeing me with it. My heart leapt into my throat as I pictured the dazzlingly-but-deadly show of purple lightning that exploded all the demon shadows into fireballs.

"I just remember being pinned against that giant tree. I resisted the demons who were tempting me to lash out at Jake and use my dark powers. Once I resisted, my Angel came in an instant." I opened my eyes to find Brooke and Abby by my side.

Bryan just stared at me, sputtering as if he couldn't find the right words. Funny, that's exactly how I felt every time I remembered that night.

Mark's face lit up like a roaring fire, eyes lifting toward Bryan. "We can work with that. Do you think you can try it again, the exact same way?"

"I can try, but there aren't any bad guys around." I shivered, feeling naked and bare with my insides scooped out and strewn all over the floor. Every Cooper in the room stared at me. Heat flashed up my neck.

Instead of staring back at them, I mashed my eyelids closed and pictured the army of wraiths behind Jake. Fear rolled over me in waves, tensing every muscle in my body. When I couldn't take it anymore, I pictured my angel with his beautiful golden eyes. *Alright, Angel. How about some angel fire?*

Bryan cleared his throat. "Is it working?"

"Not yet. You'll be able to see if it's working." Heat spread to my cheeks, but I refused to open my eyes even though I was sure they were still staring at me.

Silence blanketed the darkness hanging heavy behind my eyelids. Any embers of hope that I could summon angel fire at will sank into a slush pile at my feet.

"Nothing's happening," Brooke whispered.

"Like you could see it anyway," Bryan mumbled under his breath.

"Right, 'cause I'm not gonna kiss her."

"Shut up," Bryan hissed.

"Quiet, both of you." Mark's voiced bellowed loud enough to silence their bickering. "If you two distract Lucy, I promise I'll send you both to your rooms."

"Sorry, Lucy." Bryan wrapped his hand around mine, but I kept my eyes shut.

"Me, too," Brooke murmured.

"Try again, Lucy." Mark's tone softened around the edges. "This time, put both hands around the amethyst and concentrate. Really concentrate."

"Okay." I squeezed the amethyst between both hands and waited. Thinking back to the one good part of that awful night, I wracked my mind for exactly what I'd asked for by the tree. Was it my imagination, or did the stone warm up a little? Maybe I was on the right track.

An idea popped into my brain, so I said it out loud. "I choose light. Help me understand my Nephilim powers."

*Pffttttt…*Air whooshed around me in a stormy blast, blowing my hair back. I snapped my eyes open.

In a flash, *Boom!* there he was. The beautiful angel-man with eyes of gold shimmered in lightning-white brilliance in front of me. So bright I couldn't tell if he had wings or a white robe. He defined light itself—pure, sparkling, and mesmerizing with glints of rainbow colors, like diamond facets. I blinked, shielding my eyes from the whiteness until my gaze landed on his golden eyes. They weren't as blinding.

He tilted his head at me as if to say, *"What do you want?"*

"I just wanted to know how to use the gifts you've given me." My lips curved as my heart filled with so much peace I could barely remember why I called for him. "And to say thank you. For showing me the right path."

I tuned out the muffled gasps around me. The only thing that mattered right now was Angel. Period. He was here, and I needed to know why I'd been given this gift. Why did the world need the Seer right now? Shielding my eyes, I focused on that golden head shaking back and forth like I'd never understand.

"But I want to understand. Why me? Why now?" I couldn't tell if I'd spoken out loud or only in my head.

The whiteness around him shifted a bit. Did my angel just shrug his heavenly shoulders?

"You can't tell me? Or I just won't get it?" Were my lips even moving?

The light wavered up and down, almost like a nod. Did that mean I couldn't understand the infinite wisdom of heaven, or he wasn't allowed to tell me? A bubble of frustration gurgled inside me, curling my fingers into fists. In a flash, angel fire sparked from my fingertips.

Mark's voice filtered through the whiteness. "Good. Ask him to help you harness the angel fire."

Angel, how do I use this angel fire? My grip tightened around the amethyst.

The shimmering wall of white in front of me wavered slightly. *You don't need that stone to harness the power of my fire. I've already bound part of my soul to yours. All you need to do is open yourself up to the light.*

"That's not cryptic or anything." I mumbled, releasing the necklace.

The whiteness rumbled in front of me. *Hold your palms up and focus on the light within you. Then channel it through your hands.*

"Okay, here goes nothing." I gulped, refusing to open my eyes and acknowledge anyone else in the room. If I did, I'd surely lose my nerve.

Instead, I turned my palms up to the ceiling and searched deep within myself. Angel had given me part of his light that night, and I had to dig past all of the awful memories to find it. Pushing aside the images of Jake and his shadow army, I found the nugget of light Angel had given me. He'd said. *If you choose the light over the darkness, you'll become an angel conduit. Half of your soul with be infused with angel powers, making you a Nephilim of Light.*

Then he'd asked me if Jake was really my enemy. I'd answered immediately, *No. The darkness is my enemy. I choose light.*

At that thought, electricity coursed through my veins. I repeated the mantra over and over again in my mind, *I choose light. I choose light.*

Every hair on my body stood at attention as static sizzled down my arms. I opened my eyes as two twin balls of lightning crackled in each of my upturned palms.

"Ohmigosh." Brooke squealed as gasps echoed around the room.

"No what?" I hissed at the Coopers and Angel.

That's enough for today. Only summon your angel fire when necessary.

"But should I learn how to use it first. Like practice or something?" My words came out high and whiny.

No practice is needed. I will teach you each time you need to use the angel fire until you can do it all on your own. But you must build up your strength first. The words formed in my head as the whiteness nodded. Pearlescent fingertips reached toward my temple. Just like he'd done the first time we met, in the hospital.

Brilliant light enveloped the whole room, bursting every shadow and hint of darkness into white blossoms. Somehow my limbs were floating in the air. I felt weightless, free of all my burdens and obligations on earth.

Goodbye, little Seer. You rest now.

Suddenly my forehead grazed the ceiling. *Bam!* A clap of thunder rumbled above me. Then the whiteness faded away with a great gust of wind.

And I was falling fast.

Air whizzed around me as I plummeted to the ground. I turned my palms to the ground, trying to call up my angel fire. But it only fizzled and crackled.

Slap, my back smacked against something hard, knocking the breath from my lungs

Bryan's strong arms curled under me and we tumbled to the mats.

"It's okay, Lucy. I've got you," Bryan whispered into my hair.

My limbs went numb as the training room faded to black.

CHAPTER 4

Darkness surrounded me—still and peaceful. I floated through the universe, a bottomless void of black space. Hands wrapped around my shoulders, shaking me out of the land of nothing. Speckles of light slashed open the void. Pinpricks of stars exploding in a night sky, shooting rays of light that collided, merging into streaks of gray and color.

In a great blinding flash like a lens flare, the underground training room finally came into focus. My angel was gone. And I was cold. I could barely move, but my limbs felt lighter as if they'd been hollowed out by the strange journey.

"Lucy, wake up. Are you okay?" So much concern clouded Bryan's eyes. Too much.

It shocked my heart right back into reality. I propped my elbows up on the blue mats and eased myself into a sitting position.

In an instant, his arms were around me. "Thank God," he breathed into my hair. "Don't scare me like that. I was so worried."

"We all were." Brooke's eyes crinkled like Bryan's, and her dad didn't look much better. Abby paced back and for across the mats as if that'd help my gurgling stomach.

Bryan's strong arms found my waist, his hands cupping my sides to help me stand. The blue mats swayed like the sea.

"What happened?" A croaking sound escaped my throat.

"I'm not really sure yet. I think I'll have to check the book." Mark scratched his chin and squinted his eyes like he was trying to solve a math problem. "Get her some water."

Brooke rushed to get me a water bottle. I downed it as fast as I could.

"What book?" I asked between gulps. Two, three, five seconds ticked by. No one answered me.

"The Seer Training book. But don't worry about that now. You've definitely had enough for today." Mark turned to his son with a lost look on his face. "Why don't you take her upstairs now so she can rest?"

The idea of a training manual rolled around in my brain, but my mind was all foggy. My knees wobbled and I reached for Bryan.

"On it." Within seconds Bryan scooped me up in his arms and booked it across the room. Brooke trailed behind us, then disappeared into the locker room.

"You don't have to carry me." I could barely talk above a whisper.

"Just let me take care of you." He pressed his lips to my forehead. "For me," he whispered.

"Okay, if it'll make you feel better. I could get used to this." I nuzzled into his chest as he climbed the basement steps. "What was your dad talking about?"

He eased me past the guest-room doorway and set me down on the four-poster bed. "There's a special book the Guardian trainers have passed down for generations. It's all about how to train the Seer. He probably thinks he did something wrong or brought you along too fast. But you were doing so good."

"Was I?" My words were but a breath.

"You were marvelous." But the smile didn't reach his eyes. "Get some rest, angel girl."

That worried look on his face faded away as my eyes fluttered closed. Somewhere in a faraway place Mark's words drifted on the breeze—he wanted to talk to Bryan, and they needed to consult the book. But it all seemed so far away right now. I let myself drift off into never-never land.

><

A white fog smudged out the forest background as my white sleigh of blankets rocked back and forth between the evergreens. A figure shifted at the end of my bed. I woke with a gasp, somehow under the covers now.

"Oops. Sorry I startled you." Abby sat curled up at the foot of my bed, closing her book. "They asked me to watch you, but I thought that was kinda creepy so I decided to read."

I made an attempt to sit up. Bad choice. The room rocked on its axis again, and I slumped back down on my pillow.

"Don't move. I'll be right back." Abby dashed into the bathroom and scurried back holding a wet washcloth. She eased down next to me, pressing the cold terrycloth to my forehead. "Is that better?"

"A little." I didn't try to move my head again. Though I could've used a nice chocolate milkshake right about now.

Massaging my forehead in little circles, she stared down at me. "Listen, Lucy. There are a few things I've been meaning to tell you." She paused, gnawing on her lip.

I studied her face. "You've got a captive audience."

As her eyes met mine, a shadow crossed her face. "About James."

"Oh." The breath stole from my lungs.

"I felt guilty about not telling you James' secret." Her mouth twisted as she peeled the now cold washcloth from my forehead. "But it wasn't my secret to tell. I'm sure your brother had his reasons for not telling you."

Hadn't Will said something eerily similar the night he told me James was really my half-brother? I mashed my lips together, as if I could hold in all the pent-up anger I'd felt when Will dropped that not-so-little bomb on me. More like a nuclear explosion.

She wrung out the washcloth in a bowl on the nightstand, then turned to look at me. "I'm so sorry. I know it's a lot to ask, but can you ever forgive me?"

"I was *not* happy about the way I found out, but that's hardly your fault. Will completely blindsided me." Even now, I balled up my fists just thinking about his smug face. "Did I wish I knew before Will ratted out my brother? Of course. But I wish my parents would've told me the truth first. So I didn't have to hear about it from anyone else."

"Yeah, I bet that sucked." Her eyes were glazed over, and she continued to chew on her bottom lip, her face scrunched up like a bunny's. Maybe the only time in her life she'd ever resembled Brooke.

How could I hold a grudge against anyone in Bryan's family? I'd felt more at home here than I had in my own house back in Indiana for the past few years. Ever since James disappeared.

I reached for her hand. "Don't worry, okay? There's nothing to forgive."

"Thank you, Lucy." She exhaled the biggest sigh of relief in the history of the world. "You have no idea how much I needed to hear that. Especially since I'm sure you'll be around for awhile."

"I hope you're right," I muttered under my breath.

"You feeling any better yet?" Abby asked.

"A little." Patting the bed, I motioned for Abby to sit across from me. "Tell me a little more about my brother."

Her blue eyes lit up as she perched on the edge. "Sure. What do you want to know?"

"Were you there when he got banished? What happened to him afterward?" I inched my way upright until I was sitting up in bed, leaning against my massive pile of pillows. The world stayed still this time. Progress.

"No, I wasn't there." She gave me a headshake. "That's a Nexis ceremony they do in secret. But I was president of the Guardians when he came to us for help."

"Really?" My heart sank a little, and I tried to hide my disappointment. "I had no idea Bryan was just following in your footsteps."

She smiled at that. "I convinced Harlixton and the council to let James in. We even assigned him bodyguards until graduation."

I cocked my head at her. "But why would you do that?"

Her hands toyed with the white comforter. "For the information," she admitted at last. "We made a deal with him. On his eighteenth birthday, he came to us with stolen intel. We traded protection for all the dirt he had on Nexis. I wish we didn't have to do it that way. It only made him a Nexis target." She winced at the memory.

"Poor James." I cringed, too, but for different reasons. I'd seen everything James went through to escape Nexis. The banishment, the circle of fire, and that tortured look on his face. It was one of my earliest visions.

"Trading secrets was the only way out for him. Once Nexis figured out he wasn't the Seer, he was doomed. And he knew it." A tear droplet leaked from the corner of her eye. "They tried to kidnap him at graduation. If his guards hadn't found him, I don't know if he would've survived."

I choked up too just thinking about what Nexis must've done to my brother.

She wiped her eyes. "I begged the Montrose leaders to call in the Guardian council. They put him on a plane to Europe the next day. And I never saw him again. That's all I know."

My heart skipped a beat. "Do you have any way to contact him?"

"No, I wish I did." Her eyes dropped to the bedspread. "I wish I'd done better by him."

"Are you kidding me? You saved his life!" I tilted my head at her. "It sounds like you did everything you could. And then some."

She kept staring at the comforter and wouldn't look at me. Pink splotches broke out all across her face.

At last, it dawned on me. "Wait a sec. I get it now. You have a crush on my bro, don't you?"

"What? I—" Her mouth hung open. "How did you figure that out? What are you the Seer *and* psychic?"

"Yeah, right." I threw my head back and laughed. "One unwelcome gift is enough for me, thanks."

"Was I that obvious?" Golden hair fell across half her face as she nibbled her lip.

"Kinda." I stifled back another giggle. "Hold up. I'm missing something. Where did Maria fit into all this?"

She peered at me through her bangs. "She was his girlfriend. They were both in Nexis together."

My lips formed a big *O*. "So that's why nothing ever happened with James."

"But we were friends, even though we stood on different sides." She huffed, parting her bangs so I could see her eyes again. "I always wanted more, wanted him to renounce Nexis and join the Guardians. I just never realized how much it would cost him. I don't think he did, either. I'm so sorry, Lucy."

"Don't be." I thumped my hand on her shoulder. "It's not your fault. Nexis kicked out my brother because he wasn't the Seer. He's not me."

She bobbed her head slowly, patting my hand. "It's not your fault that you're the Seer and he's not."

I shook my head hard enough to send a pillow flying. "No, it's not my fault. That's all on my mother."

"I'm sorry I brought it up." She hopped off the bed, hugging the pillow to her chest before handing it back to me.

"No worries." I sank back under the covers. When I looked up again, she hovered in the doorway. I couldn't miss my chance. "Can I ask you one more thing? How did Maria die?"

"That poor girl." Her knuckles went white on the doorframe as if she couldn't stand up without it. "I wish I knew what happened. Whatever it was, James must've seen the whole thing. He was so afraid. He barely even spoke to me about it. His guards said he'd cry her name in his sleep. However she died, it must torture him."

With that, she left. The gloom gathered its icy tendrils and settled a fresh batch of fog over me. How had this struggle between the Three Societies become my new reality? A world where people were ostracized just for who they were. Oh yeah, and someone might die in the process.

Not on my watch. If I had any say in the matter, I'd be the Seer to finally end to this ridiculous conflict. Somehow.

><

The next day I woke up to the heavenly aroma of hot coffee and a rap-rap-rapping on the door. Stepping out of the shower, I found a fight outfit waiting on the bed for me. And a steaming mug on the nightstand with a note beside it.

Peace offering. - A was all it said. Maybe, in spite of all the Nexis/Guardian stuff between us, we were finally becoming friends.

Smiling, I sipped the coffee. Warm and creamy, with no sugar, just the way I liked it. She must've asked Bryan. Letting the warmth seep into my fingers, I downed a few more gulps. Hopefully a mega-dose of caffeine would amp me up enough to tackle training again.

My sore muscles felt even more weighed down as I velcroed the padded materials over my workout clothes. Like a walking lead balloon, I trudged downstairs to Cooperstown Gym.

Abby waited at the bottom of the stairs, eyes fixed, jaw jutting out. Lifting her chin, she gave me a hard stare. No one needed to know about our little talk last night. My head dipped as I passed. She nodded back. We were cool.

"Dad has some work to finish up before Christmas Eve, so he left me in charge." She took up a fight stance in the blue-mat quadrant next to Brooke. Fully outfitted, they were both planted in front of Bryan for some reason. "Today I'm going to teach you how to take down an attacker twice your size."

"Guess who gets to be the attacker?" Bryan mumbled against his mouthguard.

"Great." I furrowed my forehead at them. "How on earth am I supposed to take you down?"

"By leveraging your assets," Brooke piped in as a huge grin spread across her face.

"No way that's gonna work." I bit back a laugh. "First off, I don't have any assets—"

"Ahem," Bryan cleared his throat. "Yeah right."

"Okay." My cheeks burned. "At least not any that would take down an attacker. And second, I don't think I could punch Bryan. Just look at that face."

He placed his hand over his heart and turned those baby blues on me. I was gone, baby. Gone.

Abby moved in front of me, shoving sparring gloves over my hands. "You're just going to have to forget that you're lovebirds for an hour. It's not the end of the world."

"Like that's gonna happen." Brooke actually rolled her eyes at me.

I narrowed my eyes at her. "Oooh, it's on now. Challenge accepted."

Bryan took a step forward. "Just pretend I'm Will. Then you'd want to punch me, right?"

"Good one." I turned to face him.

"Or think about something Bryan did to make you mad. I'm sure he's done something. He can be uber annoying." Brooke pursed her lips at her brother.

It came to me quicker than I thought—the bio lab where Bryan tried to study me like a science project. I balled up my fists just thinking about it.

"Excellent." Abby rubbed her hands together. "Your main weapon is speed, so we'll work on fine-tuning that today. But even with speed, it'll be hard to land a punch that counts unless it's in the sensitive areas."

"Landed some of those a month ago. Solar plexus and in-step to be precise," I said, without even thinking. My moves hadn't been enough to get away from Jake.

Bryan cringed as if he knew exactly what I was thinking.

"Those aren't the best ones. The best way to catch your attacker off guard is to elbow him in the face. Like this." She winged out her elbow and popped Bryan's padded jaw. "A nose hit is good, too, but since it's unprotected you'll just have to mime today." She jabbed her elbow at his nose, then his jaw. "You try."

I mimicked her one-two motion, lifting my elbow up to his nose, then his jaw.

"Lean into it," she barked. "Leverage your body weight. Good. Now switch. Left side up. Jab, jab. Jab."

She repeated the orders, and I followed the dance until my lungs burned again. On the next pass, a spark of angel fire sizzled up my forearm and my elbow smacked dead on the bridge of Bryan's nose.

"Ohmigosh." I rushed up to him, gut-wrenching into guilty knots. "I'm so sorry. I had a weird zap of angel fire out of nowhere."

"Nice one. Your powers must've thought you were really in danger." Blood dripped down his face slowly at first, before trickling to a gush.

Brooke zipped into the bathroom, racing back with gobs of tissues. "Tilt it forward. Put pressure here."

"I know how to take care of a bloody nose. It's not the first time." He tilted his head forward, dabbing his nostrils with tissues and pinching the bridge of his nose.

"I swear, I didn't do it on purpose." I knelt to mop up the blood-spattered mats. "Did I break it?"

"No, it's fine." His voice came out pinched and muffled. "You don't have to kiss my feet or anything."

"Thanks for that." I wanted to hug him for trying to make me feel better. But I didn't want to zap him again. "Maybe we should put a hold on fight club for the day. It's just not my forté."

"I don't know." He tilted his head down, removing the tissues. "You got in a pretty good shot there." He smiled at me, almost looking like his normal self again.

I lifted my lips to smile back, but a strange odor filled my nostrils. Musty and foul just like—*Bam!* A wall of air slammed into me, knocking me off balance.

Darkness swarmed every corner of the room, graying out the light. Forming a spotlight around the three of us, with a strange red light glowing in the center. *Whoosh.* Wind howled at my face, blasting my hair back. Without thinking, I tried to call up my angel fire. It only zapped and fizzled a few sparks from my fingertips before dying out completely.

Then came the horrid shriek. A screeching whistle that carved out my eardrums.

Devoid of my powers, I couldn't protect myself from the howling demons straight from a horror movie. I screamed at the top of my lungs, clamping my hands over my ears. Sinking to the mats, I curled into a ball on the floor. Was I going insane?

With all that was left of my scrambled brain, I cried out to the heavens, "Make it stop! Please make it stop."

Strong hands gripped my shoulders shaking me, tugging on my arms and legs. But I couldn't release my protective cocoon.

"Lucy, what's going on? Are you okay?" Bryan's words barely pierced through the howling agony.

Tears streamed down my face. The Guardians moved around me, forming a circle. Murmured words rose and crested on the high-pitched wave. Words that seemed to calm and still the hellish noise. Finally, the screeching nightmare dissipated into the air as the shadows receded from the light.

Gingerly, I unfurled my limbs from their cocoon, breathing hard and fast, wiping my dripping eyes and nose.

"You're okay, sweetie. You're safe now." Bryan crouched down beside me, his hands smoothing back my hair. "It's gone. Whatever it was." He eased me into a sitting position and wrapped his arms tight around me. "Just try to breathe. It's going to be okay."

I inhaled lungfuls of stench-free oxygen, desperately trying to slow my breathing to match his.

"What was that?" Brooke crouched down to my level. "It was like someone turned on a giant fan. But not even the furnace on full blast could blow that much air down here."

I sucked in an extra breath. "You felt it, too?"

Abby nodded at me, crouching down to my level. "It was kinda freaky."

"Did you hear it, too?" I hiccupped. "That horrible shrieking?"

"Nope." She pursed her lips and shook her head. "Didn't hear anything. I just felt the wind. Did you guys?"

Brooke's voice filtered down from above. "I didn't hear anything."

Above me, Bryan moved his head, chin mussing my hair. "No wonder you were freaking out."

"Great, so you just thought I was having a psychotic break or something?" My heart pounded against my ribcage as heat rushed to my cheeks. I couldn't look at him. Any of them.

He squeezed me tight. "Never. Don't forget, we know who you are. It's a heavy burden to bear. For anyone. Especially two years before you're supposed to have any of your Seer abilities."

I gulped back the rest of the tears that threatened to overflow. "I couldn't even summon my angel fire."

"You know you're not alone, right?" He scooted me around to face him. "Even though you're the only one who can see the things you see, we're still here for you. I'm here for you."

Tears slid down my cheeks. "Thank you for that." I hugged him close.

"Tell me what happened. Wind and some kind of shrieking?" His soft breath feathered my temple. Rising to his feet, he pulled me up with him.

"Yeah." The room spun as I stood, and he steadied me. "Plus, a weird shadow engulfed the room, snuffing out my angel fire. Like all the light was drained from the world. Except for a spotlight around us. And the shrieking. The horrible shrieking …"

Suddenly his arms went slack and his face turned pale. "You're kidding."

"What?" I took a step back and stared at him.

"That's not good." His voice cracked.

I reached out to steady him this time. "What is it?"

His eyes were blank as he looked at me. "It sounds like a reckoning. Have Mom get the book." He wasn't talking to me anymore. He was talking over my head. He nodded to Abby who didn't hesitate.

"On it," was all she said. In two seconds flat, I heard two pairs of footsteps pounding up the stairs. I didn't have the energy to ask.

Turning to me, his brows scrunching together. "Can you make it to the living room, or do you need me to carry you?"

My cheeks warmed. "Maybe I should carry you this time. You look pretty shaken."

He nodded, bracing his arm around my back.

As we teeter-tottered up the stairs, I asked the question burning me up inside. "What exactly is 'the book' you're talking about?"

"It's the Guardian's Book of the Seer…" he huffed between steps. "It's got all sorts of legends … prophecies … and history in it."

"About reckonings, or whatever that was?" I cocked my head at him as we reached the landing. "That might've come in handy before now."

"Yep, it's in there." He raked his hand through his hair. "None of this is protocol. It just doesn't make sense."

I stopped at the top of the stairs. "I think it's time I saw this Seer training book."

"It's not protocol," he mumbled again. Catching my eye, he lowered his voice. "But I think you're right. It's time."

Maybe this book would explain all the crazy things I'd faced in just two days of Seer training. But if the Guardians of the Seer couldn't figure it out, how could a premature Seer ever make sense of all this otherworldly chaos?

CHAPTER 5

My knees wobbled on the stairs. My hands shook like crazy. That God-awful scream still echoed in my ringing ears. Bryan's face mirrored everything I felt. Maybe I didn't want to be the Seer any more, not if I had to deal with atrocious things like "a reckoning." Whatever that was.

Bryan herded me into the living room, easing me down on the couch in front of the fireplace. The warmth from the crackling fire seeped into my skin, steadying my nerves a bit.

Cindy rushed in carrying a cup of hot cocoa as if it would melt away the horror I'd just lived through. I sipped at the warm chocolate. Bit into a marshmallow. Breathed in and out. It all took extra effort at this point.

Cindy scurried off down the hall. When she reappeared with Brooke and Abby, she had a book tucked under her arm. I could only assume it was THE book. Plopping down next to me, she handed the book to Bryan and he ever-so-gently laid it on my lap. The Cooper sisters huddled together behind me to catch a glimpse of "the book."

Warmth radiated from the leather-bound tome. Its mere presence on my lap soothed me even more. Like maybe some kind of explanation lay hidden in the parchment pages. My fingers itched to trace the raised bronze circle in the center on the faded-green cover. Oddly enough, it looked just like the Nexis book Will tried to make me steal from the school library. A chill slithered down my spine.

Cindy opened the book, its rusty hinges creaking an ominous note. As the pages crinkled open, a dusty smell wafted up—like fresh dirt tinged with musty old books. Carefully, she thumbed through the parchment until she came to a page with a drawing. Eyes etched in ancient ink over scrawling Latin script.

I knew it said exactly what I needed. I knew it in my bones.

"Don't be alarmed, dear." Cindy glanced over at me.

"Just lay it on me. At this point I can take anything, right?" I gritted my teeth.

"This section here talks about the role of the undeclared Seer," Cindy pointed to the Latin words.

"What do you mean, undeclared? That night on the quad when my ex attacked me, I chose light." My voice wobbled as the images rushed back. "My angel said I had to choose between becoming a dark Nephilim or a Nephilim of light. And I chose light."

Cindy's eyes went wide. "Wow. I had no idea you already made your choice." She squinted down at the Latin script again, her finger landing on something. "Maybe we interpreted this wrong. Maybe this section about turning eighteen means your choice isn't permanent until your eighteenth birthday."

"Great!" I threw up my hands. "So that means I'm doomed to face horrible shrieking noises until I turn eighteen?"

Brooke gnawed on her lip as she glanced between me and her mom. "That doesn't seem fair."

"Agreed." Cindy nodded, rubbing at her temples. "Even though it's being forced on you, there are advantages to staying neutral—like peace, tenuous as it is, instead of war. However, there are marked disadvantages."

A shiver racked my body. "What kind of disadvantages?"

Peeking over my shoulder, Abby gasped. "I guess I didn't think about that, even though it seems so obvious."

"What?" I craned my neck to look at her. "Someone tell me what's going on."

Cindy patted my knee. "It seems that an undeclared Seer, such as yourself, is still subject to a reckoning from the other side. These reckonings dampen your powers until you learn to overcome them."

"But why? What does it mean?" I shut my eyes tight, bracing myself for impact.

"It's an ancient term. It has to do with balancing things out, between two sides." She flipped to the next page, a beautiful drawing of a sunset backlit with shadows. "It's like day and evening. Because you're learning how to summon your angel fire at will, the fallen angels are angry. They want their chance to tempt your with their dark powers to be their demon conduit. It can happen whenever you're training to use your powers until you get strong enough."

"What?" My eyes popped open, and my jaw unhinged. "So, you're saying every time I use my angel powers, I'm making the shadow demons mad enough to attack me?"

"Pretty much." Cindy's face went grim as she squeezed my knee. "I guess the darkness still thinks they have a chance to get you on their side. Just because they have the opportunity to equal the balance doesn't mean the darkness will come every time. But it's always out there, prowling around, waiting for its chance to tempt you back to their side."

I rubbed my still-buzzing ears and desperately tried to wrap my mind around everything I just heard. "Do they actually think some howling Tasmanian devil is gonna make me switch sides?"

"Scare tactics work on a lot of people. Fortunately for us, they've never worked on Seers in the past." She sucked in a breath, eyes wide as if she'd just said too much.

Another shiver coursed through me. "Do I even want to know what happened to the Seers in the past?"

"Probably not, dear." She pursed her lips together. "You're too young and innocent for that kind of news. Especially right now. Right after a reckoning. If you don't mind, I think I'll send you to your room to get some rest."

I gave her a blank stare. "I don't mind at all. I am kinda zapped right now."

"If you have any questions, please just let me know. I'll be happy to answer anything I can." She closed the book and tucked it under her arm, then hurried out of the room.

"Where's she going?" I glanced up at Bryan as he helped me off the couch.

He slid one arm around my back, and together we limped down the hall. "All ancient Guardian texts are kept in a climate-controlled safe. For protection and preservation."

"Like the Vatican vault?" I quipped, quirking my head at him

He huffed out a laugh. "Not quite that intense. How do you know about that? Do you have Catholic relatives or something?"

I shook my head. "No, I saw it in a Tom Hanks movie."

"Nice." This time he laughed out loud. Music to my ears. "Now you get some rest, little lady. There will be more training soon."

"Good," I mumbled, sinking into the bed.

"I'll see you later." He turned out the light and tiptoed out of the room.

I lay in bed, staring up at the ceiling. Maybe I should learn to read Latin. Then I might have some clue of what was coming next.

><

Emotions fizzled inside me as I lay in bed, unable to shut my eyes. For too many months, I'd pushed my problems back to the land of denial. My mom's betrayal. Nexis and their manipulation. The stalking Watchers who tried to brand me in a cathedral. Jake and the attack. All of the horrible visions and events collided in my brain like an internal lightning storm—striking chord after chord. Resentment. Frustration. Sheer Anger. They zapped me at random. As chaotic and out-of-control as the reckoning.

Why didn't my choice count now? It'd stop the reckonings from ever happening again. One reckoning was *more* than enough for me. I knew, in my heart, I'd never choose the darkness or Nexis. With or without demon scare tactics. The price was too high. But I didn't want to start a war over the Seer, either.

I just wanted to join the Guardians and fight against the society that banished my brother, forcing him to flee to another continent. An organization that literally tore my family apart, that caused an innocent girl's death. Nexis wanted to control me. Could they be more obvious about it? But what if the Guardians just wanted to control me, too? Deep down, that little thought niggled at my brain, forcing me to keep my guard up. Ironic, actually. Maybe the Guardians were right to keep me from joining. Stupid rules.

I punched my fist into the bedspread and stomped into the bathroom.

"I will not be controlled," I whispered to my reflection in the mirror. "I will not be put in a prison of any secret society's making."

I was the Seer in training. I needed to learn to wield my power for myself. Maybe someday I could bring down all of the Three Societies. Put an end to their feuding. But until then, this gift was given to me. I'd better learn how to use it—before anyone or any*thing* else tried to use my gifts against me.

Throwing open the shower curtain, I turned the water on full blast. Maybe a little steam would help.

After my shower, I started blow-drying my hair right as someone pounded on my door. Brushing out my tangles, I opened the door to find Bryan with an armful of gear.

"Here, get ready." He thrust the pads at me. "We're going to try something different today." Then he tramped off.

"Whatever." Dumping the gear on the floor, I yanked my still-wet hair into a tight ponytail. If a fight was what he wanted, he'd get more than he bargained for this morning.

Pffffft, pftt,
Thwack, hrumpf, thwack.

Fight sounds echoed off the concrete walls as I headed downstairs.

In the boxing quadrant, Mark braced the punching bag as Bryan pounded away on it with a fury I'd never seen before. Guess I wasn't alone in the rage department this morning.

"What's going on? Do I need gloves, too?" I hovered near the rack of boxing gloves.

Bryan dropped his dukes and wiped his brow. "Just blowing off some steam."

Mark moved in front of him. "We're going to try something a little different today. If that's okay with you."

"Absolutely." I bobbed my head. "I'm ready for a change."

Mark rubbed his hands together. "Let's try some real fight training today. Not just defensive work, but real offensive training. Think you can handle that?"

"That's exactly what I need." I strapped on a pair of boxing gloves. "Let's do it."

"Good girl." He planted his feet and motioned me to face off with him. "Now, settle into your stance. Start throwing me your best punches. Bryan will help you with your form."

"Got it." I chomped into the mouthguard, flexing my shoulders.

I scrambled through all the punches they'd taught me the last few days. I threw a right jab, left jab, alternating uppercut combo.

Mark blocked each one. Without breaking a sweat. "You can do better than that."

"Fine." I resisted the urge to growl.

Behind me, Bryan's gloves landed on my shoulders, holding me in place. "Keep your shoulder blades down and locked tight. You're giving away your punches."

I tried to shrug him off, and finally he let go.

This time I popped my elbow at Mark's chin, then punched his gut in a split-second while kicking his shin the next.

He stumbled back a step, coughing. "Better. Much better."

"From the core." A glove smacked into my stomach as Bryan barked in my ear, "Tighten your abs, babe."

In an instant I whirled around, socking him with two jabs in the gut. "Guard your middle, Cooper."

"Touché," he puffed, bending over.

"I'm liking the ferocity." Mark tapped his gloves together. "Let's see how you do with two attackers."

"Great." A shudder slithered up my spine, but I tamped it down. I shifted my stance so I could keep my eye on Mark to my left, Bryan to my right. Their shadows towered over me. How could I ever bring either one of them down? Not thinking like a loser, that's for sure.

Out of nowhere, a thought popped in my head. What if I visualized my moves first? Isn't that what all the gurus said in the movies? Closing my eyes, I visualized how to attack Mark. A spider-monkey version of Lucy flashed in my mind. She karate-chopped Mark's belly while side-tackling his leg. I blinked and opened my eyes. Then I let my body take over. I punched and kicked Mark's leg just like I'd already seen myself do.

Moments later, he doubled over from my chop-kick combo. He was totally caught off guard.

"Whoa, did that really happen?" I stepped back, blinking. Did that actually work? Something golden twinkled in the corner of my vision, and it all made sense. This was all Angel. He was right there with me, helping me. And it bolstered my confidence.

Another combo came to mind. With Mark still catching his breath, I aimed at Bryan.

He threw a jab that I caught with both hands. Instead of twisting his arm around his back like he always did to me, I kicked his shin the wrong way while simultaneously kicking his stomach. When his leg crumpled, I landed a few more blows. But a zap of angel fire zipped through my gloves like a static shockwave, knocking him to the ground.

I pinned his shoulders, locking his flailing arms to the mat with my gloves. "Tighten your abs, babe."

He shot me a smoldering look, but I didn't budge an inch.

"Very good." Mark chuckled, tapping his gloves together. "I have no idea how you learned so fast. Bravo, young lady."

"You can get off me now." Bryan tried to wriggle free.

"If you want." I loosened my grip and he slid out from under me.

"No comment." He brushed himself off, refusing to look at me.

Probably didn't want to see the triumph on my face.

"How'd you do that?" He still wouldn't look at me.

Now I turned away from Bryan, fumbling with my sparring gloves. Could I tell him everything? He'd just tell the Guardians, and who knows how they'd use it against me.

I unvelcroed my gloves and decided to give him a version of the truth. But not the whole truth. Let's see how much he could handle.

"I cheated." A smile crept up. "If you must know, I had some help."

"Really?" He stared me down, blue eyes intense. "Did you see your angel, or have a vision or something?"

Even Mark leaned in now, wiping his brow with a towel.

I shrugged like it was no big deal. "I just asked my angel to give me some cool moves. And he did."

"That's awesome!" Bryan's face lit up as he pumped his fist in the air. "I hoped it would work like that."

"You did?" Frowning, I cocked my head at him. "How could you possibly know?"

"Congratulations, Lucy. You've just started your phase three training. While you were sleeping, we reread the Book of the Seer trying to figure out a way around the reckonings." He glanced over at his dad. "Loosely translated, it said the need for a reckoning could be halted for neutral activities. I hoped that included fight training since it could be considered useful by Nexis, the Watchers, and the Guardians alike."

"Okay." I crossed my arms over my torso, my frustration mounting. "But that doesn't answer my question. How'd you know I'd see something?"

"The book said it was possible to 'obtain help from above' if the situation warranted it," Mark said. "Maybe the two-attacker approach summoned your angel's help."

"Seriously?" I shook my head, all the annoyance inside pooling at my feet. "I wish you guys would stop trying to figure out how to summon my angel. To me, it's much more organic than that. If I need him, he comes. End of story. I don't consciously try to summon him. In fact, something bad happens every time I try to do it your way."

"That's interesting." Mark stepped back, scratching his chin. "Everything we've found in the Book of the Seer about training speaks to the Seer's power to summon the angelic hosts."

With a huff, I threw my hands up in the air. "I don't know what to tell you. Except one thing, maybe. My angel never comes when I try to summon him directly. He comes on his own, or on the rare occasion I ask the big guy upstairs to send him."

"Hmmm. I wonder if we're translating that word wrong or something." With that, Mark unfastened his gear and traipsed upstairs, mumbling to himself. "Better look it up."

My jaw dangled somewhere around my collarbone. "What was that about?" I turned to Bryan.

He yanked off his pads, too. "My dad has been studying to train the Seer for all of his life. We all have. You're not what he expected. It's throwing him for a loop. All of us, really."

Fire burned through my veins. In three giant strides, I marched across the room and slammed my gear into their cubbyholes. Bryan was hot on my heels.

"Did I throw you for a loop, too?" I whirled around to face him.

"You definitely threw me for a loop. In more ways than one." He reached for me, holding me at arm's length. "But I'm glad you're the Seer. I wouldn't want you to change one bit. Not even your 'organic' methods."

"Thanks." My frustration melted a fraction.

"Don't worry about Dad," Bryan said, reaching for my hand. "You do things the way *you* see fit. Whether you summon your angel or not, he's always there when you need him. I think it's time you start trusting in that more. We all need to, angel girl. I call you that for a reason."

"Okay." I sighed, leaning in closer. "I kind of liked *babe*."

"Babe it is then." If I didn't know better I'd say I almost saw him blush. "Dad'll be looking for me. I better go."

I watched him trot up the stairs, my heart reeling from the roller coaster of emotions.

Inhaling a fresh breath, I released any remnants of anger lingering in the corners of my mind. Part of me was glad I didn't tell the Coopers every last detail of what I saw. Surely their brains would explode. I blew a kiss to the heavens, sending up my gratitude to my angel for always having my back. And giving me a secret weapon to fight for myself. If this was Seer training, bring it on.

CHAPTER 6

Visions of light and darkness played a movie through my head, hazy around the edges. A cloud of mist blew across my mind's eye as yesterday's fight floated into focus. Premonitions of fight moves before they happened. Angel hovering in the corner, quivering in brightness. Golden butterflies burst from his form and landed on my nose. They lined up in front of me, alighting on a new scene. All the visions of light I'd ever had, all laid out in a row. As if I could reach out and touch them.

My eyes fluttered open to the real world. Gray sunlight streamed through the blind slats. I rubbed my eyes, trying to picture the beauty of the dream I'd just had. But the images rolled away in a fog. Out of sight, but not out of mind.

A pang of longing seared a dull ache in my chest. Today was Christmas Eve. How could I feel so at home here, but still overcome with such homesickness? I couldn't help it. I missed my family.

"Knock, knock." Brooke appeared in my doorway, cradling a steamy cup of coffee. "I made peppermint mocha today, just to add a festive touch."

I reached for the mug and gulped down the minty chocolate comfort. "You know, I've felt more welcome here than my own home sometimes."

"Really?" A giant grin broke out on her face.

"I—uh..." I did a double-take. Did I really just admit that, out loud? My face flamed.

Brooke reached out and squeezed my hand. "You know, we like having you around, right? And not just because you're the Seer and it's our destiny to train you. There's so much more to you than that."

Like a missing puzzle piece, the truth clicked into place. Why couldn't my mother show me the warmth and compassion the Coopers had in the last few weeks? Instead, she'd nagged, prodded, and pushed me to join Nexis and be the best at ... everything. Had it always been about my abilities, because she knew I'd be the next Seer? I shuddered at that thought.

"Really?" I squeezed back. "Like what?"

Brooke dropped my hand and sank onto the bed beside me. "You challenge us, keep us on our toes. We've all been doing things the Cooper way for a long time. Then you come along and rock our world. Especially Bryan's."

We both giggled at that.

"I really wish I could stay here forever. You have no idea how good it feels to feel safe." Something about Brooke made me want to pour out my heart. Maybe because she radiated warmth, just like her mother.

She wrapped me up in a hug. "Good, I'm glad. I kind of like having you around."

I hugged her back. "Me, too."

Letting go, she pursed her lips at me. "Just don't go breaking my brother's heart."

"Ha!" A coffee-tinged gurgle bubbled up my throat. "If anyone's going to break someone's heart, it'll be the other way around."

"I hope it works out. For both your sakes." Her eyes twinkled, not unlike her brother's. "You've both had enough relationship drama for one high school career."

"And then some." I leaned in and lowered my voice. "What about you? Is there anyone you like?"

"Me?" Her cheeks pinked up. The telltale sign. "Nah."

"Your face says otherwise." I cocked my head and studied her. "Anyone I know?"

"What?" Her eyebrows quirked a little, giving her away.

"Ha, I knew it!" I clapped my hands in triumph. "Let's see, who could it be. Tony?"

She shook her head a little.

"Yeah, he's a senior. Too old for you." In a flash, an idea popped in my head. "Lenny?"

Her eyebrows quirked again, and I knew I finally nailed it.

"Aww, that's so cute." Immediately, my hand flew to my heart. "Do you think he likes you, too?"

"No. Hey, wait." Standing up, she threw up her hands. "I don't know what you're talking about. I didn't say a word."

"I won't tell anyone."

She stared me down.

"Promise." I mashed my lips together and sealed them shut.

"You better not." In two strides, she was out the door. I stared at my mug, grinning into the tawny liquid. I wasn't alone in the infatuation department.

><

After she left, Brooke's conversation stayed with me. Hopping in the shower, I let the warm water massage out any lingering thoughts. I couldn't help but wonder why my mom kept such a disastrous secret to herself. She'd always known James was my half-brother and didn't have the gift. Same as she'd known that I *did* have the gift. So why would she push him to attend Montrose anyway, even urge him to join Nexis?

Maybe she didn't think they'd banish him just because he wasn't the Seer. Yeah, I would never have guessed that one either.

With a snap, I shut off the water and toweled dry. I had so many questions that'd probably never get answered. Would I ever know the truth about my own family?

Stepping out of the en suite bathroom, I glanced at the bed. Empty. No gear deliveries today. Maybe the Coopers actually took a break from training for Christmas. Go figure.

I put on my normal, comfy clothes, combed out my long dark hair, and finished the last dregs of my coffee. Feeling like the regular old me again, I made my way into the living room.

"Perfect timing, Lucy." Abby sat curled up on the couch, aiming the remote at the TV. "I was just about to watch my favorite Christmas movie."

"No training today?" I padded across the fluffy rug and plopped down next to her on the couch. Heavenly smells wafted to my nose from a tray of scones on the coffee table.

"No training for Christmas." She handed one to me. "Try a scone. They're gingerbread."

I munched on the scone, letting the gingery-molasses tingle my tongue. "I could get used to Christmas at the Coopers. Where's Brooke?"

Abby shrugged. "She's in the basement with the punching bag. Can't imagine why she needs to punch things on Christmas Eve."

I raised my hand a little. "That's probably my fault. I interrogated her about who she likes."

"Oh, really?" Abby set down her coffee and scooched in closer. "Did you get anything good?"

"No she did not, 'cause there's nothing to tell." Brooke suddenly appeared behind us, a glisten of sweat on her brow as she plopped down next to me. "And you, little Miss Seer, weren't supposed to say anything."

I glanced from Brooke to Abby and back again. "Hey, I don't know what you're talking about. There's nothing to tell."

"That's right." A satisfied smile crawled up Brooke's face. Then she pointed the remote at the TV. "Now let's watch *It's a Wonderful Life.*"

She pressed play, and we all sat back to watch the movie. Even though I missed my own sister, it was nice hanging with the Cooper girls. That's why I didn't ask where Bryan was today. It was girl time.

As soon as the final credits started rolling, the front door burst open with a blast of cold and snowflakes.

"You guys expecting someone?" My head turned to the door. "Santa perhaps?"

A spark glimmered in Abby's eye as she nodded toward the door. Then I saw him.

My dad bustled into the foyer. Dropping his duffel bag on the hardwood, he power-walked over to me arms open wide.

As soon as I stood to my feet, he wrapped me in a rib-crushing hug.

"Surprise!" Dad practically yelled in my ear. "Wait, you're surprised right?"

"And deaf." But my lips curled up anyway. "How did you get here? More importantly, why didn't you tell me?"

"I tried calling, but it went straight to voicemail." He stood up tall, releasing me from his bear hug. "I know you'd planned to spend Christmas with your boyfriend and his family, but your family wants you home."

"But I'm having such a good time." I huffed even as I smiled up at my Dad. Under my breath I mumbled, "And Bryan's not *technically* my boyfriend."

"Well, he met me at the airport like a boyfriend would. With his parents and everything. Very official." He glanced back to where Bryan and his parents stood, huddled up in the foyer.

"Oh," was all I could say. I tilted my head at Bryan. For a guy who was waiting for the Guardian stamp of approval to date me, he sure acted like my boyfriend. Could this be any more complicated?

"Tom, welcome to our home." Cindy rushed into the living room. "It's good to see you again. It's been too long."

"Again? Too long?" I turned to my dad, my forehead doing the bulldog scrunch. They must know each other. Figured.

Before Dad could answer, Bryan barreled through his parents and wrapped his arms around me. "I think your dad likes me."

"Really?" Now I turned my worried bulldog look at Bryan.

A smile lit up his blue eyes. "This is only one surprise. I've got another one for you before you leave."

"Another one?" I could hardly catch my breath. Were my mom and sister about to walk in, too? Then it would really be like the Twilight Zone in here.

His grin faded an inch. "Good surprise?"

"Great surprise!" I squealed, hugging him tighter while eying our parents. My dad and the Coopers chatted like old friends.

"Ahem." Clearing his throat, my dad appeared by my side. "Can I talk to my daughter for a second?" It wasn't really a question.

"Of course." Bryan stiffened, releasing his hold on me.

"Fine. You can help me pack." Reaching for my dad's hand, I tugged him down the hall, closing the door to my room. Then I whirled around on my heel. "Okay, spill. What's really going on here? How exactly do you know the Coopers so well?"

"You're too smart for your own good, Lucy girl." Dad ruffled my hair, sinking onto the bed.

I lowered down next to him, perching on the edge of the bed. "You're on the Guardian Council too, aren't you?" The words tumbled out like my heart knew a truth that hadn't reached my mind yet.

Slowly, he nodded. "I should've known you'd figure it out. Being the Seer makes you that much more perceptive. I wish your mother had that quality."

"Me too. Then we wouldn't be in this mess." I couldn't help myself. I curled up into his side.

"I'm sorry I didn't tell you sooner. Can you forgive me?" He wrapped his arm around me and pulled me close.

The warmth I'd longed for ever since I woke up this morning seeped into my soul. I'd always been a Daddy's girl, even more so since I found out Mom's secret.

"Of course, I forgive you." I looked up at him. "But that doesn't mean I'm not mad. I deserve to know the truth."

Hunching down to my level, he met my gaze. "The Guardian Council wants to bring you along slowly, but I agree with you. I think you deserve to know the truth."

"Good. What exactly is that?" I asked, sitting upright and jutting out my chin.

His face softened as he nodded. "War is about to break out in Europe. I think that's why your powers have come early."

The word "war" gonged around in my brain. I shook my head to clear the cobwebs. "When you say war, what exactly do you mean by that?"

He huffed out a bear-sized sigh. "Okay, here goes. There's always some type of espionage cold war going on between the Three Societies. But when societies start stealing sacred stones from each other, it means they're planning a big ceremony to make their goals come to life. Right now, Nexis is stealing stones."

"Say what?" All the air in the room disappeared. I floated up in a vacuum, trying to just breathe as my world rocked on its axis.

"That's not all." He paused, inhaling a deep breath. Then he dropped the bomb. "They usually need a Chosen One to help them complete the ceremony." His eyes glazed over in a far-off look, then zeroed in on me. "I'm afraid this time that they want you."

In a blink, it dawned on me. "That's why Jake attacked me. What do they want with me?"

His shoulders deflated in an instant. "I'm not sure, but whatever it is can't be good."

My blood simmered in my veins. "This is crazy."

"I know, sweetie," he mumbled, head hanging low. "And it only gets worse from here."

I gasped. "Worse than siccing my ex-boyfriend on me?"

"I'm afraid so." He slumped over again. "But I want you to know that I will do whatever I can to protect you. In fact, I already did."

"Oh, Dad." The look on his face made me reach for him instinctively.

Squeezing my hand, he stared at me. "I went straight to the Guardian Council and begged them to let me tell you this."

"Let me guess, they said no." I exhaled a hot breath.

"Bingo." He snapped his fingers, ruffling my hair. "They want me to stay a double agent and they don't want to compromise that. But, that's not the point." Slinging his arm around my shoulder, he paused until I looked him in the eye. "The point is, I'm done with all of that. Pretending to be a double agent and all. The day your brother told me the truth and showed me that birth certificate, something inside me snapped. I couldn't pretend anymore. That day I chose my side. And it's not Nexis or the Guardians. I choose to fight for my children. All of them."

"Dad." Saltwater welled up in my eyes and I wrapped both arms around his middle and squeezed. My tears dampened his Colts sweatshirt. "I've always known that in my heart, but I'm really glad to hear you say it."

"Good. I'm glad you know where my true loyalties lie." Arching back, he held me at arm's length. "That's why I want you to come home."

The safe bubble, the protective cocoon I'd made in this place far away from home, shattered into a million pieces. Piercing my heart with bits of shrapnel.

"Dad, I'm scared." Memories of that night surfaced, dredging up the thick sludge of fear that seeped into every fiber of my being. The attack I wanted to keep hidden away forever. "What if Jake is there, waiting for me?"

"It's your life, Lucy. You have to live it." His tone softened, and he clutched my hand. "I know what you went through. What Jake did to you. But take it from me—you can't run from your problems. Someday you'll have to learn to face them, and I think today's that day. You're my little tiger. I know you're strong enough."

My stomach rankled. How could he dismiss my objections, my fears, so easily? "I don't know, Dad. What about my training? I want to be able to protect myself." Even as I said the words, I knew my angel would always have my back.

"I'm a Guardian too, you know." He ruffled my hair again, and my heart thawed. "Plus, I have my grandmother's journal. I'm sure insight from the previous Seer will help you. I can protect you just as well as the Coopers. I've got your back, kiddo. So please come home. I miss my sweet girl."

"What about Mom? Can you get her off my back?" My lips twitched. Wasn't this exactly what I wanted this morning? Just hearing that he wanted me home—it was the final nail in the coffin of my resolve.

"Leave her to me." He rubbed his hands together, a gleam in his eye. "I can handle that old battle-ax."

Narrowing my eyes at him, I bobbed my head. "Okay."

"So you'll come home then?" He bounced on the bed, eyes brightening.

"For you, I'll do anything." I wouldn't be the one to break his heart. Not now, not ever. Instead, I wrapped my arms around him, clinging to the father of my childhood who kissed away the booboos. Let's just hope he could keep the boogeyman away for a few weeks.

Since James' disappearance, Dad had lost his fuzzy edges, transforming into the behind-the-scenes plotter who was still on my side. Of course it made sense. He was always on my side, even when everyone else let me down.

Still, I didn't want to crawl out of this safe little hole I'd dug in the ground. Sure, it hadn't exactly been peaceful to go through Seer training, but it was better than dealing with Jake and the worst night of my life. Seer Training had saved me from thinking about reality. Did it save me, or just prolong the inevitable? Because reality was out on bail and waiting for me back in Indiana.

CHAPTER 7

Logs crackled and sparked in the Coopers' immense stone fireplace. The familiar scent of woodsmoke mingled with the piney tang of the Christmas tree in the corner. Their house even smelled like Christmas.

Luggage in hand, I stood beside my dad in the foyer, huddled up with the Coopers.

"We usually open one gift on Christmas Eve …" Mark glanced at Cindy. "But we have two farewell presents for you, Lucy."

Cindy handed me a foil-wrapped package with a smile. "Here you go. Merry Christmas."

"Thank you. It's so pretty it's almost a shame to open it." I tore into the paper anyway, uncovering a popular hardback. "You shouldn't have."

Cindy's face lit up. "Of course we should. I think you'll like that. It's one of my favorites. Don't forget to read the inscription inside."

Abruptly, she turned away to chat with my dad. Was she trying to distract him?

"Hmmm…" Now I had to take a peek. The cover creaked open, almost as if it had a rusty hinge. Inside, the pages were more yellowed than a current bestseller should've been. I flipped to the title page and my jaw dangled. It read, *A New Guardian's Guidebook*, with a note scrawled underneath. *Someday soon.* She'd even drawn the Guardian symbol.

A surge of warmth flooded through me. I hugged the book to my chest. Somehow she knew how much I wanted to be a Guardian, even though I'd never said a word since that first day here. Water welled up behind my eyes. She'd given me a promise. *Someday soon.*

Besides, who doesn't love a secret present? I vowed to read it on the plane as soon as my dad fell asleep.

Bryan inched closer to me. "I got something for you, too. Merry Christmas." With trembling hands, he placed a small black box in my hands.

Air dangled somewhere in my throat. I slid my fingers over the soft v, my breath hitching. Slowly, I opened the lid. Inside lay the sparkling Guardian amethyst necklace that they'd let me borrow during training to amplify my powers. Blinking like a fool, I stared at the swirl of tiny purple stones around the Guardian amulet.

"Bryan, it's so gorgeous. Do I really get to take it home with me?" I glanced at the Coopers, who were nodding at me.

"It's your great-grandmother Lucinda's necklace." Dad's gaze zeroed in on the purple stones. "It's nice to have it back in the family."

His words struck an awkward note, and everybody grew silent.

"Look. It matches my sweet sixteen ring." I held up my finger.

Abby leaned in closer. "A perfect color match."

"Let me see." Brooke stood on her tiptoes, peering over Abby's shoulder. "It must be a matching set."

"Here, let me put it on." Bryan leaned in closer, whispering in my ear. "Now you'll always have something to protect you. Even if I'm not with you."

I tilted my face, smiling up at him as the long chain settled around my collarbone. "Let's hope that's not too often."

His lips curved as if he wanted to kiss me. My face flamed.

"I had a chat with Mark and Cindy, and we decided to let you wear the necklace now since you're powers are early and you're still learning." Dad slung his arm around my shoulders. "I'm glad the necklace is back in the family, but you'll have to keep it hidden. We don't want it falling into the wrong hands."

"Okay, Dad." I tucked it inside my sweater, safe and sound.

"Thank you, Lucy girl." Dad swished my hair and picked up my suitcase. "We better get moving if we want to make it home in time for Christmas."

Mark yanked open the front door, blasting us with cold air. After I hugged Abby and Brooke goodbye, I followed my Dad and the Coopers to the family's Suburban.

Bryan and I sat in the back, listening to our parents drone on about nothing all the way to the airport.

><

Clutching the purple amulet to my chest, I stumbled behind my Dad to airport security. He loaded our carry-ons onto the conveyor belt. But Bryan grabbed my hand, holding me back.

He didn't have to say it. I knew exactly what he was thinking. I wrapped my arms tight around him, squishing my cheek into his chest.

"I don't want to go back home. What if something bad happens, like another reckoning or something? Or worse, I run into Jake?" Couldn't I just bury myself in his arms?

"Lay low and take a break from training. We can resume again back at Montrose." He rested his chin on my head. "You promise you'll call me if anything happens? With you know…"

"Believe me, you'll be the first person I call. I just wish I could take you home with me." A gurgle of fear rose in my throat, threatening to saw me in half. *I'm the Seer. I can take care of myself.* Maybe someday I'd truly believe that.

How did this happen? When I came to New York five months ago, I'd sworn off relationships. Bryan had wormed his way into my heart and now I didn't want to let him go.

"Me too, Angel Girl." His lips brushed my hair. "I'll see you in two weeks. Then we'll have plenty of time."

"That's true." I swiveled in his arms to look up at him.

He pulled me closer as if he couldn't let go "Don't forget how much I love you."

"I won't." I patted my necklace. "I've got proof right here."

The sea of blue burned as he crushed his lips into mine. Fierce at first, then tapering off in delicate traces.

"Ahem. Lucy, it's time to go." Dad's hands were on his hips, blocking the security entrance.

"See you soon," I whispered to Bryan, pecking his mouth one last time.

Somehow I floated away, past security. Watching his back until he disappeared into the crowd. An anchor settled in my heart.

><

Mom's shrill voice scraped my ear canals raw. "How can you be so narrow-minded?"

Rolling over in my bed, I squished my fuzziest pillow against my face. It only muted her pitch by a few decibels. What a horrible noise to wake up to on New Year's Eve.

The happy homecoming Dad and I had received only a week ago had disintegrated day-by-day. Bouts of Mom sniping away at all of us and late-night fights with Dad were the norm again. Now we were back to early morning screaming matches. A typical holiday season in the McAllen house, at least over the last few years since James left.

"Enough!" I flung off the covers and flounced out of bed. What could she possibly have to yell at Dad about, anyway? This was all her fault. Why was she the one having a fit at nine a.m.?

Padding across the hallway, I opened Paige's door and slammed it behind me. Nothing. Mom never even paused her tirade.

I stomped over to my sister's bed. "Wow, they're really going at it. Do they do this a lot?"

"All the time." Paige yawned and rolled her eyes. "Sometimes it's about James. Sometimes it's about you being at Montrose. It's never about me."

"You can't be serious." I stared her down, per usual, but her face said it all.

"I am." Her bubble-gum lips furrowed into a cute little pout.

"Aww, my poor little sister feels left out. Well, don't." I clamped her shoulders in a hug to rival one of her bone-crushers. "I'd rather have them say nothing than fight about me."

Guilt slithered its way into my brain as I hugged her tighter. Couldn't I just tell her the truth? Of course, if Mom would just do her job then everyone in the family would know by now. But she'd surely botch it up beyond belief. Even still, Paige deserved to know the truth. Maybe I should have a talk with Dad later. Before this got too messed up.

"Whatever. I just crank up the music." She pumped up a Rhianna dance song, yelling over the beat. "Then they notice me."

"That's the Paige I know and love." I bobbed my head to the pumping rhythm, spinning around the room with my little sis. For a few minutes, we were happy and carefree, just like when we were kids. If only it could stay this way forever.

A song trilled from my pocket. As I pulled my phone out, Chad's face smiled back at me.

"Hey, Chad. Nice of you to call for once." I picked up the remote and turned down the music, already dreading my best friend's yearly demand.

"Goes both ways, little girl." His voice sounded more excited than annoyed. "Paige said you'd be home. I wanted to invite you both to come over for New Year's."

I clenched every muscle in my body. "You mean like one of your legendary New Year's Eve bashes? I don't know."

Paige squealed in the background. "C'mon Lucy, it's just Chad's house. I'm sure his parents will chaperone and everything."

"Ugh. Your lil sis is right about the parents." Chad paused, then his tone turned serious. "And you-know-who is completely blacklisted from leaving his house."

"You're kidding, house arrest? If I'd known that, I wouldn't have stayed cooped up in this crazy house for a week." That little tidbit would've been useful a few weeks ago. Or maybe it was a blessing in disguise. At least I'd gotten to stay at Bryan's for ten days and get some much-needed training. And escape a week and a half of Mom tirades.

"Great, there you go again. Staring off into space." Paige snatched the phone away. "Save us from the separation anxiety, Chad. She's moping around the house, mourning the loss of her stupid boyfriend."

"Hush, you little brat." I chased her around the room, yanked a pillow off her bed, and chucked it at her.

"Fine," she huffed, handing the phone back.

Chad cleared his throat. "Ahem, back to reality. Do you really wanna be stuck with your sister at home all night? Come on, it'll be fun. I haven't seen you in ages."

"All right." I breathed heavily into the phone, laying it on thick. "But only if you promise to watch my back."

"It's a deal. I'll see you both around eight-ish." With that, he hung up on me.

"Great. What'd I just get myself into?" I cocked my head at Paige as if she was a magic eight ball, eager to answer all my questions.

She let out a high-pitched squeal and started bouncing around the room. "We're going to a party! What could be more fun than that?"

Suddenly the door burst open, and Dad walked in. "What's going on in here?"

"I told you he'd come." Paige whispered behind her hand.

"It's nothing, Dad. Just needed a little attention, that's all."
I turned my *I'm-so-innocent* smile on him, and his façade
crumbled.

"Fine. But I need to talk to you, Lucy." He angled toward
me, shooting me a serious look.

"Okay, shoot." I crossed my arms and stood my ground.

His eyes shifted over to Paige.

"You can say it in front of her. We don't have any *secrets*."
I may have over-emphasized the last word.

"Fine, if you insist." He leaned in and lowered his voice a
notch. "Your mother doesn't agree, but I've decided to let you
choose whether or not you go back to Montrose."

"Really, Dad?" Hope bloomed inside me.

He nodded. "I think it's only fair. Especially after
everything you've gone through."

"Is that what you and Mom were fighting about?" Paige
asked.

"As a matter of fact—" Dad started.

"See! Told you, Lucy. It's never about me." She turned her
bright eyes on me, lips curling into a pout.

"That's enough, Paige," Dad snapped. "Let your sister have
a chance to think about her options."

"Sorry, Lucy. I know you've had a rough month." Paige
stared at the carpet.

But I'd already tuned them out. Because the options were
equally mind-numbing. Go back to Alton High where people
thought I was crazy and let them start more rumors about what
happened in New York. Or stay at Montrose and get over the fact
that my ex stalked me there. Here I'd at least have Chad and no
secret societies to deal with. That I knew of. But with Jake's
affiliations, I couldn't be too sure about that.

Bryan and Shanda were at Montrose—the only people who
made facing my fears seem remotely possible. No matter what
happened with Bryan, Shanda would always have my back. I tried
to picture staying here in Indiana, but I just couldn't go backward.

Not now. I'd already come too far. In this new year, I had a chance to do things differently. Maybe this time I needed to face my fears and learn how to deal with them, instead of running away.

Inhaling a deep breath, I squared my shoulders and stood tall. "Thanks for sticking up for me, Dad. But I think I'd rather go back to Montrose."

"Are you sure?" He leaned down to my level. "I know it'll be hard either way."

"It will." I nodded, staring into his eyes. "But I think Montrose is the only place I can move past it."

"If you really think so." He held my gaze.

"I do." I kept eye contact, so he'd know I meant every word.

He bobbed his head. "Okay. I just wanted you to know you had a choice."

"Thanks, Dad. I appreciate that." I grinned up at him. Had I really grown up that much in the past few months?

Smiling, he reached out and ruffled my hair. "So what do you say we watch the ball drop tonight? As a family."

"Can't." Paige's voice went flat. "We're going to Chad's house."

"And you agreed to this?" Dad furrowed his forehead at me.

"What can I say? They convinced me." I pointed to my sister. "How can you say no to that face?"

Paige widened her eyes and gave Dad her famous little pout. "Chad's parents will be there and everything. And Jake is on house arrest."

"Oh, really?" Dad's eyebrows shot up and he glanced at me.

I just shrugged. "That's what Chad told me. You know I can't say no to him, either."

Dad pulled out his phone. "I'm just going to have a little chat with Chad's parents, confirm all of this. Then we'll see." He started dialing as he tromped out the door.

"It'll be completely safe," Paige called after him.

"I hope you're right," I muttered to myself.

Sure, it'd been forever since I'd seen my oldest friend. He'd probably even censor his guest list for me. But I still didn't want to face the Alton High rumor mill. Maybe if I stayed out of sight and let Chad and Paige run interference, I could escape this night unscathed. A girl can dream, right?

CHAPTER 8

As soon as I shucked off my coat, all the tiny hairs on my arms bristled. I felt exposed here, in the sleeveless gold dress Paige foisted on me. Vulnerable as prey in a hunter's scope. Goosebumps popped up like a warning siren, blaring through every nerve ending on my body. Suddenly I felt sorry for the deer population.

"Lucy, I can't believe you made it. It's been too long." Chad squeezed his way through the teenage crowd, all clad in their party-best. He hugged me around my middle, lifting me off my feet. "You're looking hot in gold. Great job, Paige."

She high-fived him. "I'm good for something."

He fluffed up his spiky black bangs and held out paper tiaras. "You have to wear them. It's New Year's."

"You're not getting off that easy." I brushed past him to the entry table, plucked up a paper top hat, and plunked it on his head.

"Yeah, yeah. Missed you, too." He tipped his hat at me, leaning in as Paige disappeared into the crowd. "How are you doing, for real?"

I opened my mouth, right as two cheerleaders passed. Nothing came out.

"Don't worry, I got your back." Hooking his arm through mine, he led me past the living room dance floor, straight into the kitchen like he was on a mission. In the breakfast nook, he slid into the booth and pulled me down next to him.

"I'm glad I came. Just hope those aren't famous last words." I shifted, fidgeting with the taffeta edge of my gold cocktail dress and adjusting my Happy New Year crown.

Chad grabbed my hand and squeezed. Hard. "I was really worried about you. Don't scare me like that again. Ever." That last word dribbled out as if he didn't even know he said it.

"I'm fine, Chad. Really, I am." I zeroed in on his soft brown eyes, filled with something I hadn't seen before. I gripped his hand like a lifeline, pulling us both out of the Bermuda triangle of what-ifs. "I've even been learning to fight while I was gone."

"No kidding?" His face lit up like Times Square. "So what? Are you Cat Woman now, ready to show Indianapolis no mercy?"

"As if I could ever pull off an Anne Hathaway or Halle Barry." We both busted out laughing. It felt good to laugh with him.

"I wouldn't mind seeing you in that costume, though. Come on, dance with me. I wanna see your new moves." He tugged on my arm, in that playful way of his.

"If you insist." I let him pull me back into the living room. It was starting to feel like old times already.

I threw my head back and let Chad spin me around the other dancers, waving at Paige as we danced by. His mom came up just as the fast song turned into a slow dance.

"Lucy, good to see you." She broke us apart for a side hug, then turned to her son. "We've got a few uninvited guests that I need you to deal with."

"Moochers." Chad rolled his eyes, spinning me around one last time. "I'll be right back. Don't you move." He waved and trailed his mom to the front door.

"Right, like I'm gonna slow dance with myself." I wound my way in and out of the swaying couples, toward the kitchen in search of hydration.

Then I saw him. And I stopped at the edge of the dance floor. The music faded away and the dance floor dissolved into a blur of bodies as I stared at that all-too-familiar chiseled face in the doorway. Angry swaths of red tinged my vision. Searing his outline into my brain.

The temperature in the room dropped ten degrees before I saw the shadows slither in with him. My heart froze, then pumped out a new beat. That sandy hair. Those steely gray eyes.

Will's mouth hung open as he stared back at me. With slow, deliberate steps, he trudged across the room.

"My God, Lucy," he breathed. "You look amazing. Beyond amazing. I'm so glad you're okay."

"What are you doing here?" I couldn't move, couldn't breathe. Caught in his hypnotic stare, as usual.

He edged closer. "I had to see you. To make sure you were okay after that night …"

And suddenly, with just those words, the darkness in the shadow's tendrils faded. Singed away by a silvery-gray light. Was this what remorse looked like?

His jaw twitched, eyes darting around the circle of Alton High onlookers. "Can't we talk somewhere else?"

"Will, don't." I flexed my fingers, if only to keep the buzzing angel fire tucked inside my body. "I don't know what you think you're doing, showing up here. But you need to leave."

"Hey, pal." Chad suddenly appeared at my side, glaring daggers at Will. "You heard my girl. Time to go."

"Lucy, please. I had nothing to do with Jake's plan, I promise. Let me explain." All of the lingering shadows backed away from him, as if they didn't want to hear his explanation, either.

I blinked, but the rays of light around Will only grew that much brighter. Maybe I should listen to them. "It's okay, Chad. I'll hear him out and then he'll be out of here in no time."

"You sure?" Chad's eyes widened at me, hands on his hips.

"I'm sure." I reached for his hand and squeezed.

"Okay, but I'll be right over here the whole time." Chad released my hand and headed for the edge of the dance floor.

As soon as he left, soft fingers wrapped around my wrist, tugging me into the dim kitchen. My insides jolted at Will's touch, but I tamped back the electricity buzzing down my arms. He wasn't here to hurt me. I let him lead me into the breakfast nook.

"I'm good in kitchens." Will's breath was hot on my neck. "We're good in kitchens, remember?"

I reached for a water bottle. Trying like crazy not to think about the last time he cornered me in a kitchen. And we kissed.

"Why did you come here, really?" I chugged down a big gulp.

"I was sitting in the airport, on layover from Chicago. And I couldn't get you out of my mind." He ran a hand over his stubbled jaw, looking more rugged than disheveled. "So I hunted down your mom's number and badgered her until she told me where you were."

"Of course." I rolled my eyes. "Why Chicago?"

"It's where my dad lives now. My parents are separated." His hand still encircled my wrist.

"Oh." I didn't know what to say to that. So, I just stared at him like an idiot, unable to move.

"I've been in agony here." With strong fingers, he drew me closer. "Why wouldn't you take my calls? Did you think I had something to do with Jake's plans? Do you really hate me that much?"

"I don't know what to think, but I don't hate you." My heart raced at his touch. The words came out fast. Too fast. "It's been hard, that's all." I hated that my voice cracked. I sucked in my wobbling lip.

"Are you okay, Lucy? Please tell me you're okay." Suddenly his hands were on my shoulders, running up and down my bare arms. Making me shiver even though I wasn't cold. "Will you tell me what happened?"

"What? I can't." I tried to push the horrible memories out of my mind, but tears still beat at my eyelids.

"Please. I have to know what happened. I haven't been able to sleep. Not knowing how you're doing. If you're okay. It's been killing me." Black circles ringed his eyes, betraying a hollowness I hadn't noticed. Until now.

I turned away from him to stare out the sliding glass door, into the dark night. And it all came back. How Jake found me in the quad, pinned me against a tree. But the angel split that tree in two. How much could I tell Will, without divulging all my secrets?

"He cornered me, but I got away. Then I tripped. Scraped my cheek pretty good." I touched my fingers to my cheekbone, remembering how they'd come back bloody. "He caught up. Dislocated my shoulder."

Will winced out loud.

"He was going to take me somewhere. Who knows where? Then Bryan showed up, the campus police not far behind him. And that was that." But we both knew it was so much more.

"I hate that you had to go through that." Before I knew it, he whirled me around and wrapped me up in his arms, cradling my head with one hand. "I wish I'd been there for you."

"Hey, mister. It's your turn to explain." Unraveling myself from his arms, I narrowed my eyes at him. "You disappeared, remember?"

His face crumpled.

"What happened to you? I didn't know what to think."

"You don't think I had anything to do with this, do you?" Those gray eyes seared into me, stealing my breath away. Melting my knees to jelly.

Tightening my core, I met his stare. "I don't want to, but part of me wonders if you were in on it with Jake and he turned on you."

"No," he breathed. He slumped forward, shoulders sagging. He reached for me like he couldn't stand on his own. "Lucy, you're too important to me. I would never do something to hurt you like that. Not ever."

I backed away from his grasp. "Then tell me the truth. Why did you go out there that night? Was Nexis involved somehow?"

"I think so." His gaze dropped to his dress shoes. "But it must've come from higher up. I went out there to tell him to back off. I even tried to arrest him. That's when it got physical. Fast. He kept saying he had a mission—"

"A mission?" I gasped, my hand flying to my mouth. "And you didn't know about that?"

"I had no clue." He shook his head. "Apparently my position doesn't count for jack squat anymore. I'm just a puppet now until I graduate."

"How long has Jake been a Nexis member?" I inhaled too fast, choking on my own fumes. "Why did Nexis send him to kidnap me now? He was my boyfriend for over a year. I don't understand."

"I don't understand either." Stepping closer, his eyes went wide. "Ever since I told her to back off of you, I've been sidelined."

"You did what?" I screeched, my jaw hanging open. "Really?"

Hanging his head, he gave me a sheepish grin. "I told you, I care about you. I don't care about who you're supposed to be. Nobody should be a pawn in someone else's game. Not me, and certainly not you."

"You really mean that?" A strange feeling undulated in my middle. Tingles danced up and down my arms. My fingers itched to trace the golden scruff on his jawline.

Will licked his lips, turning those haunting gray eyes on me. "I'd do anything to protect you, even face a rogue Nexis agent. My mom must've given Jake full discretion. Guess your ex didn't like me interrupting his plans. I doubt Nexis wanted to hurt you, either. That was all Jake."

"I'm sorry he beat you up, too. It looked pretty bad." I cringed, unable to look at Will anymore. My stomach roiled. It didn't matter who he was, I wouldn't wish that on anyone. I dug my fingernails into my hips as if I could claw out the clutches of Nexis from my life. Forever.

"Don't worry about me. I can take it." His hands slid around my waist as he closed in. "There's something I need you to know."

"What?" And just like that, he had me under his spell again. My heart cracked at the thought of someone else going through the same torment I'd survived. I guess we had something in common besides the chemistry sizzling in the air between us.

"If anyone else comes after you again, I will protect you. Whether you want me to or not." His steely eyes softened as they drank me in, sending sparks tingling down to my toes. "You mean too much to me."

"Really?" It came out as a breath.

"If I told you how much, it'd only scare you." Those gunmetal eyes pleaded with me, tormented as the shadows that morphed and changed around him—black dissolving into gray. Fading into almost white. Then twisting back to gray again.

Just then, Chad burst into the kitchen. Breaking us apart.

"Thank God," I murmured, putting some much-needed space between me and Will.

"You done yet?" Chad asked. "It's been fifteen minutes. About time for you to go, don't you think?"

"I said my piece. Now I'll be on my way." Will backed up, eyes lingering on me. "Will you pick up the next time I call?"

"I don't know. Maybe." My lips twitched. Little traitors.

"Good enough for me. Happy New Year." The tiniest smile curled up the corners of his lips, sparking a flash of silver in his eyes.

"You, too." I watched him go, mesmerized by the shadows trailing after him—shifting and swirling with ever-lightening shades of gray.

"Thanks, Chad." I hugged his side. "You're a lifesaver."

"C'mon let's go back to the party." Chad twirled me back onto the dance floor. As the music faded and the countdown began, I lost focus. The room, the faces all blurred together.

What just happened back there?

Could Will Stanton, Nexis president, really fight against the secret society he was born into—for me? Could he really become one of the good guys? I just saw it with my own eyes, the strange mixture of light warring against shadow. I wanted to write him off, out of my life forever. But every time I tried, he forced his way back in.

I had Bryan and the Guardians. I didn't need Will creeping his way back into my thoughts. Confusing me with his hypnotic charm. Making me wonder if I should even go back to Montrose.

My cheeks burned just remembering how helpless I'd been against his charisma. Nothing happened with Will, and Bryan wasn't technically my boyfriend. Even so, shame crawled over me like a suffocating blanket. There was nothing fair about this. Only torture.

CHAPTER 9

Clackety-clack went my suitcase, rolling behind me on the cobblestone path to Nelson Hall. Dusk darkened the sky as I inhaled the Montrose air. Needles of January chill stung my nose as I picked up the pace. This place still gave me the chills at night. Racing down the path, I flung open the door to my dorm lobby. I breathed a sigh of relief and my heart rate slowed. My dorm looked exactly the same. Girls clustered in groups, chatting and burying their faces in their phones.

Clunk, clunk, clunk. I rolled Pinky the suitcase through the lobby and up the stairs to the second floor. Tonight, most of the doors were closed. Including my room, 210.

A giggle leaked into the hallway. I cocked my head, listening. Then I heard it again—coming from my room. No mistaking that sound. Shanda was talking to a boy.

"Busted," I shouted, bursting into the room. "You better not be talking to that loser, Kevin, again."

"Of course not." Her smile turned into a sneer. "I gotta go. I'll call you back."

Dropping my bag on the floor I stomped over to her bed. "Who is it then? Do I know him?"

"It's not a guy." She gave me her patented eye roll.

"Yeah, right." I scoffed, rolling Pinky to my closet. "Since when do you giggle?"

She rose to her feet, sliding her phone under her pillow. "On occasion."

"Okay." I took a few steps closer. "Then why are you hiding your phone?"

In two seconds flat, she yanked her phone from its hiding spot and slid it into her back pocket. "It's none of your business. Just drop it, okay?"

"No. You're keeping something from me." My freshly buoyed hope sank to the depths of my stomach. I didn't like her keeping secrets from me, anymore than I liked keeping secrets myself. "Why won't you just tell me what's going on?"

She stepped back as if I'd stung her.

Her face twisted. "For someone who's supposed to see everything, you sure do miss a lot. Why don't you tell me what's going on?" Now her hands were on her hips.

"Excuse me?" My voice cracked as I choked on my own saliva. Did she know about New Year's Eve? How could she know I might be the Seer, unless… "How do you know that?"

Her tough mask cracked in a look of shock like she'd just realized her slip-up. Shanda raced to the door and slammed it shut. Turning around slowly, she opened her mouth, closed it. Then opened it again.

"You know who I am, don't you?" I narrowed my eyes at her.

"Yes." She met my gaze. "I know you're the Seer."

"Good." I exhaled, my shoulders relaxing. "I'm tired of all these secrets."

"Okay, Sherlock, you deserve to know the truth." She plopped on the edge of her bed and motioned for me to sit down. "Lucy, I have something to tell you. Something the Guardians asked me not to tell you, but I think you deserve to know. Only because it might make this better for you."

"What do you mean 'the Guardians'?" I just stared at her. Since when was she talking to the Guardians?

"I found out something over Christmas break. Something about why my mom left us." Her voice cracked. Her voice never cracked. This was serious.

"You never talk about your mom. I had no idea she left you. I'm so sorry, Shanda." I put my hand on her shoulder, my heart breaking for the tough girl beside me.

She gripped the bedframe, knuckles ashen. "It gets worse. My dad found out I joined Nexis. He finally told me why Mom left. She wasn't just a bad mother. She was a high-ranking Nexis official. She kept getting arrested, but Nexis always bailed her out. Eventually, she did something that threatened our family."

"What did she do?" I gasped, reaching for her hand.

"I don't know." Shanda shook her head, squeezing my hand hard. "I don't think Dad does either. It was something big enough to put us all in danger. We had to move out of our old neighborhood, somewhere safer with a secure entrance and a doorman. That's when Dad made her choose. Us or Nexis. Obviously, she chose Nexis."

"That's so crazy." I didn't know what else to say. I could only sit and stare at her.

"I guess that's why Dad put me in boarding school when he had to travel more for work." She grabbed a Kleenex and rubbed her eyes. "I always thought it was overkill. But now I know the truth. He was just trying to protect me."

"You're kidding?" I watched her stare off into space. Something didn't click, though. "What does that have to do with the Guardians?"

"I was so furious that I wanted to quit Nexis." She turned away, her jaw clenching. "So I went to the Guardians. Offered up all my secrets."

I inhaled a low whistle. "You didn't."

She mashed her lips together. "I did. I just couldn't take it anymore. I was going crazy."

"So? What'd they say?" I leaned in.

She paused, then turned my way and stared me down. "They convinced me to turn spy. For the Guardians."

"No way." My jaw fell open. Silence resonated in the room as if she'd dropped a bomb that ripped all sound from the world.

Her eyes glittered. "What choice did I have? Nexis was just going to use me to get to you. Now I at least have a say in it."

"There's more, isn't there?" I whispered.

She wiped her eyes and nodded. "Tony convinced me that it's the only way. I might get something good enough to make them leave me alone."

"Wait, so you are dating Tony Delgotto?" My heart leapt for joy. "When did this happen?"

"New Year's." Her eyes lifted back to their normal happy-almond shape. "He's been my liaison for the Guardians, and then it just turned into ..."

"More?" I curled my mouth at the look on her face.

"Exactly." Her mouth pursed in a Mona-Lisa-like grin.

Maybe it was time to spill my secrets, too. "You aren't the only one who had an interesting New Year's."

"Oh, really?" Her grin broadened as she leaned in closer. "Now who's holding out?"

"Okay," I whispered, inching closer, too. "Will showed up at my friend's New Year's Eve party."

"Say what?" she screeched. "In Indiana?"

"Keep it down," I hissed, darting across the room and turning on the fan.

"Like for real?" She whisper-screamed behind her hand. "What'd he want?"

I shrugged. "Apparently he was worried about me."

"Really? That's crazy." More screeching.

"Get this." Leaning in, I lowered my voice. "He said he stood up to his Mom, about me."

Shanda nodded slowly, her eyes glazing over. "It all makes sense now. I always wondered why Jake beat him up worse than you."

My heart ached for him—and for me. "He said something to that effect at the party. He wanted to make sure I was okay because I wasn't taking his phone calls."

"Obviously." She rolled her eyes again. "You have to admit, that boy is really into you."

"I keep trying to forget it, but he keeps reminding me." I huffed out an exasperated sigh, trying to push that tousled sandy hair and those steely gray eyes out of my mind. "We're in a mess, aren't we? What're we gonna do?"

She stuck out her hand. "Let's make a pact, here and now. We'll always put each other first. Before any secret society."

"Deal." Gripping her hand, I shook it hard. Defiant tingles shot up my arm. Steeling my resolve. "Best friends first. Secret societies last."

"To the bitter end." She pumped her fist in the air.

I raised my fist too, letting the triumph of this moment sink in.

Something twinkled in the window. A flash of diamond-speckled light. Gone in a blink.

And I knew I had more than one ally who'd put me first.

><

Dappled shadows blew across my sketchbook as I doodled my way through art class. Outside the window, clouds rolled in behind me, spilling mottled shapes on my blank pages. I raced to capture their silhouettes.

Two days back at Montrose Paranormal Academy and I still hadn't conquered the memories of the ex who followed me across five states. Not to mention the secret society that most likely sicced Jake on me.

I rolled that little tidbit around in my mind, which only made the questions blare louder in my brain. Where did Will really stand in all of this? The Stanton boy crept around like a spindly little spider, crawling in and out of trouble.

Briiing. The bell screeched, and I flinched, shaking off the lingering questions. I scrambled out of class, pummeling my way through the hall and down the marble staircase. Desperately trying to push away any more thoughts about Will and that awful night on the quad.

I had to find Bryan so I could see straight again. I needed a dose of that calm confidence right now. At times, Bryan had an enigmatic quality about him that reminded me of Will, especially when it came to his precious Guardians. But at least I knew for sure how Bryan felt about me.

Someone bumped into me, knocking me off course. My boots skidded across the marble.

"Geez, walk much?" I sputtered, till I realized it was just Shanda.

"While I'm liking the attitude, can you take it down a notch?" She cocked her head at me as she pushed open the main door. "Let's try to get to the cafeteria unscathed."

"Good plan." I huddled beside her, wind whipping my hair around as we speed-walked across the frozen quad.

"Okay, showtime. Gotta go make nice with my favorite peeps." Arching her eyebrows at me, she headed for the smoothie station.

So much for our little pact. I guess it was a *secret* pact, after all. I headed to the sandwich bar. As I reached for a tray, someone elbowed me in the side.

I smashed into the pile of trays, sending one skittering to the floor. Pain seared through my ribs.

"My bad," said a familiar voice.

Glancing up, I caught a snatch of Felicia's red hair as she disappeared into the sea of tables.

"Don't pay attention to her." A strong arm helped me up. "You know she's just jealous of you, gorgeous."

"Thanks." I turned to smile at Bryan, but stopped. My jaw dropped six inches, and I almost forgot to breathe. It was Will. "Oh, it's you."

A lizard crawled around in my stomach as I stared up at him, straight into those stormy gray eyes. *This was SO not good.*

Will's sculpted cheek curved into a sympathetic smile. He exuded calm. For some reason, that look reminded me of that night in the library, where I thought I almost trusted him. After his New Year's party crash, I wondered if maybe I'd been right in the first place.

"Yeah, right. Like anyone's jealous of me," I whispered, averting my eyes. One thing was certain. His proximity made me feel the same as always. Knees weak. Heart wild.

"If only you knew. I thought we agreed you were gonna start taking calls from me." His hand was still on my arm, zapping my pulse with its own energy.

I shrugged. "You agreed. I said maybe." As in the other side of never-gonna-happen.

"I get why you wouldn't call me at the Cooper compound, or even before New Year's." Will turned his Hamlet look on me, full of worry with a flicker of hope. "But you can't stay mad at me forever. I thought we were going to try to be friends. What if something major went down and I needed to warn you?"

"Try texting, friend. It's less invasive." I moved to turn away, but a current sizzled between us. Gluing my eyes to his.

"Maybe I will." A shadow flickered across his face for a split second. Then it was gone.

I stuck my hand on my hip. "Maybe if you stopped stalking me through my mom I would answer your calls."

He cocked his chin at me, cleft and all. "Maybe if you answered my calls I wouldn't have to use the mom grapevine."

"You're impossible," I huffed, taking a step back. Anything to break the current between us.

"And you're adorable." He closed the gap, zinging me with that infamous smolder.

Electricity fizzled up and down my arms until I forced myself to pull away.

With deliberate steps, one foot in front of the other, I walked to the cashier. Then to the Guardian table. But I felt the weight of his eyes on me. I didn't have to turn around to know he was watching my every move.

"There you are, Lucy." Bryan pecked my cheek as he pulled out a chair for me. "I've been looking for you all day."

"You found me." Was I talking to him or the waves of guilt slapping me in the face?

"Cute, isn't she?" He ran his fingers up and down my arm.

My stomach curled in on itself. No way could I eat anything now.

"Gag me, please." Tony rolled his eyes at us.

"This is gonna be a great semester. I just feel it." Bryan squeezed my hand, much like he always did when we were alone.

"What's going on?" Something was different. This guy didn't do PDA. "Why are you so amped?"

"You caught me. I've got some great news, and I can't wait to share it." His face split into a grin. "The Guardians have authorized us to have a Seer training session. Tonight."

"Here, on campus? Wouldn't that be a dead giveaway? Should we even be talking about this…?" All the air leaked from my chest. Shadows crept in, slithering in and out of my peripheral vision. "Why on earth would they risk exposing the truth? My truth?"

"It's a risk." He lowered his voice, eyes darting around the room. "But it's what the council wants. They want you to get some real-world experience. And since this was the last place—" He clamped his hand over his mouth, before he said what we were all thinking.

I flexed my fingers, if only to keep them from curling up as the blood curdled through my veins. The Guardians acted like I was their new toy. Believe me, I would never be anybody's puppet.

"We do have some advantages here, you know," Lenny chimed in, from his seat next to Tony.

"Really, like what?" I chomped into my turkey on rye with a vengeance.

"Harlixton will be there, for one." Laura gave me a small little smile.

"The other Guardian teachers and administration will be there to protect you, too." Brooke patted me on the shoulder. "We've got your back, Lucy."

Warmth pinged through my rising anger, sending it down to a simmer.

"We can finally show them what you can really do." Bryan glanced around the table.

I coughed, almost gagging on the bread. "You seriously want to expose my secret to *more* people? I thought we were trying to keep my status under wraps. It's too soon after…" I didn't have to say it. Didn't want to.

My hands trembled, my heart wild again.

"Maybe you're right." He stroked my hair as if to reassure me. It didn't help. "How about I get Harlixton to drop the rest of the staff? Just us and him."

I bit back a growl. "That's better than your first plan." But I still wanted to punch him that pitying expression right off his face.

"It will be fine." He pressed his lips into my forehead. "You'll see."

"Yeah, we'll see." I bit back the rest of my objections. Wings of heat battered my cheeks, and I put some space between us. Could I really trust him to look out for me, or were the Guardians number one in his book? From where I sat right now, I definitely felt like number two. At best.

Glancing around, anywhere but at my almost-boyfriend, I caught Will staring at me with those sea-gray eyes, weaving his crafty little web.

Enough. I ground my teeth together. I had to do this. I had to find a way to bring even an ounce of hope to the darkness surrounding Nexis. Not just so I could break free, but so Shanda could too. And Will, and everyone else duped by Nexis. Would it be dangerous? You bet. For more reasons than one. But I had to find a way to stop this never-ending feud. Maybe I was the only person who could.

CHAPTER 10

"Really, you want to do this here?" Under a black sky, shivers raced up and down my arms as I stood in the middle of the same field that witnessed James' exile. This time, brittle grass crunched under my boots, and the wind blew frost down my neck. But the memories remained.

Bryan cleared his throat. "It's the only place big enough for training."

"Who thought up this sick joke?" I mumbled to myself

Moonlight beamed down on me, and I tilted my face toward that silvery smile. My emissary of strength. Where was my angel? I'd need all the strength I could get to push me past the fear quivering in my belly.

Inhaling the wintry air, I closed my eyes for a second. Big mistake. My brother's tortured eyes stared back at me. That look of anguish on his face tormented me all over again.

Krrrh, krrk, krrh. Footsteps crunched through the frozen tundra. Headed straight toward me.

My eyes snapped open as shadowy outlines emerged on the dim horizon. My lungs seized, and my heart thumped out of control in my chest. As the figures trudged closer, I caught snatches of

Laura's red hair in the moonlight. I breathed a sigh of relief. It was my Guardian friends, not the Nexis council who banished James.

"What's going on?" I stuttered, my pulse slowing down some, but not enough.

Mr. Harlixton emerged from the shadows and laid one hand on my shoulder. "Relax, Miss McAllen. It's just me and the students. No other Guardians will be joining us tonight."

"You know this is where James got banished, right?" A ball of fear lodged in my throat. "Why are we here?"

"I truly regret having to bring you here, Miss McAllen." Moonlight glinted off his glasses as he pursed his lips together. "I'm hoping we can find a way to redeem this spot. Reclaim it for something else."

I swallowed back the acrid taste in my mouth. "If we're going to do this, just call me Lucy. And I'll call you ..."

"Raymond, if that's what you wish." A hint of a smile softened his stern face. "But only outside of the classroom."

"Deal." I shook his hand. "What's the grand plan?"

"I've instructed your friends to guard the perimeter." Raymond pantomimed a circle around the three of us. "Bryan will show me a little of how the Coopers have been training you. The Guardian elders want to know you're as prepared as you can be. I'll be giving them a full report of tonight's session."

"No pressure," I mumbled to the moon.

Raymond took my hand, then Bryan's. "Whenever you're ready, Lucy."

"Okay." Then I made the colossal mistake of closing my eyes.

Darkness crashed around me like a rogue wave, submerging me in inky nothingness. I felt like I was floating, free-falling through the universe.

I gripped Bryan and Raymond's hands—my only lifelines in the utter blackness. Torches flickered on the horizon, screaming into focus around me in a familiar scene.

Black-robed figures surrounded me. James stood in front of me, whispers hissing around us.

Fear oozed inside me, thick like black tar, gluing me in place. Shadows undulated toward me like a hand. Reaching out.

The darkness curled around James' shoulders, pinning his feet to the grass. Clenching his muscles, he gritted his teeth and nodded his head like he was ready to fight the shadows.

Then the scene faded to black. Lights brightened around me as I lay curled up on my comforter back home—crying my eyes out after I found out my brother disappeared. I choked and sobbed all over again.

But the darkness was there. Holding me too, like shadow-hands wrapped around me. I gasped deep breaths, hiccupping and hyperventilating. Then the hollowness dug into me, an ache that threatened to consume me from the inside out. Then the darkness closed in again.

A voice filtered over my head, deep and resonating.

"Lucy, hold on. You have the power. You can beat this."

The voice sounded just like James.

Warmth surged through my limbs. I turned my face heavenward. *Angel, where are you? I need you to vanquish this darkness, these horrible memories. I can't take it anymore.*

Whispered words lapped against the shores of my mind. *Little Seer, you hold the power within yourself.*

Familiar electricity crackled through my veins. I dropped the guys' hands just in time.

WaaBam! A silvery bolt shot from my right hand. The scene in my bedroom shattered into a million pieces. Flashing back to the torch-lit circle, my brother kneeling in the middle.

KerrRack! Another bolt of light from my left hand scattered the robed figures. Splintering James and I in opposite directions.

In a flash, a different memory sharpened into focus. A great tree, split in two by the same bolt of lightning. The dark night lit up like day. All the shadows screamed away, singed out of existence by a blinding light. Brighter than an exploding sun. My light. I was a conduit for the power of angels now. How could I have forgotten so easily?

I fell to my knees. Collapsed in a heap on the brown grass.

As my eyes fluttered open, the field reemerged. But I stood alone now, except for my angel, who shimmered in whiteness before me. His eyes glowed—two golden flames in a face of alabaster. Every feature shining with mirrored reflections of light from somewhere beyond this planet.

"You are stronger than the darkness. You can vanquish the shadows away all on your own." I heard his words clearly, though his lips never moved. "As long as you keep choosing the light."

I stared at his brightness, unable to look away. "Will you show me? Will you come back?"

The light around him trembled like a breeze rustling a million shards of crystal. "I will show you. Soon. You will see me again when you need help the most."

A tremor pulsated the ground. In a blast of sparks and lighting, he shot straight up into the night sky, the moon a mere speck in his wake as he disappeared into the constellations.

Voices rang in my ears. Hands grabbed mine. Blue eyes filled my vision, coming closer.

Bryan pressed his forehead into mine. "Lucy, are you okay? Lucy, talk to me."

"I, uh…" I stammered, my tongue a cotton ball in my mouth, my whole body shaking like a leaf. I could've hurt him or Mr. Harlixton with my rogue angel fire. A warm bucket of shame washed over me.

"Tell me what happened. Please, I have to know you're okay." His ragged breath warmed my nose.

"I can't." I swallowed, blinking hard. Gripping his hands as if he could bring me back to reality.

"Can you try?" Bryan hoisted me to my feet, cupping my face with his hands.

"I don't know." *Because it's too personal.* The words hung in my mind, unwilling to escape. It was my vision with my angel, and part of me didn't want to share it. The other part couldn't put it into words just yet.

Seconds ticked by. I parted my lips, just staring at him.

His face softened. He mashed his lips into mine and wrapped his arms around me.

My mind screamed, *"No."* as my body went rigid. Why didn't I want him to kiss me? The answer came in a flash. Because I didn't want him to see what I just saw, the visions, the memories. Not yet. It was too intimate.

I reached up to push him away, but strong hands came between us, landing on my torso, pulling us apart. I inhaled the cool air like a much-needed splash of cold water.

"What do you think you're doing?" Mr. Harlixton yelled.

My cheeks burned, but Raymond wasn't looking at me. His angry glare seared into Bryan.

"Yeah, what *are* you doing?" Brooke trotted towards us, the rest of the Guardians not far behind.

"I, uh, well crap." Bryan dug his fists into his pockets, eyes darting from me to Raymond and Brooke. "Only the Guardian Council knows the truth. If I kiss her, I can see her visions."

"Nowaydude," Tony exhaled three words in one breath. "That's messed up."

"It certainly is." Raymond's voice grew louder. "While I can understand why you didn't mention it to us, I don't think that's the best way to get the information you want. Did you even ask her if that's what she wanted?"

"No, I didn't. I just assumed." Air puffed out in front of Bryan as he turned my way. "Did you want me to see?"

"Not yet." I shook my head, staring at his knees instead of his face. "It's too personal."

One rough hand enveloped mine, and I recoiled.

Taking a step back, I put some much-needed space between me and Bryan.

"I'm sorry, Lucy." He hung his head, dropping his arm to the side. "I really thought that's what you were trying to tell me. I just thought it would be easier this way."

"I'm not mad." I pursed my lips, hardening my gaze at him. Somehow I had to make him understand. "It's just that it means something to me. Kissing you."

"It means something to me, too." He inched close enough for his breath to warm my face.

"Not this again." Lenny rolled his eyes. "Don't make me sic Raymond on you, man."

A laugh gurgled up my throat. "It's so weird to call him that. Maybe we should just go back to calling you Mr. Harlixton."

"Whatever makes you feel comfortable." Harlixton pushed his glasses up his nose. "Either way, all of this is still going in my report."

Bryan's cheeks blossomed pink splotches. "Great. My stupidity will be recorded for generations."

Now my cheeks were on fire. "Do you really have to write it down? This is so embarrassing."

Harlixton actually took out a notepad and pen. "Not to mention groundbreaking stuff. I'm sorry, Lucy, but this has to be done."

Bryan slung his arm around my shoulders, pulling me closer. "Don't worry. It's only me who should be embarrassed." He planted a kiss on my forehead.

"If you say so." I huddled against his bomber jacket. Maybe it would muffle the conversation they were now having about listing out my powers.

"Yes, the Seer's powers must be recorded for future generations." Harlixton clicked his pen, folding it and the pad back into his coat pocket. "Maybe we should reconvene back in the chapel so no one will overhear this conversation."

"That's a great idea, for you two." I puffed out a breath. "I just want to go to bed, if that's okay. I'm kinda drained."

In fact, I was more than just drained. I felt like the walking dead. Seeing visions and angels really sapped my energy. I had nothing left. My eyelids drooped as I made a mental note to ask Brooke and Bryan about it. Later.

"Certainly. I'll get your report at tomorrow night's chapel meeting. Just in case there are any holes to fill in." Harlixton nodded as if I was dismissed.

"Great." I murmured as I squeezed Bryan in a side hug. "I'll see you tomorrow."

"Goodnight, Lucy. I'll make it up to you, I promise." He mouthed *Sorry* as I walked away.

"Wait up, I'll walk with you." Laura wrapped an arm around my back like she knew my wobbly legs couldn't make it across the field without a little help from a friend.

><

Nelson Hall lay dark and dormant as I trudged back to my dorm with Brooke and Laura at my side. It wasn't that late, was it?

The second-floor hallway was dim and empty. Silent, except for a soft squeaking noise. *Creeeeak.* I halted in front of my door, bile rising up my throat.

The door to my room was ajar, swinging on its hinges.

"Shanda?" I croaked. No answer.

A tiny hand grabbed mine. "We'll go in with you." She glanced up at me, putting her small frame in front of me. If anything, I'd have to shield Laura, not the other way around.

Brooke inched the door open wider. "I can't see anything. It's too dark."

I tiptoed into my room and flicked on the light. And wished I hadn't. My jaw dropped.

"Ohmigosh!" Laura's shriek echoed back. "What happened here?"

All of my stuff was strewn across the room. Clothes ripped from their hangars, dangling from the ceiling fan. Dresser drawers upturned, its contents rumpled and wadded up in piles like garbage. Books littered the floor, leaving the shelves bare.

"Looks like somebody wanted something." Brooke stepped around a pile of papers, scattered haphazardly all over the hardwood floor like fallen leaves after a storm.

Yet Shanda's side of the room lay completely untouched. Her closet neat as ever. Her bed made to pristine perfection.

Seconds passed like a statue as time froze around me. Finally, I sputtered out, "Who would do this?"

"I've got two guesses." Brooke nodded her head down the hall.

"You really think Monica would do that?" Laura squeaked, her voice higher than I'd ever heard before.

Brooke rolled her eyes, planting her hands on her hips. "If she's stupid enough to resort to cyber-bullying and forcing my brother's ex on him, then yeah, I think she'd have a hand in this."

"Or at least lend her minion her master key." I pursed my lips at the thought of that brassy blond, Colleen, trashing my room. My fingers curled into fists. "She'll pay for this."

"You bet she will." Brooke gritted her teeth, looking the opposite of ferocious.

Laura held her hands up. "Before we go accusing people, let's see if anything is missing first."

"That could take hours. I'm tired enough as it is." I swallowed back a yawn, my limbs still gelatinous from Seer training. Instinctively, I patted my chest. Good. My necklace was still there. If they'd somehow stolen my Guardian amethyst, they'd really have the wrath of the Seer to deal with.

"Don't worry. We'll help." Laura went straight to work, picking up all the books around her.

I barely made a move to help her. I rubbed my eyes, blinking at the crime scene in front of me. I couldn't believe the bullying was happening all over again. At least this time, it was for a different reason, though equally as misguided.

My mind completely blanked at what to do next. So I just followed my friends' lead. Crouching over the nearest drawer, I refolded my wadded-up camis. Looks like I'd be wearing wrinkled clothes for awhile.

Brooke plucked down a sweater hanging from the ceiling fan. "You know we'll have to report this, don't you?"

"Maybe we should do that first." Laura hopped through the floor maze, putting an armful of books back on my shelf.

"Fine," I huffed, sliding my tank tops in their rightful drawer. "Go get Miss Sherry, if you must. There's no way I'm reporting anything to Monica."

"I'm on it." Laura danced around the mess and disappeared out the door.

Brooke fished some skirts off my bed. "You know Bryan's going to want to hear about this. Harlixton, too."

"Maybe I'll let you tell them. I just want to get this cleaned up." To prove it, I righted another drawer and went to work folding.

"Fair enough." She helped me clean in relative silence, muttering under her breath about mindless Nexis drones.

Couldn't say I blamed her either. I was just that drained. Too exhausted even to let my inner fury take over. But Monica and Colleen would definitely have to watch their backs tomorrow.

"Holy crap, what the—" Shanda cursed under her breath. "What the fork happened to our room?"

Petals of anger started to ignite. "Colleen and/or Monica would be my guess."

"You gotta be right, girl, 'cause my stuff hasn't been touched." She rushed to her closet, stroking her cashmere collection. "If it was, my dad would hunt down those girls until they paid back every last cent."

"Obviously they wouldn't lay a finger on your stuff. Must be some kind of Nexis code or something." I crossed my arms, aiming my newfound fury at her, the closest Nexis member.

"Hey, don't look at me." Shanda dropped the cashmere and shot me a glare. "If I was on the inner circle, they would've given me a heads up. But I do know those girls. They don't do random. There's a reason they tossed the place."

"I wish you weren't right," I mumbled under my breath.

Miss Sherry hustled her mass of frizzy hair into our circus of a room. "Lucy, Shanda, I'm so sorry this happened to you. I can't imagine who would do such a thing."

"I've got a name for you." Shanda stomped up to Miss Sherry and leaned in close. "That precious RA of yours. Monica had a hand in this for sure."

Our dorm mom backed up. "That's a serious accusation, Miss Jones. But since she does have a master key to this floor, I will have to investigate her. Along with everyone else, of course."

Shanda rocked back on her heels, a satisfied grin on her face. "Hey, that's all I'm asking."

"Is there anything missing?" Miss Sherry pried a pad from a giant pocket in her elastic-waist jeans. "I'll need a full list."

I shrugged my shoulders as defeat washed over me. "I don't know yet. I just started cleaning up."

She thrust the pad at me. "Fill this out for me by tomorrow at the latest. If you'll excuse me, I need to notify campus security."

"Thank you, Miss Sherry." I reached for the notepad, and she patted me on the head.

"Don't worry, we'll get to the bottom of this." She bustled out of the room as fast as she'd entered. At least Miss Sherry was a Watcher, so she might actually keep her word.

A phone trilled in the corner, and Brooke reached into her pocket. "It's Bryan. I'll be back."

"Thanks," I mouthed as she slipped through the bathroom to her side of the suite.

Shanda sank to her knees, wading through the books on the floor. "I can't believe this. I never should've joined that group."

I plopped down on the hardwood next to her. "Hey, this isn't your fault. You weren't even here."

"True, but this was more than a Nexis prank. This is getting serious. Fast." She turned her back on me as she gathered my toiletries and put them back on the vanity.

Something dawned on me. A horrible realization that rankled my stomach like sour milk.

"The skeleton key," I gasped, my heart banging against my ribcage. Digging through the piles of books around my bookshelf, I uncovered the remains of the puzzle box where I'd kept Harlixton's treasure. Smashed to smithereens.

"What skeleton key?" Shanda raced to my side, rubbing small circles on my back.

I threw up my hands. "It doesn't matter now. It's gone." My breath froze in my lungs. There was only one more item of value to Nexis. I rifled through the books again, scanning for the tan cover Cindy had given me for Christmas. It wasn't there, either.

"Great. Now they've got the book, too." I slumped to the floor in defeat.

"What book?" Shanda's hand paused on my back. "Don't tell me you had some secret key to a Guardian hideaway and a book on how to get there."

"Kind of." I leaned against my bed, head in my hands. "The key was for the chapel library's secret entrance. Harlixton gave it to me last year so I could sneak into the back entrance of the chapel, undetected. Then we found a secret passage, which is probably what they're really after. Good luck finding *that*."

"Cool." She breathed, her face going slack. "Does the book go with it?"

"Fortunately, no." I rubbed at the pain searing into my temples. "Bryan's mom gave me the Guardian's handbook or something, in case they ever let me join."

"Dang." She whistled through her teeth. "Did you get a chance to read any of it?"

A spark of hope ignited in my chest. "I read some on the plane. I wish I knew what it meant, though. It was a bunch of Guardian rules, but there was a section on the Seer. It had some legends and prophecies from a book in the Bible. Zechariah, I think."

"Hmm." Shanda scratched her chin. "I suspect you'd need the Guardian's Book of the Seer to really understand it."

"Or the Nexis version," I murmured, shaking my head. "I'm so stupid. How could I let this happen?"

"Hey, it's not your fault." Shanda slung her arm around my shoulder and squeezed.

"I left the book and the key out in the open. Just begging for something like this to happen." I threw up my arms, gesturing at the remnants of the break-in. "See?"

"Huh-uh," Shanda shook her head, grabbed my arms, and pinned them to my side. "You didn't make Colleen and Monica commit a felony. This is their fault."

Slowly, I nodded. "I know. You're right."

"I can't help but wonder if they know I've been spying on them." She whispered as her gaze shifted all around the room. "As part of my deal with the Guardians, I started hacking the Nexis tower security cameras in December, trying to find anything useful."

"I didn't know you were a closet hacker." The shock wore off as ideas rolled around in my brain. "Did you find anything?"

"Nope." She shook her head. "Not yet."

"Then they probably don't know what you're doing. Yet." My lips curled up, the ideas coalescing into a plan. "Look at your side of the room. It's immaculate."

Shanda cocked her head at me. "You don't think it's a tactic? Like, keep your enemies close?"

"No way." I shook my head so hard my earrings slapped my cheeks. "I don't think those girls are that smart."

"Ha!" She laughed out loud. Then her smile faded. "But you *are* thinking something, aren't you?"

"I am." I nodded, glancing at the door to make sure it was closed. And locked. I pushed myself up from the hardwood floor, and sat on the edge of my bare mattress, patting the spot beside me.

She narrowed her eyes at me but came over and sat down next to me anyway.

"Okay, here goes." I leaned in, keeping my voice low. "I'm thinking we can use your hacking skills to turn the tables on them. Somehow. Anything to stop the blond reign of terror." They weren't going to get away with this. I was done bowing down to bullies. Of all shapes, sizes, or secret society persuasions.

"So you want me to keep spying, but not *just* for the Guardians anymore." She turned a wry grin my way. "I like it."

"Right?" I waggled my eyebrows at her. "You can see if they've got the book, and what they plan to do with it. And look for this Book of the Seer while you're at it."

"That's not a bad plan, girl." Her smile widened. "Someone taught you well."

"Hey, I learned from the best." I grinned back at her. "The good news is, they've only got a few pieces of the puzzle."

Shanda's face fell. "Yeah, but they'll figure it out eventually."

I ground my teeth together at the thought of them finding the secret entrance because of me. "We'll just have to figure them out first."

The winter wind howled outside, rattling the window behind me. A small part of me wondered—was this the Montrose Paranormal Academy version of a reckoning?

CHAPTER 11

A bitter wind gnawed my exposed cheeks as I walked with the Guardian girls across the quad, dreading the chapel meeting tonight. More like an inquisition, I'd bet. Burrowing deeper into my parka, I trudged through the brittle grass with only moonlight to guide me. Part of me longed for it to snow, just like it did in Harrisburg a month ago. Probably because it was the last time I felt remotely safe.

Or maybe I just wanted to go back to the last time I was happy. When Bryan surprised me with those three precious words. But I couldn't go back in time, no matter how much I wanted to. Going back wouldn't change my reality. Bryan would still choose the Guardians over me. Nexis would continue to bully me. Will would still be an enigma.

I stared up at the soaring arch of the chapel entrance, outlined against the night sky. Brooke and Laura, oblivious to my internal musings, pushed open the door and walked right in.

Not me. I lingered in the doorway, unwilling to follow them in just yet. I still needed answers before I faced the Guardian firing squad.

Laura turned, red waves swishing. "Coming, Lucy?"

Something hitched in my chest. "Not yet. I just need a minute, okay?"

Brooke inhaled a sharp whistle. She gave Laura the oddest look, almost like she was afraid. Did she know what I'd been wrestling with? My inner war, her brother on one side, Will on the other.

Laura bobbed her head. Grabbed Brooke's hand. "We'll be down the hall."

Their whispers faded down the dark hallway.

The scent of hot wax wafted to my nose. I stood in front of the candle station, tongues of fire licking at their red glass cages. Dancing to a tune I couldn't name. Somewhere deep within, I related to their straining rhythm.

I picked a wooden wand and plunged it into the nearest flamelet. It caught fire as I watched, transfixed. Words coalesced in my mind as I stared at the growing flame.

Moving to the middle candle, I lit the wick. It sparked and caught fire—a burning symbol of my struggle.

Staring at the candle I'd just lit, a silent prayer crossed my mind. For help. For clarity. I needed to figure out where I belonged, aside from my relationship with Bryan. Or even my strange fascination with Will. If I really wanted to be the Seer, would I have to make a stand on my own?

I closed my eyes. Turned to the Maker of the universe. The one who decided to give me this wonderful, terrible gift.

I don't know what to do. Show me the way.

The chapel sanctuary faded into black. Images rushed into my mind. Me standing on a mountaintop, wind whipping around me. I jumped, free-falling into the unknown. Then I was caught by an eagle, soaring through the clouds. But it wasn't an eagle. It was more than an eagle. A white bird, radiating light brighter than the clouds. The light grew brighter than the sun. Angel.

And we soared up, up, and up. Higher than I've ever been before. Till breath was only a memory. And the heavens opened. A golden light so bright, even my angel shuddered. Heavenly music

- 111 -

swelled from above. Goosebumps popped up all over my body. It was a world full of light—immense, and beautiful. So glorious it was too much for me to bear. I wanted to run, fall down on my knees, and beg for mercy.

I couldn't take it anymore. I opened my eyes. Blinked. I was back in the chapel. The real world looked so gray now.

Snow was falling in the sanctuary, sparkling like diamonds from the Gothic-domed ceiling.

A hush fell over me. Every sound silencing for this one moment in time.

Silent flakes of white fell all around me. Made me think of Bryan. His love. But they didn't touch me. No wet splotches on my arms, no drops of water on the marble tiles. As if the glittering whiteness floated down just for me—in that unseen world only I could see. Trying to tell me something. And I felt cold all over again.

Then something really strange happened.

Flakes of iridescent black started to fall. Mixing with the white snow. Muddling the white crystals into shades of gray. Like the shadows around Will on New Year's. Was it a metaphor of some kind? Or a warning?

As suddenly as it started, the snowfall evaporated into thin air. Was that my answer? Great. Another riddle I'd have to decipher. Yet my heart felt lighter now. Free of its heavy burden. I knew it wasn't all up to me.

In one giant breath, I whispered my thanks to the heavens, releasing any remnants of my inner agony.

Low murmurs wafted down the hall. I walked toward the sound. Sharp interjections, then staccato beats pelted my ears. I braced myself.

In the library doorway, I halted. Still as a statue. Bryan and Mr. Harlixton were arguing. Loudly.

Bryan's cheeks were patches of red. Eyes hard as icebergs. "I can't believe you're making me do this."

"I'm not making you do anything." Harlixton's voice was calm and even. "This was a council decision. It's out of my hands, I'm afraid."

Bryan's gaze darted around the room, stopping on me. He held his hand up like a stop sign. "Lucy, I can't—" His face crumpled like a paper bag. He glanced at Harlixton. "You tell her."

My heart drummed wildly. "Now what?"

"Lucy, I don't know how much you overheard, but it seems like we've got a real mess on our hands this time." Harlixton crossed the room and gently placed my hands in his.

For some reason, I couldn't move, couldn't leave the safety of my doorway. I just stood there, frozen in place.

"By now I'm sure you've heard about the break-in." His palms were warm and dry.

"You mean my room?" I asked, my voice squeaking.

"No, there's been another break-in." Harlixton came closer, his face softening a crack. "Some valuable books and artifacts were stolen from my office, along with an extra key to this library. We have no doubt the secret passage you discovered last semester is their next target. Especially with the skeleton key they stole from your room."

"I'm sorry," I whispered, staring down at my snow boots.

"No, dear, it's my fault. I never should've let you have it so long." He lifted my chin with one finger. His eyes held my gaze, strong and steady as if he was trying to brace me. For something else.

I squinted at him, trying to read his expression. "What do you think they're planning?"

His stare didn't waver. "If we're lucky, they only want to use the tunnel to spy. But I'm sure they're looking for clues."

"Clues?" I stared at the dark corner of the turret, where the secret entrance lay hidden in shadow. A vision, or more like a memory, played through my mind. A glowing amethyst, hidden behind the back shelf. It felt like a dream I had long ago. I shook off the memory.

I gasped, my hands flying to my mouth. "They want the Guardian Amethyst, don't they?"

He steepled his hands, apparently unfazed. "I think so. You didn't hear this from me, but we relocated it years ago. So we can only hope they find the clues we left behind. They'll be searching for a ghost."

"That's a relief, I guess." I cocked my head at him. "But that's not what you're arguing about, is it?"

"I'm afraid not." He shook his head, squeezing my hand much like my dad would if he were here. "You see, the Guardian Council is worried. They have a new plan to hide the amethyst and get the vital information we need to properly defend ourselves. But it's a bit tricky."

"You mean like spying on them?" The words tumbled out before my mind caught up, my subconscious more aware than I wanted to admit.

"Very perceptive, I must say." His mouth curled slightly.

I choked on my own breath, spitting out the words anyway. "What does this have to do with me?"

"I think you already know." He pushed up his glasses and leveled his gaze at me. "We'll need you to be our covert operative. If Nexis is stealing stones, then they're planning something big. It's the only way to prevent the Guardians from declaring war."

"Wow. That's a crapton of pressure." Bile oozed in my gut, gurgling up my throat. I just stared at Harlixton like an idiot. Did he have any idea what he was asking of me?

"Yes, I know that, Lucy. But the only reason Nexis would steal sacred stones and risk war is if they're planning something. Soon." He pursed his lips together as if that would soften the blow.

"So, what ... are you saying Shanda's spying isn't good enough?" I clapped my hand over my mouth before I revealed anything else about our secret plan.

"Maybe you're more than just perceptive. However, I'm afraid that option isn't enough anymore." He threw up his arms in defeat. "There's no way Nexis would reveal their most guarded secrets to a new recruit. Not like they would for you, a future Seer. I think you know they'd do anything to have you on their side."

"It's not gonna work. I'm a terrible liar. Really awful." Something gurgled deep inside me like red-hot lava.

"That may be true, but you're actually not bad at acting." Bryan peeked at me out of the corner of his eye.

His words shocked me. Somehow, he'd crossed the room to stand by my side, and I never even noticed.

Squinting, I turned my anger on him. "Because I did two years of drama club back at Alton High, you think I could fool Nexis? I doubt it."

He dug his fingers into his hair. "I'm not saying I like the idea of you putting yourself in their greedy little clutches. But at least you've got a shot at getting real intel. You're the only one who does."

"So what am I supposed to do? Knock on the observatory door and say 'Hey, by the way, I want to join Nexis now?'" The realization sank in, digging its claws deep. The whole time, this was the real reason why the Guardians wouldn't let me join. They wanted me to be their little Seer Spy. The threat of my membership causing a war with Nexis was just an excuse. Another lie.

Fury roared up inside me, a captive force finally set free. *The snowflakes. The vision.* Angel tried to warn me.

"Not exactly." Harlixton stepped between us. No doubt the anger was written all over my face. "First you'll have to break up with your boyfriend. Publicly."

"What? You can't be serious." Something snapped inside me. My knees buckled. "Bryan, are you okay with this?"

Harlixton droned on, "Once you break up with Bryan, you'll have to befriend Will. Make him think you're on his side now."

And the hits just kept coming. How could this possibly be the best plan? I glanced at Bryan, but he wouldn't even look at me. Like I wasn't even there anymore. Standing two feet away.

I sidestepped Harlixton, closing the gap between me and Bryan. "This sounds a little too much like what happened with your ex-girlfriend. Colleen."

"Will's not interested in her." Bryan's jaw hardened, still unable to face me. "He's into you."

What a slap to the face. I stumbled backward, reeling inside. I had no words. I couldn't deny that. It was the truth. He knew it. I knew it. Everybody knew it. The wall of denial crumbled around me, flooding waves of guilt that puddled at my feet.

But I had to know. "Please tell me you're not saying what I think you're saying."

Bryan turned his electric gaze on me. Finally. "All you have to do is make him believe you're interested. You don't have to feel anything. For my sake, I hope you don't."

"What is happening here?" My heart beat itself against my ribcage as if it could explode any second. "You want me to break up with you, then pretend to be into your enemy just so I can use him for some stupid intel? I can't believe you're going along with this crazy plan."

"I don't want to do this anymore than you do." He reached for me, fingers tracing my jawline.

"Then don't. Fight for me." I whispered, the words all but strangling me. I promised myself I wouldn't beg, but here I was. Breaking that promise.

"I have no choice," he breathed.

And my heart burst open. Obliterated in tiny fragments. Dying embers of a love I thought we shared.

Soon those sparks would fizzle out and die. Turn to ice. It was happening already. I couldn't stop it now.

Only he could stop it.

"Of course you have a choice." My breath wobbled in my throat, but I had to say it. "You can choose me."

"Lucy, hold up." His hand traveled down my arm, making me shiver. "This only has to be a public breakup. We can still technically be together."

Salt stung my eyes, but I choked it back. "You mean talk on the phone, but never see each other in person? I don't think so. We shouldn't have to hide. Do you really think that's what I want?"

"Angel, I'll do whatever you say." His arms circled me now. Squeezing me, fingers running down my hair, cheek pressed against my forehead. "Anything to make this easier on you."

"I want you to fight for me," I whispered into his neck.

A shudder racked his body. He shook his head. "I can't go against the council. What they say goes. I'm sorry, Lucy." He pulled back, eyes searching my face. "Please, anything else."

"I shouldn't even have to ask you to fight for me." Pressure built behind my eyes. I steeled my jaw. "Who do you Guardians think you are? You can't ban me from joining, then try to turn me into a spy. I won't do it. You're going to lose the Seer. For good this time."

It was all I had left to hurl at him. An empty, hollow threat that meant nothing. I couldn't take it anymore. One more second with this Bryan, the resolute statue, and I'd really lose it. More than just my heart would explode. My anger, even my sanity, might just erupt, too.

I had to get out of there. Away from him.

I took off running.

Out the door. Down the hall.

His voice floated after me. "Lucy, come back."

The guy I loved was calling to me.

But I couldn't answer, couldn't go back.

><

Run. Run. Run. All I wanted to do was run. Down the hall. Into the sanctuary. Through the candlelit foyer. Lungs heaving. I couldn't stop now, not for anything. I pushed open the stubborn old door. Flew down the steps. Legs spinning. Churning.

But I forgot. The steps were ragged. I tripped on a rough edge. Crumpled to my knees. Face-planting into the pavement, hands first.

An evil laugh skittered to my ears. From somewhere in the night. The final nail in the coffin of my humiliation.

"Walk much, dipstick? So pathetic." Colleen. Of course she was here tonight.

More laughter circled around me. Daggers dripping with familiar venom. Hurled at my back.

Because I couldn't get up now, not even to face them. A familiar current sizzled through my veins, but I balled my hands into fists to keep the angel fire at bay. I didn't need to broadcast any more information to these Nexis bullies.

That high-pitched snicker had to be Monica, the lower rumble Kevin's. They were the pathetic ones.

How could this be happening again? The heartbreak, the humiliation. All. Over. Again.

All because I was born as the Seer, with this stupid gift everyone wanted. Or wanted to use. Not me. I never asked for this.

I couldn't hold back the dam anymore. Tears streamed rivulets down my cheeks. The salt was refreshing. Almost.

"Lucy are you okay?" An ebony hand reached down, pulling me up into her arms. "No, you're not. What happened?"

Shanda's dark eyes darted around the quad, landing on the Nexis trio. "You're seriously just going to stand there and laugh, right now? Get outta here."

"And miss the show?" Colleen stepped forward, her brassy hair swishing in the moonlight. "No way."

"You're pathetic, you know?" Shanda slung her arm across my shoulder.

"Funny, I was just saying the same thing about your little friend there." Colleen practically spat out the words.

"Burn." Kevin yelled. It echoed off every building in the quad.

Shanda rolled her eyes and urged me forward. "Are you hurt? Do we need to stop by the nurse's office?"

I could only shake my head.

Footsteps pounded behind me. Down the steps. Across the pavement. My heart thumping the same rhythm.

"Lucy, what happened?" Bryan's hand reached for mine.

"Don't." I shook him off and clung tighter to Shanda. Not turning around for a second.

He ran in front of us and palmed both hands into my shoulder, stopping me in my tracks. "Listen, I'm sorry it had to go down like that. I never meant to hurt you."

"Well, it's too late. You did." I couldn't look at him. I just stared at his shoes. Black converse, too thin for January. I hoped he got a cold from this. Something to remember me by.

"C'mon, don't be this way." He gulped, Adam's apple bobbing. "We can still be friends."

I was dead wrong. Those words were the final nails in the coffin. He was going through with the Guardian plan. Blow by excruciating blow. Step one, public break-up. Check.

How could he choose them over me? My boyfriend. The guy who said he loved me. The guy who rescued me from my ex. He'd scooped me up, made me feel so safe. How could he leave me so unprotected now?

I jerked my head, finally daring to look at him. "No, we can't. It's over."

A collective gasp punctuated the air. A note of finality hung in the frigid night air, then everything went silent.

His forehead scrunched up. Something glistened in his eyes. Tears? Maybe he finally realized what he'd done.

Now that it was too late.

No one, not even Shanda, said a word.

Bryan breathed in deep, exhaled a long breath. "I'm sorry you feel that way. I'm so sorry, Lucy."

A lone tear dripped down my cheek.

His finger stretched out to wipe it away. I almost leaned into his hand.

But we both froze. His hand dangling. Mid-air.

He backed up, converse crunching the frozen grass. "Please reconsider. Maybe we can be friends. Someday."

I wiped the tear away myself. "I don't think so. This is it for us."

I trudged past him, shutting my eyes against the stares.

Shanda hurried to catch up to me, linking her arm through mine all the way back to the dorm. Up the stairs to our room.

Until I collapsed in a heap on my bed.

An empty shell. No room for anyone but me.

CHAPTER 12

Black fog billowed around me, wrapping me in its swirling mist. An even darker forest loomed on the horizon. Pulling me in. Leaves crunched under my feet. Branches scraped my skin. Raw. Exactly how I felt. Something howled in the distance, shrieking in the night.

Notes of song trilled in the darkness. A gray fog tumbled in, grabbing onto my ankles. Pulling me out of the forest. Black branches lunged toward me. Charcoal vines snapped around my wrists. Strong tendrils wrestled me back into the darkness.

Inside I screamed. *Help me!*

The faint music jingled louder. A tune I recognized. The fog lightened. A spotlight swept by, scrubbing away the darkness.

My lids fluttered open. Blue light illuminated the darkness. I reached for my phone.

"Hello?" My voice was hoarse, not my own.

"Lucy, it's me."

I didn't have to check the screen. I knew it was Bryan.

"It's gotta be after midnight. What do you want?"

"I want to see you. Tonight. Please, just let me explain."

His tone was gruff, all rough edges. Very unlike him.

Shadowy tendrils crawled back in, curling around the ceiling, reaching for me. Just like in my dream.

I swallowed hard, an ache searing down my throat. "I don't know what's left to explain."

"Lucy, please. I have to see you." His voice cracked, a sliver of desperation. "There's more to say. I don't want this to end."

Something bloomed in my gut. Hope. A tiny ember of light still burned in my heart. For him. Sending the shadows back to wherever they came from.

"Fine, what's your brilliant plan?" My words were breathy. Muted by exhaustion.

"Thank you," he sighed into the phone. "Meet me in the parking lot. I'll pull up to the curb."

"Gimme ten minutes." My stomach clenched, the ache settling there.

"See you soon, angel." Click, the call ended.

Angel. His last word lingered like a pop to the head. Would that be the last time he called me angel? I rubbed my scratchy eyes.

Quickly, I dressed in dark colors like the Guardian girls taught me. Black jeans, my MCA hoody under my black parka, black gloves, and scarf. By tomorrow, would Brooke and Laura even be allowed to talk to me? They were Guardians, after all.

I stepped out of my room and eased the door shut behind me so I wouldn't disturb Shanda or any other prying eyes. I tiptoed down the dark hall. Was I doing the right thing?

The light in the stairwell flickered twice. It was Angel, telling me I was on the right track. I just knew it, even if my foggy mind was going haywire.

I padded across the empty lobby, into the kitchen, and creaked the window opened. I shimmied into the cold night. Jumping to the ground, I slunk across campus, skirting buildings and treelines. Staying out of sight. Much like a happier night months ago, when I'd snuck out with Brooke and Laura to find the secret Guardian tunnel. This time I was all alone, sneaking off in a different direction.

Bryan's boring black sedan purred at the edge of campus. I hopped in without a word.

He didn't look at me, just sped away from the silent school.

Silence cloaked the car, too. But I couldn't be the first to speak.

The car rumbled past the darkened shops, the swinging Betty Boop air freshener almost comforting. Except for the stoic Bryan sculpture beside me. Almost life-like, but still as marble.

"Do you hate me?" His voice came out tinny and hollow. Like it resonated from miles away.

I sucked in a breath. Held it there. Finally let it go.

"I wish I did."

He deflated like a blown tire—hissing air, shoulders slumping in stops and starts. "Good. I couldn't live with myself if you hated me."

I gritted my teeth. "I didn't say I liked you much right now."

The corners of his marble lips curled. "That's okay. I don't like me much right now either."

"Good. At least we agree on one thing."

He turned his car into a space in front of the only lit-up building on the block. The Riverdale Coffeeshop. "Is this okay?"

"Whatever." My limbs tingled, turning numb. I just sat there, waiting for him to open my door, to lead me to my doom. At least he picked a window booth.

Bryan ordered us coffees and I pointed to an anonymous pastry behind the glass display. The waitress asked if I'd like it warmed up. I must've nodded because she scurried off. She came back with a shiny coffeepot and a chocolate croissant. Like she knew what was going on here, even if my mind couldn't register the concept.

Once she disappeared, Bryan leaned across the Formica. "I'm sorry for the way things went down. I really am, Lucy."

He grabbed my hands, gripping tighter than ever. Warmth seeped into my fingertips, threaded up my arms.

I shook my head against that warmth, wriggling my hands away.

"Do you even want to hear my plan?" Each word was a soft staccato, punctuating the air between us.

"You have a plan?" I glanced up, that ocean of blue sucking me in. I could barely breathe. So I nodded.

His face brightened in the fluorescent light. "You don't have to do this forever. Let's say you spy on them for a month. Till the end of the semester, tops. Then you can come back. And we can be together."

I blinked and blinked … and blinked some more. His words just jumbled around in my brain. Not making any sense.

When I didn't say anything, he scooted closer. "We just have to keep this a secret. Until you're done with your assignment. Then we can pick up right where we left off. If you can forgive me, that is."

I closed my eyes against the blue sea. The ache inside split me open—leaving nothing but a hollow shell sitting in front of Bryan, trying to reason with him.

The shell opened her eyes. "There's just one flaw with your little plan." The ache hardened into icicles in her gut, ready to pummel him with frozen daggers. "You're telling me everything you want me to do and everything the Guardians want from me. What about what I want? Because I *don't* want to trade secrets for affection. And I *don't* want to date anyone in secret. Even you. It's duplicitous. That's just not me."

The rest of me, what was left of my heart, floated above the table. Like I couldn't watch it unfold anymore. This heartbreaking chess match.

Arms of warmth wrapped around me. Softer than any arms I'd ever known. Wings. My angel was with me, holding me above the storm below. Keeping the broken pieces together.

Bryan cringed. Arched back to his side of the booth. "I never wanted you to get within ten feet of that Mama's Boy. That was not my plan. I hope you know that by now."

It wasn't enough. The shell wanted more. "So what was your plan? Did it include not telling me about Shanda? Because I think having my roommate at my side, going double agent with me, would be a helpful little tidbit to mention."

His cheeks simmered. "Not my call either. But I couldn't disobey the Guardian council. They threatened to send you off to Europe. Harlixton and I came up with this alternative."

Floating me turned back to the fight. "Europe, really? Would James be there, too?"

"Maybe, but that's not the point." His eyes darted away like he was hiding something. "It's dangerous over there. The fighting is escalating, getting public notice. Not like over here, where everything's still covert."

"Did you ever ask what I wanted? No, you just decided what was best for me. Maybe I want to fight alongside my brother." The splintered versions of me inched closer together, almost merging back into one. "Maybe I want someone, my boyfriend, to fight for me."

"That's exactly what I did!" His eyes were wild now. Scanning me, scanning the dining room. "I fought for you to stay here. To keep you safe. You don't know what it's like over there. It's scary. And dangerous. I couldn't risk losing you. Not like that."

My heart pricked. In a rush of breath. I was me again, whole and hurting at the desperation in his eyes. "Hey, shush. I'm sorry, I didn't know. Only because you didn't discuss any of this with me."

"But the council—"

I put up my hand. "Listen, I don't care what the council says. We were in a relationship. That means you're supposed to tell me things. At least, that's what I thought. I know you've been a Guardian since the dark ages, long before you met me. But I thought we had something special. I thought we could tell each other anything. Even the hard stuff."

Tears gathered in my eyes. *Thud.* I dropped my hand to the tabletop. "Especially the hard stuff."

Suddenly his hand slid over mine and I couldn't think anymore. Couldn't breathe. All those memories, all those months last semester, came racing back to me.

And I didn't have the energy to fight anymore. It was his turn now.

"You're right, angel, we do have something special." His thumb rubbed the back of my hand, rough but steady. "I should've told you about what was going on before anything was decided. But please don't think I didn't fight for you. Because I did fight for you. I'm still fighting for you."

I wobbled on the vinyl bench, squeezing his hand like I couldn't stay upright without him. "Not hard enough. I don't want a secret relationship. I don't want to be a spy. And I don't want to use Will."

He dropped my hand and snapped back fast, rocking the booth. "What're you saying, that you care about him or something?"

I shook my head. That wasn't the issue here. "He's not the monster you guys make him out to be. He's a mixed-up kid who doesn't deserve to be used. No matter who his parents are."

"You have no idea what he's capable of." He kneaded his shoulder. "Don't think for one second that he's not using you right now. That you aren't a pawn in his twisted plan."

"I saw the shadows, remember? I know what he's capable of." The light descended around me, forcing back the memory. Illuminating a new truth. "But if he's so dangerous, why would you ever agree to the Guardian's plan? Don't you want to protect me?"

That was it—the real reason I was so upset. Because I wanted him to protect me. And I thought he would.

His jaw opened. Closed. Dropped again. "Lucy, I … of course I want to protect you. I just…"

"Can't go against the Guardians," I finished for him. "I can't win, no matter what I do. No one deserves to be a pawn in someone else's game. Not him. Not you. Not me. I'm just a weapon for one side or the other."

The fluorescent light blinked, and a surge of adrenaline pumped through me like I'd just hit on the real truth in all this madness.

I squared off, targeting my glare at Bryan. "It ends today. I want to negotiate my own terms."

He rubbed his hands together. "Now we're talking. Name 'em."

"First, I want to work with Shanda to gather the intel. But I won't manipulate Will. Period." He flinched at that, but I rumbled on. "When we're done, by the end of the semester, both of us get to join the Guardians." I sat back and waited. Chest tight. Breath shallow.

Slowly, back and forth, he wagged his head. "That's too steep. I can probably get the okay on Shanda, maybe even her joining up. But they won't let you join unless we're on the brink of war. If you got Will to trust you, as a friend, then they might go for it."

I bit into my cheek. Could a make a small concession like that? I knew how dangerous it was, walking that tightrope called Will. But I was so close to making things better. "That could work. As long as it's nothing romantic."

"I think we can both agree on that. There's just one more thing." He swallowed the dregs of his coffee, then clanked the cup down onto the table. "What about us? Are we going to make it?"

"I don't know." The icicles inside me had melted by now. Still, I shivered. I couldn't lie, not to him. He deserved better. "If you're asking me to be a Guardian puppet, then I don't think so. You can't have it both ways."

"Okay, I get that. I hate it, but I get it." He squeezed his eyes shut, only opening them in slits. Like he couldn't look at me. "So we're really breaking up? For good?"

Bile rose in my throat, but I gulped it back. "I think we have to. Unless you want to send me off to Europe."

"No way." He shook his head, threw down some money, and led me out the door into the night. "I'd rather you stay alive and spy on Nexis than risk your life on the battlefield."

"Both options suck. Wait, did you say battlefield?" The word hung like a frozen shadow in the icy air. I shimmied into his car. "Is that really what it's like over there?"

He started the car. "I'm afraid so. It's not all-out war yet. But it will be soon."

"Maybe then I could join the Guardians." The streetlights whizzed by, but he didn't answer. Even I knew it was a pipe dream, me teaming up with James in Europe, duking it out with the Nexis baddies. Yeah, right. Never gonna happen if the stupid Guardian Council had their way. Why couldn't the Seer choose her own fate?

We were back at Montrose all too soon. He parked in the back of the lot and turned off the car, never looking at me.

"Lucy, I still love you. So don't write me off just yet. Save a little piece of your heart for me."

"I hope I can. Because I still love you, too." I grabbed his hand, pulling him closer.

For a second his forehead rested on mine. Then his lips dove into my mouth, kissing me hard. His fingers burrowed into my hair, pressing me in closer. As if we could stay locked like this forever.

Lost in the moment, I forgot to think, forgot to breathe.

Did I slap him? He pulled away as if I had. My heart ached as if I had.

His breath was heavy, cheeks flushed. "Maybe we had more problems than I thought. Or else you would've told me about Will and the New Year's Eve party."

"How did you—" My gut clenched, threatening to tear in two again. "What did you see?"

His eyes landed on me, a searing look that curled my toes. "Those strange shadows around him. White and black and gray. I get it now." He shivered.

"Get what?" I gulped.

"You have feelings for him."

And it was my turn to feel like I'd just been slapped.

"See, you can't even deny it. I feel so stupid." Bryan rubbed his neck. "You're afraid you'll fall for him."

"No, that's not true. I just don't hate him like you do." I grazed his stubble with my fingertips. "And I didn't want to upset you."

He shrugged. "It seems we both have our little secrets. Maybe a break, or break-up, is just what we need right now. No matter how much I hate it."

I trailed my fingers down his neck, across his shoulder, down his arm. When I reached his hand, I entwined my fingers in his. "I hate it as much as you do."

"Really?" His eyes brightened. "You mean that?"

I nodded, and it was all he needed. His mouth was on mine again, our lips mingling.

I collapsed into him, my muscles too weary to hold me up any more. Those strong arms held me, kissing me for the longest time. Like it was the last time.

When he pulled back, the windows were clouded with fog. "I'll miss this."

"Me, too," I murmured into his mouth, pulling him back to me. "Something to remember me by."

"Believe me, Lucy McAllen, I won't be forgetting you anytime soon." He paused, lips millimeters away. "I'll be waiting for you on the other side of this."

I crushed my mouth into his lips one last time. Only because I wasn't sure I could make the same promise. Things were already starting to change.

CHAPTER 13

After that horrible debacle on the quad and the less-than-stellar breakup post mortem in a dinky coffeehouse, I didn't want to see the light of day ever again. My soul ached for what I'd lost. Every day I woke up missing Bryan, and every night I silently cried myself to sleep. As the days and weeks went by, the searing pain lessened ever-so-slightly.

Brooke sneaked in through the bathroom to check on me every single day, probably relaying whatever she saw back to Bryan. Who cared if my eyes were red and puffy, or I was a complete and utter mess? This is what he wanted. And life just hurt without him.

Every weekday I went to class and took to-go meals from the caf. Hiding out in my room. Mindy and Shanda tried to make me go to the Valentine's dance, but I just laughed bitterly in their faces. As if one month was enough to get over someone you'd said those three little words to. I didn't want to see a world without Bryan or hear the rumors going around about me this time. Part of me wondered if I'd always love him—if this pain would ever go away. Being a teenager was just too intense sometimes.

Today, I sat curled up in the hollow spot on my bed. An impact crater that fit me perfectly. It'd only taken a month to mold the mattress to my exact specifications. Dad had called a few days ago, asking if I wanted to stay at Montrose. I don't know how he knew, but he did. I guess being a Guardian spy came with some perks. But I told him no. I couldn't go home now. I couldn't admit defeat. Not yet.

Shanda hovered at the foot of my bed, pacing back and forth. I had no energy to ask why.

My heart was cracked and bruised, hanging on by a thread. It hurt so bad I almost felt numb inside. I don't know what hurt worse, the rejection or the duplicity. I thought Bryan was the exact opposite of Jake. How could I have been so wrong?

"When you're ready to move from grief to anger, let me know. 'Cause I'm *so* there already." Shanda plopped on the edge of my crater. "I can't believe those stupid Guardians."

"Tell me about it." I swiped at my eyes. Moisture I hadn't even noticed had collected in the corners.

"It's dangerous, spying on Nexis. Even I know that. And I've only been doing it for two months for the Guardians." Her low growl spoke louder than her words. "How can they put you on the front lines? They're supposed to protect you. It's all my fault."

"No way." I pushed myself up on my elbows, squinting at her. "This isn't your fault."

"I didn't do enough. I didn't get what they wanted. Now they're sending you to get it. If only I wasn't so scared." A tortured shadow crossed her face. She gripped the bedframe with all her might.

"Hey, stop beating yourself up." I patted the bed, coaxing her to sit beside me. I hated to see her look as tortured as I felt. "I don't even know what the Guardians are looking for besides what Nexis is going to do with the stones."

"Figures that they'd leave you out of the loop. Typical Guardians," she huffed, giving me her patented eyeroll. "They want the Nexis Seer's Book. They think Nexis is gearing up to perform an evil ceremony with the sacred stones. If they had a Nexis handbook, they could be prepared."

"What?" I screeched out a wretched noise. "I'm sure it's under lock and key. How in the world do they expect us to get it without blowing your cover?"

She mashed her lips together. "As if they even care about what happens to me."

"Or me." I locked eyes with her.

"Truth?" she asked, her face crumbling again. "I'm scared of what Nexis will do to me if they find out. I'm sorry you have to pay the price for it." She slumped over, burying her face in her hands.

I rubbed my hand on her back, just like she did for me in the quad. Enough was enough. This double agent insanity had to stop. First it was James, then Shanda. Now I'd somehow agreed to something I never wanted. Someone had to stand up to these guys—Nexis and Guardians both. Someone had to stop them from using people like puppets.

"You know what? I'm done letting these guys rule my life. I don't want to end up like Bryan." I could feel the fury rising in the back of my throat. I gulped it down. My throat burned like battery acid, corroding the empty pit of his betrayal. "He didn't have to break my heart just because the Guardians told him to. That was his choice."

"Sorry, girl. You deserve better than that." She laid a hand on my shoulder, lowering her voice. "We both do."

"You're right about that." I turned to my Shanda, who looked as enraged as I felt. "But you know what? I already have better. Right here."

"Ooo, you've moved to mad. Finally. What are you talking about?" She narrowed her eyes at me.

"Don't tell me you've already forgotten our pact." The corners of my mouth curled as a plan of my own began to emerge from the ashes.

"Course not." She tilted her head at me. "But if I'm gonna gather intel that's just for us, we need to figure out what we're looking for."

"I've got an idea, but you're not going to like it." I pursed my lips. "Is there any way we can stay one step ahead of Nexis? Like, find out what their plans are, for you and me, I mean."

"That's a lot sneakier than stealing one of their sacred treasures." Her eyes widened as if the gears were turning in her head, too. "That might actually work. To top it off, we could keep whatever intel we find, just in case we need blackmail."

"Exactly. Now you're thinking." I clapped my hands together, the idea taking root in my mind. Could it really work? I could be in control for once. The sheer thought was beyond delicious.

Her eyes lit up too, and she went back to pacing the room. "I'm sure these guys commit crimes all the time. The more dirt we can dig up on them the better. But you know how we'd get the juiciest details?"

"Will." I dug my teeth into my bottom lip. "Shanda, I thought you were on my side." I clamped my fists into balls of flesh and bone.

She halted, swiveled on her heel, and stared down her nose at me. "I *am* on your side. But you know I'm right."

"Why is everyone pushing this guy on me?" I dug my teeth into my bottom lip. "Maybe I can appeal to him as a friend. But I know I can't pretend to like him. That'd be too cruel."

"Ha!" She spat out. "For him or for you?"

"What're you talking about?" I stood to my feet, staring her down.

"Please, I know you've got at least a crush on him, even if you don't want to admit it." She slammed her hands into her hips and pointed her mocha finger at me. "Hey, I get it. He's got the whole bad-boy thing going on."

"I—uh, what?" I sputtered and froze like a statue. She nailed it right on the bull's eye.

Her face softened. "C'mon, you know he likes you, too."

"I guess." I shrugged. "As long as *you* know it's not going to happen. Okay?"

"You're right, my bad." She held up her hands in surrender. "I know it's too soon. But technically you only went out with Bryan for like a month, right?"

"Technically." I slumped back into my crater. "Though it felt like six months since we'd danced around it all last semester."

"I get it. Breakups are hard." Shanda eased down next to me, nudging my shoulder. "Don't let Bryan get in the way of you moving on. I don't want you to sit here and pine forever."

"Hey, I'm not pining. It's been like two days." Even the thought made my stomach reel.

"Try a week." She turned my way, rocking the bed. "I just want you to know I'm on your side. If you choose to turn double, you'll have a partner in crime. But in the end, the choice is still yours. Not anyone else's."

"Thank you, Shanda. That means a lot to me. You have no idea." If only Bryan could've said it the same way, maybe I wouldn't be in this mess. Stuck between a ditch and a bottomless pit of despair.

><

I've been numbed. Knocked up on Novocain. Life blurred and moved around me, but I'd curled in on myself again. Huddled up in my pile of blankets. A painful little cocoon that did nothing to dull the ache. The rejection was just enclosed now, surrounding me. Its arms cradling me like a best friend. Except I couldn't move. I was trapped within its cage. Powerless to escape.

"You can do this, Lucy. You're stronger than you look." Shanda's words floated from somewhere above me. Her smile reminded me why we'd become friends so fast. My real best friend. But even her warmth couldn't reach me now.

"C'mon, it's time to rejoin the living. It's just lunch. I left you off the hook for the dance, but enough's enough." She tugged on my arm, but I resisted. Her smile wavered, face tinged with that look. Pity.

I closed my eyes against the sight. Screaming inside.

And suddenly, a warmth enveloped me like a blanket around my shoulders. I opened my eyes, but Shanda was on the other side of the room now. Yet the warmth remained. A soft hug, light as a feather.

Go with her. The words played in my head. Of course it was Angel. Letting me know I wasn't alone. Where'd he been for the last month? Maybe Angel was sick of watching me mope, too. Heck, I was sick of myself by now.

"Okay, I'm coming." I bobbed my head slowly. I even let Shanda fix me up and drag me into the cafeteria.

Silverware clanged, scraping plates. Grating the inside of my eardrums. The noise was practically deafening at first. Clangs and clashes. Bits of conversation. Seconds passed as I rubbed my temples until the roar dulled.

On my own numb balloon, I floated above the crowd—the sad faces turning my way, the looks of pity hurled at me as if to say, "You should've seen this coming." By now, word had certainly gone out about last weekend's public break-up. Colleen and Monica had probably made sure of it.

Fumbling, I picked up a tray. Shuffled into line. Maybe I should've seen this coming, but I didn't. I never do.

I should've learned by now, but I guess I hadn't. That's not my way. I hold back until I think it's safe, then I throw myself in heart-first. Complete immersion. Except this time I threw myself in front of a freight train. And now I'm lying on the cold, jagged gravel. Bloodied, beaten. Half-dead, but still alive. Somehow.

That's when I saw his face. Those blue eyes cloudy and downcast, watching from a corner across the room. The bustle froze for an instant. My lungs clawed for air, but I couldn't breathe.

He looked almost as bruised and beat-up as I felt. He didn't walk away unscathed, not like Jake had. No, this time my ex-boyfriend was on the other side of the tracks, lying right there in the gravel with me.

Air came rushing back. I inhaled, breathing freely. I don't know why that heartbreaking look on his face gave me an ounce of hope, why it eased my pain a smidge. But it did.

Until he packed up his stuff and nodded at me, conceding the cafeteria.

I couldn't help it. I dipped my head, watched him walk out the door. The room suddenly felt colder.

Shanda snapped her fingers in my face. "If you don't put something on your plate, I'm gonna make you drink one of my protein shakes."

"Alright already." I rolled my eyes at her, plunking my tray down at the sandwich station. I went through the motions. Made my usual turkey on rye. Followed Shanda across the room. Not feeling any of it. Until I sat down at her table, feeling like a fish out of water. All the officers of Nexis were staring at me like I'd grown gills.

"Hey, gorgeous." Will chomped down on his burger like this was an everyday occurrence. Somehow, he managed to sear me with those platinum eyes while wiping mustard from the corner of his mouth.

"Hey," I mumbled. How would I ever get used to sitting with him and the Nexis crew if he always stared at me like that? I guess being stuck at a table with all the Nexis goons staring at me would help.

"Good choice. Now eat." Shanda pointed at my sandwich, glaring daggers at me.

I gave her a half-hearted nod and shoved down a bite. It tasted like cardboard for all I knew. I fiddled with my phone, trying to discourage anyone from making small talk.

"Still moping over what's his name?" Colleen's voice screeched like nails on a chalkboard.

I rolled my eyes. If only I'd listened to my brother. James always told me I needed to practice my poker face because I was an epic failure at hiding anything I felt. My poor little heart. Always tattooed on my sleeve.

"Excuse me?" Shanda reared back and turned all her fury at the little Nexis minion.

Will leaned across me, resting his elbows on the table to glare at Colleen. "Seeing as you were in the same boat only a year ago, I'd think you'd have more compassion."

"You're not just gonna let her walk right into Nexis though? Are you?" Monica blurted out.

Kevin elbowed her in the side. "Shut up."

Will straightened up and glanced around the table, eyes landing on me. "Well, I'm sure we can work out the same deal we worked out with Colleen. What was it, hon? Was it just a few Guardian secrets, or everything you'd ever dug up on them? If I remember, you had a file a mile thick. Like you were just waiting for them to throw you to the curb."

Colleen's jaw dropped to her collarbone. Monica choked on her water.

"I'm sure little Lucy here won't have to stoop that far." Will reached for me, patting my shoulder. "She is a legacy, after all."

My heart stuttered. In a hot second, warmth rushed to my cheeks.

"Hrmph." Monica was the first to stand up. She reached for her bestie. "C'mon, Colleen. Let's just go."

Colleen rose to her feet, lava spewing from her eyes as she followed her friend out the door.

"Nice one, man." Kevin shook his head, slinging his backpack over his shoulder. "Now my girl will be fuming, and I'll get caught in the crossfire. Thanks."

"Sorry, man. But you know Colleen." Will's chin dipped, making him look slightly sheepish.

"I know." Kevin nodded my way. "Good to see you, Lucy. Hope you feel better soon."

"Thanks?" It was more of a question than a statement. After he walked out of the caf, I turned to Shanda. "What was that about?"

"Beats me." Shanda shrugged, glancing at her phone. "I've never understood that dude. He's way better off with Monica."

"Oh, gotcha. I didn't realize that was official." I let the realization sink in. "They definitely make more sense together."

"You're going to have to keep better tabs on the Nexis dating scene if you're going to join us." Will turned that beautiful chin cleft on me.

Fireflies sputtered from the depths of my stomach. "Who says I'm joining Nexis?"

"Those girls apparently." He picked up my backpack and handed it to me.

I tried to smile at him, but my lips just twitched. All the fireflies had fizzled back into the Great Numbness. Shanda started packing up her things too, and I followed her and Will out to the quad.

My head pounded, about ready to explode with all the possible ways I'd run into Bryan. Did I have to go to class? I shuddered at the thought.

"You okay, gorgeous?" Will's steps slowed.

I shook my head. "I don't think so."

When I turned to him, his face looked different in the light of day. At first, I couldn't place the anomaly. Then it dawned on me. A strange, almost-haloed light hovered around him, even on this gray afternoon. The light was mostly white, tinged with random streaks or flecks of silver. In fact, I hadn't seen any shadows surrounding him for a long time. Just this strange gray light, that was now suddenly white. When had everything changed? Not to mention why?

"You're in no shape to go to class by yourself. C'mon. Let me walk you there." He grabbed my hand and tugged me down the cobblestone path.

"Okay, but why do we have to go so fast?" I struggled to keep up with him as he picked up the pace. I glanced back at Shanda, who stood twenty yards behind us giving me the *I Told You So* look.

"Because," Will huffed as we booked it up the stairs. "Maybe if I go fast enough you won't let go of my hand."

"Ha!" The corners of my mouth tipped skyward as I let out the first real laugh in a week. Laughter felt good. So did his hand. But it shouldn't feel good.

I tried to wriggle my fingers free, but he only clung tighter.

"Here you are, milady." He even bowed slightly as he dropped me off at the door of my English class. "It's good to see you smile."

"Thanks." My cheeks flamed for the second time today. Oh, this boy was good.

Those Guardians had no clue what they were asking of me. If I wasn't careful, I'd fall into Will's trap—not the other way around.

CHAPTER 14

The afternoon skies were brightening their gray hues, a sure sign March was almost here. But as I sat in Mr. Harlixton's class one month after the dreaded breakup, I still felt bleak inside. Heavy. Beyond bearable.

Brrriiinggg. The bell blared, jolting me back to the reality before me.

While I'd been off in la-la land, thinking about two boys at once, Harlixton had scurried out of class with the rest of his students. He wouldn't get away this time. I couldn't control much right now, but I could control who my allies were. Or at least get some answers.

I bounded up the lecture room stairs and into the hallway, skidding around the maze of marble till I found his tiny little office.

Rap, rap, rap. I knocked three times.

"Come in."

I creaked open the door, unveiling the usual clusterbomb of his office. Incessant questions swirled around me as I moved a pile of papers to clear off a seat.

He didn't say a word. Just sat there behind his desk, sipping his coffee. Staring at me with those beady little eyes and an expression that said, "You first."

If only I could dive into the dregs of his coffee mug, hide in the depths like a gnat caught in the blackness. But I was no mere gnat. If I wanted to be the Seer, I needed to figure out how to protect my gift—even in the ranks of the enemy. And I needed all the help I could get.

So I swallowed back the fear. "I'm here because I need your help. I need to figure out where to go from here."

"I see." He exhaled a sigh big enough to flutter all the loose papers within two feet. "And what exactly do you think I can help you with?"

"I don't know. You and the Guardians want me to go into an impossible situation. And I don't know what to do." I crossed my arms around my middle, curling in on myself. I had to figure this out.

"That's very true." He tottered back in his chair, gears squeaking. "I can't tell you how to live your life. That's up to you. I can only tell you what I'd do in your situation. Nexis is stealing sacred stones for some reason. You need to protect your gift."

"That's exactly what I want." I nodded, anger burning me up. As if the theft of sacred stones had anything to do with me. "I want to learn to protect my gift. Hide it if possible. So Nexis never finds out."

Whoosh, he sat forward with a start, leaning his elbows on the desk. "Don't fool yourself. Nexis already knows who you are. At least they think they do. Your only advantage right now is that they're uncertain."

"What do you mean?" I asked, chewing on my lip.

Staring down his glasses, he looked at me like I should already know this. "They don't know your gifts have come early. Keep it that way. They're waiting until you turn eighteen to see if you really are the Seer. They've got a little over a year before the clock runs out. It's the only thing you can use against them."

Tick, tock. Tick, tock. I could almost hear it in my head. "How can I do that?"

The edges of his mouth twisted. "You make them come to you. They're the ones who need to win you over. So make them work for it."

"Mr. Harlixton. I've never heard you talk like that before." A small smile crept up my face.

"Nexis really gets under my skin." He wriggled around as if to prove it.

"Me too." I eased back in my chair, my brain toying with Harlixton's little idea. Maybe I could make them come to me, even give me and Shanda all the intel we'd need to bury them.

"I know. That's why they think they have the advantage." He paused. Lowered his voices, eyes darting to the door. "They think they can control you with their scare tactics. But you have to show them you're in control. If they want you, they need to convince you."

Now my lips were curling up. "I like the thought of that. Maybe I could turn their bullying around. Somehow. But I'm not much of a bully."

"No, but you're smart. And stubborn. You don't have to be aggressive or demanding. Just stand firm, and make them come to you."

I narrowed my eyes at him, trying to crack the code. Did he mean everything he said to have a double meaning? Because I could use his pearls of wisdom on both Nexis and the Guardians. Food for thought.

"Do you really think I can do it?" My voice sounded smaller than I wanted.

"I do." His face broke into a genuine smile.

"Thank you." I breathed a sigh of relief, letting his belief in me sink into my heart. "It's nice to know I have someone like you on my side."

"About that." He cleared his throat, eyes darting around the room again. "This will have to be our last meeting for awhile. If you're going to infiltrate the inner circle of Nexis, you can't be seen hanging out with me."

"What?" My jaw dropped as every muscle in my body went taut. "Don't tell me you're going to pull the same crap Bryan did."

He cocked his head and shrugged. "It's for your own safety."

"Don't give me that!" I scraped back my chair and rose to my feet, anger boiling higher and higher every second. "You're saying I have to 'infiltrate the inner circle of Nexis' all by myself. Without any backup?"

"No, Lucy. That's not what I'm saying." Harlixton stood up too, his voice laced with soothing tones. "We just can't be seen helping you, publicly. If you get into a real jam, you can always call on us for backup. But only as a last resort."

"I can't believe this." Curling tendrils of darkness crept along the corners of my vision. I closed my eyes, the vague blackness more comforting than seeing shadows.

A ribbon of ice enveloped my wrist.

I opened my eyes to a shadowy tendril circling my arm, holding it in place. The breath hitched in my throat.

"Lucy, what is it? Are you seeing something?" His words floated above me, but they didn't touch me.

I couldn't feel anything but cold. Ice. Frozen. My entire field of vision shrouded in growing shadows.

"Look around you. Where is it coming from?"

I glanced right, then tried to look left, but my neck wouldn't budge. "I don't know. I can't move my head to see it. Like I'm paralyzed by the fear."

"That's it. It's the fear." He stumbled around the desk, resting a hand on my right arm. "We have to work past the fear. We have to find a way to control it."

"How?" As soon as he called it *fear*, all the light collapsed around me—inking every source of light with a growing blackness. "It's getting worse. What do I do?"

"I'm not really sure. But we'll figure it out." The helplessly high pitch in his voice said it all.

Here I thought Professor Harlixton held the key to unlock every secret, but he was just waiting until I was ready. But now I understood. He didn't know how to do this anymore than I did. He was figuring it all out right alongside me.

Everything clenched inside of me until I couldn't take it anymore. Electricity coursed in my veins.

A burst of angel fire sparked the shadow over his face. Wraiths of demons exploding into shrieking embers. They fizzled and died off. The light returned, a welcome relief that lapped at my toes. I smiled. Breathed the sweet, stale air again. Freedom at last.

"Better?" His eyes studied me, this strange anomaly standing before him.

"For now." My shoulders deflated as my muscles relaxed. I wanted to fall into a heap on the floor, but I braced myself on the empty chair and stood tall. "What happens when I leave here and face Nexis on my own? I can't control my visions or the reckonings. You see that, don't you?"

He paced to his bookshelf, touched a few spines, and pulled them out. "These are all the books I could find on the reckonings and how to harness your angel fire. I'm sorry I don't have more to offer you."

He thrust the hardback volumes at me. But I didn't reach for them. I just stood there, staring at him.

"Is this all you've got for me?" My question came out as annoyed as I felt inside.

"I'm afraid so. For now." He dumped the books in my arms and returned to his chair. "Only you can figure out what to do next."

I narrowed my eyes at him, sparks snapping from my fingers as they curled around the books. "Then I guess this is goodbye. Some Guardians you guys turned out to be." I shot from my perch and made my way to the door. "If you're not going to help me, I guess I'll just figure this out on my own. And you might not be happy with the results."

Pausing in the doorway, I gave him one last glare over my shoulder. But he just sat there, the corners of his mouth curling like a cat. Like my reaction was all part of the Guardian plan. Let him sit there and be smug. It didn't mean I had to play into his hands. Or Nexis'. Or anybody's.

The fire welled up inside me, stinging my eyes, my throat. I swept down the hall, boots pounding on the marble, until I reached the crowds of kids clustered up in the lobby.

I skidded to an abrupt stop, picking my way through the crowd. I *so* didn't need this right now. Gritting my teeth, I danced around the Nexis clique with Monica and Colleen sneering at me. As soon as Will glanced up, his gaze locked on mine. I wanted to melt into the floor. I had to get out of here. Fast.

I skirted past my old friends, the Guardian crew. Laura, Brooke, Tony, and Lenny all stared at me like they wanted to say something. But no one uttered a word. Bryan just gave me that pained look again like I'd been the one to break his heart. Even though we both knew it was the opposite.

I whipped around, making a beeline for the front door of Salinger, when someone stepped into my path.

Felicia stood smack dab in front of me, her auburn hair swishing as she lasered green-eyed death rays at me. Time for another Montrose Paranormal Academy reckoning. Sure, I may have told Bryan she might be a double agent Watcher spy. But, after her father attacked me with a branding iron in a church, who could blame me for spilling the beans? Apparently she did.

"I hope you're happy. You threw me under the bus only to get thrown under yourself. How's it feel, getting what you deserve?" Her new friends circled up behind her, probably the Watcher clique for all I knew.

"You did *not* just say that to me." My screech shattered the noise into silence. "I don't know what you're talking about."

She choked on her gum. "Are you serious right now? I know you're the one who ratted me out to Bryan."

My space-cadet brain tried to recall all the details. "All I did was tell him about the little Watcher symbols you signed your paintings with. And wore around your neck. You outed yourself. You need a lesson in being a little more discreet."

The chatter died down, and a hush fell over the crowded school hallway. Everyone stilled, stopped what they were doing—watching our every move.

"You got me kicked out of the Guardians. I wish my father had finished the job and marked you for the whole world to see." Felicia laughed a bitter, strangled whimper, her shoulders shaking.

"Sheesh. Way to be over-dramatic." Hot bubbles simmered in my stomach, steaming to the surface. Her father tried to brand the Seer's symbol into my arm, and she's mad at me for getting her kicked out? "You did this to yourself. Take some responsibility for your own actions."

"You little brat." Felicia snorted, her face flushing. "You ruined all of my plans, years of work. Empty promises, false secrets. It was all for nothing."

"Excuse me?" I took three steps toward her and held up my burn-scarred wrist in her face. "Who tried to brand me like cattle? Oh yeah, you and your father! So stop blaming me for *your* choices."

I stood there, shaking with rage. Still holding up my wrist so she wouldn't forget what happened last semester in that church in Harlem.

"Puh-lease," she scoffed, scooting backward. Closer to her friend for safety. Good call. "You're the one who burned down a church library. With my father in it."

Goosebumps pricked up my arms as it all came back to me in a flash. I remembered that horrible night at St. Lucy's church in Harlem. Felicia's father tried to brand me with some sort of Seer symbol. I accidentally torched the place with my angel fire just so we could get away. What an awful encounter with the Watchers, who were apparently as bad as Nexis.

Rage smoldered inside me. I arched my back, leaning in. "I didn't make you forget that you were a Watcher and join the Guardians as a spy." My blood really boiled through my veins now.

"It's times like these, I'm glad I gave you up." Her eyes gleamed as shadows slithered from the floor, circling her ankles, and crawled their way up her legs. "I saw you on the quad that night, running into the library. Someone had to point your ex in the right direction."

The weight of her words smashed down on me like a ton of brinks. "You told Jake where I was? That's low." I whispered, my stomach seizing up. Gonna hurl.

Slowly, a smile spread across her evil lips. "I told Nexis, and it looks like they did the rest. Fat lot of good it did me."

White-hot rage seared through me. Narrowed my gaze to tunnel vision. *Crash.* I slammed my bag to the floor. *Smack.* My hand shot up. Hit her in the face.

Her eyes watered, her cheek reddened.

"How could anyone be so despicable, so—" I spat out. A thousand needles buzzed through my palm as a familiar fiery tingle zinged down my arms.

Gasps went up all over the foyer as people got out their phones to snap pictures and start texting. Someone probably got the whole thing on video. At that moment, I didn't care one iota. Let the whole world see the face of evil. I just had to keep my angel fire in check. For now.

A strong arm encircled my waist. "Lucy, calm down. We need to get you out of here." Will whispered in my ear.

"Don't tell me to calm down." I grunted through gritted teeth. I was seeing red now.

Suddenly, his arm tightened around my middle, and my feet were flailing mid-air as he hoisted me over his shoulder like I weighed nothing more than a sack of potatoes.

Before I knew it, I was staring at his backside as he pushed open the front door. My eyes stung in the cold air, but butterflies whizzed around in my stomach.

He crunched across fifty yards of frozen quad then up the concrete stairs, right into the observatory tower. My face jostled against his firm back the whole time, and I tried not to stare too far south. All the pent up Felicia-rage simmered down.

Finally, he creaked open the door to the Nexis tower, but he didn't set me down there.

"Okay, okay." I flailed my feet in the air in the vicinity of his head, hopefully. "You can put me down now."

A laugh rumbled in his chest. "Not just yet, tiger."

He walked up to the back wall, shrouded in pitch darkness. An electronic beeping sound reached my ears, and before I knew it, a door that blended into the black wall opened up. Trudging through the opening, Will plopped me down on an antique leather sofa.

"Where are we?" I gasped for breath, afraid to touch my cheeks to see how hot they were.

He switched on a desk lamp that barely lit up the dim room and pulled up a chair across from me. "It's the Nexis lounge. I figured you'd be safe here. Less likely to get suspended from school, too."

I looked at my hand. Still red. "I can't believe I slapped her. Did that really just happen?"

"I can." His eyes lit up with something, maybe a hint of respect. "She deserved it, after what she just admitted. To the whole school."

"You just wanted to throw me over your shoulder and call me tiger." A little lizard of a shiver ran up my spine at the thought of it.

"I wanted to keep you from getting expelled. I figure if no one in charge saw, and you weren't at the scene, they can't prove anything. Worth a shot at least, tiger." His lips curved at his new nickname for me. "Of course, carrying you around made the plan a little more appealing."

I cocked my head at him. "You could've set me down on the quad."

"You didn't fight me." His lips twitched, making my insides quiver.

"No, I guess I didn't." I couldn't tear my eyes from his face. He was right, and I knew it. Butterflies pinged around inside of me.

"It's okay, Lucy. You can admit it." His eyes circled me, drawing out the silence so I could hear my ragged breaths against his steady breathing. "You just wanted to stare at my butt."

"You wish." I threw my head back and laughed. How did he keep doing that?

He cracked up, too. When our laughter spent itself, an awkward energy bloomed in the silence between us. We both stared at each other.

"But that's not the only reason I brought you here." His words were slow and deliberate.

"It's not?" My breath snared in my throat again.

In the dim lighting, only parts of his face were illuminated. I watched him struggle through his thoughts, eyes darting around the room.

Finally, those gray eyes landed on my face. "I'm sorry I didn't tell you about Felicia when I saw you on New Year's. I just thought it would make things worse." He gulped, Adam's apple bobbing.

"You knew what she did?" Prickles pounded my eye sockets, but I fought to keep the dam from bursting.

He sighed, running one hand through his sandy hair. "Maybe I should've told you. Now that Felicia's made a mess of it, I wish I had."

"I can't say it would've been something I ever wanted to hear. That someone could be that cruel." I inhaled, shudders racking my shoulders.

Will abandoned his chair and landed on the couch beside me. "I'm sorry, Lucy. That's why I wouldn't let her into Nexis. I know I made the right call there."

"You're kidding?" I practically choked on the words. "You did that for me?"

Something different lurked in his eyes. Not sympathy. Something more. Something I couldn't put my finger on.

"I didn't let her join Nexis, because it was the right thing to do. This group doesn't need any more monsters." His eyes widened like he'd just realized he'd said too much.

My heart thumped wildly in my chest, and my next words tumbled out before I could check them. "I think I may have been wrong about you. I've been wrong about a lot of things."

Shadow and light played across the planes of his face. In a heartbeat, he wrapped me up in his arms, squeezing me into his chest. I burrowed my forehead between his leather jacket and his black sweater. The dam finally burst, and my tears dampened the cashmere, but he didn't say a word. Not for a long time.

He inhaled a ragged breath. "Don't worry, Lucy. I've got you now, and I'm not letting go. Not this time."

A fresh batch of tears wormed their way to the surface. Because he was right. My mind screamed, *"No!"* but my heart wouldn't listen. It felt like I was beating myself against an internal brick wall. This time, my tears had nothing to do with Bryan's choice—the Guardians over me. I was crying for a different reason. My heart was letting go of Bryan. To make room for something new. It had to.

If I didn't check myself soon, I could see my heart losing itself all over again. To the guy holding me in his arms. The question was—could I really fall for Will so soon after Bryan?

CHAPTER 15

I couldn't think. I couldn't focus. The tug of war between Will and Bryan had started all over again. I stumbled out of the Nexis tower with tear-stained cheeks, not knowing which way to go.

Should I go back to class and the onslaught of questions I'd face in the aftermath of my fight with Felicia? No way. Instead, I turned toward my dorm and raced to my room.

Finally, I collapsed in a heap on my bed. And then the tears came. Clogging my nose, spilling down my cheeks.

My bruised heart was reeling, my head full of more questions than answers. The questions clawed my lungs until I could barely breathe. I couldn't do this on my own, no matter how much I wanted to be my own kind of Seer. I needed a little help right now. Rolling over on my back, I glanced up at the ceiling.

"Okay, where are you, angel?" I stared at the glow-in-the-dark stars overhead. "I could use a little help down here."

Saltwater dribbled down my chin, so I reached in my nightstand for a tissue. My fingers brushed the Bible I'd forgotten about, and my hand sparked.

"That's weird." Pulling out the graduation gift from Grandma, I slammed it on the bed. It fell open, its gilt-edged pages rustling open to a chapter I'd never seen before. Zechariah. That name sounded familiar.

I thumbed through the pages, reading the subheads. It was all about an angel who appeared to the prophet Zechariah.

I yanked the book into my lap so I could read it better.

"Whoa girl, watch it." Shanda stood in the doorway, staring at me like I'd just kicked her puppy. "Be kind to the good book."

"Since when do you care about the Bible?" I blinked, rubbing my eyes. I hadn't even noticed her standing there.

"Since now. Look, I'm just worried about you. I heard about your fight with Felicia. They sent me to check on you." Whether she knew it or not, her eyebrows arched on the word "they."

"Who sent you?" I cocked my head at her, waiting for her to say his name.

"Just people." She walked over to my bed, stiletto boots clicking, and dumped her stuff on the floor. "Whatcha reading?"

"My Bible just flipped open to Zechariah." Every nerve ending in my body tingled as I patted the bed for her to sit down.

"Didn't you say Zechariah was mentioned in the Guardian Book of the Seer? The one those witches stole?" She leaned in closer to examine the page.

"Nice one." I let out a very unladylike snort. "But you're right. The Guardian book mentioned Zechariah a lot. Something about a lampstand and some olive trees. It didn't make any sense to me."

"Let's see." She rifled through the pages again.

While she scoured Zechariah, I pulled out the books Harlixton gave me and skimmed the table of contents. In the first book, there was a whole section on the prophecies of Zechariah. Then a chapter entitled Zechariah and the Sacred Stone Ceremonies.

Shanda pounded her index finger on chapter four. "Here it is. *The Golden Lampstand and the Two Olive Trees.*"

"Huh, that's weird." I glanced over at her. "This book mentions Zechariah, and the Guardian book said something about placing a stone on the lampstand to protect the olive trees so their gifts could be used to bring light instead of darkness. That can't be a coincidence."

"You weren't kidding. That's more than weird." She squinted down at the page, reading the small print for herself.

The amethyst against my chest grew warm and I unzipped up my coat, pulling the necklace from its usual hiding place. "Do you think this could be the stone?"

Shanda's eyes zeroed in on the amethyst in my hands. "I guess so. I mean, it is glowing, after all."

Staring down at the jewel in my hands, I blinked. Sure enough, my roommate was right. The amethyst glowed brighter and brighter every second.

"Whoa, that's creepy." Still, I couldn't tear my eyes from the amethyst.

To my right, Shanda had taken my Bible and was reading it to herself. "Look, here it says, Zechariah had a vision, then asked the angel what it meant. Is that how it works?"

"What do you mean?" My forehead scrunched as my eyes flew from her face to the book. "Let me see."

There it was, in black and white. Zechariah saw a vision, just like me. Except he asked the angel to interpret it for him. Then the angel asked God, relaying the interpretation back to Zechariah. This happened again and again. My mouth lolled open. And it dawned on me.

"That's it!" I screamed, wrapping my friend in a bear hug. "You're a genius!"

"Well, duh." Shanda tried to wriggle herself free. "But why exactly?"

"Okay," I released her shoulders, keeping my voice low. "Maybe I can't control my visions. But maybe I can do what Zechariah did, ask my angel to interpret those visions. What if that's my job as the Seer?"

Her eyes widened. "Is that really all there is to it?"

"I'll never know till I find out." Nervous energy welled up inside me. It felt like my whole body was shaking from the inside out—with excitement for a change. I zipped up my hoodie and stuffed my Bible into the front pouch. Nothing could stop me now. "There's no time. I have to get to the field. Do a little training of my own. You coming with?"

"Don't even think about it." She hissed, grabbed my arm. "What're you thinking? It's broad daylight. At least wait until tonight. After curfew."

"Seriously?" I slumped back down on the bed with a huff. "Maybe you're right."

"Of course I'm right." She shot me a satisfied smile. "We'll take some time to plan it out, stay off the Nexis radar."

"Yeah, it's probably best to lay low after what happened with Felicia." My heart sank, but the urge still wriggled around inside me. I had to do something to snap me out of this funk. Figuring out how to interpret my visions seemed like a good place to start. I needed to find my own purpose, not one some secret society gave me. Until I discovered my path, I felt helpless. Useless. Like maybe I shouldn't have been given this gift. Maybe it should've gone to James. But it hadn't.

No matter how much better my brother would be as the Seer, this gift had landed on my shoulders. Now I just needed to learn how to harness my visions—or at least figure out what they meant.

><

My bedsprings creaked as I reclined against my fluffy back pillow. The pages of my bio book fluttered by aimlessly. It was no use. I couldn't focus on anything but the passages I'd read in Zechariah. The field was calling me, begging me to test out my new theories.

"Enough." I heaved the book to the floor. It made a satisfying crash. Shanda didn't even glance up from her laptop.

I couldn't stand it anymore. Time to make my next great escape.

"You ready for this?" Shanda eyed me over her laptop.

I nodded, lips curling. "It's time to test out my theory. Are you still coming?"

"I've been thinking about that." She closed her laptop and tiptoed across the room. "We definitely shouldn't sneak out together. It'll draw too much attention. Why don't you go first? I follow in five to ten minutes to make sure no one follows you."

I eyed her warily. "Why do I get the feeling you've done this before?"

Her lips curled up. "I'll say it like this, those Guardian girls are amateurs. No more banging around every time you sneak out."

My jaw fell open. "You heard me, didn't you?"

"Of course I did. I'll stay in the shadows and cover your back. We got this." She nodded to the coat rack. "Don't forget your parka."

"Thanks, Mom." I zipped up my black parka and tiptoed out the door. Slinking down the dark hall, I made my usual path down the stairs and out the kitchen window. Once my feet reached the ground, I couldn't move fast enough.

Blood zinged through my veins, fueling me as I hit the cold night air. I needed to get to the field. Someplace away from everything and everyone. Someplace I could think.

At last, I came to the clearing in the trees, that open patch of brown grass. A crescent moon slid out from behind the clouds, greeting me with enough light to help me remember. I knew Shanda wouldn't be too far behind. My muscles relaxed.

Unzipping my parka, I unsheathed my Bible and laid it down in the straw. Kneeling over it, I closed my eyes.

Lord, please send your angel to light up the sky. So I can understand the visions you've given me.

The hairs on my arms fluttered. Rose straight up.

A bolt of lightning sizzled the sky. Slammed into the ground next to me. White-hot. Scorching the grass less than five feet away.

"You called." His voice boomed—a melody in each note.

My chin quivered. The rest of me, too. Every muscle in my body went slack as a sense of awe and wonder flooded my senses. I'd never get used to seeing Angel.

He hovered before me, in all his whiteness. A glorious, dazzling white prismed around him with opalescent bits of rainbowed reflections.

"Thank you for coming." The earth quaked, or was that just my knees? I bowed before him. "Please, I want you to train me like you promised. I want to know what my visions mean. I have to know. Please, just tell me."

"Don't do that." A gentle boom blasted a gust of icy wind in my face. "That's not how it works. Don't pray to me, I am just a messenger. Stand to your feet. I will ask if the Father wishes to reveal something to you."

"I, uh, I'm sorry …" With robotic precision, I rose to my feet. But the feeling of wonder remained. I couldn't stop staring at him. The whiteness, glittering in front of me like a star descended from the heavens to glow its sheer brilliance in a frozen field.

Golden eyes focused on me again. "He will tell you one thing about one vision. But you'll have to find the Interpreter to figure out the rest."

"The Interpreter?" I croaked, my mind drawing a blank. Goosebumps shivered down the back of my neck. "That's one of the Chosen Ones like me. Right? How am I supposed to find the Interpreter?"

"They will find you. Now you must choose." Angel's white light shimmered like he was laughing at my silly questions.

"Fine," I huffed. At least I'd get something out of the deal. What did I want to know most? My head felt light and fuzzy as an onslaught of images flickered through my mind like a slide show.

James getting banished, shadows slithering in the darkness, all those St. Lucia visions. And I knew.

I sucked in a halting breath. "That vision of St. Lucia last year in my dorm room. She reached out to me, trying to tell me something. What did she want me to know?"

Static crackled in the air around me. Was he angry? Could angels get angry? My throat went dry and my hands trembled.

Wind rushed at me like a sonic boom. "He knew what you would ask. Saint Lucia wanted you to know two things. She was not the first Seer, but she was the first Seer they discovered."

"What?" My jaw dangled to my chin as shivers racked my body.

An arm emerged from the folds of white. A wispy hand, flat and vertical.

"She also wanted you to know this. If you use your gift the right way, you could be the last Seer this world ever needs." A great blue orb whirled in his brilliant hand.

I watched it twirl and twirl. And twirl. Until it stopped.

The diamonds shifted, and his hand disappeared again, the blue orb with it. A heaviness filled my chest as air seeped from my lungs. A slow leak.

I could only whisper. "No way. How could I possibly do that?"

"You will know when the time is right." His words dimmed to a low roar.

A breeze caressed my face. Comforting almost.

Those golden eyes burst into two licks of flame. "Be on your guard. Darkness comes after long periods in the light."

In a rocket-thrust of wind, he blasted off. Shooting back to his place in the heavens.

I watched his light-trail twinkle past the sliver of moon. A funny tingle wiggled up my spine, my lips curving, toes curling.

As soon as Angel was out of sight, darkness descended all around me. Like a plague. A putrid stench filled the air. An oppressive, rotting, thick cloud. All of the energy drained from my body

Opening my palms, I dredged up every ounce of strength I had left. Bursts and snaps of electricity sizzled to my hands, then crackled out like I'd been doused with a bucket of water. It was no use. My angel fire wouldn't work against a reckoning.

Shrieks split my eardrums right down the middle.

I slammed my hands over my ears. Plummeted to my knees.

Pain seared into my brain. Tears dripped uncontrollably down my cheeks until I forced my lids shut. A pinprick of red light emerged in the blackness, morphing into an expanding orb that burned brighter and brighter as dark clouds hurtled and screeched around it.

The shrieks ebbed from ghastly to ghoulish to wraith-like. The insane pitch of evil grew louder as the clouds of darkness swirled around the red light. The sphere materialized into an oblong shape, almost like an uncut gemstone. Angry words erupted from the glowing red circle, spewing venom at me like lava. Almost like this strange stone was calling to me. *Join us, and take your revenge on the Guardians. You have all this power right at your fingertips.*

Just then, familiar arms wrapped around my middle. The screams quavered for a second, and the red orb stopped growing.

I opened my eyes long enough to see the darkness tremble. Gray streaks fizzled in and out of the blackness around the red sphere. It wasn't my angel or even Bryan who held me. It was Will. The air was spiced with his cinnamon scent.

Even with the hounds of hell screeching around me I knew one thing for sure. They weren't in me, inside my head. They were on the outside of me, trying to torment me. But they couldn't really get at me, they could only try. I rocked back and forth on my heels. Will rocked with me.

At least I wasn't alone.

Will squeezed me tighter. The hellish pitches simmered until they faded away. I drew in a breath of fresh air.

Rough fingers dabbed at my cheeks, wiping away the remnants of tears.

When I opened my eyes, his face hovered close enough to examine the swirls of gray in his eyes. Streaks of gold warmed up parts of his irises as if he were lighting up from the inside out.

Something bloomed inside me, a scary-tingly feeling. If only I could curl up in his arms again. But I stopped myself for one reason. Bryan.

"What are you doing here?" My words came out raspy.

"I followed you." His eyes held mine, never flinching. Obviously, he had no shame about the truth. "Are you okay, Lucy? What just happened?"

"Believe me, you don't want to know." I uncurled from my vertical fetal position, rising slowly.

"I do want to know." He stood up in a blink, hovering over me. "I have to know. Please just tell me."

"It's a long story. Complicated, too." My knees wobbled, and I reached for him. Maybe I could catch him off-guard enough to shut him up. Or maybe I just couldn't stop myself anymore.

Pulling him close, I wrapped my arms around his abs and buried my head in his shoulder. It felt even better than I thought to rest there.

His head dipped toward mine, lips pressing against my forehead. "Don't think that's the end of this."

He circled his arms around me, too, fingers crawling up and down my back. Even through my thick parka, each tap hit a nerve deep inside me that I didn't even know existed. If his arms weren't around me, surely I'd float up into the sky like my angel.

"I hope not." I whispered the words into his coat, praying he'd never hear them.

CHAPTER 16

The night darkened around us as all remnants of angel light disappeared into the stars. The moon was our only guide as we crunched through the brown grass toward the bridge that led back to the dorms.

"Why won't you just tell me what happened?" Will reached for my hand, but I edged away, eyes on the field. Unable to pry the horror from my brain. Or the memory of Will's arms around me, shielding me as best he could.

Black combat boots planted in front of me, blocking my path. His palms came down on my shoulders.

I blinked and stood taller, trying to shrug his hands off my shoulders. He didn't budge. I tightened my abs and clenched my jaw, my feet moving into fight position.

"I saw everything, you know." He sounded eerily calm, even as those gray eyes hardened. Drawing circles around my face.

"Please." I coughed a bitter laugh through my teeth. "You didn't see anything, or you wouldn't be asking me about it. You would just know."

"I think I know exactly what happened. And I'm scared for you." His hands slid to my biceps.

"You're scared for me? That's a joke, right?" Bubbles gurgled in my stomach with an energy I couldn't name.

"No joke." Those silvery eyes softened, warming at the edges. "I'm just looking out for you. Making sure you're safe. Why don't you believe me?"

"You know why." I met his gaze full-on, my arms sagging into Jell-O. "You're the Nexis President. That's why."

"And the Guardians told you I'm pure evil, right? If I'm so evil, why are they pushing you to spy on me? It's sick." His quiet words smacked me in the face.

"You're right. It is sick." The bubbles curdled inside. I balled up my fists just remembering how easily they kicked me to the curb. And I couldn't deny the truth any longer. "How did you know?"

"It's not the first time they've done something like that." His warm breath puffed on my cheeks.

Colleen. He didn't have to say it. I just knew.

Wriggling out of his grip, I crunched up the path to the bridge over the creek. I wrapped my gloved hands around the railing. Gripping tight. The wan light of the crescent moon highlighted a trickle of water. It looked so peaceful meandering along its merry little way. That's all I ever wanted from this life. A little bit of peace.

He walked up behind me and stood at my side.

I kept my eyes on the water. "I don't know what to do."

"I think you do."

Those four words dangled in the air. I could almost reach out and grab them. But not quite.

"What do you mean?" I stared at his profile, studying his reaction.

"You aren't the only one whose life has been turned upside down this past year." His face fell, that chiseled façade crumbling. "New Year's Eve I told you my parents were separated, but I never said why."

I waited, holding my breath. Not moving a muscle.

He gulped, Adam's apple bobbing. "My mom suddenly went all gung-ho about finding the Seer and gearing up for the Nexis Nations takeover. You see, my grandpa's got a heart condition, and I think he wants to leave some kind of Nexis legacy behind."

"Oh, Will. I'm so sorry." My hand landed on his arm.

"But she went overboard. Crazy overboard. And my dad couldn't take it." He ran a hand through his hair, eyes clouding. "They fought and fought, and then he just got fed up. Asked for a transfer to Chicago."

"That's awful." I could totally relate to that.

"The thing is, I wanted to go with him." He turned this haunted look on me, face shadowed by the dim moonlight.

"Why didn't you?" My heart stuttered in my chest.

"I was torn. I couldn't leave my mom alone with Grandpa. He's too overbearing. And manipulative." His hand slid up my wrist. Bare fingers crawled under my jacket sleeves, tendrils of heat curling up my forearm. As if he could manipulate me by mere touch.

My breath hitched. Something flashed in front of me. Like a camera going in and out of focus. An eagle soaring over a bright blue globe. Much like the glowing earth I'd seen in the angel's hands. Only bigger. With two people on the eagle's back. I pulled my arms from Will's grip.

Then it disappeared, fading away into the night. A strange flash of a vision.

Will was still talking. "I have these dreams, these visions. And I just know I need to be here in New York. Even if I'd rather be in Chicago."

"What do you mean, you have visions?" I almost added, *too*, but sealed my trap shut.

"Maybe I'll tell you all about them sometime. If you tell me about your visions." He leaned closer, his mouth inches from mine. If I closed the gap, he'd have all the proof he needed.

Every muscle in my body stilled under his gaze. Scenarios, explanations, clever comebacks assaulted my brain—scrambling for something to deflect the truth. He couldn't know my gift came early. He'd tell Nexis. And the world as I knew it would come crashing down.

"I never said I had visions." Arching away, I drew the words out slowly, measuring them carefully.

"Is that right? Then how do you explain what I just saw?" Those full lips curled, chin cleft jutting out. "A lightning strike out of nowhere. Sparks flying from your hands. You falling to your knees screaming God knows what. That was a reckoning, wasn't it?"

Suddenly his hands were on my face. Stroking my cheeks, forcing me to look at him.

"How many times have you had to go through this?" His rough fingers soothed my skin. Worked my thoughts into a tangled mess. But I couldn't give in. I had to resist the tingles crawling up the back of my neck.

"I don't know." Yep. I just lied right to his face.

"Does that mean you're the Seer?"

I bit my lip. After what he just did for me, I didn't want to keep lying to him. But until I knew for sure where his loyalties really were, I couldn't take any chances. "I won't know till my eighteenth birthday. Same as everyone else."

"Don't be like that." His face fell. "We both know that's not the truth. I wish you would just trust me."

How could I be so stupid? Did he really know the truth? My lung seized, and the world around me wobbled on its axis. He'd seen too much. Bryan would kill me, the Guardians, too. But they weren't here right now. They put me in this mess.

Will didn't seem to notice my internal freakout. "It was awful for me, listening to you scream like that. Like something was torturing you. And I was powerless to stop it." His voice cracked. Almost as if he really meant it.

"You did do something. You held me," I whispered before I could stop myself. "I needed it."

"Good. If that's what you need, I won't stop. Not ever." Then he pulled away and stared me down. "I need you to know one thing."

"I'm listening." I drew in a breath, bracing for impact.

"What happened tonight—it's just between us." His eyes held mine. "I won't tell anyone. Especially not a soul in Nexis. I promise."

"Really? Not a single soul?" I narrowed my eyes at him, daring him to add a caveat. But he didn't crack.

He leaned in, lips arching up. "Let's keep our secrets for now. Shall we?"

"I think I can manage that." I tamped down a matching smirk, mixed feelings skating by in figure-eights and curlicues.

"We'll see." He dropped my hand, and I felt suddenly cold. Untethered from his warmth.

My heart clenched as my thoughts finally floated back to Bryan, where they should've been all along. Waves of guilt swarmed in my head, hurling accusations. What was wrong with me? If I could mentally kick myself, I'd be black and blue.

But it was too late. I had to keep Will from blabbing my secrets to Nexis—and keep up the charade a little longer.

So I let him walk me back. His hip bumped mine as we crossed the bridge. I scanned the woods for signs of Shanda, but she was nowhere to be found. Maybe she bailed when she saw Will?

I wanted to bolt straight for the dorm, drown my shame in a bottle of fizzy Dr. Pepper. But that idea brought back the wrong kind of memories. The time I kissed Will. Maybe this charade wasn't a charade at all. Who was I really fooling? Him or me?

><

Glancing around the shadows for Shanda, I stopped at my dorm's back window. Where was that girl? Hopefully, Miss Sherry hadn't caught her sneaking out.

"Here you are, tiger." Will's smile gleamed at me in the dark night as he dropped me off at my dorm. "Your...window?"

"That's right." I nodded at him, staring up at my kitchen window escape route. "It's top secret. Hush, hush."

His smile widened, and his eyes met mine in the moonlight. "Need a boost?"

"Absolutely not." Hopefully the darkness hid my flaming cheeks. Who knew where he wanted to "boost" me from? "Just because I'm six inches shorter than you doesn't mean I need your help. I'll have you know, I've gotten pretty good at this."

"Really?" He practically snorted. "I've got to see this."

Suddenly, nervous energy coursed through my veins. "You really don't have to watch."

"Oh yes, I do." He stepped back and folded his arms over his chest. "I want to make sure you get in safe and all."

"Sure ya do." I rolled my eyes at him as I walked toward the windowsill. *Just do your usual routine,* I told myself. Jumping for the sill, my fingers wrapped tight around the slippery brick as I hung for dear life from my fingertips. Then I made the usual attempt to pull myself up with my feeble arm strength while scrambling my feet against the siding for leverage.

"That's exactly what I pictured." His deep laughter floated somewhere behind me.

"Shut up." I turned around to shoot him an evil glare. Suddenly my left hand slipped, and I dangled from the ledge by one hand.

"Here, let me help you." Will darted below me in a second, wrapping both hands around my foot and lifting me like I weighed nothing. "We'll have to find you a better way to sneak out next time."

On quivering jelly-arms, I pulled myself through the window and stared down at him from my perch. "Next time?"

"Yes." He nodded, eyes crinkling in the moonlight. "Next time."

He lifted two fingers to his forehead and gave me a mock salute before he took off into the night.

I watched his backside as he disappeared. Two could play his little game. My heartbeat stuttered in my chest like it couldn't remember how to beat normally again. Every nerve ending in my body crackled and fizzled like a live wire wreaking chaos inside me. What was this boy doing to me?

Shutting and locking the window, I tiptoed through the kitchen, up the back stairs, down my hall, and into my room. I just hoped Shanda was all right.

Easing open the door to my room, I slipped in and shut it behind me without a sound.

Click. The desk light switched on and swiveled on me like a spotlight.

My heart did somersaults in my chest, and I squinted, shielding my face from the sudden brightness with one hand.

"Where have you been, missy?" Shanda asked in a deep voice. "You're in big trouble."

I clutched my chest, gulping in deep breaths. "Don't scare me like that, girl. What happened to you anyway?" I collapsed in a heap on my bed, peeling off my parka. My limbs were still reeling from the reckoning. And the encounter with Will.

"Oh, yeah, that." She rolled her eyes and pointed at our bathroom door. "Our suitemate came in wanting to dish about your fight with Felicia. I guess she heard us talking and thought we might still be up."

"Brooke?" I scrunched my forehead at her, hope rising up inside. If she was reaching out, maybe I could ask her about why my energy kept draining every time I used my powers.

"No, Julia." Shanda shook her head. "She asked why you weren't here, so I had to make up an excuse."

"Oh, great." My heart sank like an anchor. "What'd you say?"

"I told her you were still getting chewed out by Miss Sherry as part of your punishment." Shanda had the decency to look a little bit sheepish. "I didn't know what else to do."

I shrugged. "No biggie. Good thinking." Glad I dodged that bullet.

"Julia kept me busy for thirty minutes with her gossip girl tales." She tiptoed over to my bed and sat down beside me, whispering now. "Then I tried to follow your escape route, but Miss Sherry caught me on her nightly rounds. Did you know she does that?"

"Huh-uh." I gave her a headshake. "I wonder if that has something to do with the break-in. We've got to keep tabs on her. What time did she head out?"

"About twelve-thirty or so." Shanda pulled her phone from her pocket and made a note. Then her eyebrows knitted together. "Girl, it's 2:00 am! Where've you been for two hours?"

My cheeks flamed, threatening to give me up. "In the field. Training."

"By yourself?" She tilted her head at me. "From that look on your face, I'm not buying it. Spill."

"Okay, fine. Will showed up out of nowhere." I twisted my hands through my hair, trying to make sense of what happened out there tonight. "I don't know if he stalked me to be protective or to get intel, but he saw everything."

Shanda gasped. "What do you mean, everything?"

I shrugged my shoulders as if it didn't matter anymore, but a trickle of fear still slithered down my neck. "He saw me talking to my angel. Then he saw the reckoning." I could barely get out that last word.

"Hold up. We'll circle back to that last bit in a minute." She held up one hand like a stop sign. "Did you say you talked to your angel?"

I nodded, my eyes wide. "He told me I could be the last Seer this world ever needs."

"Whoa." She whispered, hissing air between her teeth. "That's major. And Will heard that?"

"No, no." I shook my head so hard my hair flapped in front of my face. "Thank God."

"Phew." Shanda wiped her brow, and we both exhaled a sigh of relief. "So, you have to tell me. What the heck is a reckoning?"

"Oh, it's terrible." I could barely even say the words. "It's like the screaming hordes of hell are unleashed all around you. It's awful."

"Yikes. That *does* sound terrible." She slung her arm across my back and rubbed my shoulder. "What did Will do about it?"

I slumped down and glanced away. "Kind of what you're doing now. He held me until it was over."

Her arm dropped from my shoulders, and she reared back. "Oh, so is Will your 'new man' now?" She added air quotes to "new man."

"He's not my 'new man,'" I said, mimicking her ridiculous air quotes. But my heart lifted ever-so-slightly just thinking of Will. "He's just different now. Like I'm seeing a new side of him."

"You can't be serious." She cocked her head at me with an expression that said you-can't-be-that-dumb.

"What do you mean?" My heart dropped.

Her face softened, but she held my gaze. "He's not different. The only one who's changed is *you*."

"That's ridiculous." I mumbled half-heartedly as the idea rolled around in my brain. Maybe my bestie was right.

"For a girl who's supposed to see things, you really are blind sometimes." She tsked, shaking her head at me and leaning closer. "Will's the same guy he's always been, and just as into you as ever. Trust me, he's the only decent Nexis member. Not like that moron Kevin, or those evil twins Colleen and Monica. Well, I guess Julia's not so bad when she's not gossiping like a celebrity fangirl."

I cocked my head at her. "Your point, Sherlock?"

She exhaled an exasperated breath. "My point is, you're not buying into the Guardian spiel anymore. You're finally thinking for yourself. I'm so proud of you for that."

"Huh, I hadn't thought about it that way." I slumped forward, resting my head in my hands.

"That's why Will seems so incredibly different. Maybe you're just finally seeing him for who he really is." The way she patted my knee reminded me of my grandma.

Flashes of memories popped in my head, memories of Will's face. "Now that you mention it, there's something else too. Ever since he crashed my New Year's party, I've been seeing a strange aura around him. Less shadows. More light. Maybe I'm not the only one changing. Maybe he's changing, too."

Shanda waved her hand in front of my face. "Focus, Lucy. I'm just saying, give the boy a chance. He might surprise you."

"I can't believe you're telling me to go out with Will. It's just because you're so happy with Tony." A familiar, excitement wriggled around inside me. For a moment, I felt weightless. Like I stood on the edge of a precipice, about to dive into something new. Was I really ready for something new, even with someone as amazing as Will? After all, I'd thought Bryan was pretty amazing until he dumped me on the quad.

"I am happy." A dreamy sort of smile lit up her eyes. Then she turned my way. "But I'm not telling you to go out with Will. I'm just saying, give the boy a chance."

"Fine." I huffed, hugging my arms around me. "I'll take it under advisement."

"That's all I ask." Her eyes glazed over in a faraway look.

"What is it?" I unfolded my arms and inched closer.

"Okay, there's one more thing. I need your help with my party." She sat up straight, knuckles white on the edge of the bed frame. "It's going to be mostly Nexis goons, and Daddy's not happy about it. So I invited Tony. Now I'm worried everyone will figure out we're together."

"Hey, it's your birthday. Do whatever you want." I patted her hand in an attempt to get her to loosen her grip on my comforter. "Just tell them you're trying to turn Tony or get intel out of him. They'll love that."

"Or I could just tell them you invited him." Her eyebrows arched in a mix between hopeful and desperate.

"Fine." I bobbed my head, trying desperately not to roll my eyes. "But if you want my help I want all the gory details."

She put a hand to her chest, and her face went all goopy. "Even though I like to think I'm still such a rebel, I actually like dating the good guy for a change. He's the best, especially because he treats me like I'm a princess. What's not to love about that?"

"Wait, hold on a sec." I sucked in a breath, fanning my face with my hands like a true drama queen. "Are you saying you're in love with him?"

Her lips curled up slowly. How cute. Her little secret was out.

"I can't believe it. My Shanda's all grown up." I fake sniffed and mock-dabbed my eyes. "How long have you guys been dating, anyway?"

"It's only been three months, but I just can't help myself." She hung her head, trying to hide her enormous grin, but it couldn't be contained. "I just hope the Guardians don't find out. Or worse."

"Nexis," we said at the same time.

I flopped back on my pillow. "Ugh, let's not talk about Nexis for one night. Please."

"You're right." The springs squeaked as she rose from the bed to loom over me. "Let's talk about my party."

"Right." I snapped back upright, giving her a thumbs up. "Just tell me what I need to do."

"Well, for starters," she said, pointing her index finger at me. "You need to get there early and run interference for me."

"Okay, got it." I nodded. "Can do. Next?"

"Next." She held out a second finger. "We must look fabulous." She almost squealed out that last word.

A smile lifted the corners of my mouth. "With your help, my little fashionista, we will be the most fabulous girls at your party."

"You better believe it." She danced over to her closet and started humming to herself.

"Ugh," I groaned, dissolving into a heap on my covers. "How about sleep first and then fashion?"

"Deal." She clicked off the light and before I knew it, the soft sounds of deep breathing drifted from her side of the room.

My eyelids were heavy as I rolled over and stared up at my plastic ceiling stars, but my mind wouldn't stop racing. Could I really handle a Nexis party, not to mention seeing Will again? Maybe it would be nice to get off campus and have a little fun. If only I could be sure he didn't have some other agendas. No matter what I did or where I went, there would always be someone wanting something from me. And trying to manipulate me to get it. If I couldn't stay away from them, maybe I could at least have some fun.

CHAPTER 17

March 15th had finally arrived. Anticipation gurgled in my stomach like a thousand high-kicking Rockettes. A night away from Montrose Paranormal Academy drama. What would I do with myself? By the looks of it, Shanda's fabulous seventeenth birthday party would *not* disappoint.

The Jones' condo was uber-chic, just like I pictured it. The modern living room glittered with black-and-white garlands of beads and pearls, much different than my birthday parties. Not a streamer in sight. The sleek black sofa and matching chairs were pushed up against the back wall of windows overlooking Central Park with an amazing view of the city skyline creating the perfect backdrop for the dance floor.

My knees wobbled on the stepladder, but I managed to tape the last corner of the Happy Birthday sign above the hallway. Mr. Jones lumbered down the hall, headed right for me.

"Lucy, it's crooked," Shanda practically whined. "Daddy, can you fix it?"

Mr. Jones tucked something in his jacket then reached up to adjust the silver string of letters. "There. How's that, princess?"

"Much better." Her eyes zeroed in on his jacket pocket. "What's that? Is it my birthday present?"

"I wanted you to have it before your guests arrive. Happy birthday, sweetheart." He pulled out a tiny box of pale aqua tied with a white ribbon.

"Something from Tiffany's?" Her eyes lit up like diamonds, and sure enough that's exactly what she uncovered in the box. "Look, it's the Cleopatra. Thanks, Daddy." She thrust the ring at me.

I gasped. A sideways oval diamond gleamed in the middle, surrounded on top and bottom with a curved line of mini-diamonds. An eye made entirely out of diamonds.

She slipped the ring on her chocolate finger. A striking effect.

So striking that the room started to spin, and suddenly I saw *her* again.

A fuzzy image of St. Lucia came into focus. This time her eyes were like Cleopatra diamonds. She opened her mouth, whispering words into my head.

You can be the last. You can end this. I was the first, but you will be the last.

The vision faded, leaving my brain scrambling through questions. St. Lucia was the first Seer to do what, exactly? My head spinning, I stumbled down the stepladder. A strong hand steadied me back to the carpet.

"Lucy, are you okay?" Mr. Jones asked.

I blinked up at him. Nodded. "I'm fine. Just a little dizzy. No more ladders for me."

"Yes. Let me take care of the rest of this. You girls just go get ready." He took the tape from my shaky hands.

"You're the best." Shanda hugged him, then pulled me down the hall to her room. She shut the door firmly. "You just had a vision or something, didn't you?"

"Yeah, I did." My hands were shaky and my mouth wouldn't stop running. "It was the same thing I told you about last night, except this time St. Lucia said I'd be the last Seer. Then she said she was the first, but the first at what? Until we figure out what she means, can't we just forget about it and have a fun night? It's your birthday, after all." I snapped my mouth shut, hoping she wouldn't pry any further. If she did, I might start freaking out. In front of the entire Nexis crew. No bueno.

"Fine, but only because it's my birthday. And because it's time to look fabulous." She threw open the door to her immaculate walk-in closet. Of course. Shouldn't expect anything less from Miss Fashionista.

"Here, try this one." Her eyes gleamed in the closet spotlights.

And I couldn't say no. Not tonight.

***

Muffled laughter greeted me as I ran my fingers over the black tulle and sequin number Shanda foisted on me. The things a girl will do for her best friend.

Shanda flounced down the hall in a glittering silver mini dress that highlighted her new ring perfectly. She made quite an entrance, too. The mostly-Nexis crowd hooted and hollered as she pranced in, and I trailed behind. Trying to stay off the radar.

The party was in full swing now. Standing room only. Music blaring, dancers swaying to the beat, clusters of kids yelling at each other over the roar. She was right, all Nexis—except for Tony guarding the corner by the gift table. Correction, gift mountain.

At least Colleen and Monica weren't at this shindig. Kudos to the birthday girl for that choice.

I clunked into the kitchen in my ridiculously unnecessary strappy heels, poured myself a Dr. Pepper, and surveyed the scene. Julia stood huddled in a group of like-minded girls in little black dresses, engrossed in conversation with some hot guy. Rick something.

"Five bucks says there's gonna be a catfight over Rick by the end of the night." Tony poured Mountain Dew into a clear plastic party cup, all neon yellow fizz.

"Not a chance, 'cause I'm so with you on that." I turned his way. "But who's gonna win? That's the real question."

"My money's on Madison." Tony pointed at one of the blonde girls.

"Hello? There are two Madisons vying for your boy Rick." I laughed, taking a sip of my soda. "Still, I'll bet a Dr. Pepper on my girl, Julia, there."

"Yeah, wouldn't want to cross her." Air whistled through his teeth. "Or the birthday girl, for that matter."

"You know her too well." I raised my eyebrows at him, lowering my voice. "Seriously though, I'm glad you guys are together."

"Me, too." A grin spread like taffy across his face. "She's pretty cool isn't she?"

"The coolest bestie I've ever had." The realization warmed my heart.

From across the crowded dance floor, Shanda caught my eye. I lifted my chin just to prove I wasn't a full-time member of the boys club. We had a secret all our own, just between us. No Guardian Council or Nexis conspiracy could change that.

Tony cleared his throat a little too loudly. "Shut up, here comes el maestro."

Will threaded his way through the dance floor, his golden head bobbing in a sea of black and gray.

I rolled my eyes. "You better hideout somewhere. I doubt he'll be cool with a Guardian superhero mixing it up at a Nexis party."

"Good call." His grin faded and he squared his shoulders at me. "You sure you'll be all right, alone with him?"

"We're hardly alone." My stomach did a backflip anyway. "Don't worry about me. You can resume your post at the gift table."

"Ay, ay, captain." He raised his Mountain Dew and disappeared as fast as he'd come.

I chugged my soda, bubbles fizzing on my tongue. If only they were made of iron to fortify me.

Will crossed into the dim kitchen, shadows sliding over the contours of his face. "Did you save some for me, gorgeous?"

The earth froze on its axis. At least, it felt that way with the two of us just standing there.

His gaze was a little too familiar, his shoulder a little too close. I choked back the memory of last night. His arms around me. Being too vulnerable.

I cocked my head at a 2-liter bottle of Dr. Pepper and he dumped the last of it into his cup.

"What's Tony doing here?" He took a sip, eyes trained on me.

A shiver crawled up my neck. I couldn't out my bestie. *Right, that's my cue.* "I begged Shanda to let me bring a friend."

"Since when are you and Tony friends?" He reared back, examining every inch of my face as a muscle in his jaw twitched. "I know it's only been a couple of months since your breakup. Do you like him?"

I snorted, spraying Dr. Pepper all over the counter. I rushed to wipe my face with a napkin. "Jealous much?"

Will's shoulders shook like maracas as he laughed his head off. "I'm guessing that was a dumb thing to say." He watched my face, still laughing.

"Tony's been like a big brother to me since I got here." I mopped up the sticky spatters on the countertop, trying not to laugh right along with him.

"That's good." He swiped a napkin from my hand, dabbing the spill right along with me. "You know this feels awfully familiar."

"What do you mean?" My heartbeat galloped in my eardrums. Had he figured it out already? I knew I'd be a horrible spy.

"This. Cleaning up your Dr. Pepper mess." His lips curled up.

"Oh. That." Heat licked at my cheeks. I only hoped the darkness would hide them.

He wadded up both our napkins and grabbed my still-sticky hand. "C'mon, Lucy. Let's dance."

Before I could say no, he pulled me out of the kitchen and down to the dance floor.

He lifted his hands as a fast song kicked up. Throwing his head back, he rocked to the beat. I followed his lead, trying to keep up. He was a good dancer, and he knew it, too. Every few minutes he'd grab my hand and twirl me around. Eyes dancing with the beat. A huge smile dimpled his cheeks, highlighting his chin cleft. His happiness seeped into my limbs, and I let myself fall into rhythm with him.

The music died down, transitioning to a slow song. One of the Madisons cocked her head at him, trying to cut in. He shook his head, blocking her with his hip. She shrugged, fired a glare at me, and stalked off. Poor girl. It just wasn't her night.

Did that mean it was my night?

Will's hands settled on my waist, inching me closer. I slid my hands up his firm shoulders, twining my fingers together behind his neck. His eyes lit up as they rested on my face. I inhaled shallow puffs of air.

"You look so gorgeous in that dress, Lucy. I've wanted to do this all night." He pulled me closer, his breath in my ear.

"You know, you're really great at parties." I couldn't stop my lips from curving. They forgot whose side they were on.

"I don't know about that. Didn't go so well the last time, if I remember right." He shrugged, chin stubble grazing my cheek.

"I didn't say you were great at crashing parties." Laughter tickled my throat.

"Agreed." His lips curled, but his eyes said something else I didn't want to think about. "I hope I'm not, um, I hope this is helping . . ."

"Shh," I whispered pressing two fingers to his mouth. "I don't want to think about anything else right now. I just want to have some fun."

He kissed my fingers before I slid them behind his neck again. "Then, my Dr. Pepper princess, I'm just the guy for the job."

"I thought so." The words came out too syrupy, morphing into a thick river of sludge in my gut. I didn't want to play him, but it just slipped out.

The slow song ended, and another fast beat pumped into the air. I dropped my arms like lead weights at my sides, cold without his proximity.

"You sure you can keep up?" That trademark grin spread across his face.

"Try me." I let him take my hand, whirl me around the dance floor. Black faded into silver and sequins and glinting squares of disco light. I forgot about everything else but the music, throwing my head back as he dipped me. For the first time in weeks, I was happy. It felt good for a change.

><

Blackness swirled behind my eyelids. Too heavy to open. A soft finger tapped my shoulder.

"Lucy, wake up. It's after midnight. Time to go home," Shanda croaked, sounding about as groggy as I felt.

"Can't I just stay here?" I yawned and rubbed my eyes. Arching my back, I hit my head on something solid. The arm of the couch?

"I wish, but you've gotta get back by curfew. Apparently, they're being super strict ever since some crazy people broke into our room." She narrowed her eyes and glanced at a shadowy figure behind me.

"Hey, I didn't do it." Will reached for the sky. Of course he was here now, staring down at me. Lips curved in an annoying little smirk. He'd probably drive me home, too. Perfect.

"Okay, let's go if we're gonna get back by one a.m." I smoothed down the wrinkles of my once-fabulous party dress, but they just popped right back up.

"Whenever you're ready." Will took my hand and helped me to my feet.

"Aren't you coming, too?" I scrunched up my brow at the birthday girl, hoping she could read my mind. But I couldn't dare ask why Tony wasn't the one still here. She probably had some Shanda-scheme in mind.

"I got a pass to stay overnight since Dad's in town." She waved her palm in front of her face, stifling a yawn. "So I'm off to bed. Night, you two."

With that, she turned and padded down the hall, leaving me alone in her partied-out living room. With Will.

"You shoulda got one for me, too." I mumbled in the direction of her room. Part of me wondered if she'd planned this or something.

"Don't worry, I won't bite." He got my coat from the dining room nook and draped it around my shoulders.

"Where've I heard that before?" I followed him out the front door and into the elevator. As the doors shut, his proximity became palpable. Even after hours of dancing, he still smelled cinnamony and woodsy all at the same time.

He led me through the dim concrete maze of the parking garage and opened the passenger door of a black Mercedes.

I climbed in and he took off, racing down the streets of Manhattan like someone was tailing us. Adrenaline pounded through my veins, waking up every nerve ended. The light turned red. He jerked to a stop, tires squealing.

"Hey, watch it, buddy." I bounced off the leather seat.

"That's what I get for trying to impress you." He gripped the steering wheel tighter.

"Hey," I softened my tone, reaching out to squeeze his shoulder. "You don't have to impress me. I'm already impressed. Just drive like a normal person. We'll make it back."

"You're already impressed?" Hues of red washed over his sculpted face as he turned to me.

"You're not as bad as I thought you were." I gnawed on my lip, but too late. The truth was already out there.

"I'm sure the Guardians told you I'm the worst person on the planet." In a flash, he turned back to the road, that little muscle in his jaw twitching again.

"Pretty much." I couldn't argue with that.

The light turned green, but he didn't peel out this time. His hand slid to the gearshift, and he eased up on the gas pedal. Then he stopped at another light. Glanced my way.

I couldn't help but look at him and smile as the light turned green.

"There's something I've been meaning to tell you. I tried a few times, but it didn't work out so well. I'm going to try again. And hope you don't hate me." He pulled onto the GW Bridge, hand resting on the gearshift. In no-man's land. As if waiting for me to make the first move.

"I don't hate you." Staring out the window at the dark river, I gulped down my objections, letting them swim laps in the pit of my stomach. Except they weren't my objections anymore—they were Guardian lies. Or half-truths. Because they hadn't told me the full truth about anything, least of all Will. A guy who only ever tried to help me. Tried to be with me. And I'd always pushed him away. Not anymore.

"There's only one thing left to explain." I put my hand over his.

"The initiation." He swallowed, Adam's apple bobbing, and took a deep breath. "I'm glad you ran away."

"You're glad I didn't join Nexis?" I squeezed his hand, willing him to tell me more, even as fireflies did cartwheels in my middle.

He turned up his palm and laced his fingers between mine. "I am. You're much smarter than I am." A rueful smile played across those oh-so-kissable lips. "At least about Nexis. I wanted you to join for purely selfish reasons. Mainly so you wouldn't join the Guardians. But I thought I could protect you. Now, I'm not so sure."

"I don't know how smart I am." I glanced over at him, studying the outline of his profile in the glow of the streetlights. "I just listen to my heart. Even if it means doing something dumb."

"That's not dumb. That's honest." His hand slid to my knee.

I stopped breathing for one. Two. Three seconds.

He cleared his throat. "That night, at the initiation, I wanted you to join so I could tell you more about your brother. But I shouldn't have used that info as a bargaining chip to manipulate you. Some Nexis habits die hard."

"Oh." My gaze snapped to his profile.

"I'm sorry. You deserve better than that." He stopped at another light, face dappled in the red glow.

I blinked, staring at his hand. Still on my knee. "Thank you."

He ran his free hand through his golden locks, mussing up his perfect party hair. "There's more to the story though. There's a reason why James left."

"Why he left? I thought he got kicked out." I scrunched up my forehead at him.

He gave me a headshake. "Nexis banished him because he wasn't the Seer and he'd stolen intel from them. But they couldn't kick him out of Montrose."

"I don't understand. Then why would he live in the chapel, and run away to Europe?" I stared at him as his car whizzed over the bridge.

He slowed for a car in front of us, his voice low. "I think it's because of what happened to Maria Donovan."

I sucked in a breath, tensing every muscle. Bracing for impact. "What did happen to Julia's sister?"

His jaw twitched as he stopped at another red light. "She was a Guardian spy. She was dating James. Trying to turn him. But it backfired. Big time."

"No." The truth slammed me into the seat, even as the car lurched forward. I couldn't think. Couldn't breathe. Because I knew it was true—it was the Guardian way, after all.

The city lights were more sporadic now as we approached Riverdale.

A lone muscle in Will's jaw twitched as he spilled the whole story. "I don't know what happened exactly. No one does. The security patrol says she followed them to James' banishment. When he tried to escape, she ran, too, and fell into the river. They say James reached out for her, tried to save her, and would've gone in, too. Except the guards were able to grab him and pull him back. It was a horrible accident."

"How awful. For Maria. For James." I covered my face with my hands, rocking back and forth in my seat. The second I closed my eyes, all the visions I had ever had of that night collided into one.

The field. James reaching out. The cavernous abyss. Maria falling.

And suddenly I *was* there.

On the muddy banks of the Hudson, with James on his knees.

Rocking back and forth, back and forth. Hands over his face. Sobbing as I've never seen him sob before.

I wrapped my arms around him, hoping that wherever he was he could feel it.

James looked up at me. "It's all my fault," he whispered.

"It's not your fault." I whispered back.

The gray mist rolled in and my brother faded into the shadows.

Will grabbed my hand, rubbing his finger circles across my palm. "I know, but I still should've told you sooner. Should've tried harder. Even after you ran away from me that day after junior assembly, I should've followed you. Made you listen."

"I don't know." I shook my head, trying to remember what we were just talking about. "I don't know if I could've handled it all then."

"Maybe not, but you deserved to know the truth. So you could make up your own mind." He squeezed my hand.

"I'm not sure what to do with that." Silence and miles of dark streets rolled by as my world turned upside down again.

"You don't have to do anything. I just thought you should know." He exhaled a long breath that fogged up the windshield for a minute.

"Thanks, I think." I leaned back as he pulled into the Montrose parking lot.

"They say the truth shall set you free." He turned off the car and just sat there. Staring at me.

"Not sure how that applies here." I couldn't look at him. Not yet.

"I don't know. Maybe now you'll finally be free to make up your own mind. Figure out what you really want." Will still held my hand, caressing my palm with the back of his thumb. "What *do* you want, Lucy?"

"I don't know." Tingles shot up my wrist as a strange feeling settled in my stomach. Maybe I did know, and I just didn't want to admit it yet.

Like that night in the kitchen last semester. When he kissed me. The goosebumps were still there, but my heart was a pendulum. Swinging back and forth between the guy next to me and the one who chose the Guardians over me.

"I'm so confused." Still, I scooted next to him. Until our shoulders touched over the console.

His lips curled up as he dipped his face toward mine. "I've got an idea. Why don't you come to the Nexis meeting tomorrow? There's something I want to show you."

"What? How's that going to help?" I lifted my gaze to meet his.

"Trust me, it'll be worth it. What do you say?" His gray eyes sent my heart pounding.

"Fine. One meeting. But if it gets creepy or the evil twins make a fuss, I'm bailing." Somehow I felt like I was about to give in to the dark side, but this guy put even a young Darth Vader to shame.

"Deal. I'll see you tomorrow night." Those platinum eyes moved to my lips. But he sat still. Hovering mere inches away.

My heart drummed a new rhythm, in time to his breathing. Before I could blink, let alone think, I leaned forward and brushed my lips against his soft mouth. A spark zinged straight through me, and I inched back. Did he see?

"I shouldn't." I whispered, unable to tear myself away from the proximity of his hot breath on my face.

"I know." He murmured against my mouth. "But I'll be here when you're ready."

"Thanks, Will." I breathed in a lungful of his spicy scent and touched two fingers to his lips. The look he gave me, longing mixed with contentment, made me want to give him more. Instead, I opened the door and walked into the cold night.

CHAPTER 18

"They're not going to like this, but I don't care." A muscle in Will's jaw twitched.

What was he thinking when he did that? I wanted to ask, but instead I traced the golden nameplate with my fingertip. "It says Stanton Observatory. Right here." I tapped the plaque with my index finger, raising my eyebrows at him.

Those metallic eyes were a blade. Level and steady. Trained on me. Holding me in place like he knew I wanted to run away from this place.

"You're right about that." Will led me into the dim foyer of the only place on campus named after him. Or his family at least. The one and only Nexis headquarters. With one strong arm, he steadied me as we ascended the familiar spiral staircase of the Nexis tower. In the observatory, he seated me in the back row of chairs, next to Shanda and Julia. Then he made his way up front.

"Personal escort, nice." She shot me a half-smile.

"Let's call this meeting to order." The hum of whispers grew louder until Will cleared his throat. "What's on the agenda tonight?"

He glanced at Kevin, but before Shanda's ex could say one word, someone scraped back a chair with a horrifying screech. Like nails on a chalkboard.

"Since when do we invite outsiders to attend official Nexis meetings? Especially those with Guardian affiliations." Colleen flipped her brassy hair at me, impaling me with her tawny glare.

"You can't take the prep school out of this girl," Shanda muttered under her breath.

Heat rushed to my cheeks, and I wrapped my fingers around the cool edges of my metal folding chair.

Bam! Will pounded his fist into the podium. "Last time I checked, I'm the president of this group, not you. And I'll invite whoever I want." His mouth pursed into a solid line. He wasn't messing around.

"Two and a half more months. Then we'll see." She whipped her head back toward him. Was that why Collen kept pulling all these crazy stunts? Did she really want to be Nexis president?

"Get a life," I muttered under my breath.

In the front of the room, Will squared his shoulders and cleared his throat. "Now, if there are no other objections, I'll continue. Where were we, Kevin?"

"Right, the agenda." Kevin stood up, rattling on about something.

I barely heard him. I couldn't stop staring at Will. Especially because he stared right back at me. My lips curled into a smile like they had a mind of their own. His shoulders visibly relaxed. Part of me wanted to run up and hug him like the brave defender he was. The look he gave me sent tingles shooting up my spine. Maybe this was the real Will Stanton, the one I'd failed to see from the beginning. If only I could be 100% sure.

Out of nowhere, a musty stench wafted in. I glanced around the room. And froze.

Black shadows snaked around the floorboards, uncoiling like ropes of mist and hissing as they circled the cluster of folding chairs. I gripped the edge of my seat—knuckles white, blood pounding in my ears. My eyes darted around the room as the demon snakes headed straight for me.

I sucked in a breath and called up my angel fire, electricity now coursing through my veins. *Angel, where are you? Time to help me vanquish some demons.*

No. Hold your fire. I heard the word inside my head as clear as if he spoke it out loud. My heart galloped into my lungs, leaving me gasping for breath. But I obeyed. Flexing my fingers into fist, I swallowed back the electric current.

Why not? Fear seized my throat so I couldn't utter a word.

You'll see, was all the reply I got.

The odor putrefied, curdling the contents of my stomach. I wanted to retch, or run, or both.

Will's eyes widened, then focused on our favorite blonde. He marched up to Colleen and snatched a book out of her hands. "I don't recall giving you permission to take this from the chamber."

The shadows stopped circling, almost as if they were frozen. *Chamber, what chamber?* The word rang in my ears, somehow calming me a smidge.

"Ssshh, she'll hear you." Colleen hissed, green eyes flashing at me.

"I don't care. This isn't yours to take. I'll have to return it." He tucked the book under his arm and walked away. The shadows retreated, fading away into the charcoal floorboards. The awful smell dissipated, too.

"Fine," she mumbled, crossing her arms and pouting like a petulant child.

Without looking back, he came and sat in the empty chair beside me, setting the book entitled *Age of Nexilim* in his lap.

I breathed in a gulp of fresh air, stench-free. My heartbeat slowed. Yeah, things were definitely changing that shadows retreated from this guy.

"You okay, Lucy?" He slung his arm across the back of my chair as if he did it every day.

"I am now." I nodded, my lips curling up at him.

"Good." His fingers brushed the edge of my shoulder, feathery soft.

Blurry silhouettes filed out in front of me, down the spiral staircase, until only Will remained with me in the back of the dome.

"What happened? Is the meeting over?" I glanced around the empty dome, wondering what I'd missed during my Colleen-induced vision.

I longed to throw open the observatory window and kick my feet over the side like I did last August. Talk to the moon as if she could really tell me her secrets. But I couldn't move. Not when his fingers were toying with my shoulder.

As soon as the last Nexis member left, Will cleared his throat. "It's all going to be worth it when you see the Nexis Chamber for yourself."

"Are you kidding?" My heart lifted as I turned to study his face. "Isn't that breaking the rules?"

His lips curved at the corners. "About a dozen, give or take."

"A dozen? Really?" All the air rushed from my lungs. At least one guy didn't mind breaking his secret society's sacred rules for me. The fact that it was Will, and not Bryan, just resonated that much more.

"I just want you to have choices for once in your life." Will's words struck a chord, deep in the inner nooks and crannies of my heart—in the ruins Bryan left for dead.

"Wow," was all I could manage.

"Of course, that means you'll have to spend more time with me." He reached for my hand and helped me up.

"I think I can handle that." A completely foreign feeling bloomed from the ashes. A strange, but exhilarating anticipation.

I had to admit the truth, if only to myself. I was wrong about Will. Utterly and completely. Maybe that's what he meant last night when he said the truth would set me free.

As his eyes met mine, a shockwave rippled through the pit of my stomach. I couldn't deny it anymore. The shadows around him were gone. No more black, snake-like coils like I'd seen hovering over him last year. Instead, shards of pure light filtered through the gray mist around him in a mottled halo effect. My heart dive-bombed down my throat, slamming into the pit of my stomach.

Maybe he was changing, too. Into a guy I could finally trust. But I had to be sure this time. I couldn't make the same mistake again. My heart couldn't take another beating.

"You ready for your surprise?" he asked. The gray tendrils of mist around him dissipated, fading into nothing.

I nodded, my eyes glued to the contours of his face.

His mouth quirked up and he took my hand, pulling me down the evil spiral staircase. Then he stopped suddenly, planting his feet in place. Flattened his palm on the black wall, his fingers tapped out some silent code.

Whoosh, a black door opened a gaping hole in the wall. Scratch that. A doorway.

He nudged me into the secret room, and my jaw hinged open at the sight that greeted me.

><

"Shanda? What're you doing here?" I asked, stepping into the tiny half-moon shaped room.

"About time," she hissed, slamming her fist into a button on the wall.

Swiiish. The door slid back into the wall behind me like it never existed in the first place.

Streaks of moonglow slanted across the narrow, crescent-shaped walls of stone in front of me. The room was obviously on the outer wall of the tower, with high rectangular windows as the only source of natural light.

Will headed straight to Shanda's desk next to the secret door and switched on a green library lamp, rummaging through the drawers.

"Where are we?" I asked.

"It's the officer's lounge." Shanda barely glanced up from her laptop, fingers flying over the keyboard. "Remember when I said I was spying on Nexis? This is where all the action is."

I lowered my voice. "So he knows you've been spying on him?"

"Since day one, but only because I've been spying on them, too." He pointed to the other side of the room, with an antique leather sofa. "Look familiar?"

"Stop trying to distract me." I narrowed my eyes at him.

The corners of his mouth curled as he pulled out two flashlights. "I'm taking you somewhere secret, someplace only meant for true Nexis members."

"Are you sure about this? Won't you get in major trouble?" I couldn't tear my eyes off his face.

Shanda cleared her throat and glanced up from her laptop. "He better be sure, because I just hacked your way in and fed the security cameras a thirty-minute loop. It's now or never."

Will's irises darkened as a shadow passed by his head, only to be choked out by a thousand diamond-white twinkles. A war waged somewhere deep inside this guy. I hoped to God the light would win.

"I don't want to keep secrets from you anymore." He froze, jaw twitching as his eyes darted to Shanda then landed on me. "I want you to know that I'm on your side. Not Nexis' or anybody else's. I'd choose you over this stupid society in a heartbeat, if you'll just give me half the chance."

I swallowed back the lump of fear bubbling up my throat. "Okay, Stanton, now's your chance to prove it."

"You sure you're ready for this?" The moon caught the gold flecks in his gray eyes, telling another story behind his words.

A parade of goosebumps stampeded up my arms. "Yes. I think I'm finally ready."

"You won't regret it, I promise." Those platinum eyes flashed at me.

With a gentle tug, he led me to the far corner of the room and tapped out a Morse-like code on a series of square stones. A familiar clanging of metal gears ticked behind the wall until a panel shifted back and a dark doorway loomed before us.

Uncanny. Just like the Guardian's secret passage I found last year. Without the Morse code.

"What is this, *another* hidden room?" I toed one boot through the crack, craning my neck through the dark opening.

"It's more than that. It's the secret Nexis chamber. You ready for our little adventure?" Flicking on the flashlight, he edged in front of me.

Tingles wracked my shoulders, and I tightened my leather jacket around me. Somewhere in the abyss, I glimpsed a tiny ray of light. White, yet glinting with color in every shade. The angel all-clear? After one final gulp, I nodded.

"I got your back, Lucy," Shanda called from somewhere behind me.

That was all the encouragement he needed. Flipping a switch, he ushered me into the spiraling stone corridor, now lit with electric work lamps.

"Do you come down here often?" I bit my lip, wondering what sort of horrors lay ahead of me. Luckily, the door behind us remained open. A small comfort.

"Not really, maybe a few times a year." He shook his head as he led the way down the rocky steps. "Students aren't allowed down here unless it's for something important like an induction or a grand council meeting. Sometimes you can get special permission for research purposes."

"Research? So you have a library down here?" I sniffed the musty air that smelled more like dank limestone than old books.

"Of course," Will scoffed, pausing to turn around a look at me. "Nexis dates back tens of thousands of years. We're just not arrogant enough to hide it in plain sight like the Guardians."

"I never thought about it like that." I traced my fingers along the dusty block-stone wall.

The Guardians weren't as noble and infallible as I'd always thought. After all, they'd thrown me to the wolves. Colleen, too, for that matter. Did that make Nexis nobler than I assumed? The mere idea made me shiver, and I raced to catch up to Will.

Then I stumbled, scraping my hand on the stone wall. But the rock beneath my fingertips was etched with something.

"Hey, look what I found." Shining my flashlight on the wall, I rubbed away layers of dust and grime. "What's this?"

He stood one step below me, making our faces almost even. "Just some old pictographs to remind us of our history. Carved by the early settlers who established this Nexis sect."

I gasped, unable to believe the scene before me. Carved into the stone was a depiction of what looked like the Salem witch trials. A girl, her hands and long skirts tied to a post, engulfed in flames. A look of pure horror on her face.

When I blinked, I was back there with her. Flames licking at her feet. A tortured look on her face. A crowd of angry onlookers, standing there. Doing nothing.

In an instant I stepped back into reality, landing in Will's arms.

"It's just like the—" I clamped my lips together. Too late.

"Just like what, Lucy?" He spun me around to face him.

I glanced away.

"The Guardians found something like this too, didn't they?" He tilted my chin up, staring into my eyes. "I wish you would just trust me."

My insides caught fire as if I could bust open with a million fireflies any minute.

"Trust isn't easy for me anymore." I ran my hand along his smooth cheek with the barest hint of stubble. "But the truth is, I want to trust you."

"I know." He nuzzled into my hand. "That's why you're here, following me on this crazy whim. Right?"

"Yes. We found a secret passage last semester." I finally admitted, gnawing on my lip. "I heard the Watchers have some sort of underground lair, too. Why do all of the Three Societies have secret underground bases?"

"To keep their secrets," he whispered in the silent cavern. "But I don't want to keep secrets from you anymore."

"You don't?" I squeaked out, but something inside me melted at his tone. And at that look in his eyes.

He gulped, eyes roaming my face. "I'm sure it's completely obvious how I feel about you. I want my secrets to be *our* secrets."

"Oh, O… kay." My pulse quickened as I exhaled a shaky breath and slid my hand into his. Tingles zigzagged up my arm, but I let him lead me deeper and deeper down the stone stairs.

CHAPTER 19

We halted at the bottom landing with a stone arch over a weathered wooden door. From his jeans pocket, Will pulled out an ancient skeleton key, not unlike the one Harlixton gave me many moons ago. The door opened in a series of creaks and groans. He nudged me into another dark cavern and led me into the center of the room.

I hovered next to a shadowy statue in the middle of what used to be a fountain.

"Wait right there, and close your eyes." He scurried off into the black recesses.

"If you say so." I rocked back and forth in my boots and examined the marble sculpture in the center of the dry fountain. A perfectly chiseled man lip-locked in an embrace with a Grecian woman in a long, flowing toga. Except the man had wings jutting half-furled from his back. An angel.

Was this how the Nephilim were made? I shuddered at the thought, shutting my eyes tight as the hint of a breeze wafted in.

Something clicked, echoing in the dark cavern. The blackness behind my eyelids lightened a few shades. Footsteps. Then Will stood beside me again. Holding my hand.

"Ready for your surprise? Open your eyes."

Slowly I lifted my lids. An eerie, yet beautiful sight greeted me.

"Wow. There are no words." I stood in the middle of a stone courtyard, under a domed ceiling twenty feet above. Gothic archways with lichen-covered pillars flanked the room on all sides. Old-fashioned gas lights, now electrified, illuminated the walls beside each pillar. One story above the archways, an intricately carved terrace overlooked the strange subterranean courtyard.

"So this is the Nexis Chamber." I scanned the walls for any hint of a hidden doorway. Could the Guardians ever find this from their secret passage?

"Welcome to the New York Nexis headquarters. Right now you're standing in the Nexis Chamber, where the induction ceremonies are conducted. Through that doorway is the Hall of Semigods, the meeting place for all Nexis Grand Councils. That passage leads to the library, the one behind you to the training rooms. The one on the left is the Repository."

"Sounds ominous. Is it the city headquarters or for the entire state?" A chill shivered down my spine even though the musty air was still. The idea of an entire state of Nexis bullies gathering here didn't sit well.

His hand slid around my waist. "This is the headquarters for Montrose alumni. There are these kinds of hidden, underground gathering places all over the world. For all of the Three Societies."

"Oh." My mind went fuzzy at his touch. "What exactly is a Repository, anyway?"

"It's the reason I brought you here, actually." Shadows enveloped the planes of his face as he turned toward the dark opening on the left.

With his hand on the small of my back, he led me into a dimly lit room with eight-foot-tall bookcases.

"What is all of this?" I gaped at the dark towers that were lined up in neat little rows in front of me.

Will flicked on the light, revealing the towers weren't bookcases after all. Eight-foot tall file cabinets surrounded us like mini-skyscrapers, their labels yellowed with age.

"Just records, mainly. Ancestral lineages, recruitment files, meeting summaries. That sort of thing." He pulled out a chair in front of a splintering old table and motioned for me to sit down.

Will sat on my right, jiggling his leg and refusing to look at me. "I brought you down here to prove to you that I'm on your side."

"What do you mean?" I angled my chair toward him, furrowing my forehead.

Scraping his chair back, he shot up and strode to a file tower, yanking on the drawer so hard it groaned and squeaked. He pulled out two green file folders and plopped them down in front of me.

"Do you remember the day we met last semester?" Perching on the edge of the chair, he took my hands in his, staring down at them.

"Of course." A smile tugged my lips upward, both at the memory and the way his fingers traced curlicues across my hands. "You gave me some ridiculous Nexis flyer and expected me to swoon over you."

"I don't know about the swooning part." His mouth curved and he licked his lips. "But the truth is, my parents made me invite you to that meeting."

I sucked in a breath, afraid to breathe until he finished his confession. Every muscle in my body stiffened.

"You were my Nexis-mandated mission. To get close to you. To win you over, by whatever means necessary." His shoulders slumped as he finally glanced up at me. "I'm ashamed to admit that I took the mission. Sometimes I don't even blame you for preferring Bryan at first."

I gasped, a sound the reverberated in the cavernous space.

"Here." He thrust the file forward. "It's all right here, in the Grand Council minutes."

"I, I don't know what to say." I reached for the file, tore it open, and scanned the pages until I spotted my name. It gave a full account of exactly what he had just admitted as decreed by the Nexis Grand Council. My hand flew to my mouth.

"You didn't …" I whispered.

"I did. The fact that you were James' sister only made it worse. Your brother and I were friends, and I knew what'd happened to him." A sadness washed over his face, and he hung his head. "When you came to that first meeting last year completely clueless about your own destiny, I knew I couldn't let you fall into Nexis hands. So I marched into the Nexis Grand Council and told them I wouldn't do it. I told them you deserved to make up your own mind."

Anger simmered in my gut. My fingers curled into a fist at my side. "No way. Prove it."

Sitting back, I crossed my arms over my chest and stared him down. Waiting for him to make the next move.

"I thought you'd say that." He reached for the other file and flipped to the back. "Here it is, August 31st."

"But that was the very next day." I bit my lip, reading the file. Afraid to look up at him. "But why?"

With a sharp inhale he sat up straight, scrubbing the golden scruff on his jaw. "Because I had feelings for you. Even then. And I don't want to start any kind of relationship with lies. You deserve to know the truth."

"I…uh…" My heart raced. I blinked and rubbed my eyes, but the words on the page didn't change. He was telling the truth. The file said he'd resigned from the mission the night after he'd shown me the pictures of James in the observatory tower. Nexis even gave him some kind of demerit for failing a mission.

The world tilted on its axis as the entire semester last year played through my mind. I let the file fall to the table in a spray of fluttering paper. Will wasn't the leper I thought he was. All these months he'd had feelings for me, ever since he'd met me. And I'd treated him like the plague.

"Ever since you waltzed into that campus orientation fair back in August, I've wanted to be with you." He grabbed my hand and squeezed. "I'm just hoping you want to be with me."

That was it. He'd just named that feeling swirling around in the pit of my stomach.

I wanted him.

I'd wanted him back in August, but Bryan and the Guardians had scared me away. Fireflies swirled in my gut as emotions I'd thought I'd buried began to blossom with new life. He was right in front of me the whole time, fighting for me behind the scenes. And it only made me want him more.

I finally summoned enough courage to glance up and my heart stuttered. He stared at me, eyes hungry. And I knew exactly what he wanted, too.

Edging closer, his face millimeters from mine, he paused there. Licked his lips. Waiting for me to make the final move.

If I kissed him like I wanted to, he would see the truth, just like Bryan had. What would he do, once he knew I was the Seer— that my gifts were already working, ready to use? Only one way to find out.

Closing the gap, I pressed my lips into his. A muffled gasp gurgled at the back of his throat like he wasn't expecting my surge of boldness. Or maybe it was the visions he had to be seeing by now. But he didn't pull away. Instead, he wrapped one arm around my waist, pulling me in closer. The other hand wove its way into my hair, tangling between the strands.

My toes curled. Man, this boy knew how to kiss. I sank into his arms and let his mouth devour mine.

Slowly, images emerged in the darkness behind my eyelids

A vision of the two of us, flying with my angel. Soaring above the earth. Riding a giant eagle of light. Into the stars, the globe a glittering blue dot below us.

The image faded. I couldn't breathe, couldn't think. How could this be happening? Were there two Seers?

"I knew it," he whispered against my mouth. "I knew you were the Seer."

Questions tumbled out of my mouth, even as I tried to catch my breath. "So you have visions, too? What does this mean? You're not another Seer, are you?"

"No. The truth is, I don't have visions. Not like you do. They're dreams, actually." His face lit up, cheeks dimpling as he cupped my face in his hands. "What did you see, Seer girl?"

"Us riding on my angel's back, flying around the world. Above it, too." I was alight and alive with energy, ready to reach out and kiss him again.

"You saw that? How embarrassing." He gnawed on his thumbnail, cheeks suddenly a pink hue I'd never seen on him before. "I've had that dream ever since I first saw you three years ago at your brother's graduation."

"Oooooooh, right. How could I forget I met you at James' graduation?" I whispered as goosebumps broke out all over my body. All the light faded from the room as the memory flooded back in a flash.

I was an awkward eighth-grader staring up at a golden-haired Adonis. My brother had just graduated, and we were out on the chapel lawn waiting to take pictures or something. Then Mom introduced me to the Stanton boy, and all hell broke loose. Literally.

As soon as I touched Will's hand, time slowed down. Or stopped entirely. The world spun like a merry-go-round. Then everything turned black. Morphed back into the dream I'd had the night before my brother's graduation. I'd seen this guy before. Will was dressed in black and standing next to James in St. Lucy's church library in Harlem. Their heads were hunkered over an ancient book. Then James pointed at something and ripped out the pages. My heart clenched all over again. A red stone emerged from the book—a glowing ruby. Hisses of smoke and shadow coiled around it, forming chain-like links. James handed the book to Will.

Clunk. Shadows unhinged from my brother's back as the red-hot bauble passed to Will. James slumped over and heaved a huge sigh as if an unbearable burden had just lifted off his shoulders.

The ruby sparked as the darkness coiled up again, clamping its shadowy chain around Will's neck.

Whooosh. The red stone dimmed, the blackness faded. The underground lair full of file cabinets and reality returned.

I gripped Will's hand like a lifeline. "Did you see that too?" I croaked.

A smile played across his lips. "You finally remember the first day we met. How could you forget *that*?"

I sniffed and glanced away. "James disappeared the next day. It was so heartbreaking for me, at that age that I completely blocked out all of those memories."

"That's right. I'm such an idiot. I'm so sorry, Lucy." He pulled me to my feet and wrapped his arms tight around me.

I hugged him back, willing myself not to fall apart in his arms. This wasn't a time for tears. It was time for answers. I'd just found someone else who had visions like me. And it was a major relief.

Pulling back, I peered up at him through my lashes. "How is it that you can see my visions? And I can see your *dreams* or whatever you call them?"

"You're the Seer, so that's how you can see my dreams." He held me at arm's length, specks of flickering light dancing in his eyes. "But truthfully, I didn't know I could see your visions until I kissed you. And we were holding hands when you had that last one."

"Bu—but this isn't the first time we've kissed." I stammered, my mind flying back to our Dr. Pepper kiss in my dorm's kitchen.

He cupped my cheek with one hand as his lit-up eyes landed on me. "That was for like, two seconds and you pulled away the moment I started to see anything."

"What?" I gasped, my jaw dropping to my collarbone. "You saw that?" Hot and cold shivers clawed at every inch of exposed flesh. I curled in on myself, my face flaming.

"No, tiger. I didn't see anything. That's what I'm trying to tell you." He ran both hands up and down my arms, as if he knew exactly what I was feeling. "You can tell me about it if you want to know what it means. But you don't have to."

My body flushed with adrenaline as a new realization hit me. "You mean you can interpret my visions? Does that mean you're the Interpreter?" My mouth fell open and I touched my bottom lip, because I already knew the answer deep down in my gut.

"How'd you know without me telling you?" His eyebrow quirked into that familiar V-shape, his smile returning in a flash. "You really are the Seer, aren't you?"

Heat radiated through my chest. "I can't believe this! It's so amazing." I wrapped my arms around him and squeezed him tight, feeling light for the first time in forever. Running my hands up the muscles of his back, I pressed my body close and peered up at him.

He gazed down at me with those same hungry eyes he had before. Suddenly his lips were on mine again, his hand cupping my jaw and tilting my head back to deepen the kiss. With my tongue, I explored his mouth, familiarizing myself with the spicy taste of cinnamon.

The instant I closed my eyes, the vision I saw of his dream came rushing back. This time when we flew around the globe on my angel's back, Angel's white light prismed with glints of rainbow shards and the blue of the world brightened in flashes as we flew closer and closer.

With a gasp, I tore myself away from his lips. "What does this flying around the globe dream mean, exactly?"

"You're so cute when you're trying to figure me out." He caressed the furrowed lines on my forehead with his thumb. "I think it means that someday we'll be traveling the world together. In my dreams, I always thought we were flying on an eagle. It wasn't until I kissed you that I realized that's your angel. And it changes things. Now I think it means we'll be traveling the world on some kind of mission."

"Whoa, that's heavy." I rocked back on my heels, my hands hanging loosely from his hips. It just felt good to finally be able to touch him like part of me wanted to for so long. "But you saw something, too. Didn't you, Interpreter boy?"

Growling under his breath, he rested his forehead on mine. "You have no idea what you do to me when you get sassy like that."

Heat unfurled inside, but I took a step back, letting a few feet of air cool us down. "You're not getting off this that easily. C'mon. Spill."

"You're too much." He inhaled a deep breath and ran a hand down his face. "I saw a vision of St. Lucia calling out to you. There's more to her story. She wants you to finish what she started so many centuries ago. It was her fault that Nexis discovered the existence of the Seer—and all of the secret societies by association. She was the first Seer to kiss a member of another society. Before that, Nexis and the Watchers had no idea of her existence. The Guardians were the Seer's protectors. After that discovery, all three societies clamored for her allegiance. And the war for the Seer began."

"Whoa, this is a big deal, isn't it? You're more than an interpreter. We're meant to be together, to work as a team. Aren't we?" I stared into the depths of his silvery eyes. How had I never seen the truth until this very moment?

"I've always been drawn you. Now I know why. My gift only works with yours. But you're right. It's more than that." He stared back at me with more emotion than I was ready to name.

"More?" I practically choked on the word.

He slid his hand behind my neck, pulling me closer. "We were meant to be together."

"Meant to be?" The words faltered as they fell from my lips. Those three words rattled my bones. Part of me wanted to object, or at least run screaming from the room. Instead, I stood still, waiting for him to respond.

His eyes searched mine with a new intensity. "There are all kinds of ways we can work together. As friends. As Chosen Ones in a partnership. The choice is yours. But I'd love the chance to be with you. In any capacity."

My jaw dropped at his gut-wrenching honesty. Locking my gaze on his, I grabbed a fistful of his shirt and planted another kiss on those warm lips.

Another growl slipped from his mouth as it smashed into mine. Harder, fiercer this time. His fingers curled through my hair, tugging on it to expose my neck. His lips landed soft kisses down my neck, leaving wet prints that made me tingle all over. Then his hands moved to cradle my head as he devoured my mouth once again. Closing my eyes, I got lost in his kiss. The spicy taste of his mouth on mine. The warmth of his breath on my face.

In a flash, the blackness dissolved into a new kind of vision. Transporting me into his head. A montage of moments played out in front of me. Intoxicating, and completely unnerving.

A younger me appeared, walking with James to his graduation. Will glanced over his shoulder at me from across campus, breath hitching in his throat. Then that night in the kitchen flashed in my mind. The exact moment I pulled away from our first kiss. A mixture of embarrassment and sadness pooled in him, and I felt every bit of it. The images flashed faster now. Me running from him so many times. Under the maple tree. After the initiation. At open dorms. Maybe he didn't show it, acted all cavalier. But inside, he was crushed. I felt the weight of it like a heavy yoke around my neck.

"Why didn't you tell me how much I hurt you?" I mumbled against his cheek.

"I didn't want to scare you, my skittish little Seer." He kissed one eyelid, then the other. "When I tried to force you to notice me, I thought you couldn't stand two seconds of kissing me in that kitchen. Now I understand."

"You saw my vision of Jake and Becca, didn't you?" Heat crawled to my cheeks. Now it was my turn to be embarrassed. I tried to pull away, but he squeezed my biceps and held me close.

"I did. I'm sorry. Do you want to know what it meant?" He whispered, eyes searching mine.

Slowly, I bobbed my head and resisted the urge to wriggle out of his strong arms.

His lips twisted as his face fell. "I think it was a warning. That Jake would come back. And I would be there to try and stop him."

My throat thickened as tears sprang to my eyes. "I feel so stupid. I wish I'd trusted you back then." My voice wobbled as I struggled to hold the tears at bay.

"Don't cry, gorgeous. You're not stupid, just cautious. We have all the time in the world to be together now." He brushed his lips against mine every-so-softly as if letting me decide the next move.

"I'd like that." I pressed a soft kiss against his mouth.

"I'll make you forget about anything else." He captured my mouth with his lips. Kissing me softly at first, then wrapping me up in his arms. And I almost did forget. Almost.

CHAPTER 20

Clusters of violets had sprung up in the cracks of the cobblestone sidewalk. How long had they been there, and I hadn't noticed? Such a colorful contrast to the gray skies of this late-March Monday. Today my heart was a Mylar balloon, floating above the bleakness of this gray world. Or a violet springing up out of nowhere—announcing to the world that changes were coming. Spring was almost here. A chance to begin again.

Students and teachers streamed by me, and I barely glanced up. Everything around me faded into a haze today as I trudged across the quad. Everything except the violets.

Somehow I made it to my Salinger Hall without remembering how I'd gotten there. I couldn't stop thinking about last night—that first kiss and the revelations that came with it. Will, the Interpreter. Could he really help me make sense of our visions? One question blared through my mind over and over again about those strange visions of him, of us. Was Will my destiny?

I shivered at the thought. We were both too young to think about destiny. Weren't we? How could I have a future with that guy? Or any guy, at almost-seventeen?

On the surface, it didn't make any sense. Yet somewhere in the recesses of my still-healing heart—it did. That's what scared me the most. Could I really be falling for Will? He definitely wasn't the guy I thought he was last year.

Stumbling through the crowded halls like a complete zombie, I finally made it to History of the Three Societies and took my usual seat in the middle of the mini-stadium.

Then my destiny waltzed through the door, walked down the stairs, and slid into the seat next to me. My heart pounded like crazy.

"Hey, gorgeous. Bet you forgot I was even in this class." He plopped his bag down and eased into the chair next to me.

"Yeah, kinda." I rubbed my eyes, adjusting to the strange new reality at my side. "What're you, a mind reader now?"

"Not exactly. You had this really cute, confused look on your face." Leaning over on his elbow, he tweaked my nose. "Too much?"

"Maybe a little." I scrunched my forehead at him.

Mr. Harlixton waddled down the stairs, and the loiterers in the back found their seats. He shuffled some papers at his desk, and bits and snatches of conversation resumed.

"Then this will really be too much for you." With less-than-subtle precision, Will slid his hand over mine. "Especially if you don't want the *you-know-who's* to know about the fact that you kissed me last night."

"Hey, you kissed me too, you know." I turned toward him, careful not to dislodge his hand. Something like a tiny lizard crawled up my arm. I shivered.

"Oh, I was there." A small smile rippled across his lips. "I just wasn't sure if you'd want the whole world to know."

Thirty students all grew silent. Just to watch us. Correction, they were openly staring and whispering behind their hands—even pointing. I shrugged it off. Let them gawk and gossip all they wanted. They couldn't touch me. Not anymore. No one else got a say in exactly when I could move on. That decision was all mine to make.

"Maybe I don't care what people think anymore."

Somehow, his magnetic charm had sucked me in. I kinda liked the warmth of his hand, even though it completely outed us to the entire Montrose Paranormal Academy rumor mill.

"That's good to hear." His eyes danced from my mouth to my face and back again.

Heat seared up my spine, pulling me closer to him.

"Excuse me, people." Mr. Harlixton cleared his throat, eyes narrowing ever-so-slightly in our direction. "Let's get started."

Thrusting my hand into my bag, I yanked out a notebook and banged it on the desk. Mr. Harlixton launched into a story about some ancient war, and I finally removed my hand from Will's. It felt cold and stiff as I tried to write coherent notes. I'd be lucky if I could ever decipher this chicken scratch.

My phone buzzed in my pocket, but I kept writing. Two seconds later Will nudged my elbow, jerking his head to the left. Great, he was texting me in class? No way could I focus now.

I pulled out my cell and opened his message. *Let's get together tonight. Got something to show you.*

Like the stealth spy I always knew I could be, I slid my phone under the desk and punched out a reply. *How can a girl say no to that?*

When he glanced at his phone, his face lit up.

Pick you up at 6? came his reply.

Okay, I typed back. As soon as I hit send, a shadow fell over me, and the whole room went quiet.

"Miss McAllen." Mr. Harlixton stood in the aisle next to us, voice booming. He held out his hand. "I'll take that. You can have it back after class. Needless to say, I'm very disappointed in you."

With stiff, robotic movements, I handed my cell over like a scolded toddler.

Will nudged my foot with his sneaker toe, and it actually helped a little bit. I gave up trying to write notes, hoping I'd learn through osmosis today. But it only made class drag on forever.

As soon as class ended, I bolted down the stairs, ready to retrieve my phone.

"Lucy, a word please." Harlixton handed my phone back.

I slipped it in my pocket, shoulders slumping down with it.

He waited until most of the students left, lowering his voice. "I don't think you should be meeting this boy alone. It's too dangerous."

I narrowed my eyes right back at him. "I'm only doing what I was told." Take that, Guardian-lover.

"I don't think that's what you're doing." He stared down his nose at me. "I think you're doing whatever you want to do. Which means you're just falling into his trap. Into their trap."

"You know what, you're right. I am doing what I want for once." I gritted my teeth together as fury simmered just below the surface. "I'm not letting some group, any group, tell me what to do anymore. And it feels pretty good. Besides, what do you, or any of the Guardians, care? You chose not to protect me. So I'm protecting myself."

With that, I spun on my heel and booked it up the stairs. Far away from the Guardian who hung me out to dry, then tried to judge me for making my own choices. Fire seared across my cheeks. Harlixton had lost his right to tell me what to do—along with Bryan and the rest of the Guardians.

"Hey, you okay, Lucy?" Will stood in the doorway and grabbed my hand. "What'd he say to you?"

I rolled my eyes, clenching my fingers in his grip. "Same old, this-guy-is-dangerous routine. It's getting old."

"Forget about him." Will laced his fingers through mine and gave my hand a reassuring squeeze. "You've got something to look forward to."

"What's that?" I asked as we walked hand-in-hand up the marble staircase to Biology.

"We've got a date tonight." His mouth curled up in that subtle way of his.

"A date? Is that what it is? I thought you were just going to show me something." At the top of the steps, I twirled around to look at him. I could look at this boy all day. Streaks of sunlight glinted from the arched windows, giving his chiseled cheekbones a golden glow to match that artfully mussed sandy hair.

"Technically, it's our first date." The way his eyes crinkled at the edges as he studied my face made my heart feel lighter than it had in weeks, maybe even months.

"Our first date. That *is* something to look forward to." Gnawing on my lip, I rocked back on my heels, unwilling to go to class just yet. "Hey, wait a minute. How'd you know I have class on the second floor now?"

He shrugged like Mr. Oh-so-cool Guy and kept walking, tugging me down the hall with him.

I lingered in the doorway, my fingers toying with his strong hands.

"Don't worry, you won't have to miss me for too long. I'll be right here when you're done." A smile danced in his eyes. He gave my fingers another squeeze and walked down the hall to his next class.

Somehow I found a seat in Biology, now in even more of a daze.

Did I just agree to go on a date with Will? A new tingle zapped my spine, sizzling into my toes. The scary part—I couldn't wait for my first real date with him.

><

True to his word, Will met me right outside of Bio and walked me to lunch. He even sat us at a different Nexis table with Julia, the Madisons, and that guy from Shanda's party they were all fighting over. Will slung his arm across my chair and I didn't even care what anyone thought. It felt good to have a drama-free lunch and make a few new friends.

"You ready to face the music?" Will laced his fingers through mine and led me out the door onto the quad. Rays of sunlight peeked through gray clouds as we walked hand-in-hand back to Salinger.

Heads turned our way. People gave us strange looks, but it didn't affect me like it used to. Their whispered comments just bounced right off me. I was about to turn seventeen. I knew what I was doing, and they could just butt out.

Will stopped, right before the front steps, and turned to me. "Are you sure you want to do this, being seen publicly with me, Guardian enemy numero uno?" Lines etched into his forehead as he stared down at me.

My heart clenched at the look on his face. "If I didn't want to be with you, I wouldn't have let it get this far."

The lines tightened, his eyes crinkling. "You really want to be with me?"

My insides flip-flopped, but my answer remained the same. "I want to try."

The lines in his forehead relaxed as his mouth curled. "Good. Then, I'll walk you to French."

"Thanks." I leaned into him as he rubbed my shoulders. "I might just get spoiled with all this attention."

"You'll just have to adjust, tiger." He squeezed my hand, and we climbed up the stairs together. In one fluid motion, he opened the door for me and pulled me closer into his side.

A hush fell over the marble foyer as all the students turned to stare at our entrance. I huddled closer to Will and kept walking. The teenage crowd resumed their chatter, gossiping about Montrose Paranormal Academy's newest couple.

I spotted Bryan lurking not ten feet away, hawking us from behind a bank of lockers. He jerked his head to the left like he wanted me to follow him. Then he disappeared into the empty art studio before Will saw him.

I stopped in front of the ladies' room. "I'm just going to fix my makeup. Meet you after class."

"I'll be waiting." He leaned in and whispered, "But you don't need to. You always look gorgeous." Then he gave me a quick peck on the mouth.

I curled my lips at him. "And that's why I need to reapply."

He shot his hands up, all mock innocence. "Oh no, your boyfriend likes to kiss you. Call the cops."

"Boyfriend?" I quirked my mouth at the major bomb he'd just dropped.

Running his fingers down my arms, he took both my hands in his, face full of light. "Maybe it's not the greatest timing in the world, but it's how I feel. How I've felt for a long time. I understand if it's too soon for you or you're not ready. But I am. And I can't keep it in anymore."

"Well, okay then." I stared down at our hands, entwined together. Hadn't I once thought Bryan's hands fit so perfectly in mine? Yet in a way, this felt right, too. I couldn't explain why, but in some ways being with Will felt more freeing than one moment with Bryan. And I didn't know how to make sense of that just yet. "We'll talk about it. I'm open for discussion."

"Excellent." His smile broadened, sparking the gold flecks in his gray eyes and deepening that adorable chin cleft. "I can handle that. See you in an hour."

I watched him walk down the hall, then ducked into the bathroom. After a quick touch-up, the bell rang. I poked my head out of the bathroom to find the hallway completely empty. Still, I felt the need to tiptoe all the way to the studio.

When I opened the door, I found Bryan pacing back and forth in the dark room.

"What is he, your boyfriend now?" His practically growled like Mufasa.

"Were you spying on us or something?" I shot a glare at him, stopping dead in my tracks, heart pounding.

He tried to shrug it off, but weird gray shadows swirled around him. Streaks of light clashed with the dark shadows as a battle waged around him.

"Bryan, this has got to stop. Do you have any idea what you're doing to yourself?" I gasped, slapping my hand over my mouth.

He marched up to me and stood an arms' length away. "Why, what do you see?"

I blinked, but the vision remained. "It's not good. It's like you're all mixed up."

"Tell me something I don't know." He stared at me for the longest time. "I just can't get you out of my head. Sometimes I wish I'd never fallen for you. It's too hard."

"You made your choice." I ground my teeth together, clamping my hands to my hips. "Did you really think I'd be a good little spy and get all the dirt on Nexis without hurting anyone? It's a dangerous game you're playing, messing with people at the whim of the Guardians. And I for one want no part of it."

"What's that supposed to mean?" He leaned in close. A little too close.

"It means I'm not your little spy." I backed up, fingers curling into my palms as remnants of old anger curdled in my stomach. "I can't pretend to like someone just because the Guardians told me to."

Bryan's face went white, his jaw slack. "So then you're actually into Will now? How did this happen?"

"You don't remember?" I raised my eyebrows at him, shaking my head. "You dumped me in front of the whole school. So you don't get to care about what happens next."

"But Lucy, I still care about you. Please tell me you know that." He stepped forward and reached out as if to rub my arms.

I flinched and pulled back. "I don't know that anymore, because you're my ex-boyfriend now."

He cringed, his face crumpling. "I thought we would find our way back to each other, at the end of this."

"What does that even mean, Bryan?" I practically choked on his name. "You broke my heart when you chose the Guardians over me. And now you're just gonna have to live with that choice.

Whether you like it or not." The contents of my stomach threatened to reappear. I knew just where to aim it too.

"I was afraid of that." He raked one hand through his now-almost-shaggy hair, mussing it beyond recognition. "Do you love him?"

I bit my lip, the anger seething into an electric ball in my middle. "Not that it's any of your business, but no. It's only been a two and a half months since we broke up." I wanted to add, *not yet*, but I couldn't be so cruel. Because I knew it would crush him.

"That's something at least." He exhaled the biggest sigh in the history of the world. "I heard you went to a Nexis meeting. Have you gotten any good intel yet?"

"That's what you're really after, isn't it?" I blinked. White-hot rage boiled over and I slapped my thighs. "I can't believe what a Guardian stooge you're being. Even now."

"Please, angel." Bryan narrowed his eyes into slits. "I'm no more a Guardian stooge than your new boyfriend. Will's a Nexis legacy. You better not forget that."

I leaned in, ready to let him have it, but all of a sudden my inner fury fizzled out. His words didn't burn me up like they used to. Sucking in a deep, calming breath, I took a step back. Wheels turned in my head as I analyzed the truth behind his words instead of reacting to the emotion first. Maybe I was finally getting over him.

"You're wrong about Will. Ever since I met him, Will has found little ways to break the Nexis rules for my benefit. He's not the monster you pretend he is." I bit off the next part about last night's revelation in the Nexis chamber. Some secrets were worth keeping.

"Don't tell me you're falling for their pack of lies. You're not going to join Nexis now, are you?" Bryan exhaled a hot breath.

"As opposed to your pack of lies? Please, I have no intention of joining Nexis." I crossed my arms over my chest and leveled my gaze at him. "I'm quite fed up with secret societies in general. They're kind of stupid and ridiculously demanding."

He actually rolled his eyes at me. "Demanding or not, we're helping people. And we're going to stop Nexis."

"Good, I hope you do." I couldn't look at him anymore, so I inched closer to the door. "But in the process, the Guardians are trying to exploit me. I'm sure Nexis wants to do the same. Well, I'm here to tell you I won't be exploited. By anyone, least of all you."

He stood there, mouth gaping, staring at me for five, ten, twenty heartbeats. "So where does that leave us?"

I shrugged. "I don't know. I guess we're at a stalemate."

"Funny." He puffed out one breath, then two. "I never thought we'd be here. Is there any way I could change your mind about me?"

He took two steps toward me, one finger grazed the back of my hand as if it were porcelain and would shatter any second.

Rearing back, I ran my hands through my hair, twisting and untwisting it. Bryan's eyes followed my every move. Silent. Waiting.

The idea was a tortoise, slowly crawling through my mind. My heart beat once, twice, then curdled into a stone that plummeted down my throat. Because I already knew what'd he say. But I had to ask anyway.

"Maybe if we just drop all this spying and go find my brother in Europe…" I trailed off, staring down at my little winter half-boots.

His fingertips grazed my cheek this time, sending goosebumps parading down my neck. "Angel girl, it's too dangerous. And we need the intel."

I shook my head, pulling away from his touch. "I have my answer. And I can't say I'm surprised." My stomach lurched as I recoiled from him.

He hung his head, rubbing his neck. "I'm sorry, Lucy. I don't know what to say. Maybe I should've done things differently."

"Maybe." As I stared at him, the shadows rolled in, toying with his feet. My heart sank like a lead balloon as I closed my eyes against the tortured look on his face. I knew exactly what I had to do. I had to squash whatever hope he had left. Right now. So he would let me go and one day find his own happiness.

I gulped back the lump in my throat. "All I know is I'm tired of fighting with you. I'm just done. It's really over."

"Don't say that." His voice shook as he turned those haunted blue eyes on me. "Maybe you'll feel differently when all of this blows over."

"I don't think so. Goodbye, Bryan." I turned and walked out of the room, not looking back. Not even for a second.

CHAPTER 21

Fireflies tickled my stomach as I rummaged through my closet, searching for the perfect outfit for my first date with Will. For the first time in months, I could finally admit the truth, even to myself. I liked Will. In fact, I really liked Will. Before the Guardians filled my head with lies about him, I'd always been drawn to him. Not just because he was the Interpreter and supposedly my destiny, but because he was genuine, sincere, and funny. Not to mention a bonafide hottie. Once I saw through the façade the Guardians erected, I knew I had to make my own choices and stop letting other people make them for me. Will was the first big choice I'd made since I decided to step out from under the Guardians' wing. And it felt good.

"Shanda, I need some help here." I burst out of my closet, throwing all my favorite date-night outfits on the bed in a heap.

"Where did he say he was taking you?" Shanda lugged out a giant bag of makeup. Dumping out the contents, she arranged it all on her desk, now a makeshift vanity.

"He didn't say. That's the problem. It's a surprise." I slid across the room in my slippers and plugged in my curling iron.

"Woo, I'm so jealous. You guys are at the beginning, where all the romance happens." She put her hands on my shoulders and forced me across the room. Plunking me into the desk chair, she dabbed on foundation like there was no tomorrow.

"Tony's not romantic, after only four months?" I asked, closing my eyes as she swept a base coat across my lids.

"I didn't say that."

When I opened my eyes, Shanda's lips quirked up in the barest hint of a smile.

"Aww, how cute is that?" The tingles were back, only this time for my friend.

She couldn't help but smile now. "Quiet, you. I'm working my magic here."

When she finally whirled me around to face the mirror, my heart skyrocketed through my chest.

"How in the world do you do it?" I gawked at my own reflection.

"What can I say? I have a gift, I guess." She nodded, grinning her most satisfied grin.

I looked casual but dressy all at the same time in a lacy halter with wisps of sparkle under a tailored jean jacket and a flowy black skirt with black tights. Not to mention some killer black boots—oh-so-classy, yet still somehow perfect for walking. She'd dolled up my eyes with smoky shadow and curled my long, dark hair perfectly.

"That you do. You're the best." I reached out to hug her.

"Not too tight, you'll tangle your beachy waves." She tried to wriggle out of my grasp.

"Then we'll call them messy curls, or something. The newest Shanda-inspired look." I hugged her anyway, even though I knew how much she hated PDA.

"Off you go." She herded me toward the door.

I stopped, hovering in the doorway. "Shanda, what do you think about this. Me dating Will?"

"Honestly?" She stared me down with intensity.

I knew she was trying to intimidate me. But I wouldn't back down. "Honestly."

After a few-too-many seconds of silence, she finally spoke. "I liked you and Bryan together. But after what he did, I have to admit I was wrong about him. So I'm not really sure anymore."

"I get that. It's all going very fast right now." I bit back the words that were bubbled up, afraid the truth might sound weird.

"Really? I don't believe that. You seem sure to me." Her eyes never left my face. It wasn't a challenge, more like she genuinely wanted to know.

"I am sure about Will," I whispered unable to hold it in anymore. Not from my bestie. "How can you tell?" I couldn't look away. I had to know her answer.

"Please, girl." Her eyebrows arched at me. "I know you. And I know you've been attracted to him for awhile. You were just scared to admit it."

"Seriously?" My jaw dropped, heart pounding like mad. "How long have you known?"

"You were so obvious." Her lips twitched.

"Apparently, everyone can see right through me." I slumped, curling in on myself.

"I don't know about that." She shook her head. "You just don't pretend things that aren't true. Instead, you try to hide them or bury your own desires if you don't think people will approve. I'm glad you've finally found someone who will put you first. You deserve that."

"Thanks. So do you." I grinned my freshly-glossed lips at my best friend in the world.

"I know. Tony's great about that." She smiled. A real, full smile. A rarity in the world of Shanda Jones.

I inched into the hallway. "Good. Now that we've got that covered, any last-minute tips?"

"Just be the girl we all know and love." She reached out and squeezed my hand. "The girl who wears her heart on her sleeve. Don't hide who you are or what you want anymore. Be yourself."

Tears wormed their way to my eyes. "You give the best advice. Thanks for that."

"You'll always have it. Now go on. It's almost eight. Have a great night." Her voice echoed down the empty hallway.

"You bet." I turned at the landing and waved, my heart lighter than it'd been in a long time. She had no idea how much her words meant to me. Tonight was going to be a good night. Maybe even the start of something truly magical.

><

Garish fluorescent lighting tinted the highlights of Will's sandy hair. Made it look a little greenish. Maybe that's just how I felt inside. The newness of a first date, combined with the rocking of the subway car, sent a rush of adrenaline surging through my limbs. Did he know the effect he had on me?

"Have I told you yet how incredible you look tonight?" Will edged closer to me on the subway bench.

"Maybe once or twice." I peeked over at him and let him take my hand, his warmth burning straight to my cheeks.

But his nearness wasn't the only thing burning through my brain. Memories popped into my head, unbidden, of the last time I rode the subway to the city—with Bryan. Holding onto the rail on the ride to Times Square. Running from the spies after a revealing round of elevator tag. I remembered all of it, but the emotion felt out of reach. Distant, even. Because things were different now. Bryan wasn't the saint I thought he was. And Will wasn't the bad boy with an agenda.

So I pushed away those thoughts. Focused all my attention on the guy next to me.

"Where are you taking me?" Out the window, the subway tunnel whizzed by in a dark blur, revealing nothing.

"You'll see. You're going to love it." The corners of his mouth twitched.

The car screeched to a stop. The signs outside read *Broadway Junction*. Will stood up, still holding my hand. My legs were shaking as I stood, so I gripped his hand tighter.

"Don't worry. I've got you." He led me into the press of people glomming up at the nearest door.

This must be everybody's stop. Together, we streamed out of the car with the rest of the crowd. Will held my hand tightly as we followed the pack until we reached a long corridor lined with stained-glass panels.

Then he slowed to a crawl, letting the other travelers work their way around us.

"It's breathtaking." I stared at the colorful windows, inhaling the beauty of each unique pane. Funny how it smelled like garbage with a hint of urine. "How did you know I love stained glass?"

"You're a girl. Of course you love stained glass."

I could hear the smirk in his voice. "Smart aleck." I turned and smacked him on the arm.

He grinned at that. We strolled on down the wide hallway, looking at each piece individually. Until the crowd dissipated and we were the only ones left in the subway station corridor.

That's when he picked up the pace a little. Then he stopped in front of one particular pane, a little dustier than the rest. With my fingertips, I reached out to clean off the beautiful stained glass tiles. I wiped my dirty fingers on his jacket.

"Hey, what do you think I am, your own personal napkin?" He flashed a great big smile at me. And it was contagious.

"I didn't want to ruin my outfit. You wouldn't want that, would you?" I turned my flirty pout on him.

"No, I guess not." He leaned in, slinging his arm around my waist.

"What's so special about this one?" I stared at the beautiful colored glass, snuggling closer into his side as fireflies did somersaults inside me.

"See if you can tell me that." He raised his eyebrows in that upside-down V.

I turned to inspect the stained-glass panel he seemed so intent on showing me. Each square of blue glass was accented with yellow rectangles, the colors a deep sapphire and gold. The pattern was intricate, yet I could make out distinct shapes. With my fingertip, I touched a square of yellow. Sparks singed my skin and the world around me faded to black, until only gold-tinged panes emerged from the blackness, forming the Nexis symbol.

Gasping, I stepped back. "It's marked with the Nexis symbol. Will, what is this place?" My words echoed down the empty hallway.

He cocked his head at me and grinned. "It's the Nexis Repository for all of New York City. Impressed?"

"Wow." I breathed, my fingers bumping the wrought iron crossbar. Electricity sizzled up my arm, freezing me in place. Again, the real world blacked out as the crossbars lit on fire before my very eyes—revealing a symbol I knew all too well. All the air still in my lungs. I couldn't believe what I was seeing. The Seer's symbol hovered in front of me, emblazoned in fire. Just like the red-hot branding iron Felicia's dad attacked me with last semester.

"Th—the Watchers." Words choked out, struggling to take slow and even breaths so I wouldn't hyperventilate. "Why is this place marked with the Seer's symbol?"

"What?" Now he stepped back and studied the pane, glancing up and down the empty subway hall.

"It's true." I held my wrist up to his face to prove it. The faint outline of the branding iron had left its mark.

His mouth drooped as he stared at the scar. Then he grabbed my wrist and planted a kiss on the marks. Tingles shivered up my arm.

Suddenly his jaw went slack as his eyes rolled in the back of his head. His body went rigid and he stopped breathing. Five seconds later, he keeled over, gasping for air. Is this what I looked like when I had a vision? At least he knew the truth now.

"I… uh … I had no idea." He stammered, his voice raspy. He held my wrist tightly in his hand as if he couldn't let go. "There are so many spies in the Three Societies."

I fought the urge to roll my eyes at the insanity. Instead, I ran my free hand through my now less-than-beachy waves. "Your Nexis friends broke into my room and Mr. Harlixton's office. Felicia was a double agent and her dad, the guy who tried to brand me, was probably the mastermind. My brother switched sides and stole intel. Believe me, I've seen firsthand how much betrayal is laced into the fabric of the Three Societies."

His face fell. "You're right. I don't know how it's possible, but the Nexis Repository may have fallen into to the Watcher Corps. These public repositories are unguarded, which is why I thought it'd be okay to come here."

Shivers crept down my spine. "So why did you bring me here?"

"I don't know if it's worth it now. If the Watchers have taken over, they might have planted their own surveillance. It's they're favorite thing to do, watch and wait. But I don't know what they'd do if we discovered some key piece of intel they wanted." His fingers traveled from my wrist to my hand, and he tugged me into his side, wrapping one arm around me.

"Just tell me what you're looking for and we'll decide together." The proximity to that broad chest, chiseled under his black jacket and collared shirt, made my mouth go dry.

His lips quirked into a half-smile as he stared down at me. "I have an idea about how to stop the reckonings. Some ancient writings on the subject were moved here a few years ago."

"Wow. I don't know what to say. You really want to stop the reckonings?" My heart jackhammered in my chest, and I wanted to melt into his arms. Did this guy really want to break into a Nexis sanctum to help me on our first date?

His silver eyes crinkled as a muscle in his jaw twitched. "I hated seeing you go through that. Even once." Wrapping his other arm around me, he pulled me into his chest and squeezed tight.

My breaths hiccupped in my chest as I scrunched up my face every which way to hold back the tears. I buried my face in his chest, a few stragglers dampening his shirt.

He just ran his hands down my hair, giving me all the time I needed.

Inhaling a deep breath, I let the past dissipate with my next exhale. "If that's why you brought me here, then I'm willing to take the risk." Even though my pulse sped up.

He eased me back, his eyes searching mine. "It could be dangerous if the repository is tainted by the Watchers. It may not be safe."

Gritting my teeth, I held his gaze. "So it's enter at your own risk?"

"I'm afraid so." He rubbed my arms, eyes trained on me. Waiting for the okay.

Clenching every muscle and planting my feet in fight stance, I bobbed my head at him. "Let's do it."

><

Adrenaline galloped through my veins. My hands were shaking as Will led me past the stained-glass tiles. Straight to a dirty old utility closet.

"You've got to be kidding me? This is it?" I asked.

His eyes did a little dance. "Not exactly."

Pulling me into the pitch-black room, his cell phone lit the path through a maze of storage shelves. Bleach and disinfectant soured the musty air. I held my free hand to my face to block out the harsh fumes. Then he stopped in the back corner of the room.

"Here we are." Click. He popped open a dusty electrical panel, flipping a few breaker switches in sequence. A pattern I recognized.

Swoosh, a panel slid out of the wall. Creaking and clanging on what must be a really old gearshift.

"Just like the Nexis Chamber." I gaped at his back.

"Exactly." A glimmer of a smile wavered in his bluish cell phone light. As he stepped through the opening, a wash of orange colored one side of his face.

I followed him through the new door, and my heart sank. Another spiral staircase, several stories deep, lined with fluorescent amber torches.

"Don't tell me you're afraid of heights." He gripped my hand, sliding one arm around my waist.

"Just ridiculous hundred-year-old staircases." Something fluttered in my stomach. It wasn't just the rickety stairs.

As if on cue, the wrought-iron squeaked as we descended. The roar of a subway thundered over our heads, then a blast of wind and dust pummeled into us. I clung to Will for dear life, suddenly glad he'd been presumptuous enough to hold me tight.

Finally we reached a stone archway one story below the subway platform. But my legs still wobbled.

He pulled out his trusty skeleton key and slid it into the ancient lock. Was this the same key he used to open the Nexis Chamber? I couldn't help but wonder how many skeleton keys were out there. And if the key that Colleen and Monica "allegedly" stole from my room would work on other secret Guardian locations I never even knew about. I shuddered at the thought.

Opening the heavy wooden door, Will ran ahead into the darkness. Within a few seconds, the lights buzzed on overhead.

"Here we are." He planted his feet in front of me and held out his arms, gesturing to the grand room.

Grand was an understatement. The room was cavernous, with stacks of dusty old bookshelves as far as my eyes could see.

"Whoa, you don't think this is a little much for a first date?" I cocked my head at him, eyes wide as the lights warmed up and revealed more and more old books.

His smile drooped. "You don't like it."

"You're kidding, right?" I struck a pose, flaring out my black skirt. "I love libraries and old books. I'm such a nerd like that. An over-dressed nerd, to be precise."

Taking two steps forward, he lowered his voice. "You're the hottest nerd I've ever met." His eyes ran all the way down to my boots.

I gulped as my cheeks caught fire. "Stop it." I punched him in the shoulder. "You brought me down here for a reason, didn't you?"

"Oh right, that." His eyebrows shot up as he cleared his throat. "We're going to do some research on your crazy insane reckonings. Then we'll move on to phase two. The actual date portion."

The corners of his mouth stretched up as he led me past a row of tables in the front of the cavern.

"Okay, I can get on board with that." I couldn't help but admire his sculpted backside strutting in front of me in dark jeans. "Not the worst first date ever."

"Really? What a relief." His tone was laced with sarcasm as he whirled around to face me. "Now you *have* to tell me. What was your worst first date?"

"You first, Stanton." I laughed, running ahead into the towering stacks of ancient books.

He raced after me, grabbing my hand and spinning me around. "Oh, no. You're not getting off that easy."

I batted my lashes at him. Then he leveled those unfathomable platinum eyes at me. Making my insides quake.

"Fine. You win." I lifted my hands in surrender. "It was the summer after eighth grade and this new kid asked me out. Derick something, I can't remember. He took me to a drive-in movie, except we were both fourteen. So his mom sat in the back seat. Then he spilled soda all over me, and we had to go home early."

Will tilted his head at me. "You still have drive-in movies in Indiana? How adorable."

"Shut up, you." I smacked his bicep. Bad idea. Electricity sparked through the air at that one simple touch.

He turned toward me, eyes flashing. "You better stop that, or I'm going to forget why we came here in the first place."

My heart flip-flopped in my chest. "Nice try. Now it's your turn, William Sweetcheeks Stanton."

He busted out laughing. "No way I'm telling you my middle name. I almost wish it was Sweetcheeks."

"It's either that or your first date story." I planted my hands on my hips and narrowed my eyes at him. "What's it gonna be, Stanton?"

"You sure you want to know?" He inched closer, eyes clouding over.

"I'm sure." I stared him down.

He took two steps closer, only inches away now. "That night we played Mafia and you flirted with Bryan right in front of me. And we almost kissed in the kitchen."

I could hear my own heartbeat now, thump, thumping, thumping in my ears. Will crept closer and leaned down, his breath warming my face. Lifting my chin, I froze. Waiting. His lips pressed into my forehead. Then he took two steps back.

"You sure do know how to torture a guy." His lips twitched at me like he knew he'd just won a small victory.

Tell that to my poor little heart, beating a mile a minute.

With that he walked on down the aisle, shoulders bobbing like he was trying not to laugh. Then he turned a corner and disappeared out of sight.

With a growl, I raced after him and caught up with him two aisles over. "Hey, that's not fair. That Mafia thing was definitely *not* a date." I glared at him as he pulled out one book after another, not looking at me.

"Maybe not." He scanned book titles with his index finger. "But I asked you out and you avoided me all week. So the only reason I came to that stupid dorm party was for you." With that he dropped two enormous, dusty leather books in my arms and sauntered down the aisle.

I rocked back on my heels, trying to regain my balance, and followed him down the row. "Not so fast. You're the one who asked if I was engaged. In front of everybody. Remember?"

"Yeah, that was a little over the line. But it got your attention." He still had his back turned, but I could hear the smile in his voice.

"Grrr. You're so frustrating." I rammed a ginormous old book into his back.

"Right back atcha, nerd." He turned and added two more books to the stack in arms. Then he strutted off again.

My arms turned to jelly and I stumbled on a loose stone in the floor. The top book dislodged and skidded across the tile.

"A little help here, Sweetcheeks," I called after him. If only he knew exactly what I was referring to. My cheeks sizzled.

Finally, he turned around, his lips twitching. "You know, you make it nearly impossible to stay mad at you." He picked the stray book up off the floor and shuffled back to me.

"You were mad at me?" I jutted out my lip and fluttered my best pouty-eyes up at him. Time for a taste of his own medicine.

"You better believe it. But that was six months ago. And trust me, you're worth the wait." He towered over me now.

Then he leaned down, right where I wanted him. As soon as he got close enough, I dumped all of my books in his arms and took off running down the aisle.

"You little ..." His voice faded out behind me as I ran back toward the tables. Laughing until my sides hurt.

Racing out of the stacks, I slowed my pace and leaned on the first table. Breathing hard. I didn't expect to hear footsteps behind me so soon. But he emerged from the stacks, a grin plastered across the planes of his face. Biceps bulging with the weight of four heavy books. In two strides, he plunked them on the table behind me.

First one arm, then the other, planted on either side of me. Pinning me up against the table.

I gulped, eye-level with his collarbone.

He tilted my chin up, wrapping the other arm around my waist. "It's Wadsworth, not Sweetcheeks. Now you can stop being so irresistible."

A bubble of laughter rose in my throat as he leaned in, smashing his mouth into my lips. I couldn't catch my breath, yet I kissed him anyway. He could be pretty irresistible, too.

"You sure know how to make a girl swoon, Wadsworth." My voice came out breathy.

He hung his head, touching his forehead to mine. "I knew I should've never told you my middle name. You're just gonna distract me all night, aren't you?"

"Don't worry. It's our little secret." I wrapped my arms around his neck and pulled him in for another kiss.

CHAPTER 22

Words blurred together on yellowed parchment till all I could see was a giant blob. I blinked and rubbed my eyes, but it didn't help. Nothing in these ancient Nexis books made any sense. I scraped my chair back. The sound echoed in the subterranean Repository.

"This is hopeless." I stretched my arms back to work out the kink that'd formed in my neck over the past two hours. My hands were all dusty. I almost wiped them on my skirt but thought better of it.

"Not quite the jackpot of Seer information I was hoping for." Will leaned over my shoulder, squinting at the book in front of me.

"Not quite." Narrowing my eyes at him, I turned and wiped my grubby hands all over his jacket. "Take that!"

"Hey, what was that for?" He reared back, but the corners of his mouth lifted.

"Just a little payback for this dungeon date." I glared over my shoulder at him. Would he tell me the truth if I asked? "What exactly do you think will stop the reckonings?"

Scraping his chair back, he angled toward me with those haunting gray eyes. "I think I remember some information in the Nexis Seer book. But first, we need to learn its whereabouts."

"What?" I shouted. It echoed throughout the underground lair. Lowering my voice, I said, "Won't that put a huge target on our backs?"

Slowly, he nodded. "I'm afraid so. But it'll be worth it to stop the reckonings, and we'd have some intel to trade if necessary. Exactly like your brother taught me."

My brother. His words smacked me straight in the gut, yet seemed so familiar. The implications bombarded my brain, leaving my mind reeling.

Focus, Lucy. Focus. You have a job to do. And a date to get to, I told myself.

"Great. Let's find this bad boy." Reaching one hand out, I moved to flip the page.

Suddenly Will's hand landed on mine. "Wait. I've seen this before."

His touch sparked the back of my hand, making all the hairs on my arm perk up. Then the room faded away in a sea of blackness.

Remnants of a dream floated back into my brain. And suddenly, an old memory played out before my eyes. James pouring over an ancient book in St. Lucy's Church library. Will lurked in the background.

Suddenly the scene was replaced by a totally new one. A glowing red orb appeared in the darkness, just like that night in the field. Was this the Nexis Ruby? Shadows rolled in like clouds behind the ruby, swirling in long tendrils around the stone. The red and black cloud grew bigger and brighter in time to my ever-quickening heartbeats.

Somewhere far away, amid the shadows, a familiar voice reached my ears. *You know what you must do.* Was it James, or my angel?

I wobbled in my chair, tipping back. Strong arms caught me. Rough fingers brushed the hair off my cheeks. The dim lights and the musty smell of the Broadway Repository returned. My thoughts scattered in all directions as I scrambled to put the pieces of the puzzle together. Did my destiny involve the ruby?

"Lucy, are you okay?" Will's gruff voice brought me back to the present. "What was that?"

"I remember. That's why this seems so familiar." I blinked and rubbed my eyes, biting back the last part of my eerie vision. "You've done this before, with my brother. You were with James three years ago, when he ripped out a page in this ancient book."

His eyes scoured my face. "Wait a sec. You didn't just remember, did you?"

I shook my head and let the truth spill out. Part of it anyway. "The moment I touched the book, I saw my dream from eighth grade it all over again. Right now."

"Wow." His fingers toyed with my hair as he stared at me. "Do you have any idea what he was looking for?"

I gave him another headshake, careful not to dislodge his fingers from my hair. His touch soothed me as I tried to forget the glowing ruby. And what may lay ahead in my future.

Running his hands through my hair, Will's eyes glazed over. "James said he was looking for the Watcher's Sapphire so he could display his powers. But your brother was as bad a liar as you are."

"Hey," I punched him in the arm. "Is that the worst thing ever?"

A smile crept up his face. "Not if you're trying to hide the fact that you've liked a certain someone ever since you showed your pretty little face on campus."

Oh, my heart. I clutched my chest, willing my knees not to go weak. What was this boy doing to me?

"So the Watcher's Sapphire does what exactly?" I asked in a pathetic attempt to change the subject.

"Very cute." His mouth twitched like he knew exactly what I was up to. "Didn't anyone ever tell you about the sacred stones?"

Mashing my lips together, I shook my head. "I've mostly heard about the Guardian Amethyst, and that was from the Coopers at Christmas. They never got around to telling me about the other sacred stones."

"Figures," Will huffed, rolling his eyes. "The Guardians wanted you to know only certain things. The Watcher's Sapphire, when used correctly, allows everyone around it to see what the Seer sees."

"Whoa," I breathed, stumbling toward the nearest chair. "You mean everyone could see what I see? Angels, demons, the whole lot?"

"Yep." He nodded, smoothing out the pages of the book.

"You're right. James would never want the sapphire. He was a prankster, but never a show-off." My hands shook as I tucked my hair behind my ears, a terrible question blooming in my chest. But I had to ask, had to know. "So what does the ruby do?"

Will gulped, Adam's apple bobbing as he leveled his gaze at me. "As legend says, the Nexis Ruby, in the hands of the Seer, allows access between earth and the underworld—the depths of hell."

The world spun around me as I gripped the chair tighter. Now I definitely didn't want anything to do with the ruby. "That's all in the Nexis Seer book, isn't it?"

Ever-so-slowly, he nodded, reached for my hands, and squeezed. "If we can find what I'm looking for, we can turn the Guardian's plan against them. If we get this intel, we can both join the Guardians. Together."

He barely whispered the words, but they sank like lead into my heart.

I froze to my chair. I could barely move, let alone blink. "You really want to leave Nexis?"

"I know what they're planning to do with your gifts. And I can't let that happen." His jaw hardened into steel, except for a lone muscle twitch. "You see, they need the Seer, the Interpreter, and all three stones to open the gates of hades. And set their sick plan in place for a false utopia."

Ice crackled through my limbs. "What? That's their agenda?"

"I'm afraid so." Pushing the book aside, he grabbed my shoulders and looked me square in the eye. "That's why I stopped working for Nexis. And why I want to join the Guardians."

Something clicked into place like a missing puzzle piece. "Because you're the Interpreter. That's how they were going to control me."

He nodded. "After I gave up the mission to spy on you, I'm worried they know my true intentions. If so, they'll move to plan B. And so will I." Lightly, he brushed his lips to mine, then stopped.

Sccrrrclunck. A strange clanging noise echoed through the cavern, followed by what sounded like footsteps.

"What was that?" I arched back, bumping into his nose.

More footsteps. Voices filtered above us.

"Someone's coming." His eyes darted up and down the aisles as he dug around in his jacket pocket. Then he pulled out a strange plastic bar that lit up at his touch.

"What're you doing?" My eyes went wide. Was that a portable scanner like I'd seen in spy movies?

"Scanning these pages. They're obviously important enough to give you a vision." He started piling books in my arms with one hand, while scanning pages with the other. "There's no time now. Take the rest of these books and stick them back on the shelf. Whoever is up there can't figure out what we're doing here."

"Okay," I grunted, piling the mega-books in my arms. "You're right behind me, right?"

"Right." One quick head bob and he shoved me into the stacks.

My pulse thundered in my ears as I fumbled my way through the stacks, the books heavy as an anchor in my arms. At random, I shoved one book here, filed another in the next row, and the last in the row behind. Hopefully whoever was following us wouldn't notice the books were out of place.

Footsteps clomped behind me, getting closer and closer. I raced deeper into the cavern, running straight into the unknown.

Suddenly the footsteps were louder, almost on top of me now. My heart went haywire until rough, familiar fingers laced through mine.

"Thank God," I breathed, slowing my pace for a second.

"There's no time. We've got to get out of here," Will hissed in my ear, tugging me forward. Making my legs spin faster.

With Olympic speed, we sprinted out of the stacks. He led me to a set of stone stairs built into the back wall. As we speed-climbed, I was grateful it wasn't another rickety spiral staircase.

At the top of the landing, I glanced back and caught a snatch of red hair.

"Is that Felicia?" I gasped, gaping at the bird's eye view of the stacks. She wasn't alone. A group of four black-clad figures raced through the rows with her.

"C'mon, Lucy. We've got to get out of here." Will grabbed my hand.

I shook him off. "I have an idea. You better stand back." In a split second, I reached inside myself and called up my angel fire. Little sparks crackled in my palms, but there was no time. Aiming my palms toward the lights above us, I shot a stream of lightning into the overhead fixtures.

With a pop and a shower of sparks, they fizzled out. Blackness doused the room. A grin crawled up my face as Felicia and her friends pulled out their cell phones and fumbled around in the dark. I was getting better at this.

"That won't hold them for long." Will's fingers found my elbow as he led me into another stairwell. "And put that light out."

"What?" I glanced down at my still-glowing hands. With a sharp inhaled, I sucked the energy back inside me. "My bad."

In the darkness, Will chuckled in my ear and pulled out his phone. "I don't know about bad, just interesting. You definitely bought us some time."

The ceiling roared above us as a subway car buzzed past.

"Think it's safe?" His hand tapped my palm. "No shockwave or electrocution. I think we're good."

"You're good." I whispered, biting back a giggle. At least this guy didn't want to study my powers under a microscope. He'd rather make a joke about the whole thing. A much better alternative.

Grabbing my hand again, we sprinted through the underground maze by the light of his dim cell phone.

More stairs. Then we reached another door and burst through it. Into an alleyway.

My lungs were on fire. I doubled over and sucked down much-needed breaths of cool night air, my nostrils flinching as I caught a whiff of garbage.

"We can't stop here. We have to keep moving. Your brilliant little diversion won't stop them." He tugged on my hand again and dragged me up the alley, toward the lights of Broadway. Only then did he slow his pace.

"Where…are…we?" I huffed between breaths. "What happened back there?"

Turning to look at me, something flickered across his chiseled face. "I think you're right. The Nexis Repository has fallen to the Watchers now."

The weight of his words sank in deep as the questions swirled in my brain. How did Felicia and the Watchers know we'd be there? Were they following us? But the bigger question was too scary to ask. They must have some kind of plan. Maybe they wanted to finish what they started a few months ago. Or maybe it was bigger than marking the Seer. Maybe they had plans of their own. Just for me.

><

A door burst open, spilling light into the alley. Will and I froze in our dark corner behind the dumpster. Two guys in black vests strolled out, casually chatting with each other as they each lit a cigarette. Soft strains of orchestral music trilled through the opening then died as the door slammed shut.

Will put a finger to his lips and moved against the brick wall, motioning me to do the same. I slid next to him, deeper into the shadows. He tucked me under his arm.

Something scurried near my boots, making me shiver. I started to scream. Then a second later, I stifled the sound into my fist.

"What was that?" The little vest guy said to his tall friend.

"It better not be more second-acters. I'm sick of being a bouncer." Tall guy stomped in our direction.

Will turned to me. "Just go with it." Then he pressed his mouth into mine, pinning me to the wall.

I didn't have a problem with that. I wrapped my arms around his neck and kissed him back. As I closed my eyes, images flooded the darkness. Hazy and scattered. A dark room with a stone pedestal in the center, holding a giant sparkling hunk of stone. Dim hallways. My hands gripping iron bars, reaching for Will as he sat curled up in a corner.

Somewhere, far off in the distance—on another planet perhaps—two guys were shouting at us, shooing us away.

But Will was still kissing me. And I was still seeing things. Visions that I shouldn't be seeing.

Will running up to me on a dark cobblestoned street in a foreign city, then pulling me into a black building, shadows chasing us. In a flash, the image vanished, fading into a new scene. Will and I were huddled together on a train, sitting across from James, me leaning on Will's shoulder. Staring out the rain-soaked window, I watched another scene unfold. One that made my blood run cold. Wind whipped my long hair behind me as I stood in the center of a stone dais. Light and shadow swirled around me, purple lightning sizzling, shadows exploding into fireballs. But Will stood right there beside me. I reached for his hand and held on tight.

Suddenly he jerked back, and my head bumped into concrete, bringing the world back into focus. His face contorted, eyebrows wrinkled at me. Had he seen the same things I just saw?

Fear crawled up inside my throat and seized my lungs. A bitter taste filled my mouth.

He grabbed my hand and whispered in my ear. "Run."

Then we took off. Away from tweedle-dee and tweedle-dumb-vest. Down the alleyway and out onto the sidewalk.

The street was lit with billboards and flashing marquees. Broadway.

We wove our way through the theater-goers glommed up in packs on the sidewalk.

"Maybe those guys aren't as dumb as I thought." Will slowed his pace, glancing around. "This isn't exactly what I had planned for the rest of our date. If Felicia and her Watcher minions follow us, we'll just slip into the second act of one of these shows."

As if on cue, I spotted a flash of auburn hair in the glow of a flashing sign.

"I think they're behind us," I whispered in Will's ear.

He turned, his face locked in an expression I couldn't fathom, and herded me into the nearest theater pack.

My pulse thundered in my ears. Did he see the crazy-insane vision I'd just seen? Was he as freaked out as I was?

It was like someone had just fast-forwarded my life. Everything around me seemed to move at hyperspeed. The crowd bustled around us. Heels clicking on marble. People coughing, talking, laughing. All the sounds blending together, bouncing off the floor and the yellowed walls. The lobby lights flashed. Will pulled me into a dark theater. Everything stilled and quieted as the lights went out and we took a seat in the back row.

Somewhere far away, up on a stage, a spotlight flicked on. But I just turned to Will. And stared.

"What just happened?" The words fell out of my open jaw. I tried to close it.

He shrugged his shoulders. One arm swept around my back.

"I don't know," he finally said as he turned to stare back at me. "It's obvious that the Watchers have taken the Broadway Repository, but I have no idea what they'd want with it. Maybe they've got another spy inside Nexis since I wouldn't let Felicia in. Wouldn't be the first time."

"Oh." I slammed my mouth shut and faced the stage. If he hadn't seen those visions of us, I wasn't going to be the one to tell him. No way. No how. "What exactly *did* you have planned for the rest of the night?"

"I was going to take you to a bistro where my favorite local band is playing tonight." His low voice floated above me like he'd turned to look at me. "But that's not what you're talking about, is it?"

"That would've been fun." I didn't want to look back right now, but I couldn't help it. Maybe the dark theater would hide my almost-certainly flushed face.

I could barely see him until a stage light flared, highlighting the left side of his silhouette. That solid jawline, his Adam's apple bouncing up and down, a glint of gold in one sideburn. His eyes were dark, unreadable, the rest of his face covered in shadows.

It seemed like forever that we sat like that. Staring at each other. I couldn't be the first one to speak. Not after what I'd just seen. Wasn't he the Interpreter? Shouldn't it be his job to tell me what the heck that was?

"I can't stand this anymore." His eyebrows scrunching into a V. "You have to tell me what you're thinking."

"Me?" My hand flew to my chest. "I thought it was your job to interpret these things."

"Oh." A ghost of a smile flickered on his lips, and his gaze dropped to his lap. "I guess you saw it too, then."

"Yep. That's about the size of it." I creaked back in my seat, bumping his arm that I'd forgotten was there.

"Was that the first time you've seen it?" he asked, not looking up.

"Yes," I whispered as the realization hit. "It wasn't the first time *you* saw it. Was it?"

He shook his head.

A tiny spark of something fluttered in my chest. But I swallowed hard. Crushing it like a stone. I wasn't ready for this. Yet it was here, sitting right next to me.

"When was the first time you saw that vision?" I whispered.

"Awhile ago." He didn't glance up.

Fireflies stung my throat, but I swallowed them back. "How long?"

"Maybe a year ago," he breathed.

I slumped down in my chair, its velvet scratching my neck. I wanted to curl into a ball and not talk about this. Not deal with this, ever. Or at least until I was more grown-up than almost-seventeen.

The play went on in front of us, filled with music and laughter and light. But the silence between us stretched for eons.

Finally, he cleared his throat. "This isn't exactly a first date kind of discussion."

"I think we both know this is more than a first date." I swallowed too, lowering my voice. "Even if some of us are too scared to admit it."

His head jerked up and swung my way. He turned the most haunting look on me. My fingers itched to take his face in my hands and plant a kiss on those unsteady lips. Just to reassure him. But I couldn't. This was all happening too fast. Too soon. I'd barely begun to think of Will and me as *Us*, let alone anything beyond that.

"Okay." His mouth finally decided to smile. "I can live with that. For now. But one day I'll tell you what it all means. When you're ready."

With that, he brushed his lips against my temple. I melted into his soft touch, my ribs digging into the armrest between us.

The stage lights dimmed, and the crowd stood to its feet, cheering a loud roar that matched everything I felt inside. All the hope and exhilaration I dared to think about as my mind flirted with the possibilities tied up in that vision. Mixed with a choking fear of a future I never asked for or even imagined.

Maybe it was all true and we'd be together long enough to see my brother again. But if it was true, that meant some dark and sinister things lay in wait for us. Things that made my bones shiver.

CHAPTER 23

Shadows elongated across the quad as I huddled next to Will on the cobblestone path to the caf. The evening sun was setting in the distance, painting the sky in dusky pastels. The smell of spring trees wafted on the cold breeze, but I saw only jagged edges. Every muscle in my body tensed, just waiting for someone to sneak around the corner and grab me.

In fact, all of Montrose Paranormal Academy looked different ever since our date. It felt like I had a bullseye on my back—and I had no escape.

Will slung his arm around my shoulder as we ducked into the caf. Mindlessly, I grabbed some food, shoved it on my tray, and followed him to a vacant table. Staring straight ahead, I tried not to look at anyone. But I knew they were watching me. The Watchers were everywhere, apparently.

Clang. I flinched and whirled around. Someone a table over dropped a spoon.

"Sheesh," I gasped. Anxiety fizzled through me, crackling every nerve.

"Are you okay?" he asked, eyebrows cinched. "You've been a nervous wreck ever since we got back."

"Is it really that obvious?" I cringed on the inside.

He tapped my knee—which was bouncing like crazy.

"Oh." I tried to stop my pogo-leg. "I've never been great at hiding things."

"No kidding." His lips curled in a smile that spread up his face. "I've got something that'll make you feel better. Or at least take your mind off of things."

"Wooo, intriguing. Let's get out of here." My face probably mirrored his, and my muscles unclenched.

Will wore the barest hint of a smile on his olive-toned face as he took my hand and led me out of the cafeteria. Those rough fingers laced through mine, sending a shiver up my spine. My heart danced as I followed him, feeling light and free for a change. Until I saw where we were headed. Toward the tower. A lump slid down my throat.

"What're we doing here?" I asked, trudging up the steps behind him.

"Do you trust me?" He held open the heavy door for me and led me under the spiral staircase.

I stared at him. Hard. As my eyes adjusted to the darkness, a strange, almost-haloed light glowed around the boy standing in front of me. Dim at first, growing brighter with every second. Like someone turned a lightbulb on inside him. Was it me?

"Yes," I whispered. My stomach flip-flopped and I sucked in a breath, gnawing on my lip. There were no words.

His grin deepened as he led me straight to the secret entrance. "There's something I wanted to show you. Keep an open mind, okay?" He opened the hidden door to the real Nexis headquarters.

I tiptoed behind him. The narrow room looked different now. Light from the setting sun poured through the stone-encased window slats.

"Sit there and close your eyes." Will pointed to the leather couch. "And no peeking."

"Fine." I clasped my hands together, shutting my eyes tight.

Swish. Ruffle. Scrape. Noises echoed from the other side of the room.

He laid something oblong in my lap. "Okay, open them."

It was a laptop, open to a picture of the ancient book we found on our date. "Is this the evidence you scanned on Saturday?"

He plopped onto the couch beside me, knee bumping mine. Leaning over, he pointed at some words on the screen. "You see that bit? It says the Nexis Seer book will be here at Montrose, for the next Grand Council meeting. That's next week."

"Spring break?" My heart fluttered in my chest as I stared at him. "That sounds dangerous, Will. Like, *really* dangerous."

"I'll do anything to protect you," he murmured, voice lowering. His eyes turned dark, haunted almost. "Especially now that I know the Guardians won't."

My breath hitched in my throat. "What do you mean?" My voice wavered.

Pushing the laptop to the side, he took both of my hands in his and leveled the full weight of those platinum eyes on me. "The only reason I backed down last semester was because I thought the Guardians were going to protect you. I was sure they'd make you a member so Nexis couldn't touch you."

"I thought so, too," I whispered, my cheeks flaming and my eyes darting away from him. "How could I be so stupid?"

"You're not stupid." With one finger, he tilted my chin up until I met his gaze again. "I thought they could take better care of you as a group than I could on my own."

"Instead, they kicked me to the curb." Tears pooled behind my eyes, but I held them in check.

"I just don't understand it." Running one hand through his hair, he shook his head. His face went slack, and he glanced away. "With this intel, we can negotiate our way into the Guardian ranks. Just like your brother did."

"My brother?" I croaked, hope flooding into my heart once again. "He did do that, didn't he?"

He lowered his eyes to our knees, side-by-side. "Maybe we can find him someday. Team up, you know? You're not the only one who misses him. He was kinda like my mentor."

"That's a great idea." I breathed out the barest of whispers. "But it still seems a little too dangerous."

"Going against Nexis is always dangerous. But sometimes it's worth it." He gulped and leveled his gaze at me. "I'll do anything for you. I'll choose you over Nexis. Always."

"You're serious, aren't you?" I felt the truth of his words, rattling deep down in my bones, breaking open the iron cage around my heart.

"Are you really that surprised? Don't you know how much I care about you? You've got me wrapped around this little finger here." He lifted my index finger to his lips and kissed it.

Tingles buzzed down my arm as I stared into his eyes. That beautiful face was so close to mine, close enough to kiss. "It's only been a few months, but I feel it, too. And it scares me." My voice trembled as I finally admitted the truth.

"I get it." The muscle in his jaw twitched like crazy. "It's been a lot more than a couple months for me. When we kissed in the kitchen back in September, that's when I really started to fall for you." The truth was written in his eyes.

And I couldn't deny it anymore.

Energy billowed up in my chest, tugging at the pieces of my heart. Those words were threads of hope, sewing up the giant gashes I thought might never heal. Yet here he was, sitting right beside me. Mending what once was broken.

"Yeah, I know. And I want to catch up to you." I curled into his side. "I'm getting closer every day."

One, two, three breaths hitched in his chest. I wrapped my arms around him to let him know I meant it. All at once, his muscles relaxed. He enveloped me in his arms, squeezing me tight.

"You have no idea how much I want to believe that's true." His Adam's apple scraped sandpaper against my temple.

"Believe it." I smoothed my hands down his biceps, turning him to face me. "Now tell me this plan of yours."

"Right, the plan." He blinked at me and rubbed his hands together like an excited little boy. "I know the Guardians want intel on the Nexis Seer book, so I'm hoping we can use their plan against them."

"Oooh, I like it." My lips curled up in a smile. "Go on, give me details. Don't leave a girl in suspense."

His face lit up as he reached for my hand and squeezed. "I read the pages we scanned from the Repository. They say the Nexis Seer book will be in the Nexis Chamber in preparation for the Grand Council in May. If we can break into the chamber just one more time, we can scan pages from the Nexis Seer book and trade the intel for membership. Let's just hope we don't end up on the front lines like James did."

"Front lines? What does that mean?" The anger jolted me like an electric current, balling my hands into fists at my side all over again.

"Don't tell me you didn't know." Will's face clouded over. "Right now, James is a spy for the Guardians. Done some damage to Nexis already. But if war breaks out, he'll be part of the Guardian army."

"What? You guys have armies? And James is part of one?" I spat out the word like a disease.

"The Coopers didn't tell you? The Guardians drafted James right after graduation. Probably part of his Guardian deal with Abby. She was campus president then." His forehead wrinkled. "When war breaks out between the Three Societies, spies and other intelligence agents are recruited for the fight. All three societies have military-type operatives that blend into society as law enforcement or security guards. An army just ready and waiting."

"You're joking, right?" The rage ebbed and flowed in my veins, seething with a life of its own. "Abby Cooper drafted my brother into the Guardian army and her brother never told me? James is only twenty-one!"

Will held up his hands. "Hey babe, I'm sorry. I thought you already knew this. I didn't mean to—"

Anger sliced through the air as I cut him off with one motion. "I'm not mad at *you*. I can't believe I ever trusted Bryan or his family. They knew how much it tore me up, not knowing where James was. And yet they knew all along."

"You deserve better than that." Will slid one arm around my back and squeezed my shoulder. "Once we join the Guardians, we'll turn everything around. Make your Seer status work for you."

I ground my teeth together. Anger simmered through my veins. "No need to wait. I *am* the Seer and I'm tired of being pushed around. Let's start right now."

Backing up, he looked me in the eye. "Now's not the time to negotiate anything. Let's wait until we have real intel."

"I don't think so." I shook my head, anger seething through my veins and burning me up inside. "Don't you see how they've messed with my life, tainted everything? Including our relationship."

"You've got a point there." His jaw hardened. "Besides, I'm not letting you go alone."

"Now we're talking." I let him lead me out of the tower, straight into enemy territory.

><

Nighttime swept across campus, lacing the sky with blues and deep purples. My anger fizzled in and out as I stalked across the quad, Will at my side. It burned me up inside that I'd spent ten whole days with Abby Cooper and she'd never said a word about what really happened to James. None of the Coopers told me the truth.

The moon peeked out behind the chapel's Gothic arches. The only lights came from the chapel library window. The Guardians were in there all right, probably having their weekly meeting. As usual.

"You're really going in with me?" I stopped at the chapel stairs, turning to Will. Silver moonglow highlighted the sculpted lines and curves of his profile.

"Of course I'm going with you. I can't let you face them alone. What kind of man would that make me?" He puffed out his chest, mouth lifting in that mischievous crescent smile I was beginning to love.

The fact that Will would go into that den of liars with me—stand up to the people who spread such awful rumors about him. It choked me up inside.

"The kind that breaks up with his girlfriend because he can't stand up for himself?" I mumbled, but not low enough. Chewing furiously on my bottom lip, I peeked up at him.

"Exactly." His jaw twitched ever-so-slightly. "And we're better than that. Now let's do this."

Together, we marched up the stone steps, through the antique door and into the chapel foyer. The giant stone arch greeted me, framing the beauty of the sanctuary ahead. I paused in my tracks. After all that'd happened, all that was about to go down, my heart still soared every time I entered this stained-glass sanctuary. It whispered from the depths of a simpler time when my world was far less complicated.

But we couldn't linger here. I sucked in a breath, squeezed Will's hand tighter, and led the way down the dark hallway. Voices flitted from behind the closed door and reverberated in hushed murmurs, crescendoing until I gripped the doorknob.

"Here we go," I whispered to Will as he halted beside me.

Twisting the handle, I slammed open the door and stormed into the room with Will right on my heels. But something was wrong.

"What happened here?" I gasped.

It looked like a tornado had blown through the once-pristine library. Cedar shelves were toppled over, leaning at odd angles against each other as if part of a giant domino trick. Books, the precious antique books, were strewn everywhere—their pages littering the room in piles. Yellowed, fallen leaves ripped from their homes. They could never be put right again.

All the Guardians were there, milling through the fallen stacks. Looking dazed. Everyone in the room turned to look at me. They all glared at Will.

"Lucy." Laura tiptoed through the debris, eyes narrowing at Will. "What are you doing here? With him?"

I slammed my lips together, biting back the truth. Maybe it wasn't such a good idea anymore to barge in here and share the revelation Will told me about James.

"You—" Bryan yelled across the room at Will, fire in his eyes. "Look what your insane group did. All this history, gone. Ripped to shreds. You're going to pay for this."

"Whoa, man. Just calm down." Tony stood right behind him, and Lenny jumped out from the turret to help reign in their fearless leader.

Bryan stomped around the overturned chairs and crunched up pages, but the circuitous path took all the spark from his empty threat. Brooke tumbled out from between two stacks, and they all circled up in a huddle around the door. Staring us down.

In a flash, Bryan lunged at Will. In the blink of an eye, I stepped in between them, blocking Bryan's path. His jaw dropped as he came inches from my face. Something burned in his blue eyes, surprise mixed with the tiniest hint of fear. Tony and Lenny pulled him back a few feet, but I could still see that look in his eyes.

"Someone tell me what's going on." My words came out higher and breathier than they should have. Great, now he'd think it was all about him. When really my heart was breaking at the shattered state of my beloved former oasis.

"That's a good question. Why don't we ask your boyfriend here?" He spat out the words like they were infected.

I'd never seen Bryan this mad before. Shadows swirled behind him. Puffs of dark smoke slithered their tendrils around him. I blinked and turned to Will. And saw something even stranger.

Wraith-like tendrils snaked toward Will, then suddenly bounced back like they'd hit an invisible force field. A dim, silvery light surrounded him. Dim enough so I had to squint to see it. Even though it was faint, it was still there. Making me wonder who was really good, and who was really bad now. Maybe it wasn't as simple as I'd always thought.

"Boyfriend? You're dating Will now?" Brooke's voice cracked as she stepped out from behind her brother. Her face said it all. A mixture of amazement and horror washed over her features.

The rest of the Guardians stared at me with the same look. Bryan crossed his arms in front of his chest, a smug smile on his lips.

"That was the plan wasn't it, Bryan?" I took one step closer, narrowing my eyes at him. "I just didn't exactly follow your little Guardian guidelines."

Now the Guardians turned to look at Bryan. "Nexis is stealing sacred stones. The council felt they had to take drastic action. It wasn't my call."

"So what?" Lenny glanced from Bryan to me, and back again. "Dude, I can't believe you went along with that garbage."

Bryan threw up his hands. "What else was I supposed to do?"

"I don't know, stand up to them. Tell them their plan to have Lucy spy for them is bogus." Lenny's voice grew louder. His cheeks were about as red as his hair.

Laura tugged on her brother's shirt and pulled him back, peeking at me over his shoulder.

"Since when do the Guardians play chess with people's lives like Nexis does?" Tony chimed in. "I can't believe you didn't stand up for your girl. That's what'd I'd do if—" His eyes widened as he looked at me, clamping his lips together.

I nodded at him, sealing my lips shut. I'd never blab about Shanda.

"I tried." Bryan stared at his shoes. "They threatened to kick me out, or worse, send Lucy to the front lines."

"And you believed them?" Lenny backed up and shook his head. "So instead of doing the right thing, you threw her right into the devil's arms? That's cold, man."

"Guys, he's right there," Brooke whispered, pointing to Will.

I turned to him and froze. "Sorry, babe. You shouldn't have to deal with this."

He just rolled his eyes. "Like I didn't know already. You Guardians are so unoriginal with your lies."

"I'd rather be unoriginal than a criminal," Bryan spat out, chin hardening into marble all over again. "Who breaks into a library and destroys hundred-year-old books?"

"Unless they're looking for something …" I bit my lip, still staring at my boyfriend.

His eyebrows shot up. "You don't think—"

"Think what?" Laura stamped her little foot. "What's going on here?"

I dipped my head at Will, silently asking for permission. He frowned, but nodded anyway.

"Right, golden boy. What exactly is going on with you two?" Bryan asked, lips twisting in a sneer as his head swung back and forth between me and Will.

I scooted closer to Will's side. "Just listen for five seconds."

Bryan opened his mouth, but Will cut him off. "The Watchers caught us sneaking into a Nexis repository this weekend. I'm assuming they realized what we did, blamed you for it, and trashed your poor little headquarters. Shame, really."

"Likely story." Bryan's eyes sparked with fireballs as he glared at my hand in Will's.

"He's been with me all evening. He couldn't possibly have done this." I tried to stare Bryan straight in the eye, but he wouldn't look at me.

"All evening, huh?" Bryan's jaw twitched, breaking the marble facade if only for a second or two. "Doing what, exactly?"

"Ugh, you can't be serious." Waves of disgust washed over me. My jaw dangled on its axis as I took a good hard look at this guy I used to love. Had it ever really been love? Because right now, it felt like the exact opposite.

"Bryan, what's wrong with you? Why are you acting like this?" Brooke looked as crushed as I was by her brother's insinuations.

"I'm beginning to think I never knew you at all." I took two more steps back, my stomach twisting at the sight of the shadows brewing around him. "Like how you never told me that Abby drafted James into the Guardian army. He's in Europe right now, preparing to fight whatever war is about to break out. You knew the whole time, and you never said a word."

"Are you serious?" Tony stepped back, inching closer to me and Will. "This whole time, you didn't tell her that James is stationed in Austria? I don't understand what's going on here anymore."

The rest of the Guardians backed away from Bryan a step or two.

"Guys, I can explain. I was just trying to protect you." His eyes darted from me to his sister, then to the rest of the group.

I just gave him a headshake. "No, you were trying to turn me into a Guardian spy knowing full well they'd never let me join unless I got something really big on Nexis. Not only are you willing to put me in danger, but you told all those lies about Will. It's despicable."

Brooke shook her head and huffed out a laugh. "Now, don't tell me you're starting to believe you're supposed to marry Will and bring about some Utopian dictatorship? You're falling under his spell."

"That's what you think I'm trying to do here? That's craziness! And you call me insane." Will reared back, glancing around the room.

The girls cringed. The guys shrugged. No one looked at us. Now it wasn't just the library that lay in shambles. This Guardian group was starting to crumble, too.

"It's ridiculous." I rolled my eyes. "And I'm done with all of it. From now on, I'll decide my own destiny. I don't need you or your lies to tell me what to do anymore."

I turned on my heel to walk out the door, but Tony grabbed my arm. "Don't tell me you're joining Nexis now? After all we talked about at Shanda's party."

Murmurs floated behind us as the Guardians grumbled amongst themselves. I guess Tony hadn't told anyone about Shanda or her little party. Good for him.

"Get your hands off her." Will rushed to my side in two seconds, brushing off Tony's fingers. "I've never asked her to join, and I never will. I know full well what that means."

"Good," Tony angled a head bob at Will. "That's something we can all agree on."

"You don't believe him, do you?" Bryan sputtered, his face a giant question mark of fury. "All the things I've said about Will and his family are completely true."

Will snorted. "That's where you're wrong again, Guardian de facto. Just because my family's a bit deranged doesn't mean I want to have anything to do with their plans."

I smiled at him and squeezed his hand. "I've had enough. Let's go."

We turned toward the door, and Tony followed us.

"Where are you going, man?" Lenny's face scrunched up as his eyes followed Tony.

"I'm so tired of these stupid games. The council are putting people's lives in danger. Lucy's not the only one." Tony turned toward his friends, shaking his head. "I don't know what to believe anymore. I need to figure some things out."

Together, the three of us walked out of the chapel library door and down the hall. Only silence followed us.

CHAPTER 24

Crisp spring air blasted me in the face, cooling the fire licking my cheeks as I tumbled down the chapel steps to the quad. Tony and Will followed right on my heels, their ragged breaths slicing through the silent night.

"I can't believe you just did that." Will darted ahead of me and planted his hands on my shoulders, stopping me in my tracks. "That was so bad-ass."

Digging my hands into my jeans' pockets, I rocked back on my heels as my pulse slowed its breakneck pace. "I can't either, but it had to be done."

"I don't know how the Guardians got so messed up. I don't know if I can be a part of it anymore." Tony's eyes were as wide as the silver-dollar moon behind him. "What happens next? Do you guys have a plan or something?"

"You better not be playing some stupid spy game with me." Will narrowed his eyes at Tony. "I've got a plan to protect Lucy. But it's beyond risky."

"I'm serious. I don't know what to think anymore. Lucy isn't the only one who's being strung out to dry by the Guardians." Tony ran his pale fingers through his dark curls, mussing them beyond repair.

"Shanda," I whispered, my gazing shifting from Tony to Will and back again.

Will slid his hand down my shoulders, taking my hand in his. He turned to face Tony. "If you want to help your girlfriend, we could use all hands on deck."

"I'm not going to even ask how you know about her." Tony narrowed his eyes at Will. "What kind of help do you need, and why does it involve my girlfriend?"

"Not here." Will shook his head, eyes roaming the dark campus. "We need a neutral location."

His gaze snapped from me to Will before his eyes crinkled up and he cracked an odd smile. "What about your boyfriend? Does he even know it's your birthday this weekend?"

I cocked my head at Tony. Inching closer, he winked at me three times. It looked like he was having a spastic eye episode.

"Shush, don't tell anyone." I gave him one headshake. "I only told one person. We were going to sneak off to the city tomorrow night to celebrate."

"Well, doesn't that sound fun?" Tony mouthed *tomorrow* behind his hand. Then off he went, down the cobblestone path to the guy's dorm.

Will grabbed my hand and whirled me around to face him. "What was that?" he whispered in my ear. "Is it really your birthday, or do you guys have some sort of secret code?"

"C'mon." I tugged Will's hand, leading him further and further away from the chapel. "We're meeting at a certain condo in the city."

"Oh." His head bobbed up and down in slow motion. "But that doesn't answer my question. Is it really your birthday tomorrow?"

"Yes." I huffed out a hot breath that fogged up the cold air in front of me. "I just didn't want anyone to make a big deal."

He squeezed my hand, leaning in to give me a quick kiss on the lips. "I can assure you, that's not going to happen."

"Ugh, I'm serious, Will." I pulled back and stared him down, pursing my lips in a pout.

He just wrapped his arms around my waist and tugged me closer. "What? Can't your boyfriend want to do something nice for your birthday?"

"Not fair." This close to those chiseled abs, my body started to melt into him. Two seconds later, I caved. "Fine, as long as it's nothing big enough to draw Nexis attention."

His lips curled in triumph. "We'll be off-campus. I'll keep it low key."

"Why don't I believe you?" Then I pressed my mouth into his and forgot to care.

><

Whoosh. Shanda yanked the vertical blinds closed in her dad's Central Park condo. It was seven o'clock on a Friday night in New York City and what were me and my friends doing? Sitting huddled in Shanda's dining nook, not saying a word. I guess nobody wanted to go first. Tony glared at Will, who eyed Shanda, who just stared back at me like it was all my fault her apartment was the only suitable neutral location. Yeah, so not gonna be the first to break the ice.

Knotted rope curled and uncurled in my gut. Things were starting to get serious. Fast. It wasn't just me and Will breaking into an off-campus repository for our first date. Now we were throwing Shanda and Tony into a plot that could really piss Nexis off. Someone could get hurt, or locked in a hole somewhere. Or worse.

I gulped, leaned across the Jones family dining table, and focused on Shanda. "Are you sure you want in on this? Once you're in, there's no going back."

"What, do you think I'm afraid to take Nexis head-on?" She arched one manicured eyebrow at me, mirroring my stance. "'Cause I'm not. I think it's time. Past time. They've been running our lives for too long. And I'm done putting up with it."

A smile tugged at my lips. I couldn't help it. The strong girl staring back at me had so much courage. So much resolve. Why couldn't I be like my Shanda? My insides still quaked and quivered at the thought of breaking into another Nexis repository. After all, it went so well last time.

At least we weren't all by ourselves. Will sat by my side, perched on the edge of his chair, locked in a staring contest with Tony. Who would win that battle? My new, golden-haired boyfriend? Or his dark-haired counterpart? I glanced back and forth at the dueling eye daggers. It was almost like looking at the sun, then looking at the moon. Each had their own virtues, but they were so opposite in many ways.

"Ugh. Are we gonna do this thing, boys?" Shanda asked, tilting her head toward her boyfriend.

"Of course, we are." Tony jutted his chin out at Will. "I'm just trying to figure out what Golden Boy here is up to."

Will's eyes narrowed at him, then turned to Shanda. "Lucy and I have discovered the location of the Nexis Seer book. It's going to be in the chamber next week. Right before the next Grand Council."

Tony froze, jaw twitching. "Are you saying you want to steal the Nexis Seer book?"

"Not exactly steal," Will pulled out his little scanner wand. "More like copy the good bits."

"Say wha—" Shanda blurted out, her screech echoing in the empty condo.

"I'd planned to trade it for membership into the Guardians. For all of us." Will's arm drew a path from me to Shanda, his gazing finally landing on Tony. "Do you think it'll work? Would the Guardians negotiate?"

"Wow." Tony's jaw dropped, right next to his girlfriend's. "That's a bold move, man. But it just might work."

Shanda hoisted her index finger in the air. "Except for one teeny little thing. Nexis would kill us if we got caught."

"Kill? As in murder?" I swallowed back the bile as my whole body started trembling. "They'd really do that?"

"Whoa, don't go filling Lucy's head with crazy what-ifs." Will sidled up to me and started massaging my shoulder. "They definitely won't kill the Seer. And you two won't be on the hook. I need my little hacker outside, monitoring things, and manning the cameras."

Tony arched back, swiveling his chair toward Shanda. "You've been hacking into Nexis for him?"

"No way. Hold up now." She stared her boyfriend down, shooting eye-daggers at him. "I only covered for him that one time when he showed Lucy the Nexis Chamber."

"Nice, bro." Tony glanced over at Will, smiling. "Way to win a girl over."

"It could've been worse. He could've been her super-secret spy handler." Shanda's lips curled up, and before I knew it, she'd busted out in a full-on cackle.

A gurgle of laughter bubbled up in my own throat. I tried to tamp it down, but in ten seconds I burst into a giggle-fit right alongside my best friend.

"Okay, fine. You got me there." Tony's lips twitched like he was trying not to laugh, too.

"The things guys do to impress a girl. The right girl." Will's face broke into a grin as his fingers slid through my hair, sending shivers down my spine.

Grabbing Shanda's hand, Tony leaned in, elbows on the table. "So what exactly *is* the plan?"

As if on cue, we all huddled closer to the table, eyes trained on each other. Will pulled his laptop from his backpack and set it on the table, opening it to the book page we'd scanned.

"The intel Lucy and I gathered says the book will be in the Nexis Chamber vault exactly one week from today." He tapped the screen to zoom in on the log entry.

"Yep, that's what it says." Tony's eyebrows arched at the screen, then at Will. "Now, if we could plan this operation to go down right before next Grand Council, we might have a shot."

"That's exactly what I had in mind." Will rested his arms on the table and lowered his voice a notch. "I've got a buddy who's got all the tech we'll need to crack the safe and load the files onto the cloud."

"Even from a hundred feet underground?" Tony rubbed his hands together and grinned. "Now we're talking."

"Precisely." Slowly, Will nodded, mouth curling in a half-smile.

For a moment, Nexis President and Guardian Vice President shared a glimmer of a grin. Ten seconds, max. Then the glowering took over again.

"Where are we meeting this contact of yours?" Shanda stared down her nose at Will. "Please don't say a back alley somewhere."

"We've had our share of back alleys." I patted Will's knee. His lips quirked at the memory.

"I don't even want to know." Shanda rolled her eyes.

Tony ran both hands through his hair, mussing it every which way. "If it's not a back alley, then where are we meeting the guy?"

Will lowered his voice. "Someplace public. Just a club. We can pretend we're celebrating Lucy's birthday."

"Great. At least my birthday will be good for something." I squeezed Will's knee, rubbing little circles on his leg.

Shanda's eyes lit up as she glanced around the table. "Ladies and gentlemen, it's time to celebrate Lucy's seventeenth birthday."

Those words rang in my ears as Will helped me slide into my favorite leather jacket. Seventeen meant one year closer to eighteen, when Nexis would come down on me hard. I only had one year left to outsmart them at their own game.

Shanda reached for her fabulous pink oh-so-fluffy coat.

Tony snatched the coat from her hands. "I don't know about Nexis black ops, but Guardians try to avoid being noticed when picking up off-book tech for their covert missions."

"I prefer to hide in plain sight. But if you insist." She opened the hall closet and pulled out a black leather jacket almost identical to mine. "Happy now?"

"Yes, sweetie. We can go now." He kissed her on the lips and rushed to hold the door open for her.

"How cute," I whispered in Will's ear as he pressed the elevator button. "What club are we going to?"

"You'll see, gorgeous." With that, he planted a kiss on my forehead that made me all warm and tingly inside.

Shanda tried to hide the beginnings of a grin. "It looks like you've got some competition, Mr. Suave."

"Nah," Tony scoffed as the elevator dinged. "He's no match for my rustic Italian charm."

"If you say so, honey." Shanda pecked him on the cheek.

My heart took a flying leap. If anyone deserved to be happy, my bestie definitely topped the list.

Shanda turned to Will as the elevator doors opened. "Do I need my fake ID?"

"Normally you would, but don't worry about it." Will's hand found the small of my back and led me into the car. "Let's just say, I've got connections."

I wrapped my arm around his back and snuggled into his side. "Here we go."

><

A few minutes after eight o'clock, Will parallel-parked on the dark New York street with an ease I'd never possess. Even though it was still early, 44th street was packed with black-clad hipsters, all heading around the corner to 8th Avenue. We followed the crowd.

"Is that it?" Tony pointed at a flashing red 844 Club sign down the street. "It's even Nexis colors. Figures."

My breath hitched in my throat. Shanda and I glanced at each other. Not this place again. The last time we came here for a girl's night, Shanda called me out on my feelings for Bryan. How was that only five months ago?

The line snaked to the end of the block, growing by the second. "Oh, man." Excitement faded from his voice with each breath. "Look at that line. We'll never get in."

"We'll see about that." Will grabbed my hand and pulled me close, his breath warm on my neck. "Remember, I've got connections."

"You better. Otherwise, we'll be in line till midnight and your princess will turn into a pumpkin." Tony batted my shoulder as we side-stepped a grimy puddle. A siren blared in the distance.

"Thanks, Tony." I just shook my head at him.

Shanda reached into her purse and shoved a piece of plastic in my hand.

"Just in case," she hissed, eyes flashing at Will.

I opened my palm to a fake ID that read, Maria Hernandez. "Not bad, for a fake."

"With your dark hair, you can pass for Hispanic." Shanda twirled a lock of my hair around her fingers.

"You won't need it." Will mumbled under his breath and tugged me along. We scurried past the party-goers glommed up in line, dodging evils stares and taunts of "Cutters." Will just ignored them and kept on walking to the front of the line. He shook hands with the bouncer, who lifted the rope for us.

Shanda glanced at me, eyebrows raised. "Impressive."

Bass thumped through the air around us, coming from dance floor writhing with bodies. Red laser lights strobed across the dance floor in time to the music. Will never let go of my hand as we waded through the dance floor at a snails' pace. Finally, the crowd thinned, and we reached a roped off area in the back.

Suddenly, Will pulled me close, pressing his lips into my temple.

I looked up at him. "Everything okay?"

"Happy birthday, tiger." He stared down at me, neon red swimming in his eyes.

"How'd you know?" My throat thickened, clogging with emotion.

"A little birdie told me." He shot me a sexy wink.

I glared at Shanda. "I didn't want to make a big thing out of it." Mostly because my next birthday was so monumental in the eyes of Nexis. They'd only watch me closer.

He massaged my shoulder. "Hey, I get it. But we're gonna make sure Nexis can't get their hands on you. This is as far as you should go. Tony will stay here with you girls while I get what we need."

"Yeah, right." Shanda's hand flew to her hip. "I've got the birthday girl's back."

Will glanced at Tony. "Help me out here."

Tony shook his head. "This here is a New York girl with a taser in her purse. If anyone messes with her, they'll regret it. Big time."

Will pursed his lips, looking entirely unconvinced. "I'll be right back," he whispered in my ear as he planted a soft kiss on my lips.

Taking two steps forward, he lifted the rope. Then Tony grabbed his arm.

"Not so fast. Wait up." Tony took the rope from Will and snapped it shut behind him. "You're not going anywhere by yourself. Not on my watch. I won't stand for any double-crossing. You hear?"

Will cocked his head. "Who are you worried about more, me or my contact?"

Tony held up his hands in surrender. "This is Nexis we're talking about here. God only knows what kind of nefarious things you guys do in the back room of clubs like this. It's always best to have a third-party."

"Ugh, fine." Will grumbled. "Let's just get this over with."

"Don't worry." Shanda waggled her finger at the boys. "We'll be right here when you get back. Unless you take too long and some Prince Charming sweeps us off our feet."

"That's my girl," Tony muttered, shaking his head.

As soon as the boys were out of sight behind the velvet rope, Shanda turned to me, eyes glowing in the dark. "Girl, why didn't you tell your new man it was your birthday?"

"You know why." I squinted in the dim light to make out her dark silhouette.

She leaned closer. "You and Will. Duh. You guys have been going out for what, like, a month? And yet you were never this lovey-dovey with Bryan."

I squirmed in my chair, jangling my bracelets against my jeans. "I could say the same thing about you and Tony."

"Puh-lease." She swiped her hand in front of her face. "You know what's going on there. We're totally in love. And it's amazing. Now don't change the subject."

"Grr…" I ground my teeth together. Busted. "What subject?"

"Are you in love with Will?" Her question floated toward me, dancing in time to the beat.

Beams of light strobed around us in perfect rhythm with the thumping of my pulse. And it hit me. Maybe I'd already fallen for Will and forgot to admit it to myself. Not because he said it first like Bryan did. But because he was the exact opposite of Bryan. Will was totally into me above any secret society. And that felt good, amazing even. Was I really in love with Will?

"I knew it!" She shouted over the pumping bass. "Who called it?"

My mouth hinged open, and I tilted my head at her. "How on earth do you do that?"

"Please, girl." She cocked her head right back at me. "It's written all over your face. His too, I might add."

"Really?" In a flash, my insides ignited until my whole body buzzed. For the first time in months, I had something to look forward to. Something just for me.

"That's great." The biggest grin crept across her face. "You two are made for each other."

"After what I went through with Jake and Bryan ..." My throat tightened as the grip of fear itself clamped around my windpipe.

"Don't even go there." She waved away a cloud of dry ice fog that escaped from the dance floor. "Jake was a terrible guy. Bryan wasn't ready to give up his precious Guardians for you. But Will's different. He's been waiting for you for a long time."

"True that." My mouth curled up at the thought, even as an uneasy feeling slithered around in my stomach. "But being with me might put him in too much danger."

The house lights faded, and the music died down to a dull roar.

Suddenly, shadows screeched through the air. Icy tendrils of smoke reached down, surrounding me. My lungs constricted as dark fingers wrapped their tentacles around my ribcage. Ungodly whispers screamed through my ears. Piercing cries that hissed, *You don't deserve him. He'll just betray you like everyone else. You'll only get him killed.*

"You can't live in fear." Shanda's strong voice rose above the shadows she'd just named.

Fear.

For a moment, the shadow grip loosened. I inhaled a much-needed breath.

"It's hard to put yourself out there. Believe me, I know." She stared right at me as if she knew the shadows that plagued me. "Sometimes it's worth it, though. Even if it's dangerous. If you wanna know my two cents, I think Will's worth it."

Will was worth it. Shanda's word resonated somewhere deep inside me. With those words, I pictured the look on his face when we first met. Our almost first kiss in the kitchen over Dr.

Pepper. Our first fight at the bonfire when he tried to tell me the truth about my family but I wouldn't let him. No matter how hard I tried to push him away, he'd stuck around. Worrying about me. Caring about me. Shanda was right. It was so obvious. Maybe he hadn't said the words yet, but I knew the truth. He loved me. It didn't matter that he was the Interpreter and I was the Seer. Maybe we were "destined" to be together. Maybe we weren't. But I didn't care about stupid legends or prophecies anymore. Because I knew the truth. I *wanted* to be with him. Because I loved him.

Hope surged through me. Slivers of light filtered among the wispy tendrils of darkness. I lifted my eyes to the ceiling. Four words beat a steady rhythm in my heart. A silent prayer. *I'm not afraid anymore.*

In four seconds, the shadows fled. My throat opened again. My lungs breathed easy.

"Thanks for that." I keeled over, heaving for air. "I needed a truth bomb."

"That's what best friends are for." She squeezed my hand. "I went through the same thing with Tony. The fear, the doubt, with all this secret society garbage that tries to bring us down." Her eyes glazed over as she dropped my hand, her gaze far off.

"How'd you do it?" I asked as soon as I'd regained my breath. "How'd you know you guys even had a shot to make it work?"

She turned to me. "Because he's a fighter. In that way, Tony and Will are totally alike. Will has already fought for you. So many times, just like Tony fought for me." The music swelled, and she raised her voice.

"That's true." I couldn't keep my lips from curving at the thought. A great idea in theory. One that still scared me.

We grinned at each other as dark figures appeared from behind the velvet rope. At last, the boys were back. Will had some wires peeking out from his jacket pocket. His eyes were shadowed, darting with laser focus around the room.

As soon as he was close enough, I wrapped my arm around his neck and kissed his stubbled cheek. "It's gonna be okay," I whispered in his ear. "We're together now. We're gonna be just fine."

"I hope you're right." His arms flew around my waist, pulling me tight against him, crushing bits of the contents in his pocket between us. But he didn't seem to care.

My heart was as light as it'd been in a long time. So what if the future ahead seemed scary and uncertain. Tonight, I had gotten more than I bargained for. A new realization. And some great friends to lift me up.

CHAPTER 25

The next week at Montrose passed by in a blur. Everything went back to normal, at least spring-semester normal. Bryan and the Guardians stared me down in the cafeteria. Colleen and Monica whispered whenever Will and I sat at the Nexis table. But it didn't have the same effect on me. Will and I were a team now—and nothing could come between us. Not this time.

Will and I had started training together in the gym after classes. He showed me how to block punches and kick a body where it hurt—much like the Guardian training I'd had four months ago. The athletic practice helped tone my body, made me feel strong. Being around Will made me feel strong, too.

Once we were alone in our room, Shanda and I whispered about our top-secret spring break plans. We told Miss Sherry and my parents that we were staying with Shanda's dad for the week. They totally bought it. Of course, Tony had to do a little Dad-like phone acting to make the whole thing convincing enough.

Tony and Will told everyone they were going home to see their families, but they really planned to meet us at the condo for a prep night tonight to plan tomorrow's mission. A mix of excited fear bubbles gurgled in my stomach on the drive to the Jones' condo.

Briiiing. Shanda's doorbell rang, and she rushed to the door. "What took you so long?" She wrapped her arms around Tony's neck and ushered him inside. In return, he gave her a peck on the lips. A glorious sunset lit the sky outside her condo window with swaths of pink and orange. *If I snapped a picture right now, they'd make the most romantic postcard.*

My heart did a somersault. "You guys are so cute."

She smiled at me and reached for Tony's hand. "After this mission, there will be no more hiding."

"Yeah, only because we'll be one of two places. On the run from Nexis, or safely in some Guardian bunker. That is the plan, right?" Tony looked at me, a goofy grin plastered all over his face.

"Ugh, sometimes you remind me of my brother. Stop it." On the outside, I flashed a smile. But inside my heart clenched.

"I'm sure you miss him." Shanda's eyes sparkled as dusk settled over the city behind her.

"Aren't you so sweet?" Tony wrapped both arms around Shanda and pulled her in tight. "I don't know what I'd do if anything ever happened to you."

"Nothing's going to happen to me," Shanda mumbled against his neck.

My shoulders slumped. None of us knew what would happen next. At least I wasn't the only one feeling the pressure.

Diiing. The elevator dinged in the distance.

"That'll be Will." I rushed through the foyer and straight to the elevator door.

Will's tan face greeted me when I opened the door. I smushed my lips into his before he got a chance to walk through the front door. "Missed you."

"I missed you, too, gorgeous." He kissed me back, harder this time. Then he pulled me into the corner of the foyer and pressed me up against the wall. Running his thumb along my jawline, he cupped my face and pressed his mouth into mine. I threaded my fingers behind his neck, melting into his kiss. His lips tasted sweet and a little tangy.

"Mmm … Dr. Pepper," I murmured into his mouth. "Brings back memories."

"Good memories," he whispered, pulling away to kiss my cheek, my neck, before returning to my lips. "Our first kiss."

"First of many." I ran my hands down his chiseled back. Electricity coursed through every nerve ending as I got lost in his kiss, his arms, the way his stubble scratched my face.

Finally, after who-knows-how-long, Shanda called through the open door. "Are you guys going to be out there all night? Because we've got work to do."

Will's shoulders deflated in an instant. He rested his forehead on mine. "I'd rather stay out here all night. Wouldn't you?"

Immediately my lips curled up. "Absolutely. Who knows? We might get another vision." I clamping my hands around his neck, pulling him in close again. His body felt good against mine. Anything else could wait.

He groaned in my ear. "Not fair, Lucy." He backed up a fraction of an inch, those silvery eyes on fire.

"I know," I whispered, staring up at him through my lashes. "I'll be good. I promise." Slowly, I placed my right hand on my chest, over my heart.

He sucked in a breath. "Dang girl. Sometimes I think you know exactly what you're doing to me."

Butterflies pinged-ponged through my middle. I pursed my lips together. Busted.

Leaning down, he kissed my temple. "If we play our cards right, we'll have plenty of time for us. Later."

"Now you're talking." I grabbed his hand and led him toward the door.

"There you guys are." Shanda glanced up from her snuggle session with Tony on the couch. Glorious colors painted the sky across the wall of windows behind them. They were the picture of the perfect, normal couple. If only our lives were really this ordinary.

Will scooted the coffee table closer, then copped a squat on the sofa beside Tony, motioning for me to sit beside him. I plopped down next to him, my eyes widening at all the gear he laid out on the table.

"What is all this stuff?" I gulped, trying to figure out the two black square thingies, one with wires protruding out of it.

"This is the digital combo safecracker." Will pointed at the wire thingy first, then the white scanner bar I was familiar with. "This is the portable scanner I'll use to scan the pages. And this is a hotspot that will keep the internet connection between the chamber and the office open."

Shanda pulled out a notepad and eyed Will expectantly. "I'm guessing that's where I come in?"

"You and Tony both. I need you to hack the system and keep Nexis off our trail. Tony will man the security cameras and make sure no one comes snooping around." Will held up his fingers and ticked the items off one by one, then pulled a business card from his pocket. "Plus, I scored tomorrow's security passwords."

"Got it. Just like last time. I'll take that." Shanda plucked the card from Will's grasp and tucked it into her bra. Then she went back to writing furiously on her notepad.

"What will I be doing?" My gaze flitted to the tech gear on the table. "'Cause that's really not my thing."

"Just like Tony is Shanda's backup, you'll be my eyes and ears in the chamber." Reaching for my knee, he squeezed.

A lump formed in my throat, but I swallowed it back. "I wish I could do more."

Exhaling the biggest sigh in the history of the world, Will slid his arm around my shoulder. "What we're doing is dangerous enough."

Tony grimaced as he glanced at Shanda, then at me. "I wish you girls didn't have to be involved at all. But Will is right. Both teams need a backup. No one should go in alone."

Will cocked his head at Tony. "If this goes south, I don't care what you guys see happening to us. You run. You hear me? Run."

Tony's eyes went wide. "But what about you guys? You'd be stuck in the chamber facing God-knows-what."

Will's jaw tensed, and he gripped my hand for dear life. "I'm a Stanton, and she's the Seer. They can't do too much to us. Nexis needs us."

A hush fell over the room and as the last rays of sunlight faded into darkness outside. Shanda broke the silence by flicking on a lamp, illuminating three grim faces. Mine was surely no different.

"We have our plan. I think that's enough for tonight." Shanda shoved her chair back from the table with a screech and walked into the kitchen.

"Is she okay?" Tony mouthed at me, eyes trailing his girlfriend.

"I'll go check." I chased Shanda into the kitchen nook.

I stopped in the doorway. Shanda paced back and forth across her marble kitchen tiles, running her hand through her hair.

"Shanda?" My voice wobbled all over the place. "You okay?"

She exhaled a deep breath, glancing up at me. "This is starting to feel real. What if we get caught? Or worse?"

A chill slithered down my spine. She had a point. "You're right. This is a big deal. But you're the one who's so big on backup plans. Why don't we think of a backup plan in case we get caught?"

"Okay." Slowly, she nodded. "Whatcha thinking?"

My forehead scrunched into bulldog mode, but I said it anyway. "I'm thinking if we don't come back, your dad will notice.

So maybe we send him a message to contact the Guardians if we don't get back by a certain time."

"Eeek." Shanda cringed. "Then I'll be in big trouble."

Crossing my arms over my chest, I stared her down. "I'd rather be in trouble with our parents than Nexis."

"Good point." She nodded and pressed her lips into a thin line. "But why stop there? I've got a contact at the local news station. I'm sure they'd love to know if two teenage girls go missing on spring break."

"Yes, okay." I wiped my brow and relaxed my shoulders, glad she was finally calming down. "This is shaping up to be a solid backup plan. Step one, tell Guardians if we're late. Step two, give the story to local media if we go missing for 24 hours."

Shanda reached for my hand and pulled me into a hug. "Thanks for letting me vent. Now can we have one last night of teenage normalcy before things go down tomorrow?"

"You bet." I squeezed her back. "Movies and popcorn?"

Pulling out a giant bowl, she went to work microwaving the popcorn. It was hard to believe we were breaking into a secret Nexis lair—tomorrow. Every muscle in my body twitched like it was on high alert.

Our plan was too big to fail. Bigger than when James stole Nexis documents from St. Lucy's church and got himself banished. What would Nexis do to Will and Shanda if we got caught? Icy tendrils of dread snaked across my throat in a vice grip that had me gasping for breath. Because deep down, I knew they'd get a punishment worse than being banished.

I couldn't even think about what they'd do to me. My thoughts hit a brick wall like my brain didn't even want to go there.

So, I tried to think about happier things. Maybe we'd succeed after all. Could intel from the Nexis Seer book really be enough to earn my way into the Guardians? If so, maybe I'd be headed to Europe next. Who cared if Bryan's lies about Europe were actually true? At least I'd get to find my brother. And maybe rescue him for a change.

"Lucy, wake up. It's time for bed." Will's velvety whisper hummed in my ear.

"Mmmm." Rubbing my eyes, I opened them and glanced around. The TV was dark. How long had the movie been over? Where were Shanda and Tony? Right now, it didn't matter. I snuggled deeper into Will's arms. I could stay right here all night.

His fingers wove through my hair, absently. "Are you scared about tomorrow?"

I popped upright at his question, my heart rate ramping up. "Of course I am. But I'm more scared for you and Shanda than I am for myself. Or Tony. Why, are you worried?" My muscles froze, bracing for impact.

He let out a shaky breath, his silvery eyes circling my face. "If my mom weren't so unstable right now, I wouldn't be concerned. But she's too volatile to be reasoned with."

"Why?" I croaked, reaching for his hands.

His eyes shot down to his lap as he interlaced his fingers in mine. "Before you arrived on campus, I made the mistake of telling my mom about this dream I had. It was a scene right out of Zechariah chapter 4. That's why she went ballistic and ordered me to spy on you."

"Wow. That sounds pretty intense." I squeezed his hands in a small attempt to offer some kind of reassurance.

"It's a pretty intense dream. Here, let me show you." Leaning in, he pressed his lips to mine.

Shanda's living room faded away, replaced by a new scene.

Will and I stood side-by-side in a world of clouds and light. Warmth and peace shimmered around us like tangible things you could touch and hold for your very own. I just wanted to hang out here forever. Until I noticed a golden lampstand and two olive trees standing a few feet away from us. Overhead, the clouds parted and a golden light shined down in radiant beams. Strange words boomed from the light like claps of thunder in a foreign language. As if a different angel spoke to us. Or maybe the Creator himself.

Then the heavenly world vanished, and I was on Shanda's couch again, Will's lips still on mine.

"Wow." I whispered against his mouth. There were no words to describe what I just saw.

He arched back, breaking the kiss. "At the end of Zechariah chapter 4, it says, 'These are the two who are anointed to serve the Lord of all the earth.'"

"Yikes. What does that mean, for us?" I gnawed on my lip, dread pooling in the pit of my stomach.

"It means that together, we have a lot of power. If you're a Nexis control freak, like Mom, you could wield that power in some seriously bad way." He brushed my hair back, massaging his fingers into my neck. "Does that make you want to change your mind, tiger?"

Tingles shivered down my spine at his nickname for me. But resolved solidified a fortress of steel in my gut. "No. I want to do what we can to protect ourselves. I think it's worth the risk."

His face lit up and he kissed my nose. "See? Now that's why I call you tiger. You're pretty fierce when you want to be."

"Thanks." My insides turned to mush as he grabbed my hand and pulled me up. "When I set my mind to something, I can be pretty determined. That's all."

Together, we padded down the carpeted hall, stopping in front of Shanda's bedroom door.

"True. And I love that about you." Leaning down, he pressed a kiss to my lips.

Did he just say love? I swallowed back a squeak and kissed him goodnight.

><

Rubbing my eyelids, I opened them to find myself lying in a strange white bed in a strange white room. My chest constricted automatically. Where was I? A similar image popped into my head. Of another white room, with doctors and nurses and beeping machines. I bolted straight up, knocking off the covers.

You're safe. You're not in the hospital. That was a year ago. I repeated the mantra over and over in my head and breathed in the sweet, antiseptic-free air.

Morning sunlight peeked through the blinds. Someone moved beside me.

"Morning, roomie." Shanda yawned and stretched her arms wide.

"Morning." I tried to steady my voice, racking my brain for coherent thoughts.

She cleared her throat. "You need to go take a shower. Now."

"That bad?" I cupped my hand in front of my face. Pungent morning breath greeted my nostrils.

"That bad." She sat up in bed, rubbing her eyes.

"Great. I'm going." I picked up my purse and padded across the floor to her en suite bathroom.

"Nope, not there." She threw a pillow across the room, right in my path. "I need to shower, too. No way Tony's gonna see Morning Shanda. Use the hall bath."

I'd almost forgotten the guys were here, sleeping in the Jones' guest room down the hall.

"C'mon, really?" I croaked, gesturing down to my rumpled PJs. "I can't let Will see me like this either. Seriously."

"Don't worry, the guest room has its own bathroom. And I'm sure they're not fighting over it like we are." She shrugged, mouth curling ever-so-slightly.

"Fine," I huffed and tiptoed to her bedroom door. Turning around, I pointed one finger at her. "But you owe me."

"Sure. Whatever." She shot me a grin and closed the bathroom door behind her.

Creaking open the bedroom door, I tiptoed ten paces down the hall. In a heartbeat, I flung open the door to the guest bath and slammed it shut behind me. Phew. Close one.

In the shower, I let the water stream down around me, sloughing off the city dirt and grime.

Once I dried off and wrapped my hair in a towel, the realization struck me. Oh, no. Something very important was missing—clean clothes. Hello? Why didn't I bring a change of clothes with me? Guess that's what lack of coffee does to a girl.

I could just wear my ratty old pajamas. But that wouldn't be any better, really. Instead, I wrapped a fluffy white towel around my body. Luckily, I found a comb on the counter and tugged the snarls out of my dark hair. I hadn't bothered to cut it in so long that now it hung six inches below my shoulders.

The mirror was too fogged up to see, but I didn't have any makeup anyway. I just shrugged and wadded my PJs in a ball. I still had to make it back to Shanda's room without the guys seeing. Especially Will.

Cracking open the bathroom door, I peeked out. And listened. Nothing. The coast looked clear. Cinching up my towel, I booked it down the hall with my head down. And ran smack-dab into something solid. My skin sizzled like a heatwave, but I couldn't look up yet. My towel started slipping. I gripped it tighter around me as my clothes tumbled to the hardwood. My bra flapped across his bare feet.

"Whoa, hello," came Will's voice from above. "You look good in just a towel."

My face flamed. I'm pretty sure my whole body turned red. Squirming, I tried to slip around him. Then his hand flew to my waist, blocking my path. Legions of amped-up butterflies swirled in my chest. Finally, I peeked up at him.

"Where are you going in such a hurry?" His lips were parted ever-so-slightly as he stared down at me, eyes roaming my body.

"To put some clothes on. So you'll stop looking at me like that."

He kissed my forehead. "Good idea. But there's no guarantee I'll ever stop looking at you like this."

I gulped. His eyes were dark, his jaw set in stone except for one little muscle that twitched like crazy. He was serious.

Definitely serious. So I did the only thing I could do. I raced back into Shanda's room, where I belonged.

"Nice underwear," he called through the door. "What do I do with these?"

My lungs seized up. How could I forget? My clothes were still strewn all over the hallway. *All* of my clothes.

I banged my head against the door. *Crash.* "I'll take them." I cracked open the door. Holding out my hand.

No response.

What was he doing, studying my PJs? How could I just leave my boyfriend in the hallway with my underwear?

Finally, he looped my bra and panties over my outstretched hand. "Whatever you say, gorgeous."

"Thank you," I whispered, slipping my arm back and shutting the door. The humiliation washed over me, wave after wave.

"You're welcome," came his soft voice through the door.

My heart melted into a puddle, oozing around me. Maybe that wasn't the most embarrassing thing ever.

Water hissed from Shanda's bathroom. Of course, she was still in the shower. One less person to witness my crazy antics. Though I'd probably just tell her about it later.

Gathering my towel-clad self together, I pushed myself back up and headed straight for Shanda's walk-in closet. Pulling on my all black break-in outfit, I stared at myself in the full-length mirror. Flushed pink cheeks and rivers of messy wet hair were all I could see. Sucking in a deep breath, I willed my racing heart to slow. If only I could get the last few minutes of my life back. Hopefully, that would be the only thing that went wrong today.

CHAPTER 26

Different night, same place. We stood, barely concealed in the treeline, on the edge of campus, staring at the Nexis tower. Will, Shanda, Tony, and I were about to break into the Nexis Chamber for the second time in as many months. We could only hope we didn't get caught and expelled—or worse.

A cool April breeze wafted across my face. I glanced up at the stars, feeling like something was missing. Silently, I reached out for my angel. Dozens of stars twinkled in the clear dark sky, and I knew we weren't going in alone. Tonight, there was no moon in sight. Just as we'd planned. Still, our fear hung in the air. An invisible cloud pressing down on us.

Tony whispered something to Will, and they started to divvy up supplies and flashlights.

Shanda turned to me in the starlight, her almond eyes searching mine. "I don't like that you and Will are going in by yourselves."

"I know." I stared at Shanda, my best friend in the whole world. "But you've got mad hacker skills. It'll help knowing you've got my back. And Tony's got yours."

She pursed her lips and yanked something out of the pocket of her black hoodie. "This'll keep you safe." She nodded once, then shoved a solid, oblong object into my hands.

"What's this?" I stared at the black contraption that fit in my palm. My eyes widened. "Is it—?"

"A taser? Yes," she hissed, one finger to her lips. "In case your angel fire is on the fritz. And leave your phone on. Just in case."

"Thank you," I mouthed, tucking the weapon in my hoodie pocket and hoping to God I wouldn't have to use it. I knew Shanda always had my back, but this was more than I expected. My heart swelled infinitely larger. Pulling her into my arms, I held on for dear life.

Tony swung around and walked toward us, one finger on his lips. Was he in on the taser plan, too?

Swallowing a big gulp, I bobbed my head. It was nice to know I had people looking out for me.

Lifting his binoculars, he scanned the campus one last time, then nodded at Will.

"All right, guys," Will whispered, leaning toward me and Shanda. "Remember the plan. We'll sneak up to the tower as silently as possible. I'll go first. Tony will bring up the rear."

"Got it," Shanda gulped.

I nodded, smashing my mouth into a grim line. The night seemed darker all of a sudden.

"Here we go." Will was the first to leave the safety of the treeline. I followed closely on his heels, with Shanda and Tony not far behind. Suddenly the campus went silent, too silent as we started down the hillside field. All the normal nighttime sounds were drowned out by my pulse pounding in my ears with each step down the open hillside toward the tower.

My hamstrings burned and twitched with every step as I struggled to absorb the steep terrain with my legs. I turned one last time, giving Tony and Shanda a small wave. Shanda fluttered her fingers at me. I nodded back and turned my eyes to the rocky path at my feet. One foot in front of the other. The ground beneath flattened out as we reached the base of the hill.

Our steps died to a mere pitter-patter. We were in full-on Stealth Ninja Mode now.

When we reached the side of the building, Will flattened himself against the wall, his back hugging the side of the tower. I followed suit as we made our way to the nearest door. Will punched in a code. *Click*, the door popped open.

"Nice," I mouthed.

"Thanks," he murmured. "Just one of the perks of being Nexis president."

Tony and Shanda filed in behind us, and we all tiptoed through the Nexis foyer and into the shadows as quickly as possible.

We waited. One. Two... Five seconds. Looking both ways, Will went to the back wall and uncovered the secret panel.

My lungs seized up as Will punched in the code to the Nexis office. The light blinked green, and he scanned the room before ushering us all inside. The door clicked shut behind us.

Whoosh. I could breathe again.

He turned to Shanda in the darkness. "Set it up. Quickly."

With one nod, she headed over to the desk and opened the laptop, typing furiously. Tony pulled out a second laptop and set it beside Shanda's. She whispered instructions to him.

"You okay, sweetie?" Will's hand found the small of my back.

I nodded even though he probably couldn't see. "I'm fine."

"You don't have to give me that brave face I'm sure you're giving me right now." He squeezed my hand and led me to the other side of the room. "You ready for this?"

"Ready as I can be." I couldn't keep the tremor out of my voice.

He leaned into me, lips on my temple, breath hot on my face. "I know you're scared. But I've got your back."

"And I've got yours." Without thinking, I turned to cup his chin and pressed a kiss into those soft lips.

Closing my eyes tight, I barely noticed when the blackness in front of my eyes shifted to an eerie red glow. As the red glow sharpened into focus, a ruby emerged from the shadows. Glowing like a nightlight in the dark. Hissing noises erupted as shadows swirled around the red stone, the inaudible words growing louder and louder. *Destroy me or die*, a sinister voice whispered over and over again. The ruby burst into flames.

Khrrrieickhh. A metallic crash ripped through the air, and my eyes popped open to the real world.

"What was that?" I whispered, arching back, my ears still burning as my heart found a new rhythm.

Will glanced toward the desk.

Shanda waved a handful of cords in her hands. "Just splicing into the camera system. No big deal."

"You guys about ready over there?" Will reached for my hand and squeezed, pulling me into his side.

I looped one arm around his back, letting his warmth seep into me. I could use all the reassuring I could get right now.

"We just need two more minutes and we'll be good to go." Shanda didn't glance up from her screen.

Fascinated, I watched her loop together video feed so all five cameras saw the exact same thing—nothing. Tony sat in front of the second laptop, diligently watching the live feed for Nexis guards.

She glanced at Tony, who nodded. "Okay, we're good to go."

"Wow, girl. That's truly impressive." With two fingers on my forehead, I pretended to tip my hat to her.

She shot me a wink over her shoulder. "You two better go now. Who knows how long we'll be clear."

Nodding, I grabbed Will's hand and let him lead the way to the next secret door. He punched in the code with ease, and the familiar gear-clanking sound greeted my ears.

"Be safe, but be quick." Shanda called after me.

I turned to wave goodbye to her, then Will and I descended the impossibly long and twisting stone stairs. Adrenaline coursed through my veins on hyperdrive. Every few feet, orange work lamps created shadows that made my heart leap out of my chest. At last, we reached the familiar landing, and Will did his Nexis president voodoo to open the chamber door.

This time, there was no messing around. No time to turn on the lights. Flicking on the flashlight, he walked straight to the fountain statue in the middle of the courtyard. He unrolled a piece of paper and shone the flashlight on it. Then he moved to the base of the fountain, fingers running along the cracks and seams until he found what he wanted. He pressed down.

Pop, click. A rectangle the size of a shoebox popped out form the base, metal gleaming back at me from the flashlight's beam. Scooting in closer, I peered over Will's shoulder. And gasped.

He was right. He'd uncovered a small safe hidden under the Nephilim fountain.

"Wow." I breathed.

Unfurling the paper again, Will read something off it, mouthing it over and over again. Then he punched in the code.

A red light blinked back at us. The door didn't budge.

And my heart stopped.

Grunting, Will read the code again, typing it in a second time. Another red light. He tried the code again. Same red light.

Click, click, click. Suddenly all the lights in the room flicked on. Four robed guards emerged from the shadows, more waiting in the wings.

"Run!" Will screamed, grabbing my hand and pulling me back the way we'd come. But it was too late. Two guards closed in on us, one on either side of us.

"We got 'em," one goon yelled into his walkie.

Will held up his hands, and I did the same. My knees wobbled like crazy, but I reached inside for the energy welling up inside me.

"Follow my lead. I'll get us out of this. You'll see." But the twitch in Will's mouth said otherwise.

"Maybe I can help." I flicked my gaze down to my hoodie pocket.

Two guards in front approached us, pulling out the zip-tie cuffs. "Put your hands behind your back," one said.

Slowly, I lowered my hands. Will did the same. I slipped two fingers into my front pouch and flipped the switch. The taser hummed against my belly. Then I turned on my own electric current, letting the static build in my veins.

"I said hands behind your back," the guard yelled at me.

I nodded toward Will. In one quick motion, he grabbed the taser and shot it at the guard's throat. The man jiggled and gurgled, then crumpled to the floor. I held up my hands and zapped the other guy with my voltage. He hit the floor with a thud.

"Stop." Another guard yelled behind us. "Put down your weapons."

I glanced at the taser in Will's hand. It had one charge left. Will nodded once, then turned to face the other guy and shot the distance taser. I shot an extra spark from one hand, hoping to help him out.

"Run for it!" Will yelled, grabbing my jacket and sprinting toward the entrance.

Spotlights flooded the ancient courtyard, but we kept on running.

Pfft. Pfft, pfft. A strange sound zinged by my ear. I couldn't stop now. I had to keep going.

Pfft. Something sliced into my shoulder, and I stumbled. Were they shooting at us? Will grabbed my elbow and we raced on, closer and closer to the chamber door.

Pfft, pfft. As we reached the door, I took two to the back and landed hard on my knees, then face-planted into the stone floor. Ears ringing. Head throbbing.

"Lucy!" Will bellowed. His weapon clanked to the ground as he crouched over me. "Are you hit?"

I winced, pointing to my back. But my fingers came back dry. No blood.

"Rubber bullets," he muttered, lacing an arm around my back. Pressing into my welts, he helped me up, and we limped up the steps.

"See. I told you they wouldn't hurt us." My speech sounded funny. Slurred. I blinked, seeing stars. "Hit my head pretty good."

"I know. I've got you." Suddenly I was airborne, his arms wrapped around my legs, and he was carrying me. Running up the stairs somehow.

"Not so fast." A familiar voice rang out behind us. "Sorry, but I've got to do this. You'll see her again soon."

Something buzzed into my back and legs, where Will held me. His arms went slack, and I fell to the ground. Hard.

Will dropped to his knees, body convulsing with electricity. Until he fell down beside me. The shockwave zinged through my body next. Pain sizzled through every muscle.

Will! I screamed inside my head, but everything went dark.

><

"I can't believe I let this happen." Will's face faded in and out through iron bars.

Searing pain pounded my skull as I tried to sit up, propping my elbows against a stone-cold floor. The smell hit me first. More like a stench, really. An acrid odor like melting tires and scorched marshmallows burned my lungs. My stomach lurched as darkness and light faded in and out, merging together until reality came back into focus. My new boyfriend sat huddled into the corner of the dungeon cell. Thick iron bars stood between us.

Scooting himself across the dank, dusty stone floor, Will wrapped two hands around the bars. "I was supposed to protect you, and now look what's happened. I can't even do that."

With those words, the shadows rolled in, hissing softly. So quiet I could barely hear them. They curled around Will's body. He shivered and hunched his knees to his chest.

Long wraith-tendrils of black mist wrapped around his neck, slithering up to his ears. Harsh whispers in another language sliced through the air between us. He covered his ears as if to block out the evil lullaby of strange voices.

And I couldn't take it anymore. I sat on the stone floor next to him, a chill seeping through my jeans.

"Don't listen to them." My head throbbed as I crawled across the floor and took his face in my hands. "It's not your fault. This is all my fault."

He barely glanced up, the shadows coiling around him tighter and tighter. "Look where we are. Where I've led you."

Tears sprang to my eyes. "You're not the one who brought Shanda and Tony into this. Who knows what Nexis is doing to them right now? I can't even think about it."

As soon as I said those words, the wraiths of darkness swarmed me, too. First, the stench wafted to my nose, then came the screeches. The ghoulish howls crescendoed louder and louder. Almost as loud as a reckoning. But this time the shrieks formed into words, phrases I'd told myself over and over again all my life.

You're not good enough. You'll never be the Seer. Why don't you just go back to your normal life? The last punch really hit home. My whole life, I'd just wanted to fade into the background and be a normal girl. But I couldn't do that anymore. If I stayed in the shadows and did nothing, people were going to get hurt. Or worse.

I needed to stop running from my destiny. With one hand, I reached for the ceiling—calling out to the only one who could help me.

"Angel, where are you? I need you now." Hot tears dribbled down my face. "I'm sorry I did this without you. Will you come and show me the way out?"

Crrraaackkk. A clap of thunder echoed in the Nexis dungeon, then a bolt of purple lightning sizzled through the air. Moments later, Angel materialized in front of me in all his shimmering white light.

Warm, golden eyes appeared in the white glow. Eyes that were trained on me. "It's about time you called for me."

Will's eyes went wide as he glanced from me to Angel and back again. "How am I seeing this in real-time?"

"I don't know," I whispered back. "Just go with it."

The brightness expanded to fill the whole dungeon, stamping out the last of the shadows into dying embers. "The Seer and the Interpreter together at last. I will help you both."

Tiny rays of golden light reached out in opposite directions. The golden light touched my temple first, then Will's. The light grazed my face like a finger. The moment it touched me, a comforting warmth seeped like honey from my head down to my toes. I inhaled a deep breath that smelled like sunshine itself, finally feeling free of all the doubts and fears that had just assaulted me. Standing up straight, I basked in the white and gold light. Happy memories from my childhood floated across my mind until at last, I felt like me again.

I glanced over at Will to see the same earmarks of joy washing over his chiseled features.

"Feel better?" Angel's voice boomed from the center of the white orb.

I nodded. "Thank you, Angel."

The fingers of gold faded away, and the white orb radiated sparkling shards of prismed rainbows. "You're welcome, little Seer."

The instant the angel-warmth left me, my heart sank into my chest. "I feel so stupid. I'm sorry I didn't talk to you first. We could've come up with a plan together."

"I know little one." Pieces of whiteness formed into hands that reached out for me. "You know what you must do. I will help you as best I can."

Suddenly, a glowing ruby appeared in Angel's hands. Shadows swirled around it, but they were self-contained in a dark orb. *Thump, thump, thump.* The red and black sphere grew bigger and brighter in time to my ever-quickening heartbeats.

Eeeoww, eeeoww, eeeowww. The ear-splitting shrieks slammed back, full-force as the shadows rolled in. Inch by inch, they eclipsed Angel's white glow.

Somewhere far away, in the midst of the shadows, Angel's voice reached my ears. "It is here. Tonight, I will help you fulfill your destiny."

Angel's golden eyes appeared above the ruby and I nodded, extending my arm toward him.

The ruby erupted in a great red flash, hurtling fiery sparks in every direction. Every shadow vanished in a puff of smoke. The white light faded, too.

You will know when the time is right. In a shower of twinkling stars, Angel shot through the ceiling. Leaving me and Will alone in the dark dungeon once again.

I blinked and rubbed my eyes, hoping the dungeon would fade away, too. But we were still stuck in Nexis purgatory, waiting for our sentence.

Will gulped, his face ashen. "So that's your mission? Destroy the Nexis ruby? That must mean Nexis brought it here for the ceremony."

Great. Something to look forward to. I froze as fear settled in. "How in the world are we going to do that?" I whispered.

He rested his forehead on the bars between us. "More importantly, it'll earn us both a death sentence even my mother can't stop."

Inhaling a deep breath, I peered up at him, ready to lay all my cards on the table. "All I know is, every time I try to do things on my own I end up in a craphole. Maybe this is my destiny." My words dropped like a truth bomb.

Silence filled the dungeon as something flickered across Will's face.

Through the bars, Will grabbed my hand and squeezed. "Well, if it's your destiny, it's my destiny, too."

The outer door creaked open. Footsteps clomped slowly toward us.

"Better keep quiet. The guards are coming," I hissed at Will as a familiar figure emerged from the shadows.

"I should've known they'd send you to do their dirty work." Will practically growled beside me.

"I didn't have a choice." Kevin hung his head as he slid the key into the lock. "Looks like you two lovebirds are cozy down here."

"There's always a choice." Will laced his fingers through mine as we turned to face Kevin the Traitor together.

"Not this time, I'm afraid." Kevin opened the door and stepped into my cell. Holding out a taser, he grabbed my hands. "C'mon, Lucy. Don't make me zap you again."

Did they know about my angel fire? I froze, panic icing up my veins. Did electricity short-circuit my powers?

He pushed me through the door and clanked it shut behind him.

"What're you doing? Where are you taking her?" Will's voice rose.

"I've got orders, man. Sorry." Kevin reached for Will's cell door and unlocked it. "Don't worry. You're coming, too."

CHAPTER 27

Kevin had a vice-grip on my hand as he dragged me and Will down the dark hall to our doom.

A strange sight greeted us as we made our way to the courtyard. Two black-cloaked figures flanked each pillar of the four arches. More dark cloaks shifted in the shadowy depths of the mezzanine overlooking the courtyard. I could practically feel their eyes roaming the captive audience.

Bile burned my throat, and my heart lurched in my chest. I reached for Will, but in seconds, two black-robed guards wedged between us, one yanking my elbow and the other grabbing his arm. Both poking tasers into my gut. The infamous Nexis goons dragged us past a gawking Kevin and escorted us through the archway into the one place I hadn't already seen on my Nexis Chamber tour—the Grand Council Chamber.

Ominous chanting reached my ears as I stepped through the entrance and gasped. The underground lair was enormous, with dozens of bleacher-like stone landings that descended into what could only be described as a subterranean arena. Hundreds of black-hooded figures flanked the bleachers, staring toward the arena in the center as if waiting for the main event. All the Nexis members in the country must be here tonight. My stomach twisted into a thousand knots.

"What is this place?" I whispered to Will as all hoods turned toward us.

"It's the Grand Council arena. Only used for special occasions." He yanked and pulled against the guards as they forced us down the wide steps toward the center.

The chanting muted as the guards dragged us down step after step through the middle of the crowd. I scanned the hooded faces, looking for any sign of someone I recognized, but they were all covered in shadows. Something sinister lay in store for us.

After what felt like miles of trudging down stone steps, we finally reached our destination. The guards shoved us into the middle of the arena, where three strange objects stood front and center. Three ornately carved pedestals were placed equidistant from each other. Stranger and stranger. A chill crawled up my spine as my eyes fixed on the center pillar. Goon number one pulled a chain out of his cloak and wrapped it around my wrists. I kicked and screamed, ready to call up my powers and fire into the cavern full of Nexis members, but another guard flipped on the taser until I stilled. They chained me to the stone pedestal. I could only watch as they chained Will to the pillar on my left.

One hot tear trickled down my cheek as I stared into the face of the boy I loved. We were helpless. There was nothing we could do. After tonight, nothing would ever be the same again.

A horde of black-robed guards appeared in the distance, marching toward us with torches in perfect formation. They created a circle of burning torches around us. A familiar picture that made my heart beat faster. Suddenly, applause broke out amongst the hooded crowd as a lone figure stepped toward us.

"Finally, the little Seer-in-training is ready to join us." A strange woman's voice assaulted my ears. A roar erupted from the secret onlookers.

Everything inside me clenched at her words. "I'll never join you." I practically spat out the words.

"I'm sure you think that now." She reached her long bony fingers out far enough to pat me on the head. "But I have ways of changing your mind."

My whole body shuddered. "What ways?"

"I'm glad you asked." She snapped her fingers, and two black-robed guards appeared at her side. "Where is the little traitor? Bring her here."

"Mom, stop this now. Before someone gets hurt," Will hissed through clenched teeth.

I snapped my head to look at him. "Did you just say, *Mom*?"

"I'd know that voice anywhere." He leaned close and whispered in my ear. "I've started calling her Rosalyn lately, but I don't think that'd help us now."

There was no time to chit-chat as a black-robed guard appeared to my right, dragging a dark figure between them. My heart seized in my chest. *Shanda.* She writhed in their clutches, kicking and screaming. Clawing and biting. Was that spittle? Yep, she just spat on the unlucky guard closest to her. It took four grown men to bring my best friend to Rosalyn Stanton's side.

"You okay?" I whispered, straining against my chains.

"Been better," she hissed back.

"Where's Tony?" I mouthed the last word.

Shanda lifted her head slightly, her eyes flicking up to the ceiling. For the first time in hours, a glimmer of hope bloomed in my chest.

"Now that the charade is up, it's time to get to work." Rosalyn flipped back her hood back and her blonde hair fell loose as she sneered at me. Rage and age had etched a few extra lines in her features since I met her that one time at James' graduation over three years ago. But her eyes were gray and her cheekbones chiseled, just like her son's

"Wha," my voice cracked as the question I dared not ask came tumbling out of my mouth. "What kind of work exactly?"

Firelight flickered in Rosalyn's gray eyes. "This is the Summoning Ritual. Something I've been waiting a very long time to share with you."

"No, Mom." Fear laced the edges of Will's words. "It's too soon for this. You don't even know what her gifts are yet."

She took two steps closer to her son, shaking her head. "You have so much to learn about the ways of Nexis. The age of the Nephilim is upon us. The journey begins tonight."

"Oh, great," Shanda huffed under her breath. "Get ready for crazy."

I glanced at Shanda and snickered, even as my stomach curled in on itself.

"Guards!" Rosalyn's hand shot out like a pistol. "Silence the traitor."

A guard reached out and clamped a hand over Shanda's mouth.

"Hey. Leave her alone." I lunged at the crazy lady, chains clanging and digging into my wrists. Probably a reason they shacked me with steel. I'd only zap myself if I tried to use my angel fire now. But it may be the better alternative, in the end.

Rosalyn sunk her claws into my skin and yanked me back. I winced, just as Shanda bit into the guard's hand.

"Yeow!" he yelped, jumping back.

A satisfied smile spread across her face. I felt my lips curl up too.

"Enough!" Rosalyn bellowed. "Let the ceremony begin." She pulled the black hood back over her head.

Three Black Robes stepped away from the crowd and marched into the circle, facing us.

"Thank you, my loyal Nexilim." She bowed her head and they bowed back.

They each held an object in their hands, shrouded in more black cloth. All three figures thrust their objects forward.

A chill slithered down my spine. The Black Robes were close enough to the torches that I recognized two of their faces in the firelight. Kevin stood in the middle across from Will's mom, but it was the face on the end that struck fear into my heart.

"What is Jake doing here?" I whispered to Will.

"Jake's here?" He hissed, eye darting among the Black Robes. "Where?"

I closed my eyes and pointed. "On the end, next to Kevin." Acid churned in my stomach, rising with every second that ticked by. If Jake was involved, this couldn't be good.

"That's the dean, next to Kevin." Will gasped, eyes going wide at the ebony figure beside Kevin.

My jaw dropped. He was right. I'd forgotten her face since orientation, but it was definitely her. The blood froze in my veins.

Rosalyn carefully removed the cloth from each object, revealing three rocks of similar size in the hands of Kevin, Dean Frederickson, and Jake.

"The sacred stones." I sucked in a breath, as a collective gasp rippled through the rows of onlookers. The rumors were true. Nexis *had* been stealing stones. This kept getting worse and worse. Shadows billowed down the steps toward us, so I looked to the ceiling. *Do you see this, Angel? Where are you?*

Pinpricks of white light sparkled across the ceiling above me. *Don't worry, little Seer. I will get help.*

A cold wind howled in his wake, making me feel more alone.

Rosalyn reached for the middle stone and placed it on the stone pedestal in front of me. She snapped her fingers, and two more black-cloaked figures appeared, carrying what looked like long, golden trumpets.

"Great. Let's announce our presence to the neighborhood," Shanda whispered.

The men in black flanked the stone pedestal in front of me and set down the golden trumpet. Except they weren't trumpets. They were pillars.

My heart seized. Were these the two golden lampstands from Zechariah's vision? Except they weren't lampstands. They were sacred stone holders.

Every muscle in my body clenched as I watched the whole scene unfold before me. I grimaced, wanting to tear my gaze away—but I couldn't move a muscle. I could only watch in horror as black-clad freaks placed the Guardian Amethyst on the pillar to my right and the Watcher's Sapphire on the pillar to my left. The moment all the stones were in place, the Nexis Ruby glowed on the stone pedestal in front of me. The one I'd been chained to by my boyfriend's mom. Was this really happening?

"Handmaidens, take your place," Rosalyn barked, snapping her fingers.

The three black-shrouded figures emerged from the crowd, stopping directly in front of us. Slowly, they removed their hoods, and my stomach threatened to hurl its contents everywhere. My three least favorite people stared back at me—Monica, Colleen, and my ex-BFF Becca. Monica and Colleen at least had the decency to wear solemn, almost scared looks on their faces. But not Becca. Her lips curled in a little sneer, her eyes dancing.

"Hi Lucy." Becca practically sneered at me. "Are you ready to play your part now? Finally?"

Shadows slithered at my feet, but I ignored them. I couldn't let her see me flinch. "We'll see about that."

"Yes, we will," Rosalyn growled, pulling out a gun and pointing it to Shanda's head.

I froze, still as a statute. *Not Shanda*, my heart screamed. Shanda's eyes were wide, the first sign of fear I'd seen since we got captured.

Icy tendrils wrapped around my ankles, holding me in place.

"Don't do anything, Lucy." Shanda screamed. "She'll never—" A meaty hand wrapped around her face, cutting her off.

"If you don't do exactly as I say," Rosalyn leaned in, her voice low, "I will pull the trigger."

Shadows billowed up, shifting and taking shape around me. Dark shadow-hands wrapped around my neck, forcing me to nod.

"Mom. What are you doing?" Will's cracked with a note of desperation. "You don't need a gun."

"I wish I didn't." Somehow, Rosalyn managed a smile while waving the firearm in the air. "Your little girlfriend here is finally going to fulfill her destiny. And so are you."

"It's going to be okay," Will whispered to me and Shanda. He scooted next to me until our toes bumped, but that's as far as he could reach. "We'll find a way out of this. I know we will."

"I don't think so. Remember this?" Rosalyn waved the gun around Shanda's head like it was a toy.

I cringed as the shadows formed wraiths that swirled around us, screeching and shrieking as they wove their way between me, Will, and Shanda.

"Mother, stop!" Will bellowed from my side.

The shadows reared back, making a wider berth around us.

For an instant, Rosalyn's face softened. "I always wished you would voluntarily join me in creating a new world. I never dreamed I'd have to force you to do what's good for you."

My jaw dropped as Rosalyn paced back and forth with the gun in her hand. Gasps erupted from the crowd on robed onlookers.

"How is this good for me? For anyone?" Will's eyes were wild as he stared at his mother like he didn't know her.

"Oh, no," Shanda muttered, rolling her eyes. "Don't get her started."

"You just don't get it, do you? How could you? You're only eighteen." For a moment she stopped her frantic pacing and looked at her son. "This is what I have to do to save this world from itself. Think about it. No more random crimes. No more senseless murders like what happened to your grandmother."

"Except for the gun you're waving around," I muttered under my breath.

Slowly, she turned to me, that crazy glint still in her eyes. "If you would just cooperate, we wouldn't need this." Then she turned the gun on me.

My heart stopped. My lungs froze. Somewhere in the periphery, I saw Will and Shanda lunge toward me as if to protect me, only to be subdued by their chains and their captors. But all I could see was the barrel of the gun. Pointed. Straight. At. Me.

"Ah," she breathed, drawing out the word. "I see I have your attention now. Will you agree to do everything I say? Or do I have to start shooting?" She waved the gun on either side of me—from Shanda on my right to Will on my left and back again.

Like a puppet whose string had just been pulled to the limit, I nodded. I knew if I didn't, she'd kill someone I loved. My best friend, or maybe even her own son.

"Good girl. Now, let's get started." Her voice rose as she faced the robed onlookers. "Ladies and gentlemen. We're gathered here tonight to witness the dawn of a new era in human history. Let the Summoning begin!"

A roar rustled through the crowd. The three handmaidens stepped back. All eyes turned to me, and the pedestal in front of me.

Rosalyn angled the gun toward the sacred stone between us. "Lucy, place your hands on the ruby. You're about to welcome some new beings to the realm of humanity."

I shuddered. I didn't want any new beings on this planet. No one should have to see what I saw when the shadows closed in. And boy, were they closing in now. Growing bigger, too.

Eoww. Eoww, Eoww. The shadows materialized into towering wraiths on either side of me. Their icy tentacles reached out, wrapping around my arms. Forcing my hands to obey the crazy lady's command. As soon as my fingernails scraped the dark rock, red sparks appeared.

"Ooohhh," came a collective noise from the gallery.

I stretched every muscle taut, trying desperately to resist the supernatural hands forcing mine to move. Beads of sweat broke out on my forehead, my neck. But they were too strong for me. At last, my hands enveloped the ruby. It glowed red-hot at my touch.

"Ahhh," the crowd clapped and cheered.

Beneath my feet, the ground turned translucent. Instead of rock and dirt, a whole other world brimmed below the surface. Full of fire and billowing smoke clouds. Suddenly the smoke cleared, and my heart dropped to my knees. A staircase ten stories deep, full of shadowy wraiths, materialized right under my feet. The wraiths were in formation, marching up the steps. A demon-horde ready to invade the earth, chanting their own rally cry. Whispering to me of deeper, more sinister plans than the Summoning ceremony ever dreamed of.

I gasped, dropping to my knees as tears rushed down my cheeks. The ruby's red light dimmed, and the crowd went silent. The rock returned under my feet as I sank further to the ground, straining against the chains above my head. Fear crawled around inside like a living, breathing organism, making my body quiver from the inside out. I never wanted to see that sight again. Not as long as I lived.

Whatever Rosalyn had planned paled in comparison to the demonic plans of the underworld. They were not planning to come to earth and play house with a few girls. They had plans of their own, and they had no intention of ushering in a utopian society.

"Lucy!" In an instant, Will lunged toward me, pulling at his chains. Close enough to nuzzle his toe against my boot. "Are you okay? Tell me you're okay."

"I'm okay," I croaked. "But the world won't be if your mother succeeds tonight."

"What did you see?" he hissed, eyes wide.

Strong fingers clamped around my biceps, pulling me to my feet. Five seconds later, Will was yanked to his feet, too.

"Yes, Lucy. Do tell us what you saw." An odd gleam washed across Rosalyn's face.

"I, uh ..." I trailed off, staring at her.

Her lips curled. "Better yet. Why don't you show us?" With one hand she grabbed Will's arm and placed his hand on the sapphire.

The moment his hand touched the uncut gemstone, the Watcher's Sapphire started to glow bright blue.

Rosalyn raised both arms in the air. "Behold, my son. The Interpreter." The crowd went wild as the world above and below us lit up for all to see.

Overhead, clouds of purple hovered on the ceiling, surrounding what looked like a portal of some kind. Sparkles of light shimmered in the distance, and an army of angels headed our way. Would they get here in time? Would their army be enough to tackle the demon-horde amassing at my feet?

A wave of light burst from the ruby, rippling across the ground beneath my feet. The rock floor faded away again, and the glowing staircase of demons appeared again.

"Is that what you saw before?" Will whispered in my ear.

I could only nod as hot sludge pooled in my throat.

"Oh, holy hell." Shanda's eyes were glued on the ground.

My heart fluttered like a hummingbird. "Can you see that?"

She nodded, her eyes flicked to my face. "Honey, we can all see that."

"No," I breathed, my head snapping up.

The three handmaidens in front of me had the tiniest flicker of fear in their eyes, even Becca. But the crowd was the creepiest part. Their eyes gleamed, mouths smirking, hands rubbing together. This is what they'd been waiting for. For years, maybe even centuries.

I lifted my chin to the purple sky. The lights were getting closer now, close enough to see horses and chariots of light, with my angel leading the way.

"*Gratiam, corum, domino.*" A deep voice rumbled behind me. And yet it sounded familiar.

A cheer went up from the crowd, and I turned to Will. "Who's behind us?"

He hung his head. "It's my grandfather."

"Uh-oh." The words escaped before I could catch them. The Stanton Patriarch was presiding over the ceremony. Of course.

Will turned to me. "Why is your angel and his army so far away?"

"I don't know." I shrugged. "But he usually has his reasons. Maybe they're waiting on something."

"*Gratium, corum, domino.*" Stanton raised his voice louder this time. "Let the age of the Nephilim begin." He took the sapphire in his hand and raised it above his head.

"Nexis Semigod Nations. Genesis six domination. Nexis Semigod Nations. Genesis six domination." The crowd chanted over and over again.

Suddenly, the world around me was bathed in a bluish light. Four figures came out from the crowd and removed their black robes, flanking the distance between me and Will, and the handmaidens in front of us. A flash of red hair swished in front of me.

"Felicia?" I gasped, looking around. Her father stood across from her, then Miss Sherry. I guess the Watchers had chosen sides. Luckily, my suitemate, Julia wasn't among them.

"Shut up," she hissed back at me. "You're gonna want to see this."

In unison, they all held up one hand, and a laser-beam of blue lit up the sky, aimed straight for the sapphire behind me.

The ground beneath my feet shook and crackled. In front of the pillar, the earth caved in.

Tentacles of shadow burst from the fissure like fireworks, widening the crack in the rock with shuddering force. I backed up as far as I could in my chains and let go of the ruby.

Like a clap of thunder, all the lights went out and the fireworks halted. The world returned to its usual state of cavern and torchlight.

Still, the sky glowed overhead. Butterflies danced for joy in my chest. The angels were still coming. This wasn't over yet.

"No," Rosalyn shrieked and grabbed my hands, digging the barrel of the gun into my side. She forced my hands back around the ruby, and the scene of Armageddon flickered back into existence.

The pyrotechnics resumed in the ground below me, banging and chipping away at the earth. Making an ever-widening hole.

Wraiths and shadows erupted from the pit in a screeching cloud of smoke that swirled and slithered around the stones, between the handmaidens, and into the crowd of gawkers. The cheering in the amphitheater subsided, making way for the shrieks and howls of the underworld.

"Is this what a reckoning is like?" Will whispered in my ear.

"Pretty much." I nodded.

The shadows started whispering. First in Latin, then in English. *Gratium, corum domino. Here come the fallen.*

"Except that," I hissed at him. "That's new."

The staircase of demons loomed closer now. Foul smells of rotten things, dead things, emanated from the caving earth. Along with something else I couldn't explain. All of a sudden, a wave of sadness overtook me, and tears started streaming from my eyes. Then it hit Will and Shanda and trickled out until the assortment of handmaidens and Watchers in front of me were sniffling and crying.

Then I was gripped by a fear so paralyzing I couldn't move. As soon as the feeling left me, it rippled out to everyone around me.

As wave after wave of foul emotion overtook every person standing in the amphitheater, I couldn't keep my eyes off of the scene in front of me. What once had been a crack was now an intricately carved archway, with stairs jutting up from a landing five feet below the earth.

The battalion of demons marched ever closer. In minutes they would be here, ready to do their worst.

Angel, I need you. I can't do this by myself. What do I do? My thoughts reached up, even as my eyes searched the skies above me. Angel and his brigade of light-soldiers were just on the edge of the portal. Hovering. Waiting to attack.

I'm right here if you need me, came the still, small voice.

"If I need you?!" I screamed into the night. "They're almost here. They're going to take over the world."

A laugh rumbled from the crowd, and the demon-horde marched on.

Hush, little Seer. You still have work to do. Sparkles drifted down from my angel, fluttering onto the stone.

The stone. Of course. I had to destroy the stone. I glanced at Shanda, then at Will. Their faces echoed the resolve beating in my heart. I had to make this stop. I was the Seer. I was the only one who could do it.

The moment I tried to lift a finger from the stone, all the wraiths that had been released screamed in pain and flew to my side. Black tentacles wrapped around my hands, locking them in place. Then the shadows swarmed, swirling around me like a tornado of darkness. They clawed at my hair, yanking random locks as they whirled past. They shrieked in my ear until I couldn't hear anything but ear-splitting screeches.

Then the whispers started. "You're just a little girl."

"There's nothing you can do to stop this."

"Haven't you hurt enough people by defying us?"

Hissed curses assailed my ears, trying desperately to sink into my brain. The more I tried to resist them, the angrier I became. Anger seeped into my pores, clenching my fingers into balled-up fists. My muscles tightened and clenched as my feet moved into fight stance. The rage condensed inside me into one single, determined thought. *I have to destroy the ruby. I have to destroy all the rubies.*

Angel's light flickered over my head, as if he was nodding in agreement.

How do I destroy the ruby, Angel?

A warm, comforting wind rustled across my face. *It's time. Fire at will.*

I glanced down to find the demon-horde ten steps away from making their entrance into the world of mankind.

My fingers itched to release the ruby, but the shadows still forced my hand. Since I couldn't take my hands off the ruby, I did the only thing I could think of. I called up every ounce of electricity I possessed. It sizzled through my veins at lit my body up from the inside. Somehow, I was hovering a few feet in the air, with only the chains tethering me to the pillar. Lightning sizzled from my fingertips, and I sent it straight into the ruby. Cracks broke out on the surface of the ruby. Red light seeped from the fissures.

The demons shrieked around me.

Rosalyn yelled, "No," and lunged at me.

But I wouldn't stop for anything.

Lightning flashed all around me. Once. Twice. Three times. Angel was clearing a circle of protection around me.

BOOM... a clap of thunder shook the earth, causing the ground to quake. The crowd wobbled on their feet. The demons reared backward on their staircase, halting their procession toward earth.

CRACK... a massive bolt of light crackled through the sky. *Finish it.* Angel's words roared in my mind.

A loud cry erupted from my throat as the angel fire crackled through my whole body. The lightning was blinding as it left my hands and shot into the ruby.

With a *thwap,* the ruby disintegrated it into bits. Ruby-red sparks shot through the air above me, raining down on the black-robed crowd below.

My chain snapped and an amethyst haze surrounded me, sending me soaring toward the ceiling. The purple glow took on a familiar hexagon shape. And suddenly, I the dots connected in my brain. I'd had a dream about this purple bubble right before graduation—a dream that James wanted to give me a purple stone to protect me and it would create a forcefield around me. Funny how most of my dreams came true.

Dangling mid-air in a purple diamond made of light, I glanced down at my Guardian Amethyst necklace, now hanging free. How could I forget? James wanted to find the amethyst to protect me. He'd known I'd need it one day for something like this.

Air whooshed by me as I tumbled through the sky, half-floating, half-falling toward the ground.

People were screaming below me.

"Lucy!" Shanda cried.

"My ruby!" Rosalyn yelled.

"I'll catch you." Will called, struggling against his chains.

Smack. My back hit his arms first, the force slamming us both onto the ground and breaking his chain. My ribs smashed into the stone floor, knocking the wind out of me. The laser-amethyst around me burst into an exploding shower of purple sparkles that all landed in my chest. The shape of a hexagon blinked on my black shirt—once, twice, then faded away. I clapped my hand over my heart as I lay there, unable to move or breathe.

"Lucy!" Shanda screamed, kicking free of her guards, unlocking her chains, and rushing to my side.

"Is she breathing?" Free of his chains, Will rushed to my side. With two fingers, he felt my neck for a pulse, paying no attention to the jagged scrape on his own cheek.

With a great force, air rushed back into my lungs. I coughed and sputtered, desperate for the much-needed oxygen.

"If she's not dead, I'll kill her myself!" Rosalyn shrieked in the distance.

Will and Shanda pulled me to my feet. "We have to get out of here."

"Not so fast." Rosalyn stood five feet away, gun aimed straight at my chest. "You destroyed my ruby. Now you're going to pay."

As she cocked the trigger, I froze. Ready to take the bullet. Hoping the amethyst or my angel would save me. But if they didn't, I couldn't say I blamed them. Maybe this world would be safer without the Seer.

"No, Mom. Don't. There are three other rubies out there." Will stepped in front of me, staring his mother down. "What in the world are you thinking? You can't kill Lucy. The Seer. Point blank. You just can't."

"You're right, son." She lowered the gun, her face softening.

"Thank God," Will murmured, holding out his hand. "Now give me the gun. We'll figure this out."

"Rosalyn," the Stanton patriarch hissed. "Now is not the time to go soft on me."

She nodded, her jaw hardening. "I've already got it figured out. And somebody's gotta pay." Her eyes flicked to the right, and she raised the gun again.

Bang. A shot rang out.

Shanda crumpled to the ground beside me.

CHAPTER 28

"No!" A scream ripped from my throat. "Shanda!"

I rushed to my best friend's side and sank to the earth next to her as blood oozed out from her middle. Without thinking, I pressed my hands against the wound, hoping to staunch the flow. My efforts were useless. There was too much blood.

Will knelt at my side. He wriggled out of his shirt and pressed it hard into her stomach. Her bleeding slowed. She reached for my hand, her eyes glossing over as she looked at me.

"Lucy, you finish this," she whispered. "Only you can do it."

"No, Shanda," I cried, tears streaming from my face. "I need you."

"You don't need me. You have your Angel. He'll take good care of me." Her lips were barely moving now.

How could I forget? I glanced up, and Angel hovered right beside Shanda. "Can you fix this? Please fix this," I begged, reaching for him.

My angel shook his head. "No, sweet Seer. It's time for her to go home. She's done her job."

"I've done my job," Shanda whispered, blood gurgling from her lips. Her eyes were totally glassy now, caught somewhere between earth and heaven. "I protected the Seer."

Chaos erupted around us. Sirens blared, emergency lights strobing. Walkie talkies screeched. People screamed, running in every direction as a team of fully-outfitted soldiers swarmed the underground chamber with assault rifles.

Heavy combat boots clomped down the stone steps, and suddenly Tony was at Shanda's side, kneeling over her.

"Shanda, I'm so sorry, baby." Tony whispered, his chest heaving as he cupped her face and brushed her hair off her cheek. "I got here as soon as I could. I'm not going anywhere."

"But I am." Suddenly a beautiful light enveloped Shanda, washing her in a heavenly glow. I rushed to her other side and took her hand.

"Angel's here. It's going to be okay," I whispered.

"Thank God," Tony breathed.

A soft cadence filled the air.

"It's okay. I'm ready to go home." Shanda's voice danced above me and I finally glanced up.

"No!" I screamed, an awful screeching note that clashed with the angelic symphony playing out in the sky.

The darkness of the cavern lit up with myriads of diamonds, crystallized in a sparkling array as they kissed Shanda's caramel skin, illuminating it from the inside out.

Angel hovered in the air, holding her in his arms. "I'm sorry, Lucy," came his voice through the blinding white outline. "It's her time."

"No," I croaked as sobs racked my body. "She can't leave us. What will we do without her?"

"It's time to live your destiny." Shanda's eyes were golden now as she stared at me from above, her stomach perfectly intact again. "You have to find the rubies and destroy them. You have to destroy Nexis. You're not alone. You've got me and a whole army of angels to help you."

"What if I can't?" The tears were streaming down my cheeks now.

Bronze sparkles rained from her golden eyes. "Lucy, you are the Seer. I know you can do this. This is your calling. This is your destiny."

"What's going on?" Tony grabbed me by the shoulders, but I couldn't rip my gaze away from the dazzling display in the sky. "What do you see?"

"It's Shanda," I hiccupped, extending my hand toward her. She reached for me too, but I only felt a wisp of wind as our fingers touched. "She's not going to make it."

"Lucy, tell me what's happening." Tony yanked me closer and squeezed me tight. "I have to know."

"It's beautiful. I wish you could see it." Another tear slid from my cheek, dropping on his hand.

Tony gasped, turning his face to the sky. "I don't know how this is happening, but I think I can see. It's incredible."

I glanced to my left. Will's hand touched the sapphire, eyes glistening around the edges.

Shanda outstretched her heavenly arms, one toward me and one toward Tony. "You two take care of each other. I'll be watching."

I looked at Tony, and we both managed a twisted, tear-stained smile.

In an instant, the sky brightened to an even more brilliant white as four streaks of lightning descended around Shanda.

The angels sang over her, two hovering on either side of her ethereal figure.

"I love you both." She blew us a kiss as the four angels lifted her higher, a golden ray of light in a sea of sparkling white, drifting higher like a cluster of stars dancing in the sky. In a flash of glorious light, they were gone.

Shanda's body went limp, but her lips were still moving. Tony and I leaned closer to try to hear, but there was no sound.

One last chorus of angelic music floated down from the heavens.

Shanda wasn't trying to talk. She was singing with the angels. Her chest stopped rising and falling. Her lips stopped moving. For a moment, the world stood still. Silent.

She was gone.

Tears started streaming from my eyes. I reached for her hand and clung to it.

Tony wrapped his arms around Shanda's dead body, cradling it in his arms and sobbing.

A team of gear-clad Guardians huddled around us. Tony gave his girlfriend one last hug and eased Shanda's lifeless body back onto the ground.

They were too late. They were all too late. And it was all my fault.

CHAPTER 29

I was numb. A living zombie. Things kept going on around me, but I couldn't touch them or feel them anymore. Like I was floating outside my body, watching the world go on as usual. How could anything be normal? My best friend was dead.

I couldn't go back to the dorm, couldn't stay in the room we'd shared together. As soon as I had walked into our room, I burst into uncontrollable, gut-wrenching sobs, and Will had to escort me to the lobby. My eyes were raw from all the crying. The scratchy dorm tissues didn't help either.

Within hours of the incident, Dad had shown up out of nowhere. Where'd he come from? Had Will called him? He talked with Will in hushed tones and disappeared up the stairs. He did the best he could, gathering what stuff he thought I'd need and stuffing it in my pink suitcase. But I'd probably be wearing a summer dress to Shanda's funeral unless Brooke and Julia stepped in to help out the poor guy.

"Where's Mom?" I rubbed my eyes as I stumbled out of the lobby door into the crisp April air. The sky was brightening, growing pink around the edges. When was the last time I'd seen the sunrise?

"She's in jail, sweetie." He could barely choke out the words. "They brought in all the Nexis members on suspicion of conspiracy to commit …"

Murder. He didn't have to say it. We all knew it. Me and Will, Brooke and Julia and Tony. The whole campus had probably heard by now.

My heart broke in a million pieces all over again. To think, my mother was one of those faceless Black Robes that just looked on and did nothing? I gulped as the air seized in my lungs, another sob threatening to break free. I guess Will had it worse.

I turned over my shoulder to wave goodbye to my suitemates. Brooke and Julia's somber faces reflected back at me through the lobby windows. Only a few days ago, the four of us had been chatting about our spring break plans. If only I could go back in time, back to our normal little world. But I couldn't. My whole world was shattered now. It would never be the same.

The sun peeked over the treeline, reflecting its rosy hues on the Hudson. Yet it felt colder, emptier somehow without Shanda. Shanda was so much like a sunrise, bringing light and laughter and fun to each day. Exploding into the world with boldness and color. Sure, there was heat and fire and brashness, but she made sparks fly. Made people come to life. Helped *me* come to life. No one could deny that.

Will's hand stroked my hair and Dad droned on about something, but none of it touched me. All I could do was watch the sunrise as we walked down the cobblestone, waiting with bated breath for the day to burst into life. As if it would somehow bring her back.

She wasn't coming back. I'd watched her disappear to a far better place than here. A part of me longed to go with her.

Bright flashes popped and crackled in my vision. Maybe this was it, maybe it was time to join my friend. My heart swelled with mixed emotions.

But the flashes only multiplied as we approached the parking lot, accompanied by voices on top of voices. A crowd of people swarmed the entrance, blocking out the Montrose sign. Security guards struggled to hold a perimeter, but arms and microphones and bodies reached through it. Undulating with questions and flashes.

"What's going on?" I couldn't make out anything beyond gibberish.

"It's the media. They've been here for hours," Will whispered in my ear.

"There's an investigation. They're talking about shutting down Montrose." Dad wrapped an arm around me as we approached the crowd.

"Good," I said through clenched teeth. Shanda would like that.

Two security guards peeled themselves away from the paparazzi, flanking us on each side. "Let's get you out of here." They mauled a path through the crowd and escorted us to Dad's car.

"Where are we going?" I asked as I buckled myself in the front seat, Will and my pink suitcase in the back.

"My hotel room. Excuse me, *our* hotel room now." He turned the key in the ignition and wove the car around dozens and dozens of reporters. "We can't go home. Not yet. The police won't let us. They want us both to give statements for the sentencing hearing. You and Will, especially."

I craned my neck to look at Will. "Are you staying with us?"

"Excuse me?" Dad coughed and cleared his throat, his voice turning stern. "Did you think you were staying with us, young man?"

I glanced in the rearview mirror and found Will cracking a smile.

"No, sir. My dad's flying in from Chicago to stay with me until the trial's over. We might end up in the same hotel, though." His lips quirked.

"Had you there, kid. You should've seen your face." Dad slapped his knee. "Priceless."

Will chuckled under his breath. My lips curled in the makings of a grin as I tried to stifle a laugh. Shanda would've cackled out loud at that one. And my heart sank all over again, remembering she'd never laugh again. At least not here on earth.

><

The ethereal strains of *Ave Maria* were floating over my head, up and away into the chapel's rafters as the pallbearers marched down the center aisle with Shanda's casket. But I didn't feel any of it. Throughout the whole beautiful, sad funeral for my best friend, all I wanted to do was cry. Curtis and his family sat in the front pew, and he dabbed his eyes a few times. But I couldn't muster up one tear. Not a single tear. Was I that heartless?

More like heartbroken. And numb. How could any of this be real? Shanda had been alive only a few days ago. Beautiful, vibrant, and full of life. It seemed impossible that her life could be snuffed out so quickly—by one senseless bullet. The anger churned into my fists as I curled them into fleshballs at my side. Because there was nothing else I could do. After all, I was too helpless to stop my best friend from being shot. Just a helpless little girl, without a single shred of hope to spare.

As the chapel doors opened, a brilliant burst of light colored the dimly lit chapel, illuminating the drawn faces packed into every pew. Dad reached for my hand and squeezed. Apparently, everyone was standing now, filing down the aisle pew by pew as Shanda's family led the way out. I hadn't noticed. I kept looking for something in the light. A twinkle, a hint of warmth that suggested my angel was still there. Just as well. Shanda needed him more now.

Will squeezed my shoulder as I finally hoisted my body out of the pew. Then I saw it. An extra twinkle dancing on Curtis's shoulder as he walked through the door. A spark that flitted to Tony next, pinged off his forehead, and floated above me for a few seconds, before zinging into Will.

The warmth seeped into my skin. I knew he would take care of her. She'd be okay, maybe even better off than she'd ever been down here.

A lone tear broke through the dam, tracing its way down my cheek.

Will wrapped his arm around my shoulder, smushed me into his side. "She is better off."

I jerked my head to give him my worried bulldog look.

He just shrugged. "Guess I needed to hear that one, too."

Before I could wrap my mind around what just happened, how my angel spoke to both of us at the same time, Dad stopped before we reached the foyer.

He craned his neck down the hallway and gave me an odd look. "I know you want to go to the wake, honey, but there's something we need to take care of first."

"Dad, what's going on? What are you talking about?" I studied his face.

His eyebrows were all bunched up like he was holding something in that couldn't be contained. "I can't explain out here. Let's go down the hall and talk."

"Okay. This isn't weird or anything." Like a dutiful daughter, I followed him down the darkened hallway, pulling Will along behind me.

Once we were a good distance away, Dad stopped again. And stared Will down. "This isn't any of your concern, young man."

I fought the urge to roll my eyes. "Please, not your 'young man' speech again. This is so not the time."

Will laced his fingers between mine. "Wherever she goes, I go. Sir." At least he had the good sense to nod politely.

A familiar little tingle raced up my arm, and I squeezed his hand.

"Not this time, honey." Dad gave me his serious face. "This is Guardian business."

I clamped my eyes shut. "I'm so sick of this," I whispered to the darkness. The broken pieces that were left of my heart turned to ash. *Lord, give me strength.*

Finally, I opened my eyes and stared at my Dad. "Is that all the Guardians know how to do, turn people into spies? Look what's it's done to you, to James, to Shanda." I could barely choke out her name.

His eyes softened around the edges, and he ruffled my hair. "I know this seems like the worst time to do this, but we have some decisions to make. And fast."

"Oh, Dad." I didn't know where to start, didn't have the energy.

His eyes jerked toward the library door. "There's no time for this now. There's an emergency, and you need to know what's going on."

Will cleared his throat, stiffening like a statue at my side. "It's about my mom, isn't it?"

Dad's face dropped. "I'm afraid so. But that's all I can say."

The claws of fear seized my lungs, and I forgot to breathe. I gripped Will's hand tighter.

Will ran his free hand through his golden hair, gaze darting from me to my Dad. "If that's the case, couldn't I come, too? Maybe I could help."

"No, I'm afraid they'll never allow it." Dad's face fell as he lowered his voice. "You know they're too paranoid to have a Stanton in the room."

Squeezing my hand, Will nodded. "I understand. I'll just wait out here for you, tiger."

My lips quirked as my dad cringed at the last word. But I knew Will was trying to give me an extra dose of strength. I gave him a side hug and tried not to notice my dad cringing at that last word. "I'll be right back."

Will took his post near the library door as I followed Dad inside, who shut the door behind us.

The usual collection of Guardians were huddled up in the middle of the room. Mr. Harlixton, Bryan, and his parents, along with Tony, Brooke, Laura, Lenny, and a few other teachers I didn't know were Guardians.

The door opened again and Curtis walked in, a strained look on his face. "This better be good."

My heart emerged from the ashes, and I rushed over to hug him. Strangely enough, he hugged me back, much like my own father would. For a moment we just stood there, two broken hearts trying to help the other. If that was even possible.

Mr. Harlixton cleared his throat. "I am sorry we have to do this now, but it's an emergency. Mrs. Stanton is about to be released on bail."

"What?!" Curtis roared, face ashen. "This can't be happening."

Tony's face grew red. "How could you possibly know that? The arraignment isn't until Monday."

"I know." Mr. Harlixton's voice was measured and even. "Our sources tell us that Nexis has bribed a court clerk to make sure the judge presiding over the arraignment is one of their own."

"Don't you guys have judges, too? This can't be happening." Curtis pounded his fist into the table so hard it echoed in the silent room.

"We tried the same tactic. They just had more money. I'm sorry, Curtis. It's out of my hands." Harlixton's face went pale as he wrung his hands, looking helpless for the first time since I'd known him.

Then it hit me. The truth slammed me smack-dab in the face. "She'll be free?" I croaked, taking two steps back, looking at my dad for help.

He rushed over to me, wrapping me in his bear hug. "It's going to be okay, Lucy. We won't let anything happen to you."

Hot tears welled up again. "How can you guarantee that she won't come after me? How can you guarantee anything? She's probably already ordered her little minions to put a hit on me. Even if she's locked up, what's stopping her?"

"Probably your bodyguard boyfriend," Bryan muttered, but not low enough in the silent library.

All the Guardians turned to glare at him as I shot him an evil eye. Brooke slapped his shoulder.

Tony elbowed him in the ribs. "Dude, not cool."

Curtis dropped his head and turned to me. "Lucy, I'm sorry. I didn't even think about what this means for you."

"I know. It's okay. I want her to pay, too." I glanced at him, and his eyes met mine for a moment. He didn't need to apologize. We understood each other's pain.

Mark Cooper spoke up. "Believe me, the Guardians will do everything in their power to make sure Rosalyn Stanton pays for her crimes."

"Thank you," Curtis mumbled.

"And what about Lucy?" my dad asked. "How do the Guardians plan to protect her?" Folding his arms across his chest, he cocked his head. Daring the Guardian Council to impress him. A look I knew all too well.

A hush descended on the room as every head turned to look at me.

This time Cindy, Bryan's mom, took a few steps in my direction. "We're going to send her to Europe."

Strange emotions waged war within me. Emotions I hadn't felt in days, like happiness and joy, clashed with the anger and betrayal of everything that came along with that dreaded continent. But my brother was there, so a surge of excitement won out.

"James? You mean I get to see James?" A small sort of smile played with my lips as if they couldn't decide which direction to go.

That's when a torrent of shouts erupted from the Guardians.

"You're not sending my daughter to Europe without me!" Dad roared.

Cindy shook her head. "No, of course not, you'll be coming, too."

"You can't be serious?" Bryan yelled a little too loudly. "It's not safe over there. War's already broken out. She'll be in danger."

"Don't be ridiculous, bro." Lenny rolled his eyes at Bryan. "She's in way more danger here."

Professor Harlixton held his hands up until the clamoring questions ceased. "After what happened here, under our watch, Nexis can't go unpunished for their crimes. It's inevitable. The Guardians are going to war against the Nexis Society."

A note of finality punctuated his last words. A hush fell over the room.

"It's about time." Curtis broke the silence, stepping forward. "My daughter didn't die for nothing."

"Mr. Jones is right." A surge of Shanda-esque boldness coursed through my veins as I moved into the middle of the circle, right next to Shanda's dad. "Let's face it. I am the Seer. Everyone knows it, even Nexis apparently."

Every eye in the room widened as all stares landed on me. Brooke and Laura gasped at my boldness, as Bryan shook his head at me. Tony just smiled like a proud papa.

Crossing my arms over my chest in a Dad-like move, I stared at Harlixton and the Coopers. "I refuse to be blindly led by you people anymore. I need some guarantees. If you want this Seer on your side, you'll have to meet my demands."

"Which are what exactly?" Mr. Harlixton asked through clenched teeth, glancing at the Coopers.

Narrowing my eyes, I took a good look around the room. I had the Guardians in the palm of my hand now. "If war is going to break out anyway, I want to be made a full member of the Guardians."

The Guardian leaders huddled up, and my dad marched over to them, looking like he had a lot to discuss.

My gaze landed on Curtis, and I knew exactly what I had to do. "And I want Shanda to be instated as a Guardian member posthumously. She made the ultimate sacrifice. It seems only right."

Curtis turned my way and nodded. "It is right."

The Guardian ringleaders stopped whispering and gaped at me, but made no objections.

"And Will, too." I leveled my gaze at them. "He risked everything to protect me, even turned on his own mother just for the chance to save Shanda's life. He deserves to be a member." I bit back the juicy little tidbit out Will being the Interpreter. I wasn't sure he wanted me to use that as a bargaining chip just yet.

"Now, wait a minute." Bryan puffed out his chest and squared off with me, jaw twitching like crazy. "There's no way we're letting *him* in."

I winced as he said the word "we." How did I not see this before? Now it was crystal clear to me where this boy's true loyalties lay. And they were never with me.

Cindy rested her hand on Bryan's shoulder. "Lucy, give us a few moments to consider your request. We'll discuss it and come back with our decision."

"Fine." I exhaled a breath, letting my arms fall to my side. "That's all I can ask I guess."

Curtis looked at me, eyes glistening. "If that boy tried to save my little girl, they should at least consider it."

The Guardian leaders, seven in all, made their way back to the turret and started discussing in hushed voices. My heart was half-hope, half-defeat. Because I knew exactly what they'd say.

"Thank you for sticking up for my baby." Curtis swallowed hard, squeezed my shoulder, and stalked to the other side of the room.

CHAPTER 30

"What can you possibly be thinking? Don't you know what you're asking?" Bryan grabbed my hand and yanked me into the stacks flanking the antique window. "It's too dangerous in Europe. You won't be safe at all."

The afternoon sunlight filtered through the old glass of the lead-paned library window. Slanted rays littered with dust motes cast shadows on Bryan's face—shadows I couldn't even begin to decipher. Why had he spent the past few months putting mountains of distance between us, only to go all he-man protector on me now?

I blinked and squinted at him, but nothing magically became clear. "Why do you even care?"

His jaw dropped and his mouth hung open like he didn't know how to fill the spaces he'd put between us. "You really don't know? You seriously don't think I still care about you?"

His questions bounced like darts off the protective shield I'd cocooned around my body. His words just didn't have the same effect on me that they used to.

So I shrugged. "I don't know, Bryan. You tell me."

Shadows rippled across his face, undulating like waves as he reached for my other hand. "Lucy, I'm still in love with you."

"Oh." All the air puffed out of me with that one syllable. Those glorious words should feel different. Not like this. Instead, they felt hollow and empty, an invisible hand grasping at a hologram of what we once were to each other. It just wasn't there anymore.

"Is that all you can say?" Lines etched across his face. Maybe he felt it, too.

"I—I'm sorry," I stammered. "I really don't know what to say."

"Does that mean you don't love me anymore?" he asked, peering at me.

I shook my head. "I don't know."

He took a step back, dropping my hand. "Does that mean you weren't pretending this whole semester with Will?"

"Are you kidding me?" Frustration gurgled up inside. I tried to tamp it back by balling my fists. How could we keep having the same argument, over and over? I took a second, gulped in a deep breath, and squared off to him. Maybe if I looked him in the eye, he'd finally hear me. "I'm not a very good actress. I never agreed to pretend. You know that. It's just not who I am."

With an emphatic huff, he stared down at his shoes. "I think I've always known that. You tried to tell me, but I just wouldn't listen."

The shadows elongated, engulfing the recesses of his face, drooping over his slumped shoulders.

After a few seconds, he glanced up, Adam's apple bobbing. "Are you in love with him?"

I froze. Maybe if I stood still as a statue he wouldn't see right through me. But I couldn't answer, couldn't bear to cause him any more pain.

Cursing under his breath, he stamped his foot on the thinly carpeted concrete. As if he could stamp out the truth. But it hung there, unspoken, in the musty air.

"I really screwed this up, didn't I?" He raked his hand through his dark hair, then turned a haunted look on me. "Is there any way to fix this? Can we ever go back to what we once were?"

I couldn't help myself. I reached for his hand and squeezed it tight. "I just got tired of being second-place. Sometimes you just cross a line and you can never go back."

He clamped his eyes shut, gripping my hand tighter. "We'll see."

I just shook my head. "No we won't."

Clamoring from the other side of the room broke us apart as someone called our names.

"I guess it's time for the big decision." I swung my hands at my sides as the awkwardness poured over me.

"Maybe it'll be good news for once." The corners of his mouth tipped up almost like I remembered. Like maybe he had his own plans brewing.

With halting steps, I followed his lanky form back into the center of the room. All seven of the Guardian Council members were lined up facing the rest of the group, ready to pronounce their decree. All they needed were black robes and gavels.

Well, maybe not black robes.

"We've finally made a decision," Harlixton announced from his post in the middle of the line-up. "We've agreed to welcome Lucy and Shanda into the ranks of the Guardians if Lucy agrees to several conditions."

"Excuse me," I interrupted the strange pronouncement. "What about Will? His life will be in danger if you don't give him your protection."

Harlixton leveled his gaze at me. "I wish we could do something to protect him. But I'm afraid we just can't trust him. Too many objections were raised about the likelihood of him spying on us."

"Seriously?" I choked on my own fumes. "That's only because it's the Guardian modus operandi. Just because it's your weapon of choice doesn't mean he'd do the same. Not after everything that happened."

Harlixton held up his hands and a hush fell over the room. "I understand your objections, but we just can't trust a Stanton. Any Stanton."

"You've got to be kidding me." I could hear my voice rising to a new pitch, but couldn't stop it. "I'm sure you're missing out on a lot of good intel. Isn't that all you people care about?"

Brooke and Laura gasped at my words. Even Cindy seemed taken aback.

Shaking his head, Harlixton's voice softened. "We also care about the members of our group. Subjecting them to a member of the Stanton family is just not going to happen. Please accept that."

Fury burst into flames inside me. "He can't go back to Nexis. What's he supposed to do?"

"He can join the Watchers or go it alone. It's his choice." Harlixton held out his hands and shook his head.

"The Watchers are almost as bad as Nexis," I yelled. "You're not giving him much of a choice. Me either, for that matter. Maybe I don't want to be a Guardian after all."

Someone came up beside me and rested a hand on my shoulder. I glanced over to find Tony at my side with a sympathetic look on his face. "Just hear them out," he whispered.

"Fine." I gulped back the sense of dread rising in my throat. "What are the conditions?"

Mark Cooper took one step forward. "First, you'll have to turn over any evidence you've gathered against Nexis, the Guardians, even the Watchers. The Guardian Council will decide what to do with it."

"I bet," I muttered under my breath.

"The second condition…" Cindy's softer voice rose as she moved beside her husband. "You will join the Guardian forces in Europe as soon as you're inducted as a member. If that's your choice, we will hold an induction ceremony tomorrow so you can leave the country as soon as possible. Before Rosalyn gets out on bail."

Dad walked forward, bridging the gap between us. "Don't worry, sweetie. You won't be going alone. We're going to arrange a summer abroad program that includes all the students here, as well as a few select chaperones. Myself included. That way nothing will look too suspicious."

"Let's just hope Mom gets out of jail in time to take care of Paige," I mumbled under my breath.

Murmurs undulated across the room as all the Montrose students started chattering about their summer in Europe.

Mark moved forward, inching close to me. "Even though war is being waged in Europe, the Guardian forces are prevailing. We do believe it is safer for you there than it will be here. Otherwise, we would never risk our own children's safety."

"Okay, let me get this straight." I ran my fingers through my hair, twirling it into knots. "You want all the evidence we've gathered that could possibly expose you, and in exchange I win a trip to Europe and full Guardian membership. Seems a little lopsided if you ask me."

"I assure you it's more than fair…" Harlixton droned on, but I tuned him out.

"Don't worry," Tony whispered in my ear. "I've got backups upon backups of all that evidence."

"I know, but what about Will?" I whispered back. "It seems so unfair to just leave him out there all alone."

"You know he'd tell you to do it." Tony had that same knowing look that Bryan had earlier. Could everyone see right through me? "You can agree now and talk it out with him. Nothing's official until you've done the ceremony."

"I don't know. It doesn't feel right." I ran a hand through my long hair, trying to sort out this tangled mess the Guardians were offering me. One thought kept blaring through my brain. *This is not what I wanted. Shanda should be here right now, joining the Guardians with me. It's just not fair.*

Tears sprang to my eyes, but I swiped them away and turned to the council with my best Shanda-tude. "If you want the Seer on your side, you'll let Will join the Guardians. End of discussion."

Harlixton glanced around at each council member. One by one they each shook their heads *no*. "Lucy, we've made our deal perfectly clear and there will be no more negotiations." He leaned closer, leveling a stern glare at me. "We've scheduled the ceremony for tomorrow afternoon, where we will induct Shanda Jones posthumously. I hope you decide to join us.

"You mean, I have to decide by tomorrow?" I choked out, a vice grip encircling my throat.

"Yes. Tomorrow. You know the dangers. We can't wait." Harlixton looked down his nose at me. "May I suggest you go do what you have to do to honor your friend?"

"At the expense of putting Will in danger? Why do you Guardians have to be so stubborn? I can't take this anymore." I glanced over at Dad and he nodded. "I'll meet you in the parking lot."

Without looking back at Bryan or Tony or anyone, I sprinted out of the room. Will was waiting for me in the hallway, not two steps from the door. I tumbled into his chest and pulled him into my arms.

"Hey, gorgeous. Is everything okay?" Will held me close.

"Lucy, wait." Bryan raced after me but stopped short when he saw me with Will.

I buried my head in Will's shoulder, if only to block out that horrible look on Bryan's face. "There's so much I have to tell you."

"I'm sure." He chuckled into my hair. "Did you get anything resolved with those people?"

I shrugged. "Kind of, but not really. You're not going to like it."

"Whatever it is, we can figure it out together."

"Really?" I looked up, right as Bryan turned and walked away. "It's nice to have one chapter finally over," I muttered to his retreating back.

Will followed my gaze, then glanced at me. Suddenly his whole face lit up like he knew exactly what I meant. "Finally."

I tilted my chin as my lips curved up at him.

He couldn't stop the huge smile that spread his lips wide. "Let's go find our bench and talk this out."

"I like the sound of that." We walked hand-in-hand out of the chapel, and into the waiting sunshine.

><

Our bench still sat nestled beside the maple tree, yet so much had changed since the last time Will and I had been there together. Less than a year ago, I'd thought he was some kind of creepy stalker. Now I wondered how I'd ever misjudged him so badly.

As soon as we sat down, I let the truth tumble from my parched lips. "The Guardians won't let you in. I didn't tell them your little secret, because I wasn't sure if you'd want me to. Now I wish I had."

"No, gorgeous. That's okay. It's better this way. Who knows what they'd do with two Chosen Ones in their ranks." The spring-green maple leaves dappled Will's face with shadows.

"Sometimes I wish you weren't right about these things." How I wished we could go back to silly flirty games and stupid campus intrigues. But I knew my life would never be that simple, at least not for awhile. I only hoped he knew it, too.

Will slid his arm along the bench behind me. A comforting, familiar gesture that immediately calmed my nerves.

"Don't hate me," he whispered.

"Why would I hate you?" Glancing up, I found his face scrunched with a million worry lines, completely unreadable.

The corners of his mouth crinkled. "I sort of eavesdropped a little. Heard they wouldn't let me in. Thanks for trying, though." He laid his hand on top of mine.

A cool early-May breeze picked up, and I laced my cold fingers between his warm ones. "What do I care if you listened in? I'm not a Guardian yet."

"But you should be." Those gray eyes leveled into me.

I shook my head. "No way. Not without you. There's no way I'm going to leave you all alone out there. To become mincemeat of Nexis, or the Watchers, or who knows what? I don't think so."

He squeezed my hand and pulled me closer. "Well, I don't want to become mincemeat either. But I've been thinking a lot about it, and I only see one solution. Even if it means we can't be together for now." A dissonant note cracked through his deep voice.

I inched in closer until his face was only inches away. "I won't accept that. We can find a way to make it work on our own. Who needs those stupid secret societies?"

"They will find us." His words came out strangled and choked. "Even if we could allude the Watchers and the Guardians, my mom will not stop. She'll always hunt us down."

"Because of me. Because I'm the Seer." The truth sunk into the very depths of my breaking heart, and I glared down at my lap.

"And because she alone knows I'm the Interpreter." Suddenly Will's hand cupped my cheek as he forced me to look at him. "I will do whatever I have to do to keep you safe, even if it means sending you straight into the ranks of the stupid Guardians. They're not perfect. But at least they can protect you."

Unbidden, a tear welled up and landed on my cheek. "You can't go it alone. You're the one who told me that. Everyone knows how I feel about you. They'll just use you to get to me."

Even as his eyes ignited at my admission, he set his mouth in a grim line. "You're right. That's why I've decided to make you a deal."

"Oh, great. More deals," I muttered, running my fingers along his jawline.

"This one actually benefits both of us. In a way." Now both hands were on my face as he stared at me with those platinum eyes. "If you promise me you'll join the Guardians, I promise you that I'll join the Watchers in Europe. So we can both be safe. Until we can be together again. And we will be together again. You understand that, don't you?"

I did my best to nod as another tear leaked out.

"You promise?" he asked, eyes locked on mine.

I nodded, holding his gaze. "I promise, Will."

In one swift motion, he pressed his lips into mine, all warm and soft. Tingles raced through my body and dive-bombed with the dread in my gut. I wrapped my arms around him as too many emotions exploded through every corner of my mind. If only I could tell him the truth, that I was in love with him. But it wouldn't help anything. Not when we were going our separate ways.

"You know how much I care about you, right?" Coming from his lips, those sweet little words warmed me up and cradled me in his arms.

"I know," I whispered into his soft mouth as I kissed him again. Wrapping my arms around him, I clamped my eyes shut against my own cowardice. He had to know how much I wanted to say it back to him. But how could I? It already hurt too much, knowing we only had a day left together … and weeks or even months of separation ahead of us.

So I just squeezed him tighter and melted into his arms.

CHAPTER 31

The pungent scent of burning candle wax filled my nostrils. My hands trembled at my sides, ruffling the silvery fabric of my ridiculously long dress. *This is not how I wanted to join the Guardians. Shanda was supposed to be by my side.* Swirling fireflies danced on my fingertips. I couldn't look at anything but the platinum silk flowing out from my hips and puddling in waves on the chapel tile.

Curtis stood in front of me, regal and crisp in a gray suit jacket. He took two steps down the hallway then disappeared around the corner.

The fireflies buzzed straight into my stomach. In one, two, three heartbeats it was my turn. I followed the path he laid out for me, telling myself to breathe. This was it. After hours of talking with Will, I had made my choice. And there was no going back now.

Strains of some faintly-familiar epic ballad piped through the chapel's massive organ. Each note filled the room with the pomp and circumstance this occasion called for. Today I would become a Guardian.

As I rounded the corner and made my first steps down the long aisle, I lifted my chin to take it all in. A brilliant white light bathed the room. Several lights seemed to emanate more radiance than I'd ever seen in this normally dim sanctuary. Colored rays streaked in from the stained-glass windows. But the light shining down from above was pure white like I'd only seen from my angel.

Step by step, pew by pew, the realization washed over me. A warm summer breeze wafted over me. My lips curved as I angled my gaze toward the whiteness. The white was so bright I couldn't make out any figures. Then I heard it. A chorus of extra voices, adding their own sweet refrain to the organ music. Maybe Shanda was with them, watching over me and her dad.

I made my way to the front where the Guardian Council stood on the platform facing the crowd, dressed in white robes. Mr. Harlixton motioned for Curtis and me to stand in front of them on the stage.

Harlixton held up the microphone and turned to Curtis. "Mr. Jones, please kneel before the council." Curtis dropped to one knee as Mr. Harlixton hoisted up a silver medal on a silver ribbon. "This medallion is to honor the heroic efforts of your daughter, Shanda Jones, who gave the ultimate sacrifice. And we are all humbly grateful."

"Thank you," Curtis whispered as he bowed his head.

In one fluid motion, Harlixton slid the medal around Curtis' neck, and he rose to his feet.

A round of applause erupted in the sanctuary. Pews squeaked and rattled as everyone rose to their feet in a standing ovation.

The sudden sting of tears welled up in my eyes, and one trickled down my cheek. As I dabbed at the moisture, Curtis turned and nodded at the crowd. The applause roared even louder.

"Miss McAllen, please kneel before the council," Harlixton said into the microphone. "This special gift is to acknowledge your unwavering commitment to the Guardians and thank you for bringing your unique talents to our society."

Still on one knee, I furrowed my forehead at his cryptic words and peered up at my dad. Something shiny and metallic peeked out between his fingers.

"Mr. McAllen, please present the Guardian's gift to your daughter." Harlixton nodded at him.

A strange mix of pride and sadness washed over my dad's face as he stepped forward. "I present this token to you, Lucy the Seer, to remind you of the brave choices you've made today, and of the many more you are sure to make in the future."

Whispers from the Guardian Council flitted above my head as Dad placed a silver chain around my neck. I glanced down at the outline of a circle with a cross in the middle, and wings above it. The Guardian symbol. It felt cold against my skin. Even though the trinket was light and dainty, a sense of heaviness settled on my shoulders. Too many cryptic words pinged through my brain. Dad's words. Harlixton's words. Had I made the right choice?

Dad motioned for me to rise as the applause started up again.

Harlixton raised his arms to the onlookers. "Please welcome Lucy McAllen and Shanda Jones posthumously to the Order of the Guardians."

I bristled as he announced the full name of the organization I had just joined. What had I gotten myself into here?

Harlixton motioned for me and Curtis to turn and face the crowd.

Everyone stood and cheered. Some two hundred or more people filled the chapel. I had no idea there were this many Guardians in this city alone. I spotted my sister in the crowd, sitting next to Will. Even though Mr. Harlixton said they wouldn't negotiate, I nudged them into letting Will and Paige watch the ceremony. Of course, that left a lot of questions Dad needed to answer for my sister.

Paige seemed to be taking this whole thing in stride. Even though our mom was in prison, our dad a double agent, and she'd just found out the truth about James, she was beaming and clapping so hard her hands would probably turn red. Will, on the other hand, cocked his head to the side and gave me a little golf clap. I nodded and winked at him, and he smiled for a split second, before schooling his features back into a neutral gaze.

For better or worse, this would probably be my last day at Montrose Paranormal Academy. Soon I would be jetting off to Europe with my dad to finally see my brother in the flesh. It all sounded more glamorous than it actually was. I'd have to leave Will behind for who knows how long. Could our new relationship handle the distance?

It was too late now. Tomorrow I'd get on a plane to Austria. Only time would tell.

><

Gray clouds hung low as we filed down the cobblestone path, leaving Montrose for possibly the last time. With a war looming on the horizon, the administration couldn't decide if they wanted to resume classes in the fall. If they did, I wasn't sure I could face this campus without Shanda.

Heaviness hung in the air as sadness warred with anger inside me until I was all twisted up in knots. None of this had happened the way I wanted it to. I was supposed to go to Europe to fight by my brother's side with Shanda, Will, and Tony. I guess seeing James again was one bright spot amid the horror of the past week. But the all-consuming, overwhelming stench of grief clouded everything. I could barely put one foot in front of the other, let alone think about going to Europe in a few days.

My dad's towncar waited at the parking lot curb, but I slowed my pace and let him wheel the last of my suitcases on without me. All my friends crowded around me. Will was a pillar of strength at my side. I gulped, swallowing back the bittersweet tears that rushed to my eyes.

About ten feet ahead, Dad turned and glanced over his shoulder. "You coming, Lucy?"

I mashed my lips together, a feeble attempt to keep my emotions in check. "I just need a minute to say goodbye."

His eyes drooped, and the heaviness finally seeped into his gaze. "Sure, sweetie. I understand. Take all the time you need. I'll just wait in the car."

Then he nodded at Will, who bobbed his head in unspoken assent at my father. I narrowed my eyes at both of them. No doubt they had some sort of silent agreement to protect me from whatever Nexis had in store for me next. Normally a secret pact would irk me to the very core. But not today. Dire possibilities hung over my head like a fog, shrouding my future in uncertainty. It was all hands on deck.

I turned around to face my friends as they clustered into a semi-circle in front of me. Brooke and Julia, Laura and Lenny, Tony and Curtis. Even Mr. Harlixton had shown up to say goodbye. Bryan hung back with his parents, who still tugged at my heartstrings. If only their son hadn't been so stubborn and hard-headed, things might've turned out differently. But they didn't.

"This is silly." I sniffed and wiped away the waterworks that sprang up. Traitors. "I'll see most of you in a few days."

Will squeezed my hand and my heart lurched. *Except for you. Who knows when I'll see you again.*

"I wish I could go, too." Julia rushed up and hugged me. "I hate that you guys are leaving and Montrose might be closing. I don't know what I'll do senior year without you."

"You'll be just fine. You're so good at making friends. Everyone at your new school will love you." I patted her golden-brown head, indulging her right to a life of denial. Who was I to say more if she didn't want to dwell on deeper things? At least she hadn't joined the Watcher who'd sided with Nexis.

She smiled up at me. "Thank you, for everything." Her eyes told me there was still more to uncover, locked away for another day.

Laura and Lenny ventured forward next, and Laura wrapped her tiny arms around my waist. "We'll see you in Europe in a few days. Be safe," she whispered.

"Laura, what're you doing? You're not supposed to say it out loud?" Lenny's jaw dropped as he stared at his twin. "What if Nexis spies are lurking about?"

"I—I'm sorry," Laura stammered, eyes darting around the parking lot. "I wasn't thinking."

"Calm down." I patted her shoulder. "No one heard you. Everything's going to be okay." Even as I said the words, fear clenched my heart.

Mr. Harlixton took a few steps forward. "I know this semester has been unbearable. But we will see that justice is served."

"Thank you," I mouthed as he stepped back. A nod was his only reply.

Brooke tiptoed forward, head swinging toward her family as she approached. "Don't be too hard on him. He's hurting, too." With that, she stepped back.

I couldn't help but stare at Bryan as he shuffled off to the side with his parents. Every time his eyes wandered my way, they immediately glared at Will. Part of me didn't blame him for his anger, but he'd made his own choices. And I'd made mine. Hopefully, we could coexist now that we were finally in the Guardians together.

Shaking his head at his friend, Tony walked up to me and grabbed my hand. "Life's too short to hang onto to petty stuff. Just remember you won't be alone in the Guardians. I'm going to make Nexis pay, too. You can't get all the credit."

I smiled at him. "Thanks for that. I'll need all the help I can get."

"I think you'll find the Guardians are good for that, at least." He made an attempt to smile, but it didn't reach his eyes.

"We'll see." I studied him, searching for the hidden meaning.

Lowering his voice, he met my gaze. "I just want you to know that our alliance still comes first, if worse comes to worse. I've got your back. She'd want it that way."

"Understood." I bobbed my head and he nodded back, making me wonder if Shanda had talked to Tony about our friends-first pact. Then he turned and strolled down the cobblestone path toward the dorms like nothing ever happened. Still, it was nice to know I'd have at least one ally in the Guardians since Will couldn't be there.

Curtis attempted to smile down at me, but it didn't reach his eyes. "You've done so much for my daughter. I won't forget it."

"I won't forget her, either." Salty tears burned my eyes, but he had to know my resolve. "I just wish it had been enough. She didn't deserve to die. Not for me. Not for anyone. Nexis will pay." I gulped as the tears spilled over, sizzling hot tracks down my cheeks.

"Shanda wanted you to live." His dark fingers wrapped around my shoulders as he held my gaze. "Promise me you'll honor her wishes and the sacrifice she made."

I nodded as his words sank deep into the depths of my soul. A lone tear escaped. "I promise."

"Good." With that he walked away, leaving us behind. But his words stayed with me, forming a new resolve thick as steel.

I would be the one to bring Nexis down. To dismantle the entire organization and bring it to its knees. For Shanda, for the world. And for all the Seers sacrificed on their misguided altar. I would be the Seer to change things, to turn it all around. I had to. It was either me or them.

><

I took one last sweeping glance around the Montrose Paranormal Academy campus. So many things had happened in my junior year, both gloriously good and irreparably horrendous. Shanda's death had changed things, for me and this school. So why did it feel so wrong to leave it all behind? Shanda had died here, after all. Shouldn't I want to leave this place?

The realization lapped at my feet like a wave of clarity washing over my toes. Leaving this place meant letting go of Shanda—letting go of my best friend. And that just felt wrong. I wanted to hold her in my heart forever and carry her with me wherever I went. In that way, maybe I could fulfill my promise to her dad and honor her sacrifice.

Everyone else had dispersed. Will was the only one left standing beside me.

"Let's talk." Softly, he tapped his fingers on my palm.

I relaxed the fist I didn't even know I'd clenched and grabbed his hand. Hand in hand, we walked toward what I'd come to think of as "our spot." The bridge overlooking a creek that fed the Hudson River, where we'd had our first heart-to-heart after my reckoning in the field.

I wrapped my fingers around the railing, holding on tight. As if I could hold us here, in this spot, forever. By the sheer force of my willpower.

A warm May breeze blew across the gray waters of the Hudson, bringing the smell of spring to my nose.

Will slid his arm around my back, turning me toward him. Familiar tingles shivered up my spine. "Tomorrow, I become an official member of the Watchers."

I froze, unable to tear my eyes away from the tortured look on his face. "I know we made a deal, but it still burns me up inside that you aren't a Guardian with me."

Those familiar gray eyes had me in their sights. "Don't forget who you're talking to. I'll always be your guardian. I found a way to get to Europe, but you're not going to like it."

His words made every muscle in my body brace for impact. "There's more, isn't there?"

"You know me better than you think." His words filtered through the blackness, tinged with an emotion I couldn't name. "The Watchers only agreed to take me on if I agreed to be a spy."

My breath hitched in my throat. I snapped my eyes open. "No." I breathed the word.

A shadow danced over his face. Fear danced in his eyes. "I'm sorry. It's the only way I can protect you."

I gasped, clutching my chest. Oh, my poor little heart. "But who's going to protect you?"

His jaw dropped open. "Nobody's ever asked me that before."

Pressure built up behind my eyes. "Not even your own family?" I clamped my hand over my mouth, but it was too late. We both knew his mother barely even noticed him unless it was part of her Nexis agenda. I couldn't help but wonder if his father was any better.

The veins in his neck corded. "Actually, my father negotiated the same deal with the Watchers. I guess, technically, no *woman* has ever wanted to protect me."

I wrapped my arms around his solid abs and squeezed tight, burying my face in his warm t-shirt. "You deserve so much better than what you've grown up with. I just wish I could've done more for you. To protect you." It was all I could get out before the tears overflowed. Apologies and regrets piled up in the back of my throat, dying a slow death on my unmoving tongue. I'd failed yet again.

"Hey, tiger. Look at me." He cupped both hands around my face, wiping the tears away with the pads of his thumbs. "I don't blame you for any of this. It's not your fault, okay? At least this way we can both be safe and together."

"Together?" For the first time since Shanda died, a glimmer of hope sprang up, arching my brows sky high. "You really think that'll happen?"

A small smile played with his lips. "I'll make it happen. You'll be in Europe, I'll be in Europe. We've got a much better shot this way. Especially if I get the Seer surveillance detail I requested."

"Seer surveillance detail?" My eyebrows shot to the stratosphere. "Do I even wanna know?"

"You really don't." Suddenly his hands dropped from my face, leaving my cheeks cold. Just as quickly, he grabbed my hands and leaned in closer. "No matter what you hear after today, I want you to know the truth, okay?"

Droplets of icy fear pinged the fire spreading across my cheeks. Yet I felt myself nodding, my hands still locked in his grip. Unable to tear my gaze away from the strange but beautiful expression engulfing his face. Making him glow like a ray of sunshine.

He paused for one second, two seconds. My heart couldn't take it anymore.

"What is it?" A strangled whispered crawled from my throat. I had to know.

"I love you." Joy danced on his face, lighting up his eyes and every feature I'd come to love. "I just want to be with you every chance I can get. You've been given a terrible gift, and yet you'd rather hide it away from the Three Societies than use its power to hurt people. If any of the Nexis girls had this gift, the world would end tonight. But we have a fighting chance because this gift has been given to *you*. And not anyone else."

"W—wow, Will. That's the sweetest thing anyone's ever said to me." Pinpricks of tears stabbed at my eyes, but I willed myself not to cry. His words were too beautiful to dampen with more tears.

He moved in closer, his breath a soft warmth on my face. "Just know that no matter what, I'll always love you for who you are. The bravest girl I've ever known."

"I—you know how much…" I shook my head as tears trickled down my cheeks.

He covered my mouth with his. Soft lips mingled with salt and spice. A moment so delicious I couldn't bear it anymore.

The sun burst out from behind the clouds, spilling rays of light on us. His words sank deep into my bones. They were all I'd ever wanted to hear. But the truth behind his sentiment made my heart collapsed in on itself. Because of my gifts, everyone I loved would be in danger soon. Especially him. Shanda's death was proof of that horrible fact. I couldn't be the one to put his life on the line—even if he wanted me to. It was too much responsibility.

I'd be responsible tomorrow. Right now, I lost myself in Will's arms. And his kisses that melted my bones and made my toes curl.

After five, ten, or thirty minutes, he finally broke away, dabbing my tears with his fingertips. "I know you can't say it right now. It's too hard."

"I wish I could," I mumbled into his neck, my fingers trembling as I traced his collarbone. "Please, you have to know…"

"I know how you feel. That's not what this is about." He cradled me in his arms and pressed his forehead into mine. "Don't cry, gorgeous. You just lost your best friend and now everything's changing so fast. But you're so strong. We'll get through this hell together. I'll be there, waiting for you on the other side. And believe me, it'll be worth it. Just to keep you safe."

Pulling back to stare straight into his eyes, I lifted my index finger and placed it on his chest. With slow, pain-staking strokes, I started drawing on his navy blue T-shirt. Letter by letter, I traced the words I wanted to say to him. As if they could burn through the fabric and form a tattoo on his heart. *I…LOVE…YOU.*

His breath hitched as he caught the meaning. "You have no idea how long I've waited," he murmured as his mouth overtook my lips again.

I wrapped him up tight, locking away the moment in my heart forever. I kissed him until the Hudson blurred into the sky, hoping this kiss would carry me through the next weeks and months without him. Hoping this feeling of utter bliss would travel across the ocean with me until we could see each other again.

All too soon, I'd be on a plane that'd take me far away from Will. Too far. But nothing, not even distance could keep us apart. Somewhere deep inside, I knew Will's promises were nothing like Bryan's—hollow, empty, and full of regret. Will was stronger than that. And he made me stronger.

Just like Shanda always did.

I knew what lay ahead of me—a bleak fight that I wouldn't always agree with. But even a girl who sees the supernatural needs people in this world to fight for. Bryan and the Guardians were wrong about one thing. The Seer needed some distractions. Will was the kind of distraction a girl could fight for.

I couldn't predict the future. That just wasn't my gift. But because of one boy, I was starting to figure out who I was and who I was meant to become. It just wasn't the boy I thought it'd be. But I wasn't the same girl I was a year ago.

It was time to say goodbye to the girl hiding in the shadows, trying to blend in and find her brother. Without even realizing it, I'd turned into the girl I'd always wanted to be—an independent woman who made her own choices, stood on her own two feet, and fought for what she loved.

Now I had to step out of the shadows, and into my true power. For myself. For Will. For Shanda.

For the world.

You'd better watch out, Nexis. Because this Seer is about to dismantle your secret club. By obliterating. EVERY. LAST. RUBY.

I'm nobody's property. I'm my own Seer.

And I'm about to bring the fight to Europe.

DEAR READER

Dear Reader,

I hope you enjoyed *Montrose Paranormal Academy, Book 2: Crossing Nexis*. This book was hard to write for many reasons, because I wanted to switch love interests and kill off one of my favorite characters. (Which I hope you will eventually forgive me for.) Not to mention that *Crossing Nexis* is a sequel, and we all know how those usually turn out.

But the main reason this book took so long to write is because my husband of 10 years got diagnosed with cancer in the middle of writing this book. Nine months after his diagnosis of Stage 4 Melanoma, he passed away. During the time that he had cancer, so many people loved on us and supported us. But after he died I was devastated. I stopped writing for almost two years.

A few months after this book releases will be three years from the day he went to be with the Lord. I watched him go to heaven singing praises to God. I hope this book honors him and the love and encouragement he gave me. More than anything, I know he'd be so proud of me for finally finishing my sequel.

I have no doubt Sam is up in heaven right now rejoicing with the angels.

Lucy's Story Continues ...

Check out my website to see how you can keep reading for free!

1. Want a FREE Montrose Paranormal Academy book? Go to www.barbarahartzler.com and find *The Nexis Awakening*, Book 1.5 in the Montrose Paranormal Academy series

2. Click to join my mailing list to download your exclusive free copy of *The Nexis Awakening* today! It's all about how James got banished from the Nexis Society.

3. Watch for *Montrose Paranormal Academy, Book 2: Crossing Nexis*, releasing Fall 2020.

PLEASE CONSIDER LEAVING A REVIEW

Independent authors depend on reviews. If you enjoyed reading this book as much as Barbara enjoyed writing it, please consider reviewing *Montrose Paranormal Academy, Book 2: Crossing Nexis* on Amazon or on Goodreads.
Thank you!

Visit www.barbarahartzler.com to join my mailing list to download your exclusive free copy of *The Nexis Awakening: A Montrose Paranormal Academy Prequel* today!

MORE BOOKS
By Barbara Hartzler

THE MONTROSE PARANORMAL ACADEMY SERIES

Montrose Paranormal Academy Book 1: *The Nexis Secret*

Montrose Paranormal Academy Book 1.5: The Nexis Awakening
(Exclusive freebie for email newsletter subscribers)

Montrose Paranormal Academy Book 2: *Crossing Nexis*

Montrose Paranormal Academy Book 3: *The European Conspiracy*

Montrose Paranormal Academy Book 4: *The Seer's Army* (2021)

Montrose Paranormal Academy Book 5: *The Final Crusade* (2021)

DEVOTIONAL
Waiting on the Lord: 30 Reflections

To learn more about the world of Montrose Paranormal Academy
or find me on social media, check out my website:
www.barbarahartzler.com

Or

Join my Facebook Readers Club!
Montrose Paranormal Academy VIP Readers Club

About The Author

Barbara Hartzler is the author of the Montrose Paranormal Academy Series, the story of The Seer—a.k.a. one girl with a gift to see the unseen world of angels. Not to mention the two secret societies vying for her allegiance. *Montrose Paranormal Academy, Book 1: The Nexis Secret* is inspired by Barbara's college experiences and peppered with anecdotes from her teen missions trip to New York City.

She's always wanted to write, not necessarily about angels, but the idea was too good to pass up. As a former barista and graphic designer, she loves all things sparkly and purple and is always jonesing for a good cup of joe.

So grab a cup of coffee and peruse her website at www.barbarahartzler.com. You can read her blog, explore all the behind-the-scenes extras in The Seer's Vault, or learn more about her writing journey, fun facts, and The BARBARA awards for best fiction (mostly YA).

Look for *Montrose Paranormal Academy, Book 2: Crossing Nexis,* coming Fall 2020. Or join her mailing list Barbara's Angels for all the latest updates. You can also check out her Montrose Paranormal Academy VIP Readers Club on Facebook with all kinds of MPA extras.

ACKNOWLEDGMENTS

Even a labor of love like this book had a lot of helpers along the way.

I'd like to thank my editor Rachelle Rae Cobb who came into this series after it started, but has loved it like no other. Your help and encouragement not only made this book shine, but your kind words showed me I'm not a terrible writer!

Thanks to my beta readers, Tena Redenbaugh, Erin Jacobson, Lori LeMunyon, and Carole Hayes. Your early encouragement of this book meant so much to this lonely writer who is never quite sure anyone will read the next book. Shout out to my cover designer Erin Dameron-Hill. Your work is truly amazing!

Thank you to my own personal champion, Terry Sutton. You inspire me every day to keep going even when things get hard. God knew what he was doing when he brought us together, and I'm beyond grateful.

To my beloved husband, I miss you every day. I know you're cheering my on from above. You know the rest.

To my Lord and Savior, Jesus Christ, thank you for taking care of me when I thought I couldn't keep going. You've been with me every step of the way. For that, and so much more, I am eternally blessed.

84000227R00193